TRUCK STOP
TEMPEST

KRISSY DANIELS

TRUCK STOP
TEMPEST

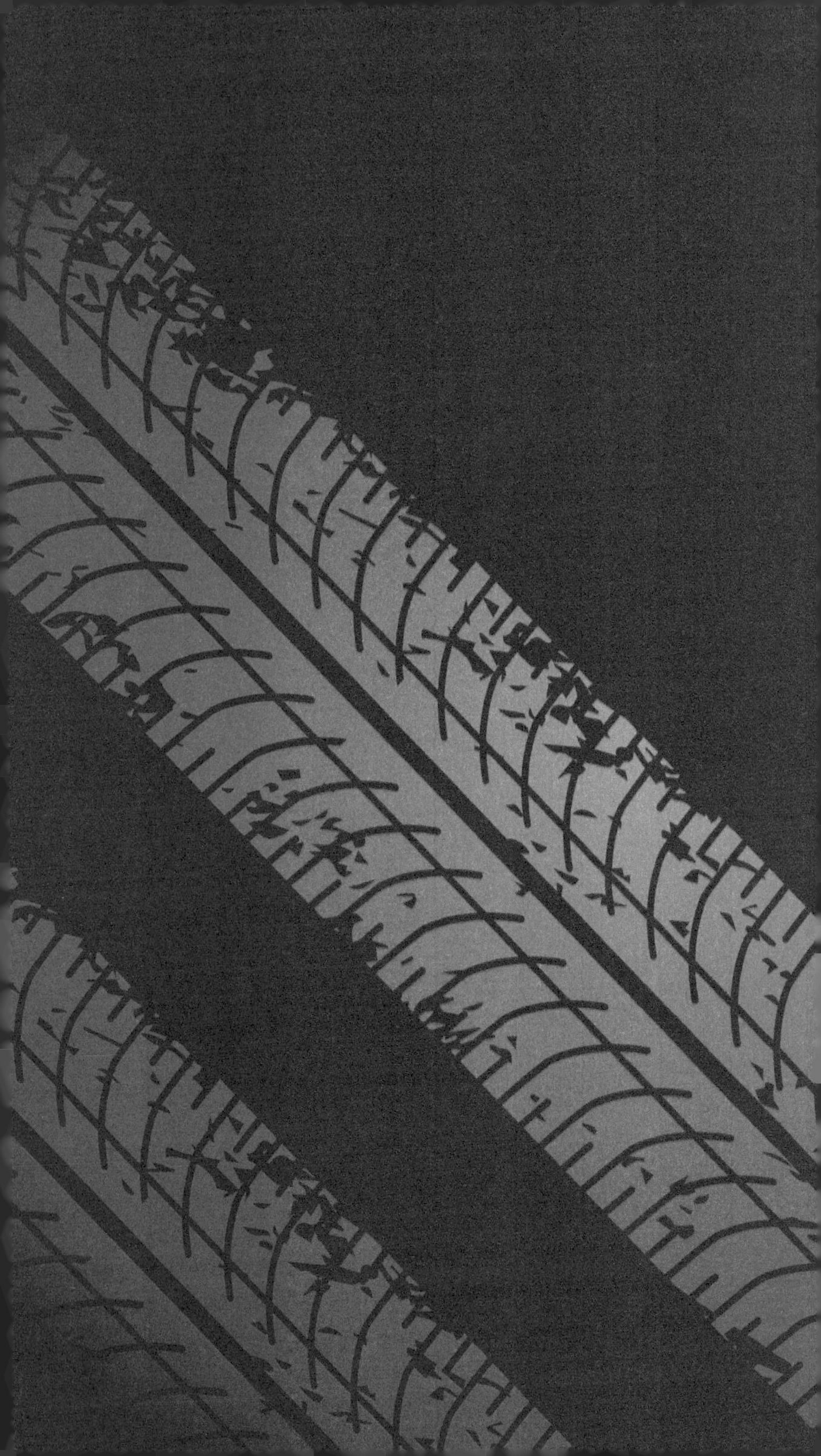

To all those taught to stay silent

Find your voice

And fucking roar!

PROLOGUE

Tuuli – 15 years ago

"STOP, JOJO! I'M NOT supposed to come here." I dug my toes into the loose dirt, but my brother only jerked my arm harder, dragging me along the driveway toward the scary house. "Ow!" I cried, trying to pull away.

He stopped walking and squeezed my wrist. "Shut your fucking trap."

My brother said the F-word a lot. I didn't know what the F-word meant, but my mom said it was bad. "You're not supposed to say that word."

He stared at the cabin. Spit. Then started walking again, pulling me behind. "I'm a guy. I can say whatever the hell I want. You're a girl. Girls keep their mouths shut."

He sounded just like our dad when he said that.

Sometimes I didn't like being a girl. I had a lot of things I wanted to say, but my dad always spanked me if I talked when I wasn't supposed to, and he would spank me, for sure, if he saw me at his secret house. "I don't like it here," I yelled, squeezing my eyes closed, hoping he wouldn't hit me.

JoJo stopped, took a deep breath, and made a fist.

Uh oh.

"Shut. Up." He turned around and grabbed my arms, shaking me hard. "Anyone hears you, we're fucked. Got it?"

I smashed my lips together and didn't yell again, even when JoJo squeezed my hand too hard, and pulled me behind a tree, and pushed on my shoulders until I sat on the dirty ground.

"Now, stay here and don't make a sound."

I looked around and started to cry. There were big trees everywhere. I didn't like the woods. Erik, the boy who lived next door to us, said there were monsters in the woods that liked to eat little girls. He always told me I had to obey him or he would drag me into the forest and leave me there for the monsters.

JoJo kicked the tree and said more bad words. Then he sat on his knees in front of me. "Stop crying. Do you want Dad or Erik to see you?"

I shook my head *no*. My brother was scary. But not as scary as Erik. Erik liked to make people scared. He liked to make me cry. He liked to make me do a lot of things.

My brother pulled a chocolate bar out of his pocket and dropped it in my lap. "Here. Don't move. Don't make a sound. I'll come get you when I'm done."

"Where are you going?" I whispered, but JoJo just walked away.

I looked at the candy. My stomach made a loud noise. My dad never let me have candy. He said candy made girls fat, and girls needed to stay small if they wanted to keep boys happy. On my birthday, Mom always gave me candy bars. She said girls couldn't get fat or spanked on their birthdays. I wished it was my birthday, then Mom would be home, and my brother wouldn't have to babysit me, and I wouldn't have to hide behind a tree in the woods.

It wasn't my birthday, and I didn't want to get spanked, so I threw the chocolate as hard as I could. Maybe the monsters would eat it, and then they wouldn't want to eat me.

I waited, just like JoJo said. I kept my eyes closed the whole time because I didn't want to see any monsters in the trees. I kept them closed until I heard a girl singing. She had a pretty voice, and she was singing about rainbows. I liked rainbows. Sometimes, I colored them for my mom, and she would hang them on the refrigerator.

I wanted to see who was singing. I opened my eyes, peeked around the tree, then snuck behind the cabin and stood on my tippy-toes to look through the window. On the TV, there was a girl singing to her dog. She had a pretty dress, and piggy tails just like me, except her hair was dark and my hair was white.

Then I heard crying.

I ran to the other window.

Erik was on the couch, watching the girl sing on the TV. His face was red and wet, and he didn't have any clothes on. He had big black marks on his arms and tummy.

I didn't like Erik, but he looked like he was hurt and sad. I didn't like when people were sad. Maybe if I was nice to Erik, he would be nice to me. I knocked on the window and his eyes got big and round. He wiped his face, and then he didn't look sad anymore. He looked scary and mad.

A door slammed, and Erik pulled his knees up high, then hugged his legs. He didn't look at me anymore.

My dad walked into the room. He was singing like the girl, but he didn't sound pretty. I never heard my dad sing before. He didn't have a shirt, and his tummy was big and jiggly. He probably ate a lot of candy bars.

Dad sat on the couch and watched the girl. Then he put his arm around Erik and pointed to the TV. He laughed about something, and then he laid down and made Erik lay down, too. Erik tried to move away, but my dad hugged him and made him stay still.

My dad never hugged me. He never hugged JoJo either. Why did he like Erik better? Erik was the meanest boy ever, and I wished he lived far away.

"What the fuck are you doing, brat?" JoJo grabbed my piggy tail and pulled hard until I moved away from the window.

I closed my mouth tight because he looked really mad. Boys were not nice, but they *really* weren't nice when they were mad. I wanted to ask what song that girl was singing. I wanted to ask why Dad and Erik were watching TV, but I didn't because my brother's face was all red and scrunchy.

He didn't talk to me all the way home. He didn't hold my arm, either. I was glad because my arm still hurt from before.

The next day, Erik found me in my room, under the bed. Every time he came to play with JoJo, I tried to hide. He always found me. I needed to get better at hiding.

Erik told my mom we were going outside to play, but we didn't play. He made me go to my dad's secret house. He made me watch the movie with the girl and the rainbow song. He scared me when the lion came on, and he told me I looked like the witch, the bad one, not the good one.

After that day, he made me go to the scary house a lot when my mom and dad were at work and JoJo was with his friends. Sometimes he hit me. Sometimes he yelled at me. Sometimes he made me sit on his lap. Most of the time, he made me lay down, and he laid next to me and wouldn't let me move until the movie was over. Sometimes, he hugged me. His hugs were not nice. They hurt, and sometimes I couldn't breathe.

He always sang the rainbow song very loud. "Somewhere over the rainbow..."

He always made me walk home alone, through the woods.

I was happy when Mom told me we were moving far away. I asked her if there was a secret house where we were going, and she just looked at me funny.

I was happy that we were moving until JoJo told me Erik and his mom and dad were coming, too.

I didn't like rainbows anymore.

Tito - 15 months ago

Smoke billowed through the large space, seeping through the vents and down the stairwell, choking precious oxygen from the room. I fought unsuccessfully against my binds, thankful that I'd been thrown to the floor where I could still pull a small amount of clean air into my lungs.

Above my head, through aged floorboards and beams, came loud crashes, and screeching, the walls and windows releasing one last battle cry before succumbing to the flames.

Screams haunted me from the far corner of the basement, those of a dead man begging for mercy. Voltolini's lawyer was their first target, and despite having lived the life longer than I'd been breathing, Mark Norton crumpled after a measly five minutes under the cut of Rafael Turner's blade, spilling secrets not even I had been privy to.

He'd yet to give up the one thing Turner wanted, Aida's location, not because he was a strong man, but because he'd been denied the vital details of her whereabouts. He did, however, spill a scarier truth, one that could bring Voltolini to his knees, and ruin a family. A truth I would most likely die for hearing.

That was if I survived the fire. Footsteps pounded around me.

A gruff voice yelled, "Time's up, Turner."

Rafael responded, "Who started the fucking fire?"

"Wasn't us, boss."

Rafael spit profanities. Fist hit flesh. A body fell inches from my head.

"The house is coming down around us. We go now."

"Not until I know where they've hidden Aida," Turner argued.

Dumb fuck.

"Won't fucking matter if we're dead. We go now. We go now!"

A deafening boom shook the foundation. Embers and shards of wood rained down. More footsteps. A boot caught me in the rib before a heavy body fell, cracking my ribs. The men surrounding me coughed and sputtered before heaving their fallen brother from the ground.

"What about Voltolini?" someone shouted.

"Let him burn," was the reply. "Let them all burn."

I fought to free my hands from the binds at my back. Fighting was useless.

"You win!" I shouted into the darkness, surrendering to my nemesis, my only worthy adversary, the Grim Reaper herself. "You win," I rasped, ready for rest. Ready for peace.

Over the years, Death and I had shared a morbid courtship, dancing around in a twisted game of cat and mouse. Year after year, hit after hit, she would follow me into the dark shadows and offer a nibble of her sweet sanctuary, only to slink away, smiling, after I offered another soul in exchange for my own.

In my world, it was kill or be killed. I'd never been ready to die, and lucky me, there had always been someone ready, although never willing, to take my place. Death wasn't biased. A soul was a soul, regardless of race, religion, or guilt.

As the old home above me crumbled, the acrid burn of paint and treated wood, old furniture, and flesh seared my nostrils. I choked on the metallic tang of blood and strained to see across the room through the sting in my eyes. I wondered if Lady Death was pleased that, for the first time, I had no alternative soul to offer.

Voltolini's enemies would escape. I would not. I had led the Marcovic Cartel to the safe house. I deserved to die.

And so, I closed my eyes, conceding. Tapping out. My only request, that Death draw out my final moments, allow me to feel and suffer every agonizing detail of my final breaths, to hurt until my black heart thumped a final beat.

Lady Death heard me. The ceiling tore open, dropping heavy chunks of fire on my head. Death heard me. And she was more than happy to oblige my wishes.

All was going according to plan until someone tugged at my feet.

From across the room, a thick, hoarse voice commanded, "Get him out of here."

More tugging. A hand lay across my chest. Heavy breaths blew in my ear. "Protect Aida, son. Take care of my princess. Then make them pay."

CHAPTER 1

Tuuli

"AND MAY THE LORD bless you and keep you…"

I closed my eyes and absorbed Pastor Davies' benediction, letting the words wash over me, pretending, for the short reprieve, that I was clean and worthy of hearing them.

As the shuffle of feet and rustle of coats and mumbled *goodbyes* and *have a good weeks* and *join us for lunch,* closed around me, I hooked my purse strap over my shoulder, shrugged my arms into my sweater, and maneuvered through the congregation toward the door, stealing one last glance at the stained-glass image of Jesus before making my getaway.

I jogged down the cement steps and hurried to the corner, hoping to catch the early bus and make it to The Truck Stop in time to have a bite before my shift started. My stomach rumbled at the prospect of a real meal.

Rifling through my handbag in search of my bus pass, I continued along the uneven sidewalk and cursed myself for not keeping the damn thing in my pocket.

"Ah, there you are." I snatched my card and looked up seconds before slamming into the figure standing before me.

Dear Sweet Mother of Mercy. My limbs locked, my insides sputtering and crackling like water dropped into a hot pan of oil.

Dark, turbulent eyes glowered down at me through the cover of his cloak. Out of habit, my gaze dropped to the ground. I hated that I still had that reaction around men. Pathetic and weak.

No more, I reminded myself, forcing my attention upward, over the scary body parked mere inches from mine.

I took in every detail, from his well-worn shoes to the running pants that clung to his thick thighs, to his signature dark sweatshirt. Tito, or Grim—as in The Grim Reaper—as I often referred to him in the safety of my private thoughts, once again had his hood pulled low over his head, hence the nickname. His chest rose and fell, sweat dripped from his half-hidden face, and puffs of white air blew from his lips with each exhale, reminding me how cold it was outside.

I shivered, as I often did in his presence, and pulled my sweater tighter around my middle.

"Hey, Tito." I forced a smile. "Going for a run?"

He didn't answer. He rarely did when I spoke to him unless reciting his lunch or dinner order. Instead, he glanced over my shoulder, then back to me, offering a nod in the building's direction. "You one of those Jesus freaks?"

Shame slammed my chest. I was a freak, but not the kind he referenced.

"Oh, God no," I said, folding, as I often did under the weight of peer pressure, or any pressure for that matter.

He shoved his hands in his front pockets, leaning back on his heels. "I saw you come out of the church."

A nervous laugh escaped my lips. "Not everyone who goes to church is a Jesus freak."

His eyes darkened. Narrowed. Burned a hole right through me. "Whatever you say."

By some miracle, under the stifling weight of his scrutiny, I managed to squeak, "You don't go to church?"

Stupid, stupid question.

"Rather be skinned alive." Such loathing in his voice.

The heavy rumble of the bus reminded me of my tight schedule, shaking me from my Tito trance. I'd have to run for it. The Sunday driver waited for no one.

"Been nice talking to you, but I gotta go." I took off at a sprint, breasts bouncing beneath my stretched-out bra, hair falling out of my meticulously pinned bun, and my purse beating viciously at my back.

I was a mere ten feet from my ride when my bag's strap snapped, spilling its guts and my hope for a meal all over the muddy ground.

"No," I screeched, skidding to a stop and gasping for air as the bus rolled away without me. "No. No. No." I squatted to retrieve my things, plucked them from the newly thawed earth, and shoved them, muck and all, back into my thrift store handbag.

Tucking the pink leather traitor under my arm, I headed the same direction I'd just come and maneuvered through the slow flowing stream of churchgoers spilled onto the sidewalk. If I kept a brisk pace and didn't die of frostbite, I could still make it to work on time.

Already a couple of blocks ahead, Tito continued to gain distance, his large, dark form growing smaller by the second. My insides warmed at the sight. What I wouldn't give to own such a powerful air of self-confidence, such a fearsome presence. What I wouldn't give for a taste of power, to instill fear rather than drown in it.

I wondered briefly, and shamefully, as I often did, how a man, more specifically Tito, would feel if he were to hold me, his thick muscles pressed against my small curves. How would he taste if I stole a kiss? Too often, I thought about his lips—whether they would be soft and gentle, or hard and forceful. I often thought about his other body parts as well, even though the little voice in my head reminded me it was wrong to have any thoughts about a man like Tito Moretti.

I hated that little voice.

Tito

That little voice. That pink, pouty mouth. Those wide, terrified, baby blues. Fuck. The girl was a damn child. A churchgoing child, no less, and, for reasons beyond my understanding, I couldn't flush her out of my head, no matter how hard I hit the bag, or how many miles of road I tore up.

My morbid attraction to her wasn't sexual, not exclusively anyway. No. Tuuli's allure was soul-deep. Maybe the draw came from her eyes. She was young, late teens, I guessed, but her gaze, when I was careless enough to hold it for more than a blink, hid wisdom that was neither earned nor bestowed. I suspected that Tuuli's erudition had been forced upon her, evident by the slump of her shoulders and the forced confidence she tried so hard to pull off.

Perhaps the unholy attraction was simply one broken soul recognizing another.

Maybe our mutual afflictions were the reason she haunted me.

Most likely, I was insane.

Didn't matter. Tuuli was a no-go. Forbidden. A big, flashing neon sign: *Danger. No Trespassing. Keep Out.* And so, I pushed forward, focused on the punch of my shoes against the wet ground, inhaling for four beats, exhaling for four. In. *One, two, three, four.* Out. *One, two, three, four.* In. *One, two, three...*continuing until I was nothing but movement, and sweat, and breathing. Until my mind numbed, the screams dimmed, and thoughts of an innocent, blue-eyed beauty faded to nothing.

I ran across town, past The Stop, and halfway up the hill toward home before the unmistakable squeal of brakes set my nerves on rapid fire.

Don't turn around. Don't turn around. Leave her be.

"Fuck!" Pulled by an invisible force, I came to a halt, and turned, hoping to catch sight, just one glimpse, of my dangerous little obsession.

Tuuli didn't step off the number twenty-seven bus like she did every Sunday. The double doors swung open, paused for a beat, then slammed shut, and the vehicle pulled back into traffic.

I stood like a dumbass, wishing I'd waited by the church to make sure Tuuli had caught her ride. "Shit. Shit, shit, shit." I sprinted to the top of the hill, busted through the door to my basement apartment, and snagged my keys off the counter. When I folded into my Mustang, I cranked the stereo to an ear-splitting level and retraced my path home, hoping she had followed the same route.

Thirteen minutes later, I found her, walking with a spring in her step, bright red cheeks, and no fucking coat. When I rolled to a stop, she walked right past. I honked. Her spine stiffened, and she continued, hurrying her pace.

I sped to the intersection and performed a U-turn, pulling alongside her again, this time with my dark window rolled down. "Get in the car."

When Tuuli's frightened gaze morphed into one of relief, topped off with a sweet smile, I damn near gripped my chest, shocked by the unusual rhythm knocking behind my ribcage.

"Hey, Tito," she said, teeth chattering. "Sorry. Didn't know that was you. What are you doing here?"

"It's freezing. Get in."

"Oh. I'm okay. Thanks, though." Her pace slowed, but only a little.

"I'm here to give you a ride. Get in."

She stopped. "Why?"

Jesus effin' Christ. Young. Naive. Definitely someone to steer clear of.

"Slade said you didn't get off the bus. She asked me to come and get you." The lie left my lips with such ease, I even believed it. "So. Here I am. It's cold. Get in."

As she scurried to the passenger side, I dialed up the heater, despite the sweaty mess underneath my workout gear.

The girl slid in, hooked her belt, and sat, stiff as a board, arms curled around her purse, broken leather strap twisted through her fingers. Without looking my way, she mumbled, "Thank you."

It was impossible to ignore the tremble in her arms.

"No coat?" I asked, gritting my teeth.

"Left it at a friend's house," she said. "She's supposed to bring it by later today."

Seems I wasn't the only one weaving stories. I ate lunch at The Stop every day. Sometimes dinner, too. I'd yet to see one of Tuuli's buddies come through. She'd never talked about friends, or family for that matter.

I took the long way around town, hoping to eradicate her shivers before dropping her at work. Tuuli didn't seem to notice. Her eyes stayed glued to the road, her bag close to her chest, and her lips pinched tight. Worked for me. I wasn't much for talking. Then again, I'd never been one to run to the aid of a girl I hardly knew, but there I sat, the reluctant hero, and fuck me, but I wanted to hear more of that soft, sweet voice. "So, Tuuli is an interesting name. Is that German?"

Her gaze sliced toward me, never connecting eye-to-eye, then shifted back to the road. "It's Nordic. At least, according to Google."

"That would explain the blonde hair, blue eyes."

Tuuli wiggled in her seat, then cleared her throat. "Why does Aida call you Tits?"

I huffed. No one had ever asked me that question. Out of fear, most likely. "Nickname Aida gave me when we were kids. In grade school, I paid a girl to show me her rack. Aida found out, gave me a fat lip. Told her I couldn't help it...I was a tit man. The name stuck."

"So, you're from New York, too." A statement, not a question.

"Born and raised."

The timid little creature turned to look at me. "What brought you to Whisper Springs?"

Death and destruction. Murder and revenge.

"Needed a change." Damn, she'd turned the tables. I'd meant to be the one asking questions. "You grow up here?"

Her moment of bravery faded and she dropped her head, knotting her fingers. "No. Born in Arkansas. Dad moved us to Idaho when I was five."

She was hiding something. Not very well, and it sure as hell wasn't any of my business, but it bothered me nonetheless. Didn't like that it bothered me. Didn't like that I wanted to keep driving and talking. Fucking hated how I wanted to coax the truth out of her. Her life was none of my business. So, with equal parts relief and disappointment, I pulled into the parking lot of The Stop.

Tuuli's hand was on the door before I shifted the car to park.

"Thanks, Tito," she said over her shoulder as she pushed out of the car.

I watched her dash to the back door of the diner. Stared long and hard at the empty passenger seat. I turned off the heater because my car's interior was fucking hot as Hades. After a bout of arguing with myself, I decided to head home rather than follow her inside. I needed lunch, but I needed a cold shower more.

Tuuli Holt and her pretty little voice clung to my skin like a New York summer. Sticky, stifling, and unrelenting. Problem was, I wasn't sure a shower could wash her away.

Not good. Not good at all.

Tuuli

"Oh, this is not good at all," The reflection glaring back at me was a grumpy, frumpy mess.

Thanks to Tito and his lead foot, I had fifteen minutes to spare before my shift started, enough time to grab a quick bite. I did not, however, have time to fix my hair. But really, when it came down to the nitty-gritty, a full belly trumped vanity by a gazillion points. So, instead of primping, I pulled my tangled mane into a low ponytail and called it good.

A wave of nausea washed over me. I folded, pressed my forehead against the cold sink, and waited for the hunger pang to pass before making my way to the kitchen.

"Hi, Charlie."

"S'up Toodaloo?"

Toodaloo. Charlie had given me a nickname my first day on the job. I'd never had a nickname, aside from *Brat.* A term used too often and too enthusiastically by my brother and his friends over the years. I refused to acknowledge the moniker as any sort of endearment. Coming from Charlie, though? I couldn't help but feel accepted, and somehow special.

I was about to ask for eggs when he pushed a bowl of soup my way. "I need your opinion. I might add this to the menu. It's kale, with Portuguese sausage. Aida's recipe."

I cozied up to the cutting board and stirred the spoon through the gold broth with long shreds of green lettuce, perfect tiny potato and carrot cubes, shiny cuts of onions, and bite-sized hunks of some type of skinny sausage. The beautiful concoction smelled cozy, like a warm house on a cold winter day, inviting you to come inside and stay for a while.

I don't remember much after the first bite, except for Charlie pushing torn pieces of bread my way, and then offering a second helping. I scraped the last piece of potato from the bottom of my bowl and sucked it between my lips. When I looked up, Charlie and Slade stood side by side, both with arms crossed, heads tilted, and brows pinched tight.

"So?" Charlie chuckled, his belly bouncing beneath his white coat. "You like it, then?"

Slade's always cheerful face twisted in concern. "You okay, Tuuli?"

"Fine. Why?" I brushed bread crumbs off my mouth and carried my dishes to the sink.

"No reason," Slade answered with a smirk. "Never mind."

"Well?" Charlie asked as I made my way past him. "What's the verdict? Yea or nay?"

I retied my apron strings tighter around my waist, to help hold up my pants, and pretended to debate the quality of his creation. "It beats Chicken 'n' Stars, gives Ramen a run for its money. I'm gonna go with a *yea*."

"Hmmm," he hummed, shooting me a wink. "I'll dump this batch, tweak the ingredients, and see what I can come up with."

"No," I waved my hand in a desperate plea. "Don't toss it. It's perfect. I lied, okay. I lied. It's the best soup I've ever had in my life. The best meal I've eaten in forever. Don't tweak it. For the love of God, don't change a thing."

"That's what I thought." The Truck Stop's famed chef turned his back and got busy with the fryer. "Get to work, Toodaloo. Got a full house out there."

With a sated stomach and more energy than I'd had all week, I headed to the dining room. Sundays were my favorite days to work. The after-church crowd was always pleasant, although skimpy with gratuities. I didn't mind. As much as I needed the cash, agreeable customers always made for a better day than good tips.

The afternoon passed in a whirlwind of burgers, coffee refills, screaming kids, and chatty geriatrics. I hardly had time to notice that Tito hadn't shown up for lunch or dinner. In my few spare moments of peace, I couldn't help but wonder if he hadn't shown up because of me.

I thought about him too much, silly waste of time that it was. I wasn't even a blip on Tito's radar. The man was scary hot, and untouchable as far as I could tell. I'd known him for months, served him lunch and dinner a gazillion times, and I'd never heard him speak more than one or two sentences to anyone other than Aida.

Our conversation earlier was the longest exchange we had ever shared, and I soaked up his attention like a love-starved puppy. Foolish, sure. In hindsight, it was obvious that he was only being polite, seeing as we had been stuck together in his car. Which reminded me...

I found Slade and Tango in the office. With one hand on Slade's lower back, the other hand tangled in her hair, Tango hummed a tune I didn't recognize and rocked Slade in a slow, gentle circle.

A jealous ache rolled through my chest.

Good Lord, they were beautiful. Always dancing. Always touching.

Tango bent for a kiss. I cleared my throat.

Slade turned her cheek to greet me. "Hey, girlie. What's up?" The woman glowed twenty-four-seven. But in Tango's arms, I could swear she was part angel, incandescent and blinding.

"Sorry for interrupting. I just wanted to thank you for sending Tito to pick me up today. My purse broke and spilled, so I missed my bus. I don't mind walking, but I'd neglected to bring a coat, and it was freezing this morning, and..."

I paused, noting the look of confusion on my boss's face.

"Tito gave you a ride?" she asked, raising her brows and shooting Tango a quick glance.

"Um. Yeah. He said you sent him because you didn't see me get off the bus."

"He did, huh?" Slade hid a crooked smile behind the guise of chewing her thumbnail.

I nodded.

"That's weird. I didn't know you took the bus." She turned to Tango, who was grinning like the Cheshire Cat. "Isn't that weird, honey?"

"Mmmhmm." Tango kissed the top of her head and offered me a nod.

Margie, our seasoned waitress, poked her head through the door. "Tuuli. A guy at table six is asking for you." She threw me a wink. "Handsome devil."

My guts dropped and bounced around a bit. I didn't know anyone in town, aside from my coworkers. Which meant someone I did know had made a trip into Whisper Springs to see me, which could only mean bad news was headed my way. My brother was the only person from Rockypoint who knew I worked at The Stop. He'd disappeared over a month ago.

I straightened my spine and said a quick prayer on my way to the dining room, asking God not to let it be my brother. Or any family member for that matter.

Even though his back was turned, I recognized my visitor immediately, his tall, wide frame unmistakable. His confident carriage sent a shiver through me. Forecasting the shit storm of white teeth, painted smile, and perfect pale skin that was about to wreak havoc in Tuuliland, I steeled my spine and battened down the hatches of my fragile, newfound independence before forcing my legs to carry me forward.

"Erik?"

"Tuuli." Steely blue eyes, in all their ass-kissing glory, took me in before settling on my face. "You've lost weight. Didn't think that was possible."

"Oh. Um." Taken aback by his insult, I floundered, dropping my gaze to the checkered tile. "How did you know I was here?" I asked his shoes. Nice shoes. Looked expensive. Shiny brown leather. Fancy thin laces.

Through my peripheral, I noticed his arms swing open. Before I could stop what was coming, he caught me in a stifling embrace, pressing me against an unforgiving chest and forcing me to inhale his expensive cologne.

My feet left the ground. An *oof* left my lips. I dangled in one of his famous hugs. Except it wasn't a hug *per se*, but more a reminder that he was bigger and stronger, and more powerful than I would ever be. Erik's hugs were never about intimacy or emotion. Only control—or pretense, when others were around.

When satisfied, he dropped me to my feet with an "Umpf." Not gentle. In fact, harder than necessary, another reminder that he could break me if he so desired.

He curled long fingers around my neck, and said, "I've come for my girl."

I jerked away. He pulled me right back, asserting his power with more aggression. His eyes would've been pretty if I didn't know what was hiding behind the congenial mask.

"I've come for you, Tuuli. This charade is over; get your things."

He didn't own me. He didn't know anything about me or the promise my brother had made. I was never going back. Not alone. Not with him. Not ever.

I cleared my throat, forced a lifetime of conditioning down deep where it couldn't control me, and I found my voice. "You don't understand."

Tito

I understood Tuuli had a life outside of work. I understood that her life did not and in no way should have involved me. I had no business giving two fucks. But when I stepped through the door of The Stop, the cowbell rattled, the cacophony of happy diners filled my ears, and my eyes fell on that young, forbidden angel, dangling in the arms of a large, clean-cut suit. What I couldn't fathom was why my face heated, or why my heart banged erratically, or why, for the love of all that was holy, I wanted to pound my chest like a damn gorilla and charge the pasty motherfucker who was holding the girl who wasn't mine.

Fuck. My head was fucked. I pounded my temple once, hoping to rattle some of the shit loose. My usual table, hidden in the corner, was otherwise occupied, by said motherfucker, I assumed. So, I retreated to the opposite corner, parked my ass at a dirty table, and tried my damnedest not to watch the interaction between Tuuli and her friend. Intimate friend, judging by the way he held her.

Busying myself with a menu, I tried, unsuccessfully, to keep my attention off the couple. Tuuli stared at the floor more than usual. She seemed two sizes smaller, two souls smaller next to the douche.

The more I watched, the more I realized that she wasn't into the guy, and he, apparently, seemed to think he was her world.

Margie approached. "Hey, Tito." She wiped the red laminate with a bleach-soaked towel. "Ready to order?"

I nodded *yes* before asking, "What's up with Dolph Lundgren over there?"

Margie looked over her shoulder. "Not sure, sweetie. Never seen him before tonight. He came here looking for Tuuli."

"She look happy to see him?" Not sure why I asked. Maybe I needed confirmation that I wasn't reading Tuuli's body language wrong.

"Well." Margie turned to assess the situation. "Now that you mention it, no. She looks like she wants to curl into a tiny ball and roll away."

"That's what I thought," I mumbled.

Tuuli jerked free of the guy's grip and shook her head. He clamped his fingers back around her neck and pulled her closer.

Lady Death whispered in my ear, "I want that one."

I shoved off my chair and decimated the distance between us, reaching earshot in time to hear Tuuli say, "Get your hands off me. I'm never going home. And I'm not your girl."

I didn't give the guy time to respond. I hooked an arm around Tuuli's shoulder and pulled her against me, effectively freeing her from his hold. "Hey, Tuuli," I said, tapping her chin, forcing her to look at me. "Who's your friend?" I held her gaze, hoping like hell she understood my game.

I hated the meek fucking expression on her face.

Tuuli stared at me, flushed, unspeaking, so I offered a hand to the dead man. "Tito Moretti. You are?"

The man's jaw hardened, his eyes narrowed, and his pale face reddened. After an excruciating pause, he shook my hand and said, "Erik Meyer." His gaze sliced to Tuuli, then back to me.

I held his hand past the point of polite, let Tuuli go, and nudged her toward the kitchen. "Charlie needs your help in the back. Said it was an emergency." I didn't watch her retreat. Instead, I dropped my friendly facade and sized the fucker up.

A wicked smile spread across his face, revealing perfect white teeth. "Moretti? What is that, Italian?"

"What that is, is none of your fuckin' business," I warned, stepping even closer.

He didn't shy away. Stupid move.

My skin ignited head to toe.

Erik asked, "Is there a problem?"

The guy was too white, from his hair to his skin, and even his teeth. White, and clean. Too damn clean. Creepy as fuck, but in a pretty way.

"You laid your hands on my girl," I gritted through my clenched jaw. "You lay hands on her again, you'll be fishing your fingers outta the lake. Got me?"

Unfazed, Erik pulled his wallet out of his pocket, tossed a roll of bills on the table, and sauntered past me toward the door, but not before pausing to straighten his tie and say, "Don't know what game you're playing, but Tuuli is not your girl. She was mine before she was born."

Had we not been surrounded by clueless diners, I would've taken a swing, for shits and giggles. Instead, I hid my fisted hands in the pocket of my sweatshirt and watched the guy exit the building and stroll to his Mercedes SUV. He glanced my way before disappearing behind the tinted glass.

His vehicle was not the first clue that something wasn't kosher with the guy. It was the most glaring, though. Why the hell was a douche his age driving a Mercedes G-class modified with bulletproof glass?

I walked outside and watched the vehicle blend into the dark night, pissed that I hadn't caught his plate numbers.

"Thanks," Tuuli's soft voice cut through the hard vibes rattling my nerves.

I didn't turn around. I didn't move because if I moved, I would've gone to her, and if I'd gone to her, I would've touched. Touching meant dirtying, and I didn't want to be the man that dirtied the sweet, churchgoing angel.

I didn't turn around. "You need a ride home?"

"Um. I have to finish my shift."

She didn't answer my question.

Walk away, dumbfuck. Walk away.

"After your shift, do you need a ride home?" I asked again, unable to hide the agitation in my voice.

"No, Tito," she huffed, mirroring my ire. "I don't need a ride home, but thank you, again. For everything."

The cowbell rattled. She'd fled back inside. The sky darkened around me. I trekked up the hill, parked my ass at the kitchen table, and fired up my computer, dead set on finding a reason to take that Erik fucker down. Instead, I pictured Tuuli standing alone at the bus stop, or worse, sitting in the metal petri dish on wheels next to a drunk perv.

I grabbed my keys and drove back down to the diner.

Then I waited for Tuuli's goddamn shift to end.

Yeah. I was fucked.

CHAPTER 2

"NICE TO SEE YOU again," the woman next to me said, her voice soft and melodic.

"Good morning." I offered my hand.

"I'm Joyce." Sliding her warm palm against mine, she shook my arm with vigor.

I stared down at our joined hands, fascinated by the stark contrast of my ivory palm encased in her ebony fingers. "I'm Tuuli." I lifted my gaze to meet a pair of exotic green eyes.

Joyce was beautiful. I guessed in her late sixties. Dark, flawless skin. Hair cut short, tight to her scalp, enhancing her features. She wore a plum-colored suit with a paisley blouse underneath the blazer. Red tainted lips spread into an inviting smile. "It's about time we introduced ourselves."

"Yes, it is. Thank you for saying hello."

Joyce and I occupied the same pew almost every Sunday. Over the past few weeks, we had exchanged glances and smiles, but I'd never reached out.

"I figured it was time, seeing as we both seem to prefer the back row." She leaned closer, her exotic, green eyes playful and comforting. "I need to stay close to the ladies' room if you know what I mean."

I preferred to stay close to the exit, but Joyce didn't need to know that silly detail.

My new friend moved her handbag from between us, set it on the other side of her lap, and inched her hip closer to mine. "Tuuli is a beautiful name."

"Thank you." Shame coiled through me, sinister and cold. If she knew the truth, my name would sicken her.

The band started to play. Joyce jumped to her feet and bounced on her toes for a few beats, then turned and gestured for me to stand. She clapped in rhythm, and when the lyrics kicked in, she sang along, loud and proud.

I rose, eyes glued to the woman next to me, enthralled with her infectious joy.

Without taking her eyes off the stage, she leaned into me. "That handsome boy behind the drum set is my grandson."

I nodded but didn't speak. I couldn't form a syllable through the lump in my throat.

Joyce raised her hands in praise. I stared at my palms. Palms that had touched the *enemy* and remained unscathed.

Guilt weighed heavy on my shoulders, crushing my spirit. My eyes filled with tears, and two bars into "Glorious Day," I was a blubbering mess.

I braved a glance at Joyce who seemed lost in the lyrics. So free, so full of the Holy Spirit, I wanted to hug her tight and soak up her positive energy.

There was no way the woman next to me was bad. She wasn't dirty. I didn't feel damned or disgusted for having touched or spoken to her. She'd made me feel...loved. She didn't know me, but I sensed that she wanted to, and I wanted to know her better. I wanted to know all the people surrounding me.

My tears fell harder with each beat of the drum. I couldn't stay. Not with the lyrics or the anticipation of Pastor

Davies' sermon. I couldn't stop the flood of emotion leaking down my face. I could not open my heart to the word of God when I was so full of self-hate.

I snatched my purse off the pew and bee-lined for the exit, heading left toward the lake, instead of right toward the bus stop. No way was I about to get on public transit in my emotional state. Everyone would stare and see me for what I was, weak and pathetic. So, despite the cold wind whipping through the tree branches and biting through the thin fabric of my cardigan, I headed toward work, on foot, again.

Halfway down Sunnyview Boulevard, where the houses tripled in size and the lake came into view, my tears dried, and I'd crammed the guilt back into the dark hole in my gut. I would go back to church next week, head held high. Maybe I would get there early enough to have coffee and talk with some of the people. I hoped Joyce would be there, and still wanted to sit next to me.

When a dark figure at the bottom of the hill caught my attention, an odd flutter rose in my chest, halting my brisk pace.

Even from a distance, Tito was recognizable. Larger than life. Focused. Inspiring.

His strides didn't falter, motions didn't slow, even with the steep incline.

Heat flooded my veins. My insides buzzed with anticipation, cosmic and utterly ridiculous.

The wind picked up as if challenged by his drive. Tito only put his head down and plowed through the gusts, rising higher, and closer to me. *Me*, who hadn't budged since laying eyes on *him*. Me, who stood shaking under the cold force of the wind—or maybe because of the sheer force of his raw, frightening beauty.

Feet planted firmly on the cracked cement, I waited, silent, nervous, anxious. Would he see me? Would he stop?

My fingers tingled, imagining the feel of his sweaty skin.

One block away. My cheeks heated.

Head down, he came closer. Closer.

See me.

A large gust blew hair across my face, temporarily blinding me, stinging my eyes, sticking to my lips.

I freed my face from one obstacle, only to be blindsided by the dark eyes that greeted me an arm's-length away.

"What's wrong?" Tito asked, foregoing pleasantries like, *Hello*, or *Hey*, or *What's up, Tuuli?*

Breathless and acutely aware that I should not have been the winded one, I mumbled, "Um. Nothing. Why?"

Tito pulled up the sleeve of his shirt and looked at his watch. "You're out early."

"Early? I don't understand."

"Church," he snapped. "It doesn't end for another thirty minutes."

His clipped tone made my head spin. I couldn't grasp what he was getting at, so I said, "Oh." I'd intended to elaborate, but he didn't give me a chance.

"You okay? Did something happen?"

"I'm fine. Why?"

Tito invaded my personal space, not touching, but enveloping me in his body heat nonetheless. "You've been crying."

"Oh. That." I waved my hand back and forth, the international gesture for, *oh, it was nothing.* "Girlie stuff. That's all."

An exhausted breath escaped his lips. His shoulders dropped along with his chin, and he stepped back, shaking his head as if disgusted with himself.

"Are *you* okay?" Drawn to him, I inched closer. Somewhere between *you're out early* and *girlie stuff,* it dawned on me that he knew when church ended. Meaning he'd paid attention. Meaning he'd maybe, possibly, although I couldn't understand why, timed his run so that he would bump into me again after the service ended.

"Me?" He smirked. "Yeah. Fine. Fine." Hands shoved deep inside the front pocket of his pullover, legs set at a wide stance, head cocked slightly to the side, he asked, "Why aren't you taking the bus today?"

The heat of his gaze burrowed straight through me, striking body parts unfamiliar with that level of burn. I trembled, my nerves under rapid fire.

Above his head, a squirrel ran across the telephone wire, giving me an excellent excuse to avoid the weight of his stare. "I needed to walk."

"With no coat, again," he said, looking over his shoulder, no doubt to see what had caught my attention.

"Oh, yeah. Forgot to grab it this morning."

"I'll walk with you." Tito turned and nudged me with his elbow. "I'm not much in the mood for a run today."

That small, thoughtless gesture, that tiny nudge made ridiculous things happen to my insides. Everything encased inside my skin started to buzz like I had been a house with no electricity, sitting in the dark, cold and quiet, and my power had just been restored.

Tito flipped the switch.

Even though he scared me, I didn't fear for my safety. He scared me because Tito seemed the type of person that would challenge me, rile me to the core, and I would either shrivel and die under the pressure, or grow wings and soar. He terrified me because, for some odd reason, Tito felt like a test.

A life lesson I didn't want to fail.

Tito

I'd failed miserably.

The prior evening, and again that morning, I'd convinced myself to stay away from Tuuli. Talked myself out of running the route that led past the church or timing my strides to happen by as she headed to the bus stop.

Somewhere along the line, however, my head and feet suffered a major miscommunication, and my legs led me straight to where I knew she would be.

Hell wasn't hot enough for bastards like me.

"Are you cold?" I asked, lifting the bottom hem of my sweatshirt, preparing to offer the tiny girl a shield against the biting wind.

"No. I'm good. Thanks, though." She grabbed my wrist and stopped me from undressing.

Fuck. Those cold, small fingers seared my skin.

"Why'd you leave early?"

"Hmm...Truth?" She turned her palms face up and studied the pink skin.

"Yeah. Truth."

Tuuli stopped and faced me, arms dropped to her sides. "Sometimes, I don't feel worthy of being in church. Sometimes, I feel like bad things are squeezing my heart so tight it's going to implode, create a black hole, and suck everybody in."

Her confession struck me hard, a lightning bolt searing my insides from head to heart to gut. I related, too well.

"That's dark." I had nothing more to offer, other than truths that would scare her.

She started to walk again, her usual bouncy sway missing from her strides. "My turn for a question."

"That's fair, I suppose."

"Were you coming to meet me?"

Her bold inquiry caught me off guard. Before thinking, before taking a breath to come up with a convincing lie, I confessed, "Yes."

"Why?" she asked, gaze to the ground, windblown hair hiding her features.

"That's two questions. It's my turn."

"Fine," she laughed. "If that's how you wanna play it."

I didn't want to play at all. She was a child. That simple fact should've stopped me from asking, "That guy from the other night. He your boyfriend?"

"Umm." She opened her mouth to speak, shook her head, then mumbled, "It's complicated."

"It's not a complicated question. The answer is either yes or no."

"No."

Good. "But he used to be?"

"That's two questions. It's my turn."

I expected her to ask again why I'd come to meet her. She didn't.

"How'd you get the scar?" She raised a finger and tapped on her temple.

My hand lifted, a defense mechanism, and I tugged the hood of my sweatshirt further over my face. "House fire."

"You were inside the house?"

I wasn't going there. Ever. Not with Tuuli, not with anybody. "That's two questions. My turn."

We continued with the back and forth, keeping it light with surface level probes. Worked for me. I sensed her secrets were locked as tight as mine.

Two blocks away from The Stop, Tuuli threw me for a loop when she asked, "Why no girlfriend?" And then added, "Someone as hot as you should have girls lined up for miles."

She thought I was hot. Fuck. I was fucked.

"It's complicated." Knowing that answer wasn't sufficient to warn her off, I further explained, "I'm complicated. Don't do relationships."

"Oh." She dropped her gaze back to the ground, where it stayed until we entered the diner.

Tuuli beelined for the back room, but not before mumbling over her shoulder, "Thanks for walking me to work, Grim."

Grim? I shook off the weird vibes plucking my nerves and headed for home, dead set on a shower, where I definitely would not be jerking off to the mental image of Tuuli, the forbidden fruit.

I cussed under my breath. Who was I kidding? I wouldn't be able to think straight until I jerked off thinking about Tuuli.

Tomorrow was another day.

Tomorrow, I would stay away from her.

Today? Epic failure.

Tuuli

I'd failed miserably at hiding my blush when Tito came to the diner for his evening meal. Fortunately, he hadn't looked at me once, not even to recite his dinner order. Unfortunately, his lack of common courtesy had my guts twisted in knots.

Since our morning game of twenty questions, I'd battled unease, my heart thumping two beats behind pace. He had come to meet me at church, on purpose, but then he'd warned me away. I didn't understand. The man was so confusing. Brooding and closed-off one minute, over-concerned and protective the next.

The burn of bleach stung my eyes as I wiped down the table next to Tito. I sucked up my insecurities and spoke first, asking why he hadn't touched his club sandwich.

His gaze sliced to mine, features set hard. "Not feeling it today, kiddo."

Kiddo. Ouch. You didn't call someone you were attracted to *kiddo.* How stupid I'd been. Wishful thinking was a fool's luxury. I hated being a girl sometimes.

The cowbell jingled, announcing new customers. I knew the voices without having to look. The group of college boys came in for breakfast once a week, usually on Monday mornings, and always hungover. Judging by the volume of their speech and the obscenities they spewed, tomorrow would be no exception.

I did my best to encourage them to the far corner of the diner, where they wouldn't disturb our other guests, but they insisted on sitting in my section, therefore, taking the table next to Tito.

I took their drink orders, ignoring the lewd remarks about my blonde hair and perfect tits, and managed to evade a wandering hand aimed for my butt.

My cheeks burned. Partly because of my crude admirers, but mostly because Tito had to bear witness. He still hadn't looked at me. I knew because I checked every five seconds.

I brought their drinks, and with a fake smile, patiently took their orders in-between blatant advances. Wasn't the first time I'd dealt with assholes, inebriated or otherwise. Wouldn't be the last.

I scribbled the last order and headed to the kitchen, for a breather, and a minute to gather my wits.

"Toodaloo!" Charlie shouted over his shoulder. "How's it goin' out there?

"Good, Charlie. Except for the frat boys at table three."

He dropped the fry basket into the oil, then turned to face me. "Want me to take that table?"

Charlie, bless his heart, never failed to step in when a customer made any of us feel uncomfortable.

"No. I've got it under control." I'd dealt with worse, much worse. Erik, for example.

Charlie gawked through the service window. His whole body jiggled with his chuckle. "Looks to me like Moretti has it handled."

"What?" I screeched, sidling up to the chef and rising on my tiptoes to see over the ledge.

Sure enough, Tito, still hooded, sat next to the guy with the wandering hand. His two buddies shifted nervously in their seats, faces pale. They started to scoot from the table. Tito halted their escape by slapping a hand on one of their wrists. Both pulled a wad of cash out of their pockets, dropped it on the table, and scurried out of the diner, leaving their friend behind.

Charlie grabbed their order and tore it into pieces, huffed, then mumbled, "That's my boy," before heading back to the fryer.

Tito scooted from the table, waited for the third drunk to slide free, patted him on the shoulder, and waited for the guy to make his exit. Then, as if nothing had happened, he returned to his seat, picked up his sandwich, and started to eat.

I didn't know if ovaries could explode, but I was pretty sure mine had detonated.

When I loosened my grip on the counter, dropped my heels to the ground, and turned around, Slade stood behind me, arms folded, her electric smile lighting the room.

"Whatcha looking at?" she asked, fully aware of who I'd been spying on.

"Oh. Um. Sorry. I was just taking a quick break." I tried to scoot around her, but she stepped to the left, blocking my direct path to the door.

My face heated a thousand degrees, and I resisted the urge to flee.

"I have a feeling those jerks won't be back. As in...ever."

She'd seen the whole thing.

Charlie laughed. "Tito probably scared them straight out of town."

"What's that supposed to mean?" I asked.

With a smirk and a head shake, she responded, "Oh, nothing. It's just that those Triple T boys get a little overzealous when it comes to the ladies in their life."

"Triple T boys?" I asked.

She lifted her hand and raised three fingers one at a time while ticking off the names, "Tango, Tito, Tucker."

Charlie laughed. "Corny."

Slade shrugged. "I know. Corny. But cute. And accurate." She challenged me to argue with a raised eyebrow.

I wasted no time reminding her, "I'm not his lady."

"You're not?" She smirked.

"No. I hardly know him."

Slade stared down at me wearing a crooked smile like she knew a secret and wanted to share, or like she was waiting for the lightbulb over my head to blink because I'd just realized the solution to a major life crisis.

I huffed, done with the conversation, and, more accurately, not willing to admit I was giddy over the fact that Tito had possibly defended my honor.

Maybe he liked me.

Or maybe that's how he was built.

He would've done the same for Slade or Margie.

I made my way back to the dining room. Back to work. Waitress mode: on. Pathetic girl with a crush mode: off.

The drunk bunch had left three stacks of money on the table.

I felt the weight of Tito's stare as I shoved the folded bills into my apron. The tip had to be close to a hundred dollars. For a table I hadn't even served. I wondered what he'd said to scare them off. Shameful, really, how much the gesture thrilled me.

I avoided Tito for as long as I could, ten minutes at least.

When I approached to clear his table, he turned his head to stare out the window. Only, when I followed his gaze, he wasn't staring out the window at all. He was looking at me through the reflection in the glass. Our eyes met, he looked away, and I pretended the exchange hadn't happened.

I didn't ask if he was done eating. I didn't ask if he wanted a drink refill. I didn't ask if he wanted the bill. I mumbled, "Thank you," trusting he knew what the gratitude was for, and carried his dishes to the kitchen.

When I returned, he was gone.

When my shift ended, he was outside, waiting for *me*.

Tito

I waited outside for Tuuli. Grateful for the cool air and dark sky. Gave me room to think and time to clear the shit in my head. I'd tried to go home. I had. Only, I couldn't, in good conscience, sit in my safe apartment, while Tuuli rode the bus, surrounded by God knows what kind of riffraff.

I tried to talk myself out of waiting for her. Then I realized I was going to hell anyway, so what difference would it make if I committed a few more sins? I'd pulled my car around back, where I knew she'd exit, and I waited.

Fuck. She was still a kid. Every time she was near, I struggled to keep my hands off, reminded myself she was off limits. Yet, I woke every morning anxious to see her face, aching to hear that sweet, soft voice.

The back door opened. I wiped my sweaty palms on my pants. She came outside, turned, and locked the door. Charlie would be inside closing up the place, and it irritated me that he hadn't come out to see her safely to the bus stop.

Then again, maybe Charlie didn't know she took the bus. I only knew because I'd obsessively watched since the night Tango had carried her out of the bloody motel room where I'd killed the last surviving member of the Markovic Cartel. The night she had tried to defend Aida from Rafael Turner, a man twice her size, putting her own life on the line.

I'd have a talk with Charlie. Tomorrow.

For the time being, I would see her safely home.

Tuuli searched for something in her purse and hadn't noticed my car yet. I opened the door and stepped into the cold night air, blowing a low whistle to catch her attention.

The timid little bunny looked up, and swear to Christ, when she smiled, my knees buckled. Thank fuck I'd stayed behind my door.

"I'll give you a ride home."

Whatever she'd been looking for was forgotten and she made her way to my car. I jogged around to the passenger door and pulled it open.

When her breast brushed against my arm, I damn near groaned out loud. She was a baby, making me nothing more than a pedo pervert. Fuck.

Under Voltolini's command, I had tortured, dismembered, and disposed of pedophiles. I'd agreed to help Tucker and Aida take more of them down. Yet there I sat, pining over a child myself.

I had to shake this kid.

And I would. After I saw her safely home.

I turned up the heat and the stereo and made my way out of The Truck Stop parking lot. Tiamat's "Love in Chains" belted through the speakers and I chuckled. Fitting.

Tuuli turned, eyes bright. "What's funny?"

"Nothing." I shook my head. "Which way am I going?" I asked, pausing at the intersection.

"1415 Apricot Lane."

I turned the volume up a notch, discouraging conversation, and drove into the night toward Tuuli's home, where I would drop her off, then head to a local bar and drink her out of my system.

When I pulled in front of her house, she twisted in her seat to face me, turned the volume down, and stared at me long and hard.

Damn, how I wanted to stare back, get lost in those wild blue eyes, let her see the real me. Instead, I said, "What?"

My guts twisted at the hurt on her face. Her brows drew tight before she dropped her gaze to the console between us. Good. I couldn't let her see how she affected me.

"Nothing," she mumbled. "Um. I just..." She shook her head and reached for the door handle. "Thank you. That's all." She slipped out, closed the door, and ran to the gate leading to the house. With one hand on the picket fence, she glanced at me over her shoulder.

I hated being the reason for that sad expression. Hated myself for wanting to be the reason for her smile. So, I drove away before seeing her safely inside. I drove away before getting out of the car and acting on my urges.

CHAPTER 3

Tuuli

EVERY NIGHT FOR A week straight, Tito came for dinner at The Stop right before closing time. He would wait in his booth for my shift to end, offer to drive me home, and refuse to take no for an answer.

I didn't understand why, but I didn't question his motives, either. I liked that he drove me home. I appreciated that he never invited himself inside. Not that I would've allowed him in, but I liked that he didn't ask. Because if he asked, I would have to say no, even though I wanted to say yes. I wanted to ask him in so badly my chest ached.

I couldn't invite him in because the house on Apricot Lane was not actually my home.

One week had passed. One week of warm rides in a hot car next to a ridiculously hot guy, rather than long walks home, alone, with no coat.

Sunday had come too soon, but not soon enough. I sat in my usual spot in the same pew I always occupied. I straightened the hem of my skirt and admired the silky sage and pink print. I usually wore my work uniform to church, seeing as I had to head straight to The Stop after the service ended. But I'd been given a rare Sunday off, and I took advantage, wearing my new dress and heels. I'd even taken time to put on mascara, blush, and lip gloss.

The worship band played their last song, a gritty rock version of "Amazing Grace," and Pastor Davies gave his benediction. For some reason, the guilt that usually accompanied his sendoff didn't settle on me as it had in the past. For some reason, I didn't feel the need to rush out ahead of everyone else. Maybe because leaving meant going home alone, which meant hanging up my new clothes and most likely not having an occasion to wear them again for a long time.

When I made my way outdoors, I stopped at the top of the stairs and raised my face to the sun. Warm tingles danced across my cheeks. The sky was clear save a few puffs of white. The breeze had a chilly bite to it, but all in all, I couldn't have asked for a more beautiful day. Spring was coming. I loved spring.

I started down the steps and nearly tripped over my feet when I saw the tall figure across the street leaning against a tree. Black shoes, black running pants, black sweatshirt. He had one foot propped against the bark, both hands tucked in his pocket.

His face wasn't hidden. He'd been waiting. Watching.

For me.

I was so thankful for my new dress.

Tito didn't smile. His slow perusal up and down the small stretch of my body, however, seemed to express that he liked my outfit, too. His gaze landed on my face. His chest rose and fell. He looked away. Shook his head. Pushed off the tree and jogged across the street, stopping at the sidewalk.

I met him where he stood. "Hi."

He looked over my shoulder, then jerked his chin toward the church. "Why?"

I waited for him to say more. He didn't.

"Why do I come to church?" I asked, confused.

Tito nodded.

"I don't know. I like it. I'm happy when I'm here."

"That the only reason?"

Oddly, I was compelled to speak from the heart rather than cower at his sharp tone.

I started toward the bus stop. "Here, I'm reminded that I'm loved. That I have a Father who loves me. I'm reminded that life isn't about me." I sucked in a breath and stopped, turning to face him. "I come to church because I'm learning that no matter my past, no matter my sins, how big or small, I'm forgiven, and in God's eyes at least, I'm clean. There's hope for a better life, for a better me."

"Sins?"

"Yeah." I started walking again, taking it slow, because the heels, regardless of their price tag, were doing a number on my feet. "I have a past I'm not proud of."

"You're just a kid. How many sins could you have racked up?"

And there it was—*a kid*. I laughed, despite the claws tearing my heart to shreds. Of course, Tito saw me as a child. Everyone did, why wouldn't he? I was small and slight, with a personality to match. "I'm twenty. Not a kid."

"Wait." Tito stepped back and scrubbed a hand over his head. "You're twenty?"

I nodded. "I know, I look young. Nobody takes me seriously, everybody talks down to me. What's worse? Even when I was a child, I wasn't allowed to be."

It hurt, knowing he thought me young and naive. It hurt enough that I felt that familiar ache in my muscles, the ache that hits right before an ugly cry. "Listen, um...I gotta go." I stepped out of my shoes, scooped them off the ground, and took off, shouting over my shoulder, "I don't want to miss my bus." I ran toward the bus stop. Away from Tito. Away from the emotions he evoked.

"Wait." He caught me halfway to my destination. I was out of breath. Tito wasn't. He was, however, breathing heavy, from anger, judging by the burn of his glare and the tight grip of his fingers around my bicep. "Jesus Christ, Tuuli. Why the hell are you running from me?"

"I don't want to miss my bus," I mumbled, telling half the truth. Mostly, I ran because I didn't want him to see me cry. Ashamed, I looked to the ground. My feet were small compared to Tito's. They were also cold and dirty from running barefoot. Great. I ruined my pedicure.

"Look at me," he ordered, ducking his head to catch my gaze. "Look at me, please."

I raised my chin then my eyes to meet his, which were crinkled with worry.

"What'd I say?" he asked, voice soft, controlled.

There was hope in his haunted eyes. Beauty in his scarred face. A soft glow hidden behind the dark mask he wore. A warmth I longed to bask in.

"Why'd you run?" he repeated.

The familiar roar of the bus's engine grew louder behind me. I was out of time, and dear Lord, I was out of my mind, with want, and fear, and unbearable urges. The rap, rap, rap in my chest beat like a final countdown, and I feared if I didn't act, didn't do something, I would cease to be, disappear like a fading apparition.

I dropped my shoes, gripped the sides of his hood, and pushed up on my toes, pressing my lips to the rough stubble surrounding his mouth.

I pulled away, then kissed him again.

"I like you, Tito," I whispered before scooping my shoes off the ground and sprinting to catch the bus.

Without looking back, I found a seat, tucked my feet under my rear, closed my eyes, and pressed a trembling finger to my lips. He hadn't kissed me back. Not really. But he hadn't pulled away either. Funny thing was, his response didn't matter. I had taken the initiative. Acted on impulse. Conquered fear. I had kissed a man who was dark and dirty, and the earth hadn't opened up and swallowed me whole.

Father had been wrong.

Daddy Dearest had lied about so many things.

Adrenaline could be to blame, or perhaps the lingering tingle of his stubble on my skin, but the slow burn I suffered every time Tito was near exploded into a full-blown blaze.

Didn't matter that he thought me a child. Didn't matter that I'd been lying to him. Didn't matter that we were polar opposites. I stole a taste, a kiss.

I wanted more.

Tito

I wanted more. I wanted more. Fuck me; I wanted more. She wasn't a kid. She was legal. I sure as hell didn't deserve that bit of good news, but I'd take it.

The timid little bunny—of legal age—came out of her hole and kissed the scary beast. A fissure in my tight chest opened wide, releasing pressure, filling me with pride, or hope, or fuck, I hadn't a clue. She'd kissed me. I'd let her. Without reciprocation. Kissing her back would've soiled the beauty of the act, her act, hers to own because I could see in her frightened gaze that it took courage for her to press her lips to mine, to speak those words: I like you.

I absorbed the sweet innocence of her kiss, but more so, her confession. She liked me. I couldn't fathom why. I wasn't sure why I liked her, too. But I did, or I wouldn't have been standing outside the church like a crazy stalker waiting to see her. I wouldn't have chased her to the bus stop, or climbed in after her, or parked my ass in the seat next to hers.

I needed more Tuuli more than I needed to breathe.

She'd yet to notice that I'd followed, and I watched, silent, while she closed her eyes, touched her pink lips, and smiled. Tuuli stayed that way, lolling her head to the side to rest on the window.

When I could no longer stand the silence, I whispered, "I'm sorry."

Tuuli's eyes met mine, wide and blue, giving the sky one hell of a run for its money. The surprise on her face faded to relief. "For what?" she whispered back.

"For upsetting you."

She shook her head as if she couldn't process my words. "What are you doing here?"

Stalking you. I sunk deeper into my seat. "I'm hungry. Thought I'd head downtown for a bite. Was hoping you'd join me."

A small smirk played on her face. "This bus doesn't head downtown, Tito."

"Oh." I scratched my temple and dropped my chin to my chest. Smooth one.

"But if we get off two stops down, we can walk," she said, offering the pathetic dog a bone.

"Good. Yeah. We can walk."

The bus reeked of body odor, exhaust, and cheap vinyl. The ride was loud, bumpy, and I'd counted three unsavory characters when I'd entered. I decided then that Tuuli would never ride the bus again.

"Why don't you have a car?"

Rolling her head to look at me, she sighed and said, "I do. Or, I did, but it's back in Rockypoint. Where it will stay."

I waited for an explanation. She studied me for a moment before shaking her thoughts away and saying, "It's a long story. I'll get a new one soon. Saving up. Almost there."

Rockypoint was a small town, about an hour north of Whisper Springs. I wanted to probe. I refrained. Her story. Her timeline. I assumed that, like me, there were things she needed to keep private, and she had damn good reasons for needing to do so. So, I didn't pry.

Before the bus screeched to a halt, Tuuli slipped her feet back into her nude-colored heels. Shamefully, I watched, admiring the arches of her small feet, the smooth curve of her calves. Her skin was pale, but flawless, like rare, opulent china. My fingers were rough and worn, but damn if I didn't want to drag them up the length of her legs anyway.

I licked the dryness from my lips, smiling when I tasted the remnants of her lip gloss.

"This is us." Tuuli nudged me with her elbow and pushed to stand.

I followed her off the bus and into the fresh air. We headed toward downtown Whisper Springs, the small, yet slowly expanding city nestled on the rim of Lake Willow.

My uncle owned most of the city, from real estate, to media, to hospitality and entertainment venues. Carlos Rossi was the king of Whisper Springs, making my cousin, Tango, the prince and heir. As a kid, I had stayed with my cousin every summer. Defiled three of my aunt's dance students in Lakeside Park, and suffered my first broken arm thanks to a skiing accident on the very water we were heading toward.

"Where should we eat?" Tuuli asked, bumping my shoulder while she avoided a deep crack in the cement.

"Somewhere close. You're not wearing a coat again."

"I'm fine," she said, her body tightening against a shiver.

Jesus, what did the girl have against outerwear?

"Here," I said, pulling my sweatshirt over my head.

Tuuli stopped in her tracks. "Really, I'm fine."

I held my hoodie toward her anyway.

"Listen. I don't expect you to understand, but I haven't bought myself anything new in a long time." She looked down and smoothed her hands over the fabric at her waist. "I'll probably never get to wear this again. It feels good to dress up, and I don't want to cover up with a coat. I might sound stupid and immature, but I need to enjoy feeling pretty for one day."

God, she had no clue how gorgeous she was, make-up or not, dress or not. Another personality trait I found attractive. I tugged my sweatshirt back on. Tuuli watched, smiled, and whispered, "Thank you."

"You're pretty every day, Bunny," I said, then tucked her under my arm.

She didn't pull away, and damn, that felt good. She did, however, ask, "What are you doing?"

"Keeping you warm," I replied, and then steered her into the first restaurant we came across.

It wasn't until we'd started on our three-bean soup and meatball subs that she asked, "Why did you call me Bunny?"

I only smiled.

I had smiled four times by the time we finished eating.

Tuuli

By the time we finished eating, Tito had smiled five times. The last was only half a grin, but I'd take it. He had a beautiful face, and when he was happy, his eyes crinkled at the corners. The warm, olive shade of his skin seemed even darker in contrast to his white teeth. And his eyes…dear Lord, his eyes, they burned, glowing like molten glass still being shaped over the fire.

The conversation stayed casual, neither of us breaching our unspoken personal boundaries. When I stole a glance outside, the sky had darkened, and minuscule drops of water dotted the sidewalk.

"It's raining," I said, crinkling my napkin between my fingers. "I should head home."

"No. Not yet." He swallowed his last sip of coffee. "Something I wanna show you. It isn't far."

I glanced at the large, farm-themed clock hanging over the counter. If I stayed with Tito, I'd miss the last bus. Meaning I'd have one long, miserable walk home, meaning I for sure would freeze, and undoubtedly ruin my dress. On the other hand, I could call a cab. Did people do that anymore? Or was Uber the better option? I had no idea. Also, I had no cell, so Uber was probably a no-go, anyway.

"Okay." I pushed from my seat. "But I'll miss the last bus home. I don't have a cell. Could you call me a cab when we're finished?"

Tito stared at me. Blinked. Opened his mouth to speak. Changed his mind. He thumbed through the wad of cash he held, then mumbled, "You don't have a phone?"

"I do. Or, did."

His shoulders bunched. "Let me guess. You left it in Rockypoint?"

My brother had smashed my cell in a fit of alcohol-induced rage, but I wasn't ready to discuss my brother with anyone. "Yes. I'll get one soon. Saving up for it."

"Almost there?" he asked, dropping money on the table.

I laughed. "Yeah. Almost there."

His hand landed on my lower back while he guided me outside. "So, you're saving for a car and a phone. Anything else?"

Pretty much everything a girl needed to live on her own. "That's about it."

We made it halfway down the block when Tito stopped. "You're limping."

My attempt at ignoring the pain and hiding my misery had failed. "Blister. New shoes."

"Fuck." His eyes sliced to mine. "Why didn't you tell me?"

A lie formed on the back of my tongue. Before the fabrication left my lips, he turned his back to me and said, "Hop on."

"What?"

He squatted. "I'll carry you...it's only a block. Hop on."

"A piggyback?"

"Yeah. Get on." He wiggled his fingers behind his butt.

Oh, Lord. Well, options were limited. Die of embarrassment or suffer for vanity. I'd never had a high threshold for pain, so I hopped up, wrapped my arms around his thick neck, squeezed my thighs around his trim waist, and prayed my skirt was covering my backside. Like I weighed nothing more than a rag doll, he tucked his arms under my legs and scooted me higher.

"We good?" he asked.

"All good." I laughed into the thick, black cotton covering his head.

Two blocks later, we reached our destination—a tall building with a security entrance. Tito crouched. I slid to my feet.

"What is this place?" I asked, slipping out of my heels while admiring the mammoth steel and glass construction, but mostly admiring his strong fingers while they punched a sequence of numbers on the keypad.

The door eased open and he stepped aside, allowing me entrance first.

"You'll see." Once again, his hand rested at the small of my back, a small gesture that made me feel larger than life. He guided me toward a set of elevators, typed numbers into another keypad, and pressed the large "P."

The elevator doors opened into a foyer, empty except for two large planters filled with lush green foliage. A steel-plated door opened into a grand, open, airy, living space. We entered a state-of-the-art kitchen with stainless steel appliances and black granite everything else. A wall-to-wall window with a slider door opened onto an enormous deck that seemed to stretch over Lake Willow.

"Whose home is this?" I asked, taking in the barren, pristine surroundings.

Tito leaned his shoulder against the polished cement column that separated the kitchen space from the living area. "It could be mine. All I gotta do is sign on the dotted line."

"Yeah, right." I laughed. "This is the penthouse. It has to cost well over a mil."

Shoving his hands into his pockets, he mumbled, "Closer to two. Your point?"

"Guess I don't have one. It's just...I don't even know what you do for a living." I gestured to the gorgeous staircase, floating white steps with a polished steel banister. "And you're showing me a ridiculously lavish home, with a view of...well...everything, and I guess I'm just surprised. Why did you bring me here? I don't understand."

The brooding man shrugged away from the column and walked to the window, pressing his forehead to the glass. "I guess I wanted to see it through someone else's eyes before I made my decision."

"Through mine?"

"Yes," he said without hesitation.

My guts floated, gravity be damned. "Why?"

He turned to face me. Voice thick with irritation, he said, "Because you'll be honest with me."

"Fair enough." He'd offered a soapbox, laid it at my feet. I'd make the most of the opportunity. "You really want my opinion?"

"More than anything."

I nodded. Choked down my trepidation. "Okay. Well. Nice homes are great. Really. I have nothing against them. I get the whole buying in a nice neighborhood and all that, you know, for safety and security reasons and whatnot, but this? This is over the top. This is gloating. This feels a lot like you're telling the world, *'Look at me, I'm richer than you.'*"

"Showing off?" He leaned back against the window, arms crossed, glare focused and challenging.

My throat dried, all the menacing, broody vibes heating the air. "Yes. Exactly. Showing off."

A huff. "Maybe it's nothing more than an investment."

I was losing steam. "Maybe."

"Oh, come on. Don't tell me you wouldn't love waking up to this view every morning."

With him? I'd give my left arm for that opportunity. "Sure. I'd feel like a princess. But honestly, I'd be happy to wake up in a soft bed. I'd be content with reliable warm water for my showers. A working toilet."

The mood changed in a heartbeat, his inquisitive glare morphing into something more akin to concern. "You don't have those things?"

"What? No. Of course I do." I waved my hand frantically in front of my face as if that would erase my almost-slip. "It's just...I mean...There are so many people who don't have those things, and to them, this place would be, well? A slap in the face. With the money it cost to buy these digs, you could probably buy ten struggling homeless mothers their own place. I guess my point is, if you can afford to buy a place like this, you have too much money."

"I work damn hard for my money. Bleed for it."

And he was back to brooding.

I wanted off my soapbox.

"I'm sure you do, but you can't take it with you when you die, so you could use it to change a life, or maybe even save a life."

Was that a smirk or a sneer? I couldn't tell.

"This how all churchy people talk?" he asked, pushing away from the window and prowling around me like a panther ready to pounce.

Self-preservation kicked in, and I took slow steps, putting distance between us. "I'm going to ignore that question."

I should have kept my mouth shut.

"Do you like the penthouse or not?"

"It's the most beautiful home I've ever seen."

Tito

The penthouse wasn't the most beautiful home I'd ever visited. Swear to my maker, though, with Tuuli standing in front of the window against the backdrop of the lake and mountains, in her spring-colored dress with that nervous smile and adorable bare feet, the lakeside home became the most welcoming real estate I'd ever occupied.

Over the years, I'd laid my head in many different varieties of square footage, ranging from ramshackle to ridiculous. Not once had I ached to share my space with another human being. Never had a woman looked more at home than the petite, blonde angel blinking her ridiculous wide eyes at me. Sweet, innocent, fucking timid little bunny. I wanted nothing more than to scoop her up and stroke every inch of her pure porcelain skin.

Like a beast stalking his prey, I inched forward, drawing closer, careful not to scare her off. As we stood toe to toe and her pert little nose twitched and the heel of her left foot bounced incessantly, I drew my cell from my pocket and dialed my uncle's number. While I waited for him to answer, I raised my gaze from her delectable body to her lips, then up, hoping she would meet my gaze, yet terrified of what she might see. After a gnaw on her bottom lip and a nervous bounce, she finally looked me in the eye.

I winked. "Will you help me decorate?"

She laughed through her nose. Dropped her gaze to her feet, where she scratched her left foot with the bottom of her right. "I...um...I don't know anything about decorating."

Fuck me, but those pink toenails were hot as hell.

Carlos answered. "Tito, boy. Nice to hear from you."

"Hey, Uncle Carlos. I've decided to buy." I brushed a stray hair off her cheek.

Tuuli's eyes narrowed. She took a step back and too far away, leaving my hand hanging in the air.

"Great, kiddo. Come by tomorrow. We'll get the ball rolling."

"See ya tomorrow." I ended the call.

In a voice frail and full of disappointment, she said, "So, you're a showoff, then."

Knife to the chest.

She didn't know me. Perhaps the time had come to offer a small piece of my reality. "That's not entirely true."

I hated that she wouldn't look at me. "Come here. Maybe this will help you understand." I grabbed her hand and led her up the staircase, through the upstairs hall, and to the third story master suite. The room may as well have been sitting on a cloud. Wall-to-wall windows. Three-hundred-and-sixty-degree view of Whisper Springs. Open. Bright. Breathtaking. Even the master bath boasted a million-dollar view.

Tuuli remained silent, taking in her surroundings. She pushed open the slider door to the deck and gasped when she stepped outside to the private oasis with the outdoor shower and swimming jacuzzi.

"I've spent too damn many years underground. Or in windowless rooms, in front of computer screens, dealing with dangerous people and their vile shit. Don't get me wrong. I love working. I'm the best at what I do. But my job can be suffocating."

I shoved the hood off my head and tapped at the scar on my face. "This? This right here. The day it happened? Thought it was going to be my last day on Earth. Thought I'd take my last breath in a musty basement surrounded by the darkest people you'd ever want to meet."

I looked away, avoiding the pity on her face.

"My uncle offered me this place, knowing what I've lived, knowing what I need."

"And what is it you need?"

"Air." A thousand pounds of pressure left my body with the simple confession. "To me, this place is air, it's oxygen, and light, and freedom. Do I need twenty-thousand square feet? No. You're right. Nobody does. But I need to breathe, Bunny. I need to fuckin' breathe."

Her gaze dropped again to my feet, her head bowed.

"Look at me."

She did, stepping closer in the process. So close, I could smell the rain on her hair. Lifting a small finger to my face, she traced the outline of my scar, those blue beauties studying every inch of my mug.

Her lips parted on a sigh, her shoulders relaxed, and her gaze rested on my mouth. She wanted my lips. Fuck if I didn't want to devour hers.

I couldn't resist a second longer. I slid a hand around her neck, tangling my fingers through the silky mess, and I pulled her close, ducking to meet her halfway. I kissed her soft and slow, tender, and with no intentions, no underlying goal other than tasting and feeling and being closer to a soul that called to mine.

Tuuli was soft and pliant and so damn small in my arms. Petite and modest. The complete opposite of every woman I'd ever touched. White and pure. Tuuli was perfect. So goddamn perfect my chest hurt.

I would muddy the beauty in my arms. I would ruin her; there was no doubt. A noble man would've sent her on her way. A worthy man would never have lured the innocent to his den. I was no more noble than I was worthy of her kiss.

I didn't want to break her. I didn't want to stain her with my sins, so I broke the kiss before our kiss became more.

I was not, however, ready to let her go.

I pulled her close and held her small frame against my deadly planes. "When is your next day off?" I mumbled into her hair.

"Tuesday," she answered into my shirt.

Two days. Fuck. Could I wait two days? "Do you have plans?"

"No."

"Good. I'll pick you up at nine."

"It's a date," was her simple reply. No, *Where are we going? What should I wear?* No batting her lashes, sexual innuendos, or lovelorn expectations. Just blind trust, bright eyes, and a chest-piercing smile.

I called a cab. After paying the driver, and seeing them off, I lifted my face to the crying sky. Cool pellets of rain batted my cheeks and rolled down my neck, soothing the burn below the surface of my skin.

Then I ran, pushing through the dreary afternoon until I was nothing but movement and sweat and breathing. Until my mind numbed, the screams dimmed, and images of an innocent, blue-eyed beauty were all that haunted me.

CHAPTER 4

Tuuli

"HOW YA DOIN' TODAY, Toodaloo?" Charlie asked, eyes red and moist from the sting of freshly chopped onions.

"You know how they say you are what you eat?" I poured myself a glass of orange juice. Not the breakfast I needed, but I was grateful nonetheless.

"Mmhmm," Charlie mumbled, his knife moving in a blur against the wood board.

"Well, today, I'm Cheez Whiz," I deadpanned. "That's how I'm doing."

Electricity had been a no-go since I'd moved into my brother's home. My supply of nonperishables had dwindled since Tito started driving me home, leaving me two options for last night's dinner: canned cheese and crackers, or a can of tuna. Tuna would've been the healthy option, but the can opener had rusted through and snapped in half three days ago.

Charlie laughed. "So, you're a gooey mess, but morbidly delicious."

"Sounds about right." I gulped my O.J.

"Oh, hey," he said, pointing his knife my way. "There were a couple of calls for you this morning."

"Me?"

"Yeah, you."

Weird. "You sure about that?"

"Don't know anyone else named Tuuli."

Not good. Definitely not good. "Did they leave a message?"

"No." Charlie swiped a knuckle under his eyes. "The guy was a gentleman, though."

"Thanks, Charlie." I pulled my apron strings tight before tying the knot and scooted past the giant, wondering who my mystery caller might've been. I wasn't left to ponder long because when I entered the dining room, Erik stood at the counter in a light gray suit that looked hand-tailored, and shoes that were too pointy. His platinum hair was slicked back and set hard into perfection. Try as he might, no amount of designer clothing or beauty products for men would mask the trailer trash bully I knew him to be.

"What do you want?" I forced my gaze upward, then higher still, into his stone-cold eyes. Held my ground for a good ten seconds before wimping out and busying myself with the menus.

"That's no way to greet an Elder, Tuuli."

My insides vibrated. "You are not my Elder. I no longer belong to your church."

He merely flashed his over-bleached set of porcelains and said, "That's a good one, little girl." Laughing, he pulled at the knot on his tie. "You and me, we are the church. We are the future, or have you forgotten?"

"How could I forget? You seared it into my skin and brain for years." I winced at my outburst, bracing for a strike that didn't come. Eyes to the ground, I whispered, "My brother said—"

Long fingers clamped around my arm, silencing me with the threat of pain. Erik tilted his head but didn't dare lower himself to my level. "I know all about the deal you made with your brother. Had a nice chat with him yesterday. Straightened a few things out."

"Yeah?" I yanked my arm free, praying he wouldn't turn violent in public. "Straightened what out, exactly?" I hadn't seen or heard from my older sibling in months. I didn't dare let Erik know I was out of the loop.

"He told me why you're working in this shit hole. Told me about his promise to free you from your duty. Problem with that arrangement, Tuuli, is that you were never his to set free."

I knew where the discussion was headed. My opinion, my voice, no matter how loud, would make no difference. Regardless, I opened my mouth to speak.

Erik silenced me with a hard glare. "Hold your tongue, girl. You've forgotten your place. I'm done with the games. Get your things; you're coming home with me."

"No," I snapped, taking a step back, surprising myself.

The cowbell rattled, drawing Erik's attention to the door. Fearing his retribution, I took the opportunity to put more space between us and stepped behind the counter.

Tucker came my way, holding a squealing Lucia in his arms. Tucker, who was tall, blonde, and blue-eyed, would've been perfectly acceptable to Erik if it weren't for his dark-skinned, ebony-haired daughter.

Oh, no. No. No. Please. No. Keep walking. Don't…

"Hi, Tuuli. Mind holding her for a sec?" Tucker settled the baby in my arms. "Be right back."

He didn't wait for me to answer before jogging through the double doors toward Slade's office.

A strange rumble rose from Erik's chest.

Lucia made a funny noise, and I looked down at her hair, all fuzzy and soft, and the dark shade of her skin. Her green eyes widened when they met mine and her chubby face cracked in a wide grin, effectively cracking something in my chest.

"What the fuck you been doing here, Tuuli? Making friends?" Erik mumbled.

My heartbeat thrummed loud between my ears. I was so angry I wanted to scratch his eyes out or grab a fork and stab him in the throat. Even though the counter separated us, I took another step away from the horrid man.

Tucker burst back into the room. "Thanks," he said, snatching his daughter from my arms. "I had to grab some papers from the office." He took Erik in, shifted Lucia against his chest, and stepped around the counter to offer his hand. "Tucker Slade."

Erik straightened his shoulders and acted the gentleman, shaking Tucker's offered palm. "Erik Meyer."

"You Tuuli's brother?" Tucker asked innocently. "You two look almost identical."

Horrified, I sucked in a breath and waited for the inevitable explosion.

Eerily calm, Erik laughed. "No, sir." He shot a glance at me.

The cowbell rattled again, but I didn't look to see who had entered.

Erik continued his exchange with Tucker, stating, "I'm Tuuli's fiancé." He then rapped his knuckles on the counter, said, "See you tomorrow, love," and headed toward the door, leading my gaze to the mountain of rage standing behind him.

Tito's molten eyes bore a hole straight through me.

As Erik made his exit, Aida and Slade came through the door. I stood, speechless, disgusted, and dangerously close to fainting.

Without so much as a word, or a grunt, or even a disappointed grimace, Tito turned on his heel and left.

"Hi, Tuuli," Slade grabbed her niece from her brother's arms. "Who was that hottie?"

"Her fiancé," Tucker chimed in.

My stomach roiled. That cheesy grin would've been gorgeous if he hadn't been talking about Erik.

Aida crossed her arms and quirked one of her perfectly formed brows at me. Although she'd been nicer to me since she'd given birth, I was still terrified of the woman.

"He's not my fiancé," I said. "The jerk refuses to take no for an answer."

"Explain," Aida ordered.

My drama was nobody's business. Deep down I knew that, but I'd been raised to obey. So, obey, I did. "We went to school together. He's been after me since we were kids. That's all. Erik is used to getting what he wants. He hasn't figured out that I'm a person, not an object."

Aida eyed me suspiciously, making my skin crawl. Then again, she always looked at me like she knew my life was a lie. What I couldn't figure out was why she hadn't confronted me.

"Good," Slade said, peppering the baby with kisses. "Clean-cut suits are not your type." She lifted her head and winked at me like we shared a secret.

Aida, of course, not missing a beat, asked, "What's that supposed to mean?"

"I suspect she's more attracted to the tall, dark, and brooding type," Slade said. "Right, Tuuli?"

I chose that moment to grab the coffee pots, decaf and regular, and start my rounds. I also chose to ignore Aida when she blurted, "Tits? Oh, hell no. He'd destroy the little mouse." I also ignored the snickers, and ssh's coming from Tucker and Slade.

I ignored them because their opinions didn't matter. At least, that's what I tried to tell myself. Truth? Maybe they mattered too much. Perhaps I feared they believed me unworthy of Tito.

So, I tried to convince myself that they didn't matter.

And Aida's words didn't cut deep.

Tito

Cut deep, hearing the words, "my fiancé." Not a *woe is me, my heart is broken*, kind of pain. More like an, *Aw, fuck, I have to kill another piece-of-shit lowlife* sting. I had hoped that Whisper Springs would grant me a reprieve from the innate call to murder I'd lived with for so many years. I was tired of fighting. Tired of killing. Just plain tired.

That Erik character raised all my hackles. The guy was a fraud, any fool could see. The poser had pissed on my territory. For that act alone, there would be consequences.

One thing I knew sure as shit: guys like that pretty boy in the expensive suit didn't respond to warnings. Punks like Erik needed to be taken down, swift and hard.

Tuuli didn't want him around. I'd make sure he respected her boundaries.

I followed the fucker outside to his Mercedes, watched until his vehicle disappeared, then trekked up the hill to my apartment, fired up the coffee pot, and settled into the sofa with my laptop.

Two hours later, I'd learned everything I needed to know about Erik Meyer.

I continued to dig.

Another hour in, I'd decided I wasn't so tired of killing.

I sat in the dark. Alone. Raging. Struggling to make sense of the facts I'd uncovered.

The screams grew louder, ricocheting against the confines of my skull. Riotous bastards.

I dialed Tango. Three rings in, he picked up. "Cuz. What's up?"

"I need to spar."

"Great. Meet me at Dad's. Five-thirty good?"

"Now," was all I needed to say.

No hesitation. "I'll be there in twenty."

I made it to my uncle's home in ten. Waited on the front porch for Tango to arrive. Followed him in silence to the basement gym.

My cousin loosened his tie and threw it to the corner while kicking off his shoes.

I ripped my sweatshirt over my head, toed off my Nikes, and attacked. Tango was ready, dodging an uppercut.

"This how it's gonna be?" he asked, working at the top button of his shirt.

I snarled a warning.

"That bad, huh?" he huffed, working at his cuffs.

I paced, knocking at my skull to quiet the noise inside.

"At least let me get my shirt off. Don't wanna bloody this one."

I was a geyser ready to blow, steaming to release the unbearable pressure searing my insides. I paced until Tango came at me, muscles bunched, an unholy fire in his eyes.

He was never one to shy away from the promise of a good old-fashioned fist to face.

Tango didn't dodge the next strike or the next. He took my assaults like a champ, then came at me, clipping my jaw, throwing a weak jab to my gut. Fucker was holding back. Pissing me off.

"Hit me," I screamed, pounding fists to chest.

"Not without gear," he shouted back, shaking his head.

"Afraid I'm gonna blemish that pretty mug?"

"No." He jogged to the corner of the mat to grab headgear and gloves. "Afraid you might kill me." A set of leathers landed at my feet. I kicked them away. Didn't want protection. Didn't need it.

Then again, the gear wasn't for me. Few men had seen me fight. Where Tango fought with his head, I surrendered to blind rage and instinct. Meaning I was never allowed in the ring.

I didn't fight to win.

I fought to kill.

So, unless sanctioned by Luciano Voltolini, I didn't fight.

At that moment, though, I sure as hell needed to hit someone.

Tango didn't see me coming. He took a pound to his right temple and fell, face to the mat.

"Motherfucker," he grunted, pushing to his knees.

"Get up," I ordered, pounding at my skull, the voices taunting me.

"No." He sat back on his haunches.

"Get up and fight." The room spun. Bloody images whirled in my head.

"Not gonna happen." He covered his face with one hand, held up the other in surrender, halting my advance. "I don't trust your mood right now."

The screams amplified. Time for them to shut the fuck up. Turning to the bag, I swung, the impact vibrating my arm, adrenaline spiking my blood. I hit again. Again. Blow after blow I attacked the heavy bag until I was nothing but sweat and heavy breaths. Until the voices disappeared. Until my muscles failed to work. Until I fell to the ground, depleted of oxygen, purged of anger, and free to think clearly.

I lifted my lids and stared at the knotty pine ceiling.

"Ready to talk?" Tango huffed, falling to his ass at my side.

"Just needed to blow off steam," I said, wiping sweat from my brow.

"No shit?" Tango laughed. "Hadn't picked up on that."

"Sorry about your face."

"No, you're not. You've always been jealous of my good looks." He slapped my chest and draped his arms over his knees, waiting for me to spill.

My eyes, my lungs, my chest burned with fury and an urge I didn't understand. A call to protect the little bunny who'd wandered into my den.

"It's Tuuli." Her name on my tongue was the sweetest drug, unfurling through my bloodstream like a snowstorm in the desert, cooling the hot spots, temporarily soothing the scorch of the sun. "Friend of hers came to The Stop. She wasn't happy to see the guy. Creepy fucker. So, I looked into him."

We shared a stare-down before Tango blinked and looked away. "Aww, fuck," he said, smoothing back his hair with a rough scrub. "Slade was right. You like her."

"Fuck off." Should've kept my mouth shut and dealt with Erik on my own.

Tango dropped his head between his arms and chuckled. "Never thought I'd see the day. My untouchable cousin, googly-eyed over a girl."

I let the *googly-eyed* comment slide. What I had to say would shut his trap.

"In fact," he continued. "I've never seen you—"

"The fucker has been in Branson, Missouri the past two years, fighting child abuse charges. Fuckin' rape charges. Youngest was seven. He walked because the boys either changed their stories or disappeared."

"Shit." Tango fell back on the mat and rubbed his hands over his face. "No wonder your head is such a fucking mess right now."

Tango, my parents, and Luciano, were the only people who knew what I'd survived as a child.

"That's not all. He has ties with a white nationalist group in Ridgedale."

As expected, Tango didn't take the news lightly. "Fuck. We can't get free of this shit, can we?"

I nodded in agreement. Several months back, Aida and Tucker had trouble with a group of white supremacist dickheads at The Stop. Jonas Carver, the group's apparent leader, had been arrested in Seattle on unrelated charges and there hadn't been any trouble since.

"This Erik guy tied to Carver?"

"They belong to the same damn church. The Christian Brotherhood of Faith in Rockypoint."

"Think Tuuli knows?"

"I suspect she does, although she hasn't said a word about it. I've seen her around the guy. She's scared shitless of him."

"Send me his specs. I'll pass them on to the security team, make sure he doesn't step foot in the door again."

Tango was overzealous when it came to Slade and her safety. Case in point: The security team he'd hired to watch the diner. The Stop had seen its share of trouble recently, so I couldn't fault his motivation.

"Appreciate it."

"Listen. I don't know our little waitress very well. What I do know is that Slade is fond of her. She works hard. Is always on time. Never calls in sick. Gives me more time with my girl. But Tuuli is quiet and skittish as all hell. Not sure she can handle the likes of us. If you're just looking to get laid, man, I gotta ask you to back off. She leaves her job because of you, we'll have Slade to deal with. And trust me, that won't be pretty."

"Not sure what you're trying to say, cousin." I knew damn well what he was getting at. I didn't date. Never had time, or the desire. Of course, I had physical needs. Just like every other man. Back home, Luciano's girls were willing and available, twenty-four-seven. When doling out a grand an hour for pussy, it was in my best interest to find a dark corner, get shit done, and send the ladies on their merry way. A win-win for everyone involved. Aside from the lifelong tug-o-war between Aida and me, that was the extent of my experience when it came to female companionship.

"All I'm trying to say is that you better be sure."

I wasn't sure of anything except for the ache in my gut.

Part of me wanted to cut Tuuli loose. I was trying hard to shake trouble, didn't need more worry, especially in the form of a tempting little pixie. Problem was, the thought of never seeing her again made me want to bloody more faces.

"Next time you wanna talk, can we skip the foreplay and get to the good stuff?" Tango poked at the darkening bruise on his cheek. "How the hell am I going to explain this to Rocky?"

"Tell him the truth. You've gone soft, and your cousin kicked the shit out of you."

"Ha." Tango pushed to his feet, then dropped a hand to help me up. "I gotta get back to work. Don't forget we're having dinner at Aida's tonight."

He pulled me into a hug, slapped my shoulders, and headed up the stairs. I attacked the bag again, finding a steady rhythm, sated, knowing there would be extra eyes on the diner when I couldn't be there.

Why the fuck did I care?

Tuuli was good. I was the worst kind of bad. We would never work.

Church girls didn't fall in love with executioners.

Despite the razors of truth slicing my insides to ribbons, I couldn't ignore the spike of adrenaline that hit me every time I thought about seeing her again.

Selfish fucking bastard.

Tuuli

Selfish bitch.

I should never have agreed to a date with Tito. Not when so much about my life was a lie. He deserved to know the ugly truth about my family. Yet, there I stood, primping and giddy about a date I had no business agreeing to.

Challenging as it was with no electricity, and the stormy sky offering little in the way of natural light, I managed to apply a light coat of makeup and make my hair presentable. I shimmied into my favorite jeans, topped them with a babydoll cami and matching light blue cardigan, and tightened the laces on my well-worn Doc Martens before heading out.

After Erik's visit the day before, Tito hadn't returned to the diner or shown up to drive me home. He had, however, arranged for Charlie to give me a ride, which I gratefully accepted because of the torrential downpour.

I prayed our date was still on and hurried to get to the house before he arrived. The mile-long trek toward River Drive proved muddy and difficult to navigate, slowing my pace, but when I cut through the property that once belonged to the Brighton Wood Mill, I made-up for lost time and reached the main highway before the bus screeched to a halt.

Forty minutes later, I stood in front of 1415 Apricot Lane. The large blue house with its wraparound porch, white picket fence, and pristine yard, was my favorite dwelling on the entire block.

Sledgehammers pummeled my chest at the familiar roar of Tito's engine. The beautiful black car rolled to a stop at the curb. When he exited the Mustang and jogged around to greet me, a warm tingle settled in my cheeks.

Dark-blue jeans hugged his thighs, and a black, long-sleeved T-shirt showed off—much too well, in my opinion—his outrageous physique. No hood covered his head, leaving his scar on full display. He'd cut his hair, leaving it short on the sides and longer on top, arranged to look messy, but artfully so.

"Hey," he sighed, assessing my outfit, then resting his gaze on my face. "You didn't have to wait outside."

"Hi." The greeting left my lips, breathy and slow.

A rare, unreserved smile spread across his face.

A thousand bombs exploded in my chest. Those deep dimples branding a permanent tattoo on my temporal lobe.

"Ready?" He opened the door, gaze dropping to my boots, lingering.

I should've taken time to wipe the mud off my shoes. "Am I dressed okay? You didn't say what we were doing today."

He blinked, then shook his head as if dispelling a thought. "You're dressed fine. Perfect." Leaning closer, he whispered, "Beautiful."

I settled into the car seat and hooked my belt. When he sat next to me, a rush of cologne filled my senses, warming me deeper than the heat blowing through the vents.

Tito inhaled, then exhaled, his shoulders relaxing. "Get home okay last night?"

I nodded.

"I'm sorry I wasn't able to pick you up. Had a dinner I couldn't back out of."

"No need to apologize. It's not your responsibility to drive me home."

"I like driving you home," he mumbled, turning his attention to pull away from the curb.

The deep rumble of the engine made my insides tingle.

"You hungry?" he asked.

"Starving." I'd burned off the measly banana calories halfway through my hike.

"Good. I know a great place in Hollow Falls. They make the best Spanish tortilla."

I'd never heard of a Spanish tortilla, but my mouth watered regardless. Food was food. Anything would be better than canned cheeses and Chicken of the Sea.

Hollow Falls was the neighboring town west of Whisper Springs. The two cities, once separated by miles of farmer's fields, were now connected by new housing developments, car dealerships, and mini-malls. The half-hour drive passed in a blur of speeding cars and lighthearted conversation.

Tito pulled into a parking lot hidden behind a large brick building that housed the restaurant, a tattoo parlor, and an antique store.

The sign above the door read, La Caverna.

When we entered, Tito grabbed my hand and led me to the corner of the dining room. The dark-stained wood tables were held together with wrought iron rivets and decorated with mason jar candles.

As soon as we sat, the waiter brought a wood cutting board with a loaf of rustic bread. "Morning, Tito." He wore a smile that boasted a crooked tooth and infectious joy.

"Morning, Max." Tito leaned back into his chair. "How's the hip?"

Max winced. "Little stiff. Mother Nature is brewing something nasty today." He shot me a wink, then headed back toward the kitchen.

My stomach growled, and I hoped the Spanish guitar playing over the speakers was loud enough to mask the embarrassing rumble.

"How'd you find this place?" I asked, admiring the brick walls and ambiance.

Foregoing the cutting knife, Tito pulled a hunk of bread off the loaf. "I come here with my uncle. He's friends with the chef." He set the bread on my plate, then ripped off a hunk for himself, took a bite. Chewed. Swallowed. Took another.

So, I did the same. I'd never been served bread without the neat little slabs of butter. I'd never tasted bread so full of flavor that it didn't need butter. It didn't take long to realize there were no menus on the table. It also didn't take long for Max to return with small cups of dark coffee. Shortly after, he returned with another cutting board. On the board sat something that resembled a thick pancake, but smelled of garlic, fried potatoes, and the promise of a happy, happy stomach.

"What is this?" I asked, embarrassed by my lack of culture.

"Spanish tortilla." Tito winked, cutting a wedge from the pie. "Potatoes, eggs, garlic, onion, and a shit ton of love." He set the slice on my plate, then filled his own. "Never had it?"

I shook my head *no*.

Tito's face cracked into a wide smile. "Well, then. You're in for a treat."

Max returned, once again, with two plates, each containing two fried eggs and lemon wedges.

"Did you call ahead our orders?" I asked.

Tito shook his head. "No. No menus here. Chef serves whatever he's in the mood to cook, and people eat it. They don't like that setup, they don't come."

I cut into the potato concoction and lifted it to my lips. Tito watched, halting his own bite midair.

I shivered at the explosion of flavor. Salty, buttery, potato heaven. Hint of garlic, but not overpowering. The texture was dense and comforting, like a promise that you'd never feel the pain of an empty stomach again.

"Good, yeah?" he asked, face beaming with anticipation.

I didn't bother with an answer. Instead, I took another bite. Then another. I sipped my strong coffee in-between chews, then dug into the eggs, mimicking Tito by dipping my hunk of bread into the yolks.

I sopped the remaining oil and flavor-filled crumbles off my plate with the butt of the bread, then popped it between my lips. "You eat this good all the time?"

Tito laid his fork down and leaned back in his chair, crossing his arms over his chest. The scrutiny in his gaze triggered alarm bells.

"You eat that fast all the time?" he asked, voice gruff, his mood shifting into a dark zone.

I looked at my plate. "No."

Had I made a fool of myself? No doubt I'd suffer for my binge. I sure as heck wouldn't regret it, though.

"Look at me," Tito ordered. Or maybe it wasn't an order. Maybe his deep voice or the dark inflection that marinated his words made every syllable sound like a command.

On impulse, I obeyed, raising my eyes in a slow drag to meet his.

Those eyes. Dark and stormy. An exotic clash of browns and greens warring over prime real estate.

"Why do you do that?" he asked.

"What?" I feigned interest in my napkin.

A heavy hand covered mine. "Look at me."

Again, I did as ordered.

"Whenever you feel uncomfortable or challenged, you look down."

With great will, I held his gaze. "I. Um. Sorry. Habit. It's how I was raised. Eyes down. Don't argue. Obey your Elders."

"Elders?" He laughed. "How old do you think I am?"

"No. I mean, Elders, as in, the men who are leaders—" I clamped my lips shut before spilling my ugly truth. "I mean, yeah, you know, like people older and wiser. Parents, aunts, uncles, teachers, you get the picture."

Not missing a beat, he argued, "You started to say men who were leaders? Leaders of what?"

"Leaders in the church. The um, the church I grew up in." I'd said too much already, but I couldn't stop rambling. "We were punished if we disobeyed or showed any disrespect. Um. But. I don't belong to that church anymore. I don't agree with their beliefs. That's why I moved to Whisper Springs. To get away."

Tito's face hardened, eyes narrowed. The weight of his scrutiny was suffocating. "Punished how?"

I wanted to flee. "Let's talk about something else."

Stone cold silence. My breakfast threatened to make a reappearance. After agonizing seconds, his glassy eyes cleared.

Tito leaned over the table, jaw clenched, his face inches from mine. "Listen to me, Tuuli. When we're together, when we're talking, you hold your head up. You look at me. Whatever the fuck is happening between us, you hold your head high. If you don't like what I've got to say, look me in the eye and stand your ground. Got me?"

I nodded, biting my lip to hide the quiver.

He grabbed my chin and stole a kiss. A simple, sweet assurance. Then he held my gaze again. "Your eyes are full of secrets and stories. They are devastating and beautiful. Please don't keep them from me." With that, he pushed away from the table, pulled cash out of his wallet, and dropped it between our empty plates. "Come on. Let's hit the road."

My legs moved to follow. My guts, my heart, and my head lingered, not ready to leave the spot where I'd caught a rare glimpse of the real Tito Moretti.

The man who would most likely ruin me.

Tito

I would ruin her. Knew it deep. Didn't fucking care.

With my fucked-up head and Tuuli's unsettling confession about her upbringing, we were, without a doubt, a match made in hell. Any fool would agree. However, I'd never been one to cower from a challenge.

Then again, I'd never been one to lose my head over a woman. So where did that leave me?

On a date with a girl I would inevitably destroy. Or, quite possibly, fall victim to.

"Where are we going?" Tuuli asked when we'd settled in the car.

"I have something to show you."

"Another luxury condo you plan on buying?"

"No." I couldn't decipher her tone, unsure if her question was a dig or a poke. Didn't care much. She'd be happy when we reached our destination. "The other day, you said you don't know what I do for a living. But you've never asked, either."

"I figured you would tell me in your own time."

"I like that you don't pry."

Her face turned three shades of pink. God, the girl wasn't used to receiving compliments.

"I could explain my job, but it'll be more fun to show you."

We drove back through Whisper Springs, then around the lake, and pulled on to the private road that led to Aida's new obsession: the mansion.

"Isn't this the Clarkson Mansion?" Tuuli asked, leaning forward to take in the full view of the home.

"It is. You know it?"

"Oh, yeah. There are rumors it's haunted. Kids from school used to sneak up here and scare the crap out of each other."

"You've been here?" I shifted to park. Pulled the brake.

Tuuli fell back in her seat, shook her head. "My parents were overprotective. I wasn't allowed out at night."

"Come on." I unfolded from the seat and jogged to her side of the car. She was already heading toward the front door. I snagged her hand and pulled her around the back of the massive home. "My office is around back. Private entrance."

"Your office?" She stopped in her tracks, motioning toward the home. "You work here? I thought this place was abandoned."

"It was vacant for years. Aida and Tucker own it now."

"No way."

"They're turning it into a group home for at-risk teens." Although I wasn't lying about the plans Aida had for the home, I wasn't entirely honest either. Only a handful of people knew the true purpose of the mansion we were renovating—a safe-haven for rescued children. Sex slaves, more accurately.

For the past few years, Tucker had been rescuing girls from the sex traffickers that plagued the highways. He spent many nights trolling websites and social media outlets, trucking apps and radio waves, searching for the fuckers who pimped underage girls. He would take down the johns and take the girls to a home in Montana where they would be rehabilitated. So far, none of the kids he'd rescued had returned to the streets, like so many often did.

Aida bought the Clarkson property for its size and privacy, so Tucker could continue his plight and remain close to home. I agreed to help, in part, because Aida hadn't given me a choice. But mostly because I needed an outlet and taking down sick fuckers who hurt helpless children gave me the perfect opportunity to channel my ever-burning rage.

I was the best at what I did. Programming. Hacking. Security. I would help Tucker locate his targets. Help take them down. He'd lost his stomach for violence the day Lucia was born. With my skills, violence was no longer necessary. I had other ways to hurt the pedophiles. The pimps? They were another story. But I'd been working on ways to bring them down, too.

It would be months before the home was ready to receive girls. But I'd already set up my equipment and started work on security around the property.

The door to my office opened by code. I punched the numbers on the keypad. With a satisfying thunk, the door swung wide, revealing a long hallway that led to another door. Another code entered, and that door opened into what would be my second home for the unforeseeable future.

I keyed the necessary digits, waited for the green light, and pulled the handle. At the sound of my voice, the room lit in a warm glow.

Tuuli pushed past, bumping me out of the way. I took the opportunity to study the way her jeans hugged her ass. Then spent my attention on her expression as she spun a three-sixty, taking in the room. Monitors, keyboards, the wall-to-wall equipment that would soon control every square foot of the manor.

"Tito," she said, breathy and awed.

I liked the way my name sounded on her lips.

"Did this room come with the house?"

"No. I built this. This is what I do."

"Are you a computer genius or something?" She brushed a finger over one of the many keyboards lined up on the main desk.

I couldn't help but laugh. "Or something."

"I don't understand. You said this would be a refuge for troubled kids. Why the NASA level security?"

"I'll work security for the home, but I'm a private contractor as well. Some jobs require more of..." I gestured around the room with a sweep of my arm, "this."

"Well, now I understand your need for an open, airy penthouse to call home. It's stifling in here. No windows. No natural light."

"When I'm working, I need the seclusion." I stepped behind Tuuli. Damn, her hair smelled good. Like sugar cookies.

"Can I see the rest of the place?" she asked, leaning into me.

My chest constricted at the contact. My fingers tingled with the need to touch. My head spun with images conjured of us naked.

I should never have brought her to my office. My workspace was forever tainted with her scent, her face, the sound of her sweet, sweet voice.

CHAPTER 5

Tuuli

LIGHTNING CRACKED OUTSIDE, sending a flash of blinding light through the room. My heart danced in my chest, and I waited, counting. *One, two, three, four, five, six…* Boom. Thunder tore through the dark sky, rattling the glass and shaking the foundation. My whole body vibrated with nervous energy.

"So much for a tour of the grounds," Tito said, peeking out the window.

He came back to meet me where I stood, on the gigantic mat placed in the center of the large gym. In one corner, weights were stacked on iron racks. In the opposite corner, three treadmills and four elliptical machines lined the walls. To my right, punching bags, three hanging from the ceiling, two on the ground yet to find a home.

I was completely out of my element, but enthralled, nonetheless.

"You work out?" Tito asked, throwing a fake punch at my shoulder.

I held my arms away from my body and looked down at my slight build. "Do I look like someone who works out?"

Tito pretended to inspect me, lifting my arms higher, squeezing my biceps. His eyes met mine before he smiled and said, "I think if I sneeze, you might blow away."

On impulse, I hugged myself, putting distance between us.

"Hey. Hey," Tito snagged my elbow and settled back on his heels, holding me steady, urging me closer. "Don't do that shit."

I sagged against him and laughed, a pathetic attempt to hide my insecurities. "I'm jealous of you."

"Me? Why?"

"You have so much self-confidence. People take one look and know not to mess with you. You're untouchable." Except, I was touching him. He touched me, too, his tenderness erasing the memory of every ugly touch that came before.

"You could do that, too." He raised both hands to cup my face and tapped a finger on my temple. "It's all about what's going on in here." He pulled away and laid an open hand over my heart. "And here."

Tito dipped his chin and moved his hand to my jaw, tilting my head. He leaned closer, forcing me to meet his gaze. "There's a beast hiding inside you just waiting to be released."

I swallowed a giggle. "How do you know?"

"I know because my beast can sense her." He slid one hand to my hip and lowered his face to my neck with an inhale. "My beast can smell her."

Oh, God. My heart.

His lips grazed the sensitive skin. "And taste her."

A shiver tore through me. The sky outside lit up again, and I counted in my head. *One, two, three, four*...Boom! Thunder rocked the building.

The storm was getting closer.

I shivered, and before I could cower in fear, Tito's lips met mine. Strong arms coiled around my body, his beard scratching my skin and his fingers curling into my back, pressing hard.

Rain pelted the windows, the ceiling, the ground outside. Tito pulled me closer against his tense muscles.

I softened for him, opened for him, relaxed my jaw, and let him in. Joyful and willing, I surrendered to the strong, scary man, allowing his exploration.

Tito slid one hand to the curve of my rear, bent down, scooped my leg up his thigh, then lifted me, urging my legs around his waist. When I complied, he lowered to his knees, then laid me down, never breaking our delicious contact.

Tito kissed me. Touched me. Kissed me harder. And I let him. I loved his mouth, and his lips, and the rough drag of his hand up and down my ribcage.

I closed my eyes and absorbed every detail. Committing the moment to memory. Committing *him* to memory.

With a groan, Tito pulled away. He braced his left arm at my side. His right hand tangled in my hair, pulling tight. "Kiss me," he ordered, voice strained, breaths heavy.

"I am."

He huffed, dropping his head. "No, Bunny. I'm kissing you. Kiss me back."

"Tito...I—"

"Kiss me back."

The man growled, the room spun. I landed above him, straddling his waist. He held my hips tight, his hazel eyes burning bright. "There. You're in charge. Now, kiss me."

My cheeks blazed. From the first time we'd met, I'd wanted his mouth, dreamt of us, imagined a million different scenarios where I was kissing Tito.

Now I had him, and shamefully, I didn't know how to take charge.

As if reading my mind, he whispered, "Don't think about it. Just do it."

I feared if I didn't try, I'd never get the chance again. So, I leaned forward, planted my hands on the mat, caging him, and I dipped my head, planting a kiss on one cheek, just above his mouth, and then the other.

Tito chuckled. "That's a start."

I pressed my lips to his, smiling, mostly from embarrassment, but also heady from the power he'd granted me and the thrill of having the man between my legs. I couldn't waste the opportunity. I dragged my tongue across the seam of his mouth, urging him to open. When he did, I dived in, with my mouth, my tongue, and my teeth. I curled my fingers into the longer hair on top of his head, holding him steady while I took what he offered.

I was wild, ravenous, delirious with want. I kissed. I licked. I sucked. I claimed what I wanted, how I wanted; only, what I took wasn't enough. I craved more. Ached for more.

Tito's hips bucked underneath me. He curled his fingers into my ass and started to take over, but I tightened my grip on his hair and held him still, not ready to yield control. Power was rare. Beautiful. Freeing. And for a fleeting moment, dominance was mine.

My breasts ached. A low flame burned beneath my skin. The throb between my legs became unbearable, and I arched my back, pressing my core harder against the beautiful man between my legs.

Tito.

Oh, God.

Tito was thick and rigid, meeting my grind with soft thrusts. Rubbing, riling, taunting, and tempting. The ache was no longer only between my legs; it was everywhere. My face. My head. My heart. Pounding. Pounding. Pounding. A relentless rhythm of sex and need and selfish pleasure pumped through my veins, loud and erotic and all-consuming.

I rocked my hips against the hard length of him—greedy, selfish, unabashed—and soon we were no longer kissing.

Face buried in his neck, his arm clamped around my head, I moved against him, a slow mating dance, lustful, sinful, and I didn't care; I didn't want to be good, not in that moment, not in Tito's arms. I wanted wild and writhing and mindless, and I never, ever wanted to stop.

Tito

Stop. Stop. Stop.

I heard the words. Wasn't sure where they came from. My head? My mouth? They were there, getting louder. Pissing me the fuck off.

"Stop. Fuckin' hell, Bunny. Stop."

Tuuli collapsed on top of me, chest heaving, face buried in my neck, wet lips pressed against my sweaty skin.

"Fuck," I grunted, rolling us over, pushing to my hands and knees above her wild little body. I struggled to replenish my own oxygen. Those flushed cheeks and rosy lips were temptation enough, but that damn hair splayed beneath her like a tattered halo? Fuck me. My head was a mess.

I'd never lost my mind with a woman. I'd sure as hell never ceded control.

Her eyes filled with liquid, and she slapped her palms over her face. "I'm sorry. I'm sorry. I didn't mean to. I just. That was. Oh, God." She shook her head. "I'm not that kind of girl."

I knew where the conversation was headed, and no fucking way would I let her diminish the hottest bump-and-grind I'd ever experienced.

"Don't do that." I dropped my forehead to hers. "That was the best fuckin' kiss of my life. Don't make it bad. Don't you dare make it dirty."

She nodded in agreement, then peeked between her fingers. "Why did you stop?"

"Why?" I huffed, frustrated beyond measure, and barely holding my shit together. "Because I was two heartbeats away from tearing off your clothes and turning that kiss into something dirty, that's why."

If I hadn't stopped, she'd be lying beneath me, wearing bruises, swollen lips, and a blanket of regret.

I watched a tear slip down the side of her still hidden face. My guts twisted. I pried her fingers away and captured her hand in my own. "You okay?"

Lips curled between her teeth, she mumbled, "Mmm... hmm."

"Why the tears, then?"

Her gaze dropped to my mouth, then my chest, then snapped back up to meet my eyes. "I'm not a virgin."

I fought not to laugh at her confession or the worried expression on her face. "Neither am I."

"I've been kissed. I've had sex. But..." She turned her head away from me and stared at the weight rack.

"But, what?"

She swallowed. Sucked in a sharp breath. "I didn't want to give myself to those boys. At the time, I didn't know how to say no. Didn't think I could say no. I did what was expected of me. I didn't kiss them back. I just laid there, and they did their thing. And they left. And I hated everything about the act. Hated myself for letting it happen. But I thought that was what girls were supposed to do. I was raised to obey men, no matter what. I know that's messed up. That's part of the reason I left home. I couldn't live like that anymore."

I released her hand and dropped to my ass at her side. "Why are you telling me this, Tuuli?" I didn't mean to sound harsh, but I hated hearing she'd been used that way, and part of me feared that I'd made her feel used.

"I guess I'm telling you because I like you. I think you like me, too. And I definitely like what just happened. But you see, that's the problem. The next time I give myself to someone, I want it to be forever. And I'm afraid if I keep getting the chance to kiss you, I won't be able to say no because unlike those boys, when you kiss me, I feel you deep down, and I want more, and part of me is afraid that I won't be able to say no to you, but mostly, I'm afraid to say no because I don't want you to go away. I want you to want me. I don't want you to go away and find another girl to have sex with when I do say no."

I finally turned to look at her. She was sitting up, legs crossed in front of her, tears rolling down her face. When our eyes met, she released a half-laugh, half-sob.

"I know. I sound crazy. I'm sorry." She tucked her feet under her and pushed to stand. "Maybe you should take me home."

The room lit up with a strike of lightning that seemed to hit right outside.

Tuuli crouched back down and counted, "One, two..."

Boom. The thunder cracked. The windows vibrated, and Tuuli covered her ears.

Clearly, she was terrified of lightning storms, and she was doing a shit job of hiding that fact, evident by the cheesy smile she faked before whispering, "Ooh. It's almost right over us now. Think it'll pass soon? It should pass soon, right?"

God damn, the girl was cute. Crazy as fuck. But cute. And I couldn't help but pull her into my arms and hug her until the trembling stopped.

I rested my chin on her head and rubbed her back. Yes, she'd just rambled on about forever, and sex, and liking me. No, I was not ready for a conversation about relationships, or celibacy, or liking her. I was, however, content to have her in my arms, despite my blue balls. I definitely liked how her hair smelled. I would never forget the way she kissed me.

And the voices hadn't bothered me all day.

Tuuli

The bothersome voice in my head told me to run. Count my losses before he could crush me because that's what he was. A crush. He'd never be anything more. Men like Tito didn't fall in love with girls like me. Men like Tito fell in love with women who graced covers of magazines. Women who knew how to kiss back, how to satisfy a man's needs. I hated that little voice. But I couldn't deny that, for once, she was right. I wasn't a child, but I wasn't woman enough for Tito.

And besides, having sex meant he would see me naked. Meaning he would see the ugly reminders of my family ties. Then he would know who I was. What I was.

Lightning struck again, and before I could count to *one*, thunder followed. I summoned my inner beast, but she seemed to be more terrified of the storm than I was, and I shivered again, even in the safe space against his chest.

Maybe there was no beast. Maybe Tito had only made her up to make me feel better. He always seemed to say the right things.

Until he said, "We can make a run for the car. I can take you home if you're ready."

Definitely not the right thing to say. Me, outside with the elements? I'd rather be dipped in blood and locked in a lion's den.

"No." Reluctantly, I pulled free of his arms. "Not in the storm. It can't be safe to drive. Let's do something else. Let's talk."

"We've been talking all day," he said, shoving his hands into the front pockets of his jeans. He dipped his chin and raised his eyes to mine. "I haven't talked this much in months."

"Why?" I asked, pushing, breaching the unspoken agreement we had not to pry. He had, in a sense, given me an opening.

I waited out the long pause, studying his broad shoulders, his thick neck, the tick in his jaw.

His mouth dropped open. Then slammed shut. "Never mind."

"All right then," I searched the room for something, anything, to keep him from taking me outside, even though the car was only a few feet from the front door.

I walked over to one of the heavy bags hanging from the ceiling and gave it a shove. It barely moved. "You know how to use these?"

Tito chuckled behind me. His voice drew closer as he said, "Yeah. I know how."

"Show me."

He stood at my side, lifted my hand, and molded my fingers into a fist. "You ever throw a punch?"

"No."

He studied my fingers, brushing a thumb over my knuckles. "Never? Not once?"

"No."

He dropped my hand. Looked at his own, flexing and stretching his fingers. "Seriously? You've never been so mad that you needed to hit something? Or someone?"

"Yes. I mean, no. I mean, yes, I get mad, but no, not enough to want to hit someone." Okay, that was a lie. I'd fantasized punching my brother in the face more than once. I'd also, at least a thousand times over the years, imagined different ways to hurt Erik, every time I'd watched him bully some kid, or the times he had wrestled me to the ground and made me kiss him, or had forced me into his lap and made me sit still while we watched movies, or until he had finished his homework, or until my father came home.

I hadn't fooled Tito. He gave me a scolding look and said, "Liar."

"Sure. I've thought about it. But I don't like violence." I'd seen too much brutality.

"Violence is necessary sometimes."

"I disagree."

"Liar," he said again.

"You don't know me well enough to call me a liar, Tito."

"Tuuli. The night I met you, you had defended Aida by attacking a man five times your size."

"That's different. He was going to hurt her."

"There's no difference. Violence is violence, regardless of our motives. You could've run for help, or quoted him scripture, but you chose to go for the kill."

He was right. Had I been stronger, or had a weapon even, I would've done anything in my power to keep that horrid man from hurting Aida. "Are you going to hit the bag for me, or what?"

"Make a deal?"

"Sure." I refrained from rolling my eyes.

"You hit the bag once, with everything you've got. If you can tell me it doesn't feel good, I'll drop the subject."

"You'll drop it. Then I get to watch you?"

He nodded, chewing his bottom lip.

"With your shirt off," I added.

He released his lip and almost smiled. "Now you're pushing."

"Fine," I said, conceding. "Shirt on." I held up my fists and stepped closer to the bag.

Tito grabbed my arm and turned me back toward him. "First things first. I don't want you to break a bone." He repositioned my fingers, showing me the safe way to ball my fist and the correct angle to hold my wrist. Then he stepped back, arms crossed, and nodded for me to proceed. "Make it count. Think of something, or someone, that makes you angry."

I already pictured Erik's face on the leather. Not his smug, fake smile, but the face he reserved for me when we were alone. The expression of domination. I pulled my arm back and thought of the time he made me stick my hands down his pants and touch him while he reminded me that I was his, and when we were married, I would have to do whatever he asked. I remembered how, when I tried to pull away, he held my arm and made me stroke him. I remembered how when my dad walked into the room, Erik shoved me off the kitchen chair, and instead of helping me off the floor, he stood toe-to-toe with my father and told him that I was a slut, and if I kept throwing myself at him, he wouldn't be able to marry me because he was pure, and he would only marry a pure woman. I remembered how my dad patted him on the back, told him he was proud, and then took me to my room, slid his belt from his pants, and made me hold onto my dresser while he struck me, over, and over, and over.

My entire body vibrated with rage. I hit the bag as hard as I could, releasing a strange guttural noise from deep in my throat. I gave it my all, and still, the bag barely moved. My insides, however, had shifted something fierce, like there was another me inside my skin and bone frame, another me that was waking from a deep sleep, stretching and yawning, and coming back to life. God, it felt so good.

Too good.

I stepped back and inhaled, savoring the rush.

I heard a chuckle, then Tito's deep voice brought me back to Earth. "Amazing, right?"

Life-altering. "No."

I walked away from the bag, despite wanting, or needing, rather, to hit it again and again.

I didn't dare look him in the eye, certain my exhilaration was evident. I sat, cross-legged, in the middle of the mat, and waited for him to make the next move.

Much to my surprise, and enjoyment, Tito gripped the back of his shirt, pulled it over his head, then tossed it my way. The moment his back was turned, I brought the soft cotton to my nose, savoring the scents of rain and laundry soap. I even caught a whiff of my vanilla body spray, and that made me happy. So damn happy.

Tito hit the bag with one hand, then the other. Slow at first, finding a rhythm. He glanced my way twice before a mask fell over his face and his breathing changed. His eyes darkened, sweat coated his bare back and chest, and his strikes came harder, quicker, more aggressive with each blow. His feet moved with mesmerizing grace. His muscles coiled and bunched, a heady and terrifying sight. I watched, silent, frozen, captivated by his raw, animalistic beauty.

Tito was gone. Not sure where. In the zone. In hell, perhaps. He wasn't in the room with me though. His physical form, yes, but his heart, his head, his soul—a million miles away.

I couldn't help but wonder what damage he could do were those strikes aimed at another human.

I watched, hypnotized by his focus, his power. Those muscles. Lean. Raw. No doubt carved from years of hard training. I suspected he'd been a fighter at some point in his life. I'd watched my brother and his friends fight in their makeshift rings back home. They were clumsy, and stupid and fueled by nothing but ego. Nothing like Tito. His strikes were calculated, and precise, backed by passion and fury. My heart broke for him because he seemed to unleash a lifetime of bad memories on that bag.

Minutes rolled into an hour. The storm passed. At some point, I laid down on my side. At some point, I fell asleep.

Tito

She'd fallen asleep clutching my shirt to her chest. I wasn't sure how much time had passed. I'd started hitting the bag, got lost in the zone, and next thing I knew, I was laying on the ground, a sweaty, spent mess. When I could focus my eyes, all I saw was Tuuli, despite the fact that she was the smallest thing in the massive room.

I didn't wake her. I couldn't take my eyes off her. God, she was beautiful. Peaceful. I took advantage of her unconscious state. Studied her breaths, the slow rise and fall of her chest, the way her hair draped her face and neck like silk.

Waking her and driving her home would've been the right thing to do. Instead, I ran to my car, snagged a clean shirt and my jacket out of the trunk, then quietly laid beside my sleeping beauty and covered her with my coat. I didn't touch. Not right away. I managed to withhold my desire for three excruciating minutes before I tucked my arm under her head and pulled her against me.

Then I closed my eyes and pretended I was good enough for the churchgoing angel in my arms, and that I wasn't pissed about her earlier rant, and that I hadn't released all my pent-up frustration on the heavy bag.

"Tito," a soft voice whispered.

I blinked the world back into focus. Blonde hair and a bright smile waited for me on the other side of my sleep haze.

"We fell asleep."

"Why are you whispering?" I asked, rubbing my hand up and down her back to make sure she was real.

"I don't know," she said, laughing.

She rolled out of my arms and pushed to her feet. I stretched, then propped my head in my hand and watched her walk to the window and peek outside.

"It stopped raining."

"Yeah? You ready to head home?"

Her shoulders rose and fell. "Sure."

She wasn't ready to go. I wasn't ready to let her go.

"Can I take you to dinner first?"

Tuuli tapped on the window before turning around and asking, "Really? Are you sure?" like she thought I was eager to get rid of her or something.

"I at least owe you dinner." I pushed to the sitting position and rested my arms on my knees. "You know, after checking out the way I did," I gestured over my shoulder to the punching bag.

"You don't owe me anything," she said, coming my way. "I liked watching you." She crossed her ankles, then lowered herself to the ground in front of me. "Think you can teach me to do that?"

Fuck, yeah. I'd take any chance I could get to have my hands on her. "I'd love to teach you."

Her eyes darted from me to the window, to the ceiling, to my chin.

"What?" I asked, ducking my head to catch her gaze.

A rush of air left her lungs. "You never said anything after I rambled on about sex."

What could I say without breaking her heart? Without losing her. Relationships were not my thing. Love? Definitely not my thing. Sex with no strings used to be my thing until the night I met Tuuli.

I had no clue how to verbalize my feelings. So, I showed her. I slid a hand around the back of her head, tangling my fingers in that gorgeous hair. I pulled her close, and I kissed her. I continued, giving all I had, and soon, I was crawling over that small body, urging her to lay down, pressing my hips between her thighs. She opened for me, her mouth, her legs. She offered herself, and without prompting, she kissed me back, and I fell into that dangerous fog of lust and want and selfish pleasure. My cock was hard and thick between us, and I made sure to move, grinding into her warm body, showing her how she affected me.

I waited for the right moment when her body softened beneath me—giving in. I pushed her to the point where I knew she questioned her vow, until I knew she would give herself to me without hesitation, and then I broke the kiss. I found her eyes, and I ground my erection between her legs before pushing to hands and knees above her.

"I told you before, I don't do relationships. I'm not capable of falling in love. I don't know what this is between us. I do know that I like spending time with you. But you have to know what you do to me. You have to know that if I kiss you again, or you kiss me again, it will lead to more. If I'd kept going just now, you would've given in. You can't deny that. There will come a time where I get lost in the moment, lost in my own head, and I won't be able to stop. Or maybe you won't want to stop. And we'll fuck. Then I'll be the guy who made you give up your vow. I'll be the guy who made you dirty." I paused for a breath, and to make sure she heard my next words loud and clear. "I respect that you want to save yourself for the right guy. Whoever that man is, he's one lucky bastard. But you have to know it won't be me. I'm not built that way. And goddamn, Bunny, I don't want to be the guy that ruins that for you."

She looked so vulnerable, with her innocent eyes, her flushed cheeks, and her wet lips. She understood what I was trying to say. The wonderment I was used to seeing was gone. Now, there was nothing but a sad ocean of blue blinking up at me. My words cut her deep. It hurt me to say them, knowing she might never want to see me again.

Tuuli held my gaze. She swallowed.

And then she forced a smile.

"You just said more to me in thirty seconds than you have in the past two months."

I sagged against her, resting my head on her chest. Her arms came around me, and she stroked my hair.

"So, what now?"

"You tell me," I inhaled her vanilla scent one more time before pushing to my feet and offering a hand to help her up.

"Friends?" she asked, voice void of any confidence.

I nodded, trying to appease her, knowing we'd eventually crash and burn. I couldn't be friends with a girl I jacked off to daily.

I waited for her to break. Expected a lip quiver, tears to fall, or at least watery eyes. She gave me nothing but that sweet smile, and that soft voice. "Can we eat now? I'm starving."

CHAPTER 6

Tuuli

MY MOTHER ONCE TOLD me I could learn everything I needed to know about a person by studying how they acted when they thought no one was watching. Mom had been right. She had also unwittingly created a monster. A curious, sneaky, quiet monster.

Two days after that conversation, I learned all the best hiding places in our house, all the secret nooks and crannies of my father's church and the entire surrounding property. I was small. And patient. And I learned to hide. And listen. And watch.

The first thing I remember learning was that my father was a liar. He never wrote his own sermons. He watched pastors on the internet, some well-known, most of them not, and twisted their words to fit his agenda. I also learned where he hid the Holy Bible. The real one. Not the fake scriptures he passed out to his followers. When I was twelve, I started reading the real Bible. Didn't take long to realize that the life I'd known was the biggest lie of them all.

I'd also discovered that my father had private meetings with the boys of our church. Training sessions, he'd called them. The boys had always left his office looking sick, or sweaty and tired. Erik had more meetings than any of the other kids, spending hours locked in Dad's office. Erik was the only boy that had ever came out with a smile on his face.

I learned that my brother, despite being the loudest supporter of my father and his beliefs, had sex at least twice a week with a dark-skinned girl in the old hunting cabin at the far end of our property. Sometimes, the girl would bring friends. Every time, he paid her. I used to wonder how he got the money until I discovered he'd been filming their sexual escapades and posting the videos online.

Old habits were hard to break, and when Officer Caldwell came into The Stop to meet Tucker and Aida, I happened to be cleaning the table behind where they sat, mouth closed, eyes down, ears open. I wasn't intentionally eavesdropping, my mind still wandering aimlessly in Titoville, but when I heard the name Jonas Carver, my focus narrowed to their conversation.

When Aida grabbed the officer's arm and dragged him to Slade's office, I told Margie I was off to use the ladies room. Only, I didn't go to the bathroom. I slipped into the utility closet, squeezed between the two metal storage racks in the corner, and pressed my ear to the vent in the wall. From that spot, I heard everything that transpired between the three.

"Jonas Carver is being released as we speak," the officer said.

"He's getting out?" Tucker asked. "How?"

"New team of lawyers."

"Fuck." That came from Aida. She always cussed when she didn't have the baby with her.

"Thanks for the heads-up," Tucker said.

I waited for them to say their goodbyes, holding my trembling fingers over my mouth, shaking my head in disbelief. I stayed hidden in my private little corner of the storage room, trying to make sense of the news.

Jonas was being released? What did that mean? Was he back in town?

My head spun. Bile rose in my throat. I needed to leave. The moment he disappeared, I should have left Whisper Springs and never looked back.

I didn't want to leave my job. I also didn't want to cause grief to the people I'd grown to adore. Staying would mean hurting them. So, I squeezed out of my hiding place and headed to the back room, where I gathered my things, took a final look around, then dragged my feet to the kitchen. Aida and Tucker were nowhere to be seen. Charlie whistled a tune from the walk-in.

"Charlie," I mumbled to his backside, "I just threw up. Think I have the flu. I'm heading home."

He mumbled something while I retreated, tail between my legs, making my getaway before having to conjure more lies.

When the bus dropped me off in front of 1415 Apricot Lane, I gave the gorgeous home a good, hard look. I wondered about the people inside. Was their life a lie, too, hidden inside the pretty exterior? Or was it only my family whose public and private lives were two different worlds?

The air was ripe and electric with the promise of an incoming storm, so I ran the rest of the way home. Unfortunately, I wasn't fast enough to beat the downpour. I hung my wet clothes on the shower rod, slipped into my baggiest sweats and sweatshirt, hid my purse in the hole under the carpet where I stashed my savings, double-checked the locks on the windows and doors, and curled up underneath my pile of blankets on the ratty couch.

The weight of shame was a heavy and stifling burden, and I was suffocating under its heat, despite the chill in the room. I curled into a ball, and I cried.

Pellets of rain pinged on the metal roof. I pulled the blankets over my head and prayed. Prayed for forgiveness. Prayed that Jonas would not come home before I could catch a bus out of town. Prayed that I would fall asleep before the thunder came.

Tito

A jolting crack of thunder pulled me from my reading. My thoughts immediately filled with the memory of Tuuli trembling in my arms, her brave face, and her feeble attempt to hide her fear of the storm.

The dark living room lit up with a bright flash. Rain beat against the windows. I checked the time. Tuuli's shift would end soon.

Fuck. I shouldn't care.

Last week, we'd agreed to be friends. She'd asked that I not come into the diner for a few days, give her time to adjust, get over her *crush*. Although I knew her feelings for me were more than a crush, I agreed, not because I was respecting her wishes, but because I needed time to digest our new arrangement as well.

Worst fucking week of my life.

I missed seeing her face every day. Missed having her next to me in the car while I drove her home. Missed how she filled the silence and quieted the voices.

As the storm grew closer, the rain fell harder, and agitation crept over me like a nagging itch, the words on my computer screen blurred. I could not, in good conscience, let Tuuli get home alone.

I jogged to my car, tore down the hill, and waited at the back door. Eight o'clock came and went. The last customer rolled out of the parking lot.

Like a lovesick jackass, I waited.

Eight thirty passed, still no Tuuli. Eight forty-five, the dining room lights went dark. Eight-fifty, the back door opened, and swear to my maker, my heart skipped three beats when Charlie and some guy I'd never seen before appeared. No fucking Tuuli.

Charlie shook the guy's hand then came my way, holding a knife bag over his head, like that would protect the giant from the downpour. He ducked to look in my window. "Hey, Tito. Need something?"

"No. I'm waiting for Tuuli. Thought I'd drive her home."

"She's not here, buddy. Left ten minutes after her shift started, said she was sick."

That nasty, aching boom in my chest amplified. "Thanks."

"No problem."

I started to roll up my window, then paused. "Hey, Charlie. Who's the new guy?"

"That handsome dude is my nephew, Eli. He's joining the crew. Summer's coming. Need all the help we can get." He turned and ran to the driver's side of his Tundra.

I glared at the building until the buzz in my head cleared. Then I drove until I was parked in front of 1415 Apricot Lane. Fuck. What a sap.

Lights from the television screen flashed through the thin curtains of the front window. I caught movement, the shape of a figure settling on the couch. Tuuli, I guessed, judging by the shape and size.

I convinced myself she was okay. Waited a while longer. Waited for the television screen to go dark. Watched her form through the curtain rise from the chair and pass into the next room. She turned off the lights, and, I assumed, went to bed.

I forced myself to drive home and do the same.

The next morning, I broke my promise about giving her space and settled into my usual table at The Stop for breakfast. If she complained, I'd simply say I was hungry and leave it at that. Only, Tuuli didn't greet me with her usual bright smile.

Slade came my way with a coffee pot and two mugs. She then scooted into the seat across from me. "Morning."

"Morning," I grunted, not caffeinated enough for Slade's level of perky. "Tuuli still sick?"

Slade filled my cup first, then her own. "Haven't heard from her. Called the number we have on file, but it's been disconnected."

Fuck.

"You haven't heard from her?" Slade asked, cup held to her lips.

"No. Why would I?"

"Because, grouchy goose, I've seen the two of you together. I know you've been driving her home, and I know you don't grace us with your presence every day because of Charlie's cooking."

I adored Slade. Was happier than hell that she and Tango had found each other again after years apart, but I sure as shit wasn't about to open up to her about my issues. "Afraid you're sorely mistaken, doll. There's nothing between me and the little bunny." Fuck. I realized my slip the second it left my lips.

"Ha!" She pointed at me. "You've given her a nickname. You're smitten."

I couldn't look at her face, all proud and beaming, so I stared out the window and tapped a beat on my coffee mug with my thumbs. "Who says *smitten* anymore?"

"I do. And trust me, that girl is smitten, too."

When I didn't respond, Slade continued, "Want to know how I know?"

I didn't. Not really. The conversation was awkward enough.

"She's given you a nickname, too."

That got my attention. Tuuli had never called me anything other than Tito. Well, except for that one time…

I cringed when Slade said, "Grim" at the same time the word played in my head.

"Grim? What the hell kind of nickname is that?"

"Seriously?" Slade pointed to the window. I looked, catching my reflection. Black sweatshirt. Black hood covering my head. Scary fuckin' mug. Okay, Grim made sense. The only thing missing was a scythe.

"You could at least take that cloak off when you sit down to eat. You scare my customers."

I looked around the busy dining room. Not a single soul was looking my way. One fucker, seated two tables over, was mentally undressing Slade, though. Couldn't blame him, the girl was every man's wet dream come to life. Regardless, I rapped my knuckles on the table to catch his attention. One look was all it took. The guy blanched, turned in his seat, then pretended to be busy with his cell.

My stomach chose that moment to grumble. I wasn't wholly convinced it was from hunger, though. "You gonna take my breakfast order or what?"

"No." She smiled.

I wanted to scream or throw the sugar jar through the window. "Why?"

"Because you're going to drive by Tuuli's house and make sure she's okay. It was strange the way she ran out of here yesterday."

My rage turned to worry. "What do you mean?"

"She was fine when she clocked-in, then out of the blue, she tells Charlie she has the flu. Trust me, that girl did not have the flu. Take it from a mom who's experienced the horrors firsthand."

Fuck. Even if I wanted to argue, I couldn't, because my gut told me something was up.

I took a sip of my coffee, set down the mug, then leaned over the table and kissed Slade on her forehead. "Fine. I'll check on her."

"Good boy," Slade said, flashing her famous smile.

"Yeah, yeah," I mumbled, making my way to the exit.

Fifteen minutes later, I stood at the door of Tuuli's house. I pushed the doorbell button. Waited. Pushed it again. I slipped my hood off my head, then pounded on the door. I tried to look in the windows, but the curtains were all drawn. "Can I help you?" a frail voice said from behind me. I turned to find a small woman wearing gardening gloves, rubber shoes, and a green flannel jacket. White hair popped out from under her wide-brimmed hat. Tuuli had never mentioned a grandmother.

"Hey. Hi. …I…Um…I'm looking for Tuuli."

"Tuuli?" she asked, brushing a clump of mud off her left knee.

"Yeah. She, um, didn't show up for work today. Thought I'd come by to make sure she was okay."

"There's no Tuuli here, son."

I rubbed at the pain gripping the back of my neck. My insides twisted something fierce. "You mean she's not home?"

"I'm sorry. I think you have the wrong house." The woman's concerned expression held no similarities to my bunny.

"I don't understand. I drop her off here every night after work."

The woman looked over her shoulder at my Mustang. "I recognize the car. Thought it was odd you'd drop off a young girl then drive away."

"I'm sorry. I'm still confused. She gave me this address. Told me she lives here."

"No." The woman raised her arm and pointed east. "She always walks that way after you leave. Sorry I can't be more help."

"Thank you," I mumbled, holding back a chorus of profanities and jogging down the porch steps.

The woman offered a sympathetic grin as I passed, her gaze darting from my eyes to my scar, and back again. She still watched as I opened my door.

"Have a nice day," I said before dropping back into my seat.

Could I be any more of a fucking chump?

"Fuck. Fuck. Fuck!" I yelled, pounding my steering wheel.

Tuuli

"Fuck. Fuck. Fuck!"

Jolted from a deep sleep, I shot upright, struggling to free my arms from the tangled bedding, unable to focus through my swollen eyes.

"What the hell are you still doing here, brat?" came a deep, gravelly voice.

Icy prickles danced across my skin, my body vibrating with nervous energy.

Oddly enough, I wasn't scared. I was angry. Wiping sleep goo from my eyes, I mumbled, "JoJo. How nice of you to show up."

"Jesus, Brat. Don't call me that. We're not kids anymore." Jonas crouched, brushed the hair off my face, and held it in a fist on top of my head. "You look like shit. Why the hell are you sleeping on the couch?"

"Because I've seen the things, and the women, you've done on that bed," I blurted, surprised by my brazen response. "Don't want any part of me touching any part of that freak-fest." I blinked up at him, half-expecting a slap across the face, and not caring one iota. "Where have you been?"

"Prison." He dropped my hair. "You didn't know? I left you messages."

Lordy, the man was dense. I refrained from rolling my eyes. "You destroyed my phone, remember?"

Jonas fell backward onto his butt and roughed his hands over his shaved head. "Yeah. Right. Sorry." He lifted his blue eyes to mine. "I can't believe you're still here. Why didn't you bolt? You had an out. I've been gone for months."

He mentioned nothing about my end of the bargain, and why I was even living in his trailer in the first place. I wasn't about to remind him.

"I had nowhere to go," I said, giving him a partial truth. Because the whole truth, especially the part involving Tito, would've pissed him off. Pissed-off Jonas scared me to death.

"Why were you in prison?"

"Nothing you need to worry about." He studied the small living space. My heart stuck in my throat when his eyes landed on my Bible. He leaned forward and plucked it off the floor, then thumbed through the pages. "You reading this shit?"

I didn't answer.

I waited for him to explode. He only huffed and tossed the book into my lap.

"The place looks nice."

"I did the best I could with no electricity."

Regret shadowed his eyes before he slammed them shut and pushed to his feet.

"I need you gone." He pulled his shirt up his torso and over his head, revealing his ugly, hate-filled tattoos. Swastikas. Devil's faces. Quotes from Dad's scripture. Pin-up girls wearing combat boots and nothing else but a confederate flag. He had gained weight, his muscles thicker, more defined than the last time I'd seen him.

"Are you kicking me out?" Unbelievable.

"No, dumb-fuck. I've got friends coming over."

I stared at him, unsure why I needed to leave because of his friends.

Then he grabbed his crotch, in a crude and disgusting gesture. "Need to get laid, brat. Been awhile. Pretty sure you don't want to hang around for that show."

"Oh. Oh. Right." I stood, gathered my blankets, and shoved them in the small closet next to the bathroom.

Jonas looked through the cupboards, then the fridge. "There's no fucking food." He turned to look at me. "No wonder you're so damn skinny."

I closed my eyes and sucked in a breath, imagining Jonas as the punching bag at the mansion. "No electricity. Couldn't keep things in the fridge. No car, so I couldn't haul many groceries."

"Right. Sorry about that, too." He scratched the back of his head. "Goddamn. Why the hell didn't you get out of town, or go home? Christ, kid, you could've frozen or starved to death out here."

He pulled a wad of cash out of the back pocket of his jeans and tossed it on the small coffee table. "Here. Go buy some food. I'll call about getting the electricity turned back on."

Again, I stood staring, not trusting his subtle, and grossly out of character, gestures of kindness.

"What?" he barked.

"The nearest store is miles away. It's pouring rain."

His truck keys landed on the table next to the cash. "Take my Chevy. Give me four, no, make it five hours. I've got a shit ton of fucking to do."

"I didn't need to hear that."

"Fuck off. Just get dressed, brat."

I obeyed. Not because I'd felt obligated, but because I really did not want to be anywhere near the trailer when his *relief* arrived.

I didn't bother to change out of my baggy clothes. When Jonas locked himself in the bathroom, I grabbed my purse from its hiding spot. I lifted the carpet in the corner of the living room and found the envelope containing my emergency cash. I didn't trust him not to search the place. With Jonas home, I'd have to get my own apartment sooner rather than later. Which was doable with my savings, as soon as I found a new job.

I shoved the large wad of cash he'd offered into the middle pocket of my purse, snagged the keys, and left without saying goodbye.

Had I known what I would return to, I would've turned east onto I-95 and disappeared with my brother's truck.

Tito

"That his truck?" Tango asked when a red Chevy came into view.

Tucker shifted in his seat, stiffening. "Sure as shit is."

We passed the rusted contraption halfway up the pothole-riddled driveway. The front end of the vehicle was smashed against a boulder—one wheel bent, the bumper hanging crooked. The windows were thick with filth like it had been sitting for months. The tire tracks, however, looked fresh.

I fought off a violent shiver and chalked-up the weird vibes to being tired.

Sleep had eluded me, and I'd spent half my day debating whether to look for Tuuli. Went for a run. Hit the gym. Passed through the diner five times to see if she'd shown up for work. Couldn't wrap my head around the fact that she'd lied about where she lived. Pissed me the hell off, to be honest.

I'd been on edge all day and had finally decided to head home and do a full work-up on the little beast when Tango and Tucker wrangled me into joining them for a "drive," insisting they needed backup. Sounded intriguing, so I pushed thoughts of Tuuli down, tucking them away, and settled into the back seat of Tango's Rover.

My nerves were worn beyond their limit by the time we reached our destination on the edge of the wooded property. "Tell me again who we're visiting?"

Tucker turned to look at me from the passenger seat. "Jonas, the punk who almost ran Aida down in the parking lot last fall."

That snapped me out of my Tuuli funk. "The racist shit who tried to kill you?"

Tucker huffed. "He was released yesterday. High-tailed it out of Seattle, headed straight for home. We're just gonna pay him a little visit."

The fucker had messed with Aida. I couldn't fathom how he was still breathing. "We dusting him?"

"No," Tango snapped.

"Crippling him?"

"No," he repeated.

"Can I break a fuckin' bone at least?"

"No!"

Tango clearly wasn't feeling my level of ire. "Would it be a problem if my knife accidentally slipped and nicked an artery? I'm feeling a bit twitchy."

"Tito. We're not killing anyone. Just reminding him to steer clear of The Stop. Christ, you've been a miserable fuck all week. What crawled into your boxers?"

A little white bunny with a viper's tongue. Sure as shit wasn't gonna share that bit of intel with those meatheads. They'd never let me hear the end of it.

Tucker backhanded Tango's shoulder. "It's Tuuli. Leave him alone."

Tango's eyes met mine through the rearview. "You missing your girl, cousin? Slade says she's been sick. Missed her past two shifts."

I opened my mouth to argue, then figured it'd only give them cause to rib me more. Instead, I focused on the trailer home up ahead and tried to get my head in the game.

The moment we pulled up to the shabby dwelling, I jumped out of the Rover, adrenaline cranking my gears, moving me forward.

The front door hung crooked, the top hinge torn from the frame. Plywood steps bowed under my weight, threatening to snap, and I paused at the threshold, hackles raised. The place reeked of death. A scent I knew too well.

The living room was a wreck. Curtains ripped off the wall. Sofa overturned. Carpet torn. Women's clothes strewn across the floor. A familiar pink and green dress lay at my feet.

Despite Tucker's warnings not to enter, I made my way inside, drawn to the pink handbag lying on the kitchen counter and its contents spread across the worn laminate. Leather satchel. Broken handle.

All the blood in my body drained to my feet. I rifled through the contents and found a driver's license.

Tuuli's picture smiled up at me. "What the fuck?" I stumbled backward, bumping into Tango.

My cousin shouted orders, but I couldn't register a word with the blood-beat banging through my ears. I stormed down the short hallway, the knot tightening in my gut, kill-rage coursing through my veins.

If she was hurt...

I slowed my pace at the end of the hallway. The door to the bedroom was open wide, revealing the carnage. Three naked bodies. Two females. One, brunette and pale, the other, brown skin with ebony waves. Neither one of them were Tuuli, and I fell to my knees in relief.

Both women had bled out on the floor, judging by the stains beneath them. The man, however, was spread across the mattress, wrists bound behind him, ass and thighs bloody, rope tied around his neck, steak knife sticking out of his shoulder blade.

The dead man's head was turned to the side. Eyes open wide.

I stepped over the bodies, searched the small room, under the bed, then made my way back down the hall and into the bathroom. A Truck Stop T-shirt hung on the shower rod next to a small pair of khaki pants.

Mother fuck.

Tango came behind me, laying a heavy hand on my shoulder. "Don't touch anything. Christ. Stop leaving your DNA all over the crime scene."

"She's been here."

"Who?"

"Tuuli." I turned and smacked her ID against his chest. "She's fuckin' been here."

Tango yelled, "What the hell?" At the same time, the first wail if sirens reached earshot.

"We need to go. Now." Tango grabbed the back of my neck and yanked me toward the door, where Tucker was already sliding into the SUV.

"We can't leave. We have to find her."

"I know. I know. We will," he promised, pushing me onward. "But think, cousin. We can't be here when the cops show up. How's that gonna look?"

He was right.

Only, I didn't give a fuck. Because Tuuli had been in that trailer. Where the fuck was she? Voices rattled in my head, wailing, inviting the darkness. I tried to shake them off.

Tango must've sensed my distress because he squeezed harder and slammed me against the passenger side door. "Get in. Keep your shit together. We'll find your girl. I promise."

I crawled into the back seat, every nerve in my body screaming for me to stay.

He headed toward the main road. When we passed the old Chevy, I got the same chill as before. Something wasn't right about that damn truck. I turned in my seat to get a better look.

Swear to Christ, when I saw movement inside, I aged ten years. I didn't bother asking my cousin to stop the car. I jumped out, falling ass over elbow in the gravel, and landed against the front tire.

I pushed to my feet and yanked on the handle. Locked. Without considering the consequences, I punched a hole in the window, fumbled for the latch, and pulled the door open.

A guttural noise escaped my lungs. Tuuli sat, curled in a tight ball against the driver's side door, hugging her knees, eyes vacant, body trembling, blood stains on her arms.

Tango stormed my way, screaming something fierce.

"She's here!" I yelled over my shoulder. "She's in the damn truck."

That shut him up.

I climbed into the cab, inched my way across the seat, and tucked her against me. She didn't fight, but she didn't relax. My internal temperature spiked.

"She hurt?" Tango asked.

"Don't think so. Can't tell yet."

"Unlock the door behind her. I'll take a look."

I stretched an arm around her trembling body and pulled the lever. Tango jogged around the other side of the truck and opened the door, slow and steady. Tucker stood in the road, waving down the police cruiser and yelling for an ambulance. I closed my eyes and pressed my lips against the top of her head while my cousin gently inspected the girl in my arms.

"Don't think it's her blood. I don't see any wounds."

"Tuuli," I whispered into her hair. "Bunny. You're safe. I'm here. I'm here."

"They made me watch." Her voice was so faint, I wasn't sure if it'd been my imagination.

Tango and I exchanged a glance. He'd heard her, too.

"What'd you say?" I whispered against her hair.

"They made me watch," she said again, louder.

"They made me watch." She dropped her legs to the floor and twisted to face me, eyes wild, unfocused.

"They made me watch." She pounded my chest with one fist, and then the other.

"They made me watch." She struck again. Then again. And again, throwing more aggression into each hit.

"They made me watch. They made me watch. They made me watch. They made me watch..."

CHAPTER 7

Tito

I WAS STILL A baby the first time I killed a man. A week away from my twelfth birthday. I remembered hovering inches from the pedophile's face, watching the fight and the life drain from his gray eyes. My fingers weren't long enough to fit around his thick neck. My body trembled from exertion. Twice, he had wrestled free of my hold. Thankfully, what I had lacked in size and experience, I made up for in conviction—and an unholy amount of hatred.

I didn't kill Father Mulligan for my own benefit, however. I ended his reign of perversion to protect those who would come after me. The boys who wouldn't be strong enough to defend themselves.

I remembered vivid details of the expression on his wrinkled face as the old man finally gave way to fear and accepted his fate—death at the hands of a child. One of the countless souls he'd ruined.

What I remembered most was that he had shown no hint of remorse, not one goddamn lick of regret for all the innocent lives he had defiled.

Didn't matter. I would never regret my actions either. I hadn't ended him to prove a point. I ended him because nobody else would. Not the church. Not the parents of those children brave enough to speak up.

Aside from my first kill, I had never kept a tally of the souls I'd delivered to Lady Death.

As I stood inside the waiting room at Whisper Springs Medical Center, I started to count. There were ten people. Three women and seven men who I would strike down without a second thought, just to burn off steam if I couldn't get to Tuuli soon.

I fucking hated hospitals.

I sat, unnoticed, in the corner chair of that stifling room, listening, waiting, watching. Three men wearing hand-tailored suits sat at the far end of the space. I pegged them as lawyers. There were two cops, who wouldn't sit but paced from the nurses' station back to the waiting room, warily eyeing the heavy-set, balding man who sat like a king five chairs down from me. I recognized him from the intel I'd dug up on Erik Meyer. Jeremy Carver, leader of the Christian Brotherhood of Faith Church. Jonas's father.

A small blonde woman cried quietly at the fat man's side, hands in her lap, gaze fixed on the wad of tissues bunched in her delicate fingers.

At one point, she asked, "How could this happen?"

To which the man replied, "He was a damn fool. That's how." His lips curled in disgust. "We don't need this mess," he snarled, leaning toward the woman. "Don't you dare cry for that boy. Pull your shit together." He pushed to stand, and the lawyers snapped to attention when he waddled their way.

Not until Jeremy moved out of earshot did the woman rise. Never taking her eyes off the floor, she headed to the nurses' station. She was striking. Small and graceful, platinum hair, enormous blue eyes. Dressed entirely in designer threads. Ridiculous fucking rock on her finger.

For the life of me, I couldn't imagine what she was doing with the inflated fuck-twat, but whatever. Wasn't my business. I was there for one reason and one reason only. Answers.

Fine. Two reasons. Answers, and to make sure Tuuli was okay, despite being angrier than shit about her deception.

Fuck, she better be okay.

I sighed a breath of relief when Roger strode through the emergency room doors, sent a chin nod my way, and walked toward the frustrated men in blue. They exchanged quiet words before he came to greet me.

"Hey, Rog," I grunted.

He eyed my bandaged hand but didn't voice his thoughts. "Hey, Moretti."

"Everything get cleaned up at the trailer?"

He spoke low, keeping our convo private. "Hell, no. Place is a mess. Gonna be a long night. Found bunkers around the property, most of 'em empty, but a couple stocked with rifles and hand grenades, military-grade."

Officer Roger Caldwell ate lunch at The Truck Stop several times a week. Sometimes with his wife and children. They were a young family of four. His eldest daughter was special needs, so he also worked private security for Tango whenever he could to help make ends meet. Nice guy. Good cop. Always sat in Tuuli's section.

"How's our waitress doing?" he asked.

"Nurse said she'd let me know as soon as there was any news." I leaned forward, elbows to knees, hands clasped. "What's the story with that guy?" I jerked my head toward the bald man, who had pulled one of the suits aside. "Your buddies look like they're itching to take him out."

"Whenever he makes a public appearance, his posse isn't far behind. Trouble inevitably follows."

That ever-present knot tightened in my gut. "What the fuck was Tuuli doing in Jonas's trailer?"

"I promise, we'll get that sorted as soon..." Roger continued to speak, but my attention was drawn to a small figure wearing a baggy sweatshirt, hair tucked into a Mariners baseball cap, and a pair of baggy sweats, hem dragging on the floor over a pair of Doc Martens.

The tiny little beast sauntered right past the cops, who were busy watching Carver, right past the front desk, and right out the motherfucking door.

Roger continued talking. I didn't hear a word he said. "Excuse me, Rog." I pushed to my feet and slapped a hand on his shoulder. "I just remembered I have an appointment. Call me as soon as you hear anything about Tuuli?" *Or when you realize she snuck out, right under your nose.*

"Sure thing, Moretti."

I jogged through the slider, looked right, then left. It took a few blinks to adjust to the darkness, but I found her, sticking to the shadows, halfway down the block, like she was out for a Sunday stroll.

I ran to my car, fired her up, and rolled onto the street, parking half a block ahead of the escape artist.

When I hopped out of my car and headed her way, Tuuli stiffened, then looked around as if searching for an escape route.

Silly little beast. There was nowhere for her to hide.

Huffing in defeat, she pulled the cap off her head. "What are you doing here?"

What was I doing? Seriously? Christ, I needed to hit something.

"What the hell do you think?" I locked my fingers around her arm, dragged her back to my car, and not so gently nudged her into the passenger seat.

I drove several blocks before I was calm enough to speak. "Gonna tell me what the hell is going on?"

Tuuli rubbed her eyes. Her head rolled to the side, and she stared out the passenger window. "I lied to everyone."

"Lied about what?"

"Everything."

"Everything? What does that mean?"

Her face scrunched and fat tears rolled down her cheeks.

I was beyond frustrated, and despite my urge to offer comfort, I pushed. I needed answers because my gut was raw and my nerves jagged. "What were you doing in that trailer?"

Tuuli leaned forward, face buried in her hands, body heaving.

"Were you living there? How do you know Jonas Carver?"

Tuuli continued to sob. I remained unaffected, my anger an impenetrable field of protection against the heart-wrenching look on her face.

"Why did you sneak out of the hospital? Why aren't you answering me?"

I didn't give her a chance to answer because the more questions I asked, the faster the pieces clicked into place. The trailer. The blonde woman. The fat man. The lawyers. Tuuli disappeared the same day Jonas was released from prison. The Christian Brotherhood of Faith.

I yanked the steering wheel to the right and threw the car into park.

I was out of my mind with rage. I didn't want to accept the truth that smacked me right in the kisser. I turned in my seat and pulled her hands away from her face. "What the fuck is going on?"

She couldn't catch a breath.

I grabbed her chin and forced her to look at me. "Why were you in that trailer? And fuckin' look me in the eye when you say it. What's your connection to Jonas?"

Tuuli trembled, but hell, I broke a little when she lifted her red, tear-soaked eyes to meet mine.

Fuck, my heart split in two when she spit out the words, "He's my brother." She held my gaze for a brave spell, blinking through the torrent of tears. "He was my brother." Her face crumbled. "They made me watch him die. I couldn't do anything but watch those monsters tear him apart."

She batted my hand away, yanked on the door handle, and before I could wrap my head around the situation, she was halfway down the street.

I took one deep breath, then another.

If Jonas was her brother, that fat man in the hospital was her father. That woman, who'd been sitting mere feet from me, with familiar blue eyes, was her mother. How the fuck did I not know? How had she slipped past Tango's radar? Tuuli Holt was the daughter of one of the country's most prominent White Supremacist leaders. Her brother had threatened to kill Aida.

I'd dismembered the last guy who'd hurt the people I loved.

The lying little beast had infiltrated my family, and I'd just let her go.

Hell, no.

I stepped out of the car and cracked my neck. Drawing a deep breath, I stared at the dark sky and welcomed the blackness that closed around me.

Tuuli

The black sky closed around me like a collapsing tunnel, burying me under its filthy rubble. I pushed forward, unsure of my destination, knowing only that I had to keep moving. Away from Tito. Away from the images of blood and skin, Jonas's blue eyes begging for help, the grunts and taunts of his masked assailants, and that terrifying voice panting in my ear, "You're next, beauty. Gonna fuck that ass up real good. Then you can run home and tell Daddy this was all for him."

Crushing shame consumed me. The ground passed below in a dizzying blur. Run. Run. Run.

A pair of arms enveloped me. My feet left the ground, the world spun, and I landed on my back in a patch of wet grass.

Angry eyes invaded my field of vision. Hot breaths heated my face.

"You don't drop a bomb like that and run away. No fuckin' way. You spew bullshit like that, you damn well stick around and face up to it. Hear me, little viper?"

A jackhammer battered my chest. Jonas's screams grew louder, clanging in my head like loose change in a dryer. Tito was above me yet seemed a million miles away.

"Tell me what the fuck is going on."

I gasped for breath, struggling to get back to my feet.

His heavy body fell across mine, smashing me into the wet ground. "Are you one of *them*? Were you trying to hurt my family?" He grabbed my wrists and pinned them above my head. "Tell me."

I wanted to speak, purge my guilty conscience. He'd never forgive me. None of them would. I was crumbling under the weight of my deception. I wanted to confess, but the words wouldn't come. I couldn't find them through the screams in my head.

"Tito." I choked on my plea. "Tito, please."

"You fuckin' little liar," he groaned through gritted teeth. "You've been lying to us this whole time. Did Jonas put you up to it? He make you get a job at The Stop? What was the plan exactly?"

"Please," I begged, choking on my tears. "I can't."

So much blood. So much screaming.

"What was your game, Tuuli?" His face hovered inches from mine. His voice vibrated with disgust and hate.

"I can't. I can't. He won't stop screaming." I tried desperately to shake the images, the noises, from my head. "Oh, God. Make it stop. Make them stop screaming."

In a breath, his weight was gone. I rolled to my side, pounding at my skull, desperate to dull the noise. I shoved my palms into my eyes, a futile attempt to rub the images away. They wouldn't go away.

I didn't want to see them anymore. The blood. The knives. The bodies. The masked men.

Gonna fuck you up like your daddy fucked us up.

"Stop."

You're next, beauty.

"Tuuli. Stop."

Jonas's blue eyes, wide and lifeless, focused on me through his torture. His bloodied lips mouthing, *Tuuli, I'm sorry. Tuuli, I'm sorry. I'm sorry. I'm sorry.*

"Fuck." Tito yanked my fingers from my face, holding them between us with one hand. His other hand locked like a vise around my jaw, squeezing hard and holding me still. "Breathe. Just fuckin' breathe."

Through the dark, I heard his words—rough, angry, and violent. Through blurry eyes, I registered the shape of his face, vibrations of rage the only barrier between us. Still, his touch grounded me. His presence soothed me. His strength pulled me back from the spinning abyss.

"Breathe with me. You can get through this. It'll pass."

I attempted a slow and steady inhale, only to choke on tears.

"Breathe in for three, out for three. I'll do it with you." He pressed his forehead to mine and started to count, "Inhale. One, two, three."

I sucked in shaky breaths.

"Good. Now blow it out. One, two, three."

I blew wet breaths at his face.

"Again," he ordered. "Breathe in. One, two, three."

I focused on his voice and my intake and output of air.

"That's it, Bunny. One. Two. Three," he repeated, over, and over, until the tears stopped falling, until the world stopped spinning, until Tito's was the only voice I heard.

I don't know how long we stayed that way, heads together, eyes locked. I don't remember walking back to his car or driving to his apartment. I remember the numbness thawed when Tito parked and said, "You'll stay with me tonight. Tomorrow, you're gonna tell me everything. Then, you're on your own."

On my own.

No job. No home. No money.

Everything I'd owned I'd left behind in Jonas's trailer. I would never step foot inside that pit of death again.

On my own was too daunting a concept to process, considering the events of the day.

I followed my reluctant savior inside his home. He tossed his keys on the kitchen counter and led me down the hallway into the bathroom.

He stood in the doorway, pointed to the tub, and grunted, "Take a shower. You're a mess."

I brushed past him, closed the door behind me, and stood at the sink, taking stock of my reflection. Red-rimmed, swollen eyes mocked me—blue like my brother's, our only common trait. Tangled hair. Muddy and ugly. Dirty. Ruined.

As much as I wanted to melt into a puddle on the floor, I stepped into the tub and washed away the bloody mess.

Tito

What a bloody fucking mess. I should've cut her loose. I should've driven her back to the hospital, handed her over to Roger, and washed my hands of her.

Perhaps I would have if she hadn't started screaming about the voices.

I knew those damn voices all too well. Angry as I was, I could not leave her to fight those demons alone.

She'd just been through hell. A hell of her own making, most likely, but torment nonetheless, and I wouldn't let her slip into the abyss until I had the answers I needed.

I waited to hear the shower run, then grabbed a T-shirt out of the bedroom and laid it on the sink. I scooped her soiled clothes off the bathroom floor, carried them outside, and tossed them in the trash. Then I parked my ass on the sofa and fired up my laptop.

I couldn't fathom how Tuuli had slipped under Tango's radar. He'd had every one of Slade's employees screened after the attack outside the diner last year.

After a five-minute probe into Tuuli's family, it became clear how she'd passed the background check. Like her mother, Tuuli didn't share her father's last name. No father listed on her birth certificate. Not one financial record existed that tied her to the bloated bastard. Bank. School. Dentist. Doctor. Nothing.

Her parents had never married. Had never shared an address.

If Jeremy Carver was her father, DNA would be the only way to prove it.

Tuuli's mother, Ingrid Holt, however, had collected state assistance for the entirety of Tuuli's childhood, worked as a cashier at several different large chain grocery stores over the years, and was currently collecting a decent monthly disability check that was mailed to an address that shared a property line with the Brotherhood Church.

A soft, shaky voice startled me.

"Thank you for the shirt."

Pale, bare legs passed my field of vision. My crew neck hung like a burlap sack over her slight frame, falling off one shoulder, the hem reaching below her knees.

She curled into the armchair across from me, pulled the cotton over her legs, and rested her chin on her bent knees. "Are you Googling me?"

I huffed. There was Google. There was the deep web. Then there was my web. "Something like that."

"That's not necessary. I'll tell you everything you need to know."

"Little late for divulgence, sweetheart." I waited for a response, a pathetic apology, crocodile tears, hell, even a cringe or a lip quiver. Got nothin'.

"You're a White Supremacist?"

"No. I told you. I left the church."

"Jeremy Carver is your father?"

"Yes," she answered, staring at the floor.

"You sure?"

"Yes. Why?"

"There isn't a single lick of evidence stating that he's related to you in any way."

Her gaze lifted to mine, confused and wary. "I don't understand."

Liar.

"You don't use his last name. Why?"

"My mother always said it was to protect us from my father's enemies."

Convenient.

"When you told me about your father's church, why didn't you mention it was The Christian Brotherhood of Faith?"

"That's not exactly information I'm proud to share." She reached down and picked at her toenail. "And I was afraid to tell you."

As she should've been.

"Why did you come to work at The Stop?"

She shivered and tightened her arms around her shins. "I had to get away. From my father, the church, Erik. I begged my brother to help me. I'd thought it would be hard, that I would have to bribe him, but he'd told me I could stay at his trailer. He even promised to help get Erik off my back. All I had to do was get a job at The Stop and find out everything I could about the big blonde guy and the crazy pregnant chick who hung out there all the time."

Aida and Tucker.

"Did he tell you why you were supposed to keep an eye on them?"

"I asked. He said it wasn't my concern and that he'd let me know when the time was right."

"Were you aware that he'd threatened to kill both Tucker and Aida?"

Tuuli blanched. "No."

"Do you know why Jonas was arrested?"

Her eyes snapped to mine. "No."

"You know nothing about the videos? The young girls?"

"Girls?" Her face crumpled, tears welling. "Oh, God. No."

If she was bullshitting me, the girl was good. Her whole body trembled.

"You lived in that shithole with him for how long, and you want me to believe you didn't have a clue what he was up to?" I closed my laptop and set it aside, giving her my full attention.

"He was never around. After a couple weeks, he stopped checking in with me. One day, he said he had business in Seattle and he'd be gone for a few days, but he never came back. I waited for a week. I thought maybe he forgot about our deal. I was going to look for another job, catch a bus out of town, maybe, but then that man attacked Aida. After that, I got a raise. A good raise, and I liked everyone at the diner so much, and you were there, and..."

"And what?"

She sucked in a breath. "You know."

Yeah. I knew. She liked me. She had stayed because of me. Fucking little bunny.

Too bad I couldn't stand the sight of her. Although, those damn pink toenails peeking out from under my shirt were distracting as hell and sending blood to places it had no right going. When had I developed a foot fetish?

"Tell me something."

Her head lolled to the side, her cheek taking the place of her chin against her knees. Her swollen eyelids lifted, then closed, then lifted again. "Hmm?" she sighed.

"Why'd you make me believe you lived in that nice house?"

"I was embarrassed." Her red-rimmed eyes fell closed again.

I watched her chest rise and fall, listened to the soft, raspy breaths expelling from her lungs. Jesus, she was small.

So breakable.

I watched, nauseous from the emotions battering my insides.

"I'm sorry," she mumbled, halfway to dreamland.

She was sorry? I was sorry. For letting her in. For letting the goddamn little bunny burrow her way under my skin.

I stared at her slight frame. Watched her body loosen. Her lips part. Her breaths deepen. Fuck, she smelled good. Fuck. I was pathetic.

Before long, she started to whimper, her face twisting in fear.

Fuck.

I pushed off the couch and scooped her up. She was so damn light, and damn me to hell, I liked that she smelled like my soap.

I carried her to my bedroom, stood bedside, holding my little obsession, wondering when I'd become such a sap. I'd never been soft with a woman. Never once had I let a girl stay the night in my private space. I sure as hell had never wanted to curl around another human being and protect them with everything I had.

For the life of me, I couldn't figure out why I wanted the girl in my arms. The fraud. The broken creature.

As I laid her down and she curled into a tight ball, it hit me.

She was damaged. I was damaged.

She was alone. I was alone.

I was so damn angry about her deception. But when we were together, something in my icy interior thawed. The dark abyss didn't feel so hopeless. The voices kept their fucking mouths shut.

Tuuli

"Keep your fucking mouth shut."

Jonas clamped a sweaty hand over my lips, squeezing so hard my jaw popped. "If he sees us, we're dead," he whisper-growled in my ear.

I wanted to ask why he was in my hiding spot—the small alcove above my father's office. I wanted to ask why his camera was pointed through the hole in the ceiling. Instead, I shivered violently against him and watched the scene unfurl below me.

The boy's face was red and wet, and snot bubbles swelled in and out of his nose. He could no longer scream, his voice having lost all steam, releasing nothing but a wheezy cry.

I knew the kid—Riley. I'd seen him around school. He'd started coming to church three months ago. He had spiky black hair, pale skin, and never-fading dark circles under his eyes. He never smiled. He didn't have any friends as far as I could tell. He started fights all the time.

He wasn't fighting my father, though.

He couldn't. He was stretched across my dad's heavy oak desk, bare butt hanging over one edge, his hands pinned to the other in handcuffs that were secured with metal chains to the legs of the antique. His pants pooled on the floor at his ankles.

Dad held his favorite belt, one end wrapped around his wrist, the buckle end striking Riley's broken skin over and over.

I wanted to scream. I wanted to tear through the ceiling and help the boy. I couldn't move with Jonas's full weight on top of me, pinning my face to the floor, where I couldn't see anywhere but through the crack, couldn't see anything but the brutality of a scene I'd lived over and over. The only difference was I'd never been chained, or half-naked. Dad had never hit me hard enough to leave permanent physical marks.

My father dropped the belt. His face was red, his eyes sleepy looking, his breaths shallow. He stared for a long time at the shaking boy before licking his lips, unbuttoning his pants, and rubbing his hand up and down his crotch. He stepped closer to Riley, then half-groaned, half-whispered, "Time to earn your place, boy," and pulled the zipper of his fly down.

I tried to scream again, my whole body quaking with the force.

Jonas rolled onto his back, pulling me on top of him, spitting out, "Fuck. Fuck. Fuck," into my ear. He pressed his face to my wet cheek, "Show's over, brat. Cover your ears."

I cried, and screamed silent, "No. No. No's" into his hand.

"Tuuli. Shh. I'm here. You're safe."

I bolted into a sitting position, sweaty, crying, and about to vomit. I barely registered the fact that Tito was next to me. I threw the blankets off and stumbled down the dark hall to the toilet.

I didn't puke. There wasn't food in my stomach to purge. Instead, I braced my hands on the porcelain seat, arms locked, and stared into the bowl, tracking the little ringlets my tears made as they dropped into the water.

Tito's bare feet passed my periphery. He sat on the edge of the tub, elbows to knees, head in his hands. "I'm going to ask you a tough question. I need the truth."

I swiped a swelling tear from my eyelash and nodded, feeling every agonizing inch of distance between us.

"Did your father hurt you? Was he abusive?"

I retched, fighting another wave of nausea. "Why would you ask me that?"

"You were talking in your sleep. And it sounded like..." Tito huffed, stood straight, pounded the wall, then mumbled, "Never mind," before pushing past me, retreating.

What I said next stopped him cold. "He was abusive. All the men were. But he never sexually abused me, if that's what you're asking. He never—" My voice broke. God. I hated revealing my ugly past, but once the bucket of truth had tipped, there was no stopping the runoff. "He never touched me because he likes boys."

The air shifted. Every muscle of his bare torso rolled before going rigid. "The fuck'd you say?"

I didn't elaborate. Deep down, I knew I was as guilty as my father for not telling anyone what I'd seen all those years ago. What I'd always known, even though I didn't fully understand the depths of his abuse. Then again, I'd only been a child. Jonas had made me promise never to tell. He'd said my father would kill us. I had believed him.

I had never returned to my favorite hiding spot after witnessing what really happened during my father's private meetings. I had never gone near my father's office again.

Avoidance and denial—a warm, fuzzy blanket to a guilty soul.

Tito turned, and I could swear he trembled. A full-bodied, violent shiver. I hated the way he looked at me like I'd just admitted to killing kittens for pleasure.

I straightened, too, reflecting his glare. "Now do you understand why I didn't want anyone to know who I was or where I came from?"

I pushed past where he stood bone stiff and hunted for my clothes. I needed to leave. I needed to put the past twenty-four hours, hell, the past twenty years, behind me. Forget my family. Forget the Truck Stop. Forget Tito.

Start fresh. On my own terms.

"Where are my clothes?"

"In the trash. I tossed them. They were ruined." He scratched the stubble along his jawline, stared at the floor, eyes unfocused. "Your father fucks boys?"

"You threw away my clothes?"

"Yes." He fisted his hands at his sides, the muscles in his arms flexing, twisting in short spasms. "He's hurting kids?"

I didn't want to talk about my father. "You do realize I have nothing to wear, right? Everything I own was in Jonas's trailer, including my ID, my bank card. Everything. And you have to know I can never step foot in that place again; I can't. Not after—"

"Tuuli."

I didn't want to think about the blood. The dead girls. "You said I have to leave this morning. How am I supposed to do that with no clothes?"

"Tuuli."

"Go get them, Tito!" I yelled, surprising myself, but continuing regardless. "Go get my damn clothes out of the garbage. I know you're mad at me, I know I'm a freak, but at least let me leave here with a little dignity."

"Bunny." He breached my personal space, his feet caging mine, his arms wrapping around me. He slid one big hand up my spine and gripped the back of my head, smashing my face against his chest. "Just shut up and give me a fuckin' second here."

His chest rose and fell, and I wanted nothing more than to melt against all that skin. He was heat, and strength, and the opposite of every man I'd ever known. He held me like I was precious, not a possession. Delicate, but not weak. His hold was tight, but not tense. He shivered like he needed the connection more than I did.

His voice came at a low rumble. "I don't want you to leave. Fuck. You're not leaving. You're right. I was angry. I'm still angry. You dropped one helluva bomb last night. I need time to process. We'll figure this out."

"I never meant to hurt anyone. You have to believe me. I had to get away. I just wanted out."

He sighed, leaning on me as much as I leaned on him. "I don't know what to believe. But I promise you're out. You're never going back there."

I closed my eyes and let Tito soothe me with his muscles, and words, and heartbeat. I started to relax, my pulse slowing to a healthy rhythm, my thoughts quieting.

Until Tito said, "You're never going back there because I'm going to kill Jeremy Carver and burn that church to the ground."

CHAPTER 8

HARD TO SAY WHEN I turned the corner. Could've been the second I believed Tuuli was missing. Or when I found her driver's license inside the trailer bloodbath, or maybe it was the moment she broke down in Jonas's wrecked truck and beat the ever-loving shit out of me.

Most likely, I had gone soft the moment she outed her father as an abuser. No doubt, the past nights I had spent holding her in my arms and helping her breathe through the aftershocks of her nightmares had something to do with my change of heart.

Hell. Could've been the bravery she showed two days ago when she'd called Tango, Slade, Tucker, and Aida over to my place and stood before them, profusely apologetic, confessing everything about her family and her reason for coming to work at The Stop. Or the next morning, the way she bit her quivering lip to hold tears at bay until after she'd given her statement to Officer Caldwell about the murders.

The catalyst to my revelation wasn't as important as the fact that somehow, at some point, for whatever reason, I had turned a corner. Fuck me and my lone soldier, live for me, die for me bullshit. I wanted to be the guy Tuuli saved herself for.

No other man would lay hands on her. Not while I was living and breathing.

I headed to the kitchen, barefoot and bare-chested, still wet from my shower, and sated for the time being because, yes, I'd jerked off again.

Tuuli stood at the counter. I slowed my approach, appreciating the scene, palms sweaty, throat dry as sandpaper, ticker pounding an atomic countdown in my chest.

Tuuli flipped through the morning paper, left heel bouncing erratically over the top of her right foot. The shirt she wore, although five sizes too large, rode up the back of her thighs, revealing too much naked real estate. I knew there was nothing under that lucky shirt of mine. Her only bra was hanging on my towel rack, and I'd thrown away her only pair of panties the night of her attack. She hadn't asked to borrow any of my boxers. So, I knew, if I lifted the hem of that shirt, I'd find nothing but sweet, smooth, creamy skin.

I could've stood for hours, watching her read, watching her fidget and wiggle. I was a mindless, feral dog, panting over the piece of tail wagging in my face.

I could've watched forever. Instead, I dragged my ass to the fridge, popped the lid off the OJ, and chugged.

"When do you move into your new place?" she asked my back.

Sweet Jesus, that voice. I took another swig to lubricate my vocal cords before turning around to answer. "We close next week."

"Oh," she mumbled, chewing on her bottom lip. Tuuli looked down at the shirt she wore and smoothed her hand over her torso. "I need clothes, so I can get out of your hair."

That constant low rumble in my chest rolled into a full-blown earthquake. She couldn't leave. "You've got nowhere to go."

"I'll figure something out."

Didn't she get it? I would not lose her again. I scratched the top of my head, then fisted my hair to keep from screaming. Breathe in. *One, two, three.* Out. *One, two, three.* "I've figured it out for you. Stay here."

"What? No. That's not a good idea, Tito. I've imposed too much already. I need to find a job. A place to live..." she rambled on about her clothes that had been left behind in Jonas's trailer and affordable apartments on the wrong side of town.

The more she talked about leaving, the larger the dent in my chest grew. I hadn't touched her in the ten days she'd been with me, except to quiet her demons, but for the time being I needed to quiet mine. I decimated the space between us and claimed her mouth, holding her tight, absorbing her trembles, her heat, the press of her soft tits against my chest.

Fuck. Fuck. Fuck. Couldn't she see we needed each other?

Tuuli didn't fight like I'd expected, and damn, her compliance drove me insane. I held her boneless body, kissing, smelling, tasting, just fucking connecting. I bent low, cupping her ass, and hoisted her onto the counter. When her legs cinched around my waist, a moan escaped my lips.

There was no going back. I wanted her. I wanted the connection. The buzz, the high, the fear, the ache, the uncertainty, the promise of things to come. I needed to keep her close. Needed to protect her from all the shit the world spewed. Needed to feed off the good she made me feel.

Tuuli broke the kiss, pulling away with parted lips and lowered lids. Breathless, she whispered, "I can't stay here, Tito. Not after everything—"

"Don't leave." I fisted the hair at her nape and pressed my forehead to hers. God, I wanted to crawl inside her skin. "I can't let you go."

She jerked back like she'd been slapped. I captured her lips again, then mumbled into her mouth, "I'm fuckin' keeping you."

"But—"

"I can't stand the thought of another man touching you. When you're ready, let it be me. Please, let me be the only one."

She grabbed my shoulders and pushed, holding me at arms' length, glassy eyes aimed at my chest.

I tapped her chin. "Eyes up here."

She didn't lift them. I didn't push. I was throwing enough at her already.

I heard the gears grinding in her pretty little head. She wanted to speak. She wanted to argue. Plead her case.

I couldn't let her talk her way out of *us*.

I dipped, capturing that worried gaze. "I don't know what this is, or what the fuck we're gonna call this thing between us. But we're something, you and me. We're something I can't turn my back on. You know it. I know it. I'm not letting you disappear again."

"But you said—" She dropped her face into her hands and groaned. Her shoulders rose and fell before she looked at me again. "We agreed to be friends. How is living under the same roof going to make things any easier for us?"

"Jesus Christ. Did you hear what I just said to you?" I backed away, fisting my hair. "I'm so fuckin' over the friend stage. I've never so much as taken a woman on a date, let alone have one spend the night. Now, I'm begging you to shack up. Do I look like the kind of fucker who begs? I don't know what to call this. I don't know what the hell I'm doing. All I know is that I'd never been so scared in my life as I was when you disappeared. I've never been so goddamned angry at someone for lying to me. I've never let a woman get under my skin the way you have, and Bunny..." I rubbed the ache in my chest. "You're burrowed deep. Scratchy and uncomfortable as it is, I want to keep you there."

"You want to be more than friends?"

"That's what I'm saying."

"More than friends...without sex?"

"Sounds ridiculous, I know. But yes. No sex until you're ready."

"You would do that..." Her eyes liquefied and she choked on her words. "For me?"

I swallowed the profanity that barreled up my throat. I didn't understand the pull between us. Vulnerability was giving me indigestion. There was no doubt my right hand and I were about to set out on an epic getting-to-know-ya adventure because I wasn't the kind of guy to push any woman into sex, especially Tuuli. I wouldn't bring that issue to the ring.

Tuuli wasn't a battle I wanted to win. She was the prize. I was only fighting myself.

"Only for you."

She let out a sob, then reined in her emotions, swiping the moisture from her face. Drawing in a slow, steady breath, she hopped off the counter. "I have to show you something. After that. If you still want me, you can ask again. Okay?"

Tuuli

"Okay." Tito nodded, watching me back away, worry pinching his brows.

Every nerve in my body exploded under rapid fire.

"You need to understand how crazy my family is." I crossed my arms and grabbed the hem of the tee. "You think you want to be with me?" I pulled the shirt over my head. "You need to know what you're getting into." With a sigh, I turned my back to him, pulling my long hair over my shoulder, exposing my bare skin. I stood naked, shivering, hugging myself, allowing Tito time to study my tattoo. The hate symbol. A bold font number fourteen, black and ugly, permanently etched on my skin. Underneath the number, in a smaller font, a 100% symbol.

His breath caught. I didn't look over my shoulder, certain I'd find disgust on his face.

"I was eleven when I started my period. In The Brotherhood's eyes, the day a girl starts her period, she becomes a woman. She's fair game. To celebrate, Jonas and Erik held me down, while my dad and Erik's father branded me."

I choked on the bile rising in my throat and pinched my eyes shut, trying to block out the memory.

"Fuckin' purist breeders," he mumbled. "You didn't want this, and they gave it to you anyway."

"You know what it means?" I asked, dropping my head in shame.

"I've seen it before. I know what the mark represents." The heat of his breaths hit my neck. "The number fourteen symbolizes the fourteen words—*We must secure the existence of our people and a future for white children*. The 100% represents the purity of the white race."

"I'm prime breeding stock. I'm expected to consider it an honor if any member of The Brotherhood wants to use my body for any purpose. Erik has been my saving grace. He laid his claim on me when we were children. Sick as his obsession is, he protected me."

"But he didn't protect you. He let other men touch you." His voice sounded pained.

I looked over my shoulder and found nothing but compassion in his expression. He lifted a finger to my shoulder and traced an X over the image.

My skin exploded in goosebumps. "Erik disappeared for two years. Nobody knew where, how long he'd be gone, or if he was ever coming back. I believed I had no choice when those boys wanted to be with me."

I reached over my shoulder and dug my nails into the blemished skin. "I've spent the past nine years hiding. I never made friends in school. I was afraid they would find out who my father was. Who I was."

Tito growled his disapproval over my shoulder, then pressed a kiss on the ugly numbers. "This mark does not define you."

My entire body vibrated under that simple gesture.

He stepped around to my front, wrapped one arm around my waist, and lifted the other hand to my chest, laying it over my heart. "This defines you." He kissed my forehead and tapped my temple with two fingers. "And all the beautiful, brilliant things you have going on in here define you. This tattoo doesn't change the way I feel about you."

I melted against him, my breasts smashed between us, his naked flesh searing me, his words freeing me.

He walked backward, pulling me with him until his calves hit the back of the sofa. We fell into the cushions. I settled on his lap, my bare butt on his thighs, my knees hugging his hips.

I was naked but felt no shame. Exposed, but had never felt more protected. He didn't look at my breasts, and I could tell he wanted to, but I loved that he was trying so hard to keep the exchange from becoming sexual, even though his arousal swelled between my legs. His eyes burned with need, his cheeks flushed.

"I want you, Tuuli. All of you. Please, stay here with me," he urged, rubbing warm, calloused fingers up and down my bare back.

He wanted me. I would never understand why, but I would never doubt his sincerity. He'd taken care of me every day for the past two weeks. Every time I woke with nightmares, he'd crawled into bed, made me breathe through the panic attacks, then held me until I fell asleep again. He'd fed me when I couldn't get out of bed, hiding from the world, from the voices, the images that haunted me. He could've turned his back the second he found out who I was, but he'd never left me alone, not once.

Yes, he was quiet and brooding. Yes, he was scary and terrifying. But I couldn't deny that Tito Moretti was also a blessing. We were brought together for reasons bigger than the both of us.

I threw my arms around his neck and squeezed, offering every ounce of gratitude, relief, and contrition I could pour into that hug. His arms tightened around me with equal fervor and didn't loosen until I rolled my head to the side and kissed his neck.

"Thank you," I mumbled against his warm skin.

Tito

The skin on skin was torture. Beautiful, bloody torture. "Thank you for what?"

"For not freaking. For not making me feel like a freak." She sighed, curling tighter against me. "Thank you for not leaving me on the street when you found out who I was."

God, she smelled like vanilla and sweet, naked skin. My entire body vibrated with need.

"I wish I had told you everything from the beginning. I was afraid and ashamed. I've wanted to be with you since the first day you came to the diner. You scared me. Terrified me, really. But there was something about the way you looked at me like you knew what was inside my head, like you recognized the mess. You looked at me like none of my ugliness would faze you because you're indestructible."

Indestructible? Not by a long shot. Brick by brick the girl in my arms was breaking me down. A crack here, a dent there, leaving my walls weak and vulnerable. I cupped those blushing cheeks, making sure her eyes were right where they needed to be. On me. "You get that I'm in this for the long haul, right?"

Her face crinkled. Her gaze dropped. But damn, when she recovered and lifted those blue beauties back to me with a nod, I couldn't have been prouder.

When she whispered, "Please, don't ever let me go," something epic and painful happened in my chest, making my pulse race and my eyes blur. Part of me wanted to spill my guts, share my burdens, lighten my soul. Confess. But I feared my truths would break her, ending us before we began.

"Tito," she murmured into my neck.

"Yeah?" I pulled a white strand of silk through my fingers.

"Make love to me."

Jesus. H. Christ. Every muscle in my body tensed. My hard dick jerked in response. "But—"

She raised her head and pressed a finger over my lips. "I know what I said about waiting." Her cheeks flushed and her gaze dropped to my chest. "That was mostly a lie because I didn't want you to see my back, my mark. But I've wanted you from the beginning. You're the only man I've ever wanted."

"Bunny." I dipped my head. "Look me in the eye when you ask me for things. Don't be afraid. Don't be ashamed. Please. I need those eyes."

Sweet fucking Lord, when she lifted her burning gaze to mine and whispered, "Please. I need you," I was done for. I captured her mouth, savoring the sweet softness of her lips.

When she broke the kiss and whispered, "Please," I tucked my arms under her ass and rose from the couch, urging her legs around my waist. We hit the bedroom, I set her on her feet, and I took a long, greedy gander at her naked body.

Ethereal. Flawless.

A blinding beauty, rendering me speechless.

Tauli

I couldn't find my voice, which didn't matter anyway because when I smiled, he sighed and stepped closer, dropping his mouth to mine, stealing my oxygen. He trembled, squeezing me tight, pinning my arms between us. We stayed that way for a long time, Tito holding me upright and in the perfect position to take what he needed. Only he was giving more than taking, offering his mouth, his body, his soul through that kiss.

When he broke away, he stared at me long and hard, eyes soft, lips parted. He brushed a thumb over my bottom lip and asked, "Is this real? Do I finally get to have you?" like I was a precious gift. Not trash. Not a tool, but a beautiful, magical gift. And I knew, no hesitation, no question, that Tito was the right man, the one I should have saved myself for.

My pulse beat violent and thunderous in my ears, the fire in my cheeks growing hotter with each boom, boom, boom.

I stood naked and exposed for excruciating moments, shivering, not from cold, but the raw emotion on Tito's face.

Or maybe I trembled from the adrenaline racing through my veins. Either way, I couldn't wait for his body to follow through with the promise in his eyes.

My breasts ached, tightening to painful peaks.

He scratched the stubble on his jaw. His nostrils flared. A dark glow covered his cheeks. His breaths remained steady, while mine...Oh, God, was I even breathing?

I couldn't understand why he hadn't groped me. Why he hadn't pushed me to the floor or shoved me on the bed, or why he wasn't already thrusting inside me like had happened every other time.

With every other boy.

But Tito wasn't a boy.

Tito was confidence and savage beauty. He was quiet and controlled, and dear, sweet Jesus he was killing me, burning me alive with the heat of his stare. Why wasn't he doing anything? Was I too small? Too inexperienced? I pulled my arms up, covering my chest.

"No. God, no. Don't do that." He skimmed a finger across my cheek before pushing my arms back down to my sides. "Please. Don't be shy. You're beautiful. So goddamn beautiful. Just let me look at you."

I swallowed the emotion bubbling up my throat and blinked the sting from my eyes.

"Don't move," he rasped, stepping behind me.

Through the silence, I heard movement. He tossed his pants on the bed, and then his boxers.

His breaths grew louder, heightening my arousal. From behind, he grabbed my hand, laced our fingers, and squeezed. "I'm not used to having a woman like this, all mine, all night. I want to take my time. I need to savor you." He scooped my hair over my right shoulder, then pressed his lips to my ear. "It's been torture having you so close for so long, and not acting on every impulse. Sweet fuckin' torture." His teeth sunk into the base of my neck. When he closed his mouth and sucked, my knees buckled.

Tito hooked my waist and pulled me against his chest, holding me steady and upright while he licked and nibbled. With calloused fingers, he traced a slow path up my sides, scorching me, then cupped my breasts, kneading, massaging, rolling the tight buds between his fingers, pelting me with hot, erratic breaths.

I'd never ached so deep, never craved so hard, never burned so hot. I was helpless, mindless to do anything but take, take, take.

His lips traveled up my neck, then to my jaw, my cheek, the corner of my mouth. "Kiss me," he commanded, his mouth against mine.

I turned my head, and I kissed him. Soft and slow, savoring his tender touch, his flavor, his desire...for me. I could have died in that moment—taken my last breath with no regrets because in that moment I was beautiful, and whole, and desirable, and nothing would ever be as perfect as the way Tito cherished me. The way he held me tight and kissed me, trembling with want, with unbridled desire.

I couldn't imagine a more perfect moment.

Until he slid a hand down my abdomen and worked his fingers between my legs, his thumb brushing the sensitive spot. I jerked against him. A noise I didn't recognize escaped my lips. My body folded at the flood of sensation, my backside pressing against his erection. I wanted him to stop, the emotion unbearable. I never wanted him to stop, the pleasure, intoxicating. I wanted to cry and scream, and beg, and pray. I wanted to hold his hand down and make him continue or pull it away because I was either going to burn to ash or burst into a million shards of brilliant light.

Tito was everywhere. His lips on my neck. One hand on my breast, one hand between my legs. When he pressed his palm against my clit and slid a finger between my folds, instinct took over, and I ground against him. That's when I felt her, clawing through the nerves, taking over.

My beast.

Tito

My beast was so damn close to taking over, throwing her on the bed and devouring her soft little body until there wasn't an inch untouched, unclaimed, unmarked. Fucking hell, I trembled with restraint. I'd kept him in check until the moment she started to fuck my hand, her little body writhing against me, her hips bucking, the soft moans escaping those pink, wet lips. She hadn't a clue the danger she was in.

I'd never been gentle when it came to sex. Never wanted to take my time. Never needed to explore, taste, smell, mark another human being like I did the beauty in my arms.

If I didn't stop, if she didn't slow things down, neither one of us would survive the day unscathed.

I dropped my arms and stepped back, drawing one deep breath and then another. I was dizzy from the lack of blood flow to my brain. My cock throbbed like a son of a bitch. I fisted myself, a pathetic attempt to relieve the building pressure. Tuuli's hair fell down her back, nearly reaching her waist, and swear to my Maker when the light hit those soft waves just right, she looked every bit an angel. An exquisite, glowing gift from Heaven.

She hadn't turned around. Her shoulders rose and fell, and I knew she was trying to pull herself together. I didn't want her composed. I wanted her undone.

I stepped around, admiring every inch of ivory skin. When we stood toe to toe, she reached out, laying a shaky hand on my chest. Her nipples were so damn hard, my dick jerked. I brushed a knuckle across one tight bud, watching it pebble more. Her lips parted on a soft sigh, her face so pink with desire I had to swallow a moan.

"You're trembling," I said, offering a soft kiss. "Do you want to stop?"

"No. No. Please don't stop. I'm just nervous. Nobody has ever touched me the way you touch me," she whispered.

"I'm nervous, too, Bunny."

"Why?"

"I don't want to hurt you. I'm afraid I'll lose control and scare you, and that's the last fuckin' thing I wanna do. You have to tell me if I get too rough, or if I make you uncomfortable in any way. Promise me."

"I'm not afraid."

"Promise."

"I promise."

"Good." I dropped to one knee, more than ready to continue my exploration. She trembled when I kissed her stomach. Wiggled against me when I traveled lower.

Fuck. Fuck. Fuck. Her pussy was untrimmed, her blonde hairs so damn light and pretty. My fingers curled into her hips when her scent reached me—that fucking raw, wild scent of arousal. I yanked her closer, burying my nose and inhaling deep, craving more. She was a drug. A goddamn mind-altering, addictive drug, and I needed more than to smell her. I needed to taste. Gorge myself.

I dropped lower to the floor and held her tight while I raked my tongue up her crease.

"Oh. Oh. My. No…Shit." Tuuli's legs buckled, and I held her tighter.

"Hold on to me, baby."

Her fingers curled into my hair, fisting tight. So compliant. I dove in again, working my tongue up and down her folds, teasing her clit. The innocent little angel rolled her hips, writhing and needy. She was wild. So damn wild and responsive. I needed more. I needed her open for me. I slid a hand down her thigh, gripped behind her knee, and urged her to hook her leg over my shoulder.

Sweet hell, she was wet, so damn soft and sweet. Mine. All mine, body and soul. No inhibitions. I offered my mouth, she fucked my face. I squeezed her ass, she pulled my hair. I slid a finger inside her tight opening, she cried my name. And when I knew she was on the verge of losing control, when I couldn't wait another moment to be inside her, I sucked her clit between my teeth and made her come, and that goddamn, innocent little bunny released her beast, holding my head between her legs, trembling and shaking and riding out her orgasm, grinding hard against my mouth. When she came down from the high, her leg collapsing, I caught her spent body over my shoulder and dropped her on the bed.

Her tits bounced. Her hair splayed across my black duvet. Heavy-lidded, she smiled up at me. Then she spread her legs, inviting me in.

Fuck. I'd been scared of hurting her? We were zero for three by my count. My mouth would be bruised, I was sure I'd have two bald spots where she'd ripped at my hair, and what the fuck was she doing to that traitorous organ in my chest?

I grabbed a condom out of the nightstand drawer and fumbled to put it on. Tuuli watched, lips parted, eyes hungry. When I crawled over her, she sighed like she'd waited her whole life for our bodies to come together. I kissed her once, pressing my cock against the soft flesh between her legs. I wanted to take it slow. Ease into her. Draw out the pleasure. But when she curled her fingers around my neck, her blue eyes meeting mine, and begged, "I need to feel you inside me," I sunk deep, pushing inside until she took all of me.

Her gasp and her sweet pleas had me moving when I wanted to stay pressed against her, absorbing her heat and the tight fit where our bodies were one. I moved inside my precious angel, giving her everything I had—my lips, my voice, my eyes, my strength.

I loved how my body covered hers. I loved the contrast between her ivory glow and my dark features. I loved her whimpers, her breaths on my neck, the scrape of her nails on my skin, and the way her hips met mine with equal urgency. I loved how she looked at me like I was her fucking world. I loved that I didn't have to ask for her eyes. I had them. She gave them freely, holding my gaze like she was afraid I'd disappear if she looked away.

And I fucking loved how after I came inside her, after I grunted my pleasure into her neck, after we clung to each other, sweaty, and breathless, I didn't want her to leave.

CHAPTER 9

Tuuli

"YOU READY?" TITO ASKED, voice gruff, eyes worried.

I nodded. Turned away. Chickened out. Turned back.

Strong arms wrapped around me. "You can do this, Bunny."

Lordy, how I wanted to believe him.

Two days ago, Slade had come to Tito's door holding brand new uniforms and begged me to come back to work at The Stop.

My first instinct was to tell her no.

But she had offered me a lifeline, and, in a sense, a chance to earn back my dignity.

My brother's murderers had walked away with my entire savings. Three thousand dollars. I couldn't refuse Slade. I needed the job. As much as I wanted to hide in Tito's apartment, where I was safe, warm, and fed, I needed to stand on my own two feet.

"Okay. I can do this." I forced the words, not wholly believing them, but determined to make them truth eventually. "I'm good. I'm ready." Faking a smile, I kissed his cheek, then left him alone in Slade's office.

"Toodaloo," Charlie sang from the kitchen as I passed the service window. "Glad you're back."

"Me, too," Slade chimed from behind the counter.

"Me, three," Margie shouted from table five.

"Me, four!" an unfamiliar, but friendly voice shouted from somewhere near Charlie.

Slade came closer and bumped my hip, her ponytail bouncing behind her. "Hey, girl. Thanks for coming back. We've missed you."

Words of gratitude lodged in my throat, stuck behind a thick lump of emotion. Forgiveness was not easy to give, yet she'd handed me a clean slate, no conditions.

"I'm sorry about your brother," she whispered, pulling me into a hug. "I know how it feels to lose a family member. If you need to talk, I'm here, okay?"

"Thank you," I mumbled, moisture pooling in my eyes.

She stepped back, holding me at arms' length. "If you ever need a minute, go lock yourself in my office."

A deep voice rattled over my shoulder, "You must be Tuuli."

I turned to find a pair of exotic green eyes, amped by a set of sinful dimples.

"Hi," I squeaked, shaking his offered hand, struggling to hold the eye contact because wow, the guy was so beautiful it almost hurt to look.

"Tuuli, this is Charlie's nephew, Eli. He's joined the crew." Slade smiled and winked. "He's a jack of all trades. Cooks. Cleans. Even waits tables when we need help."

"Nice to meet you."

"Glad to finally meet the famous Toodaloo." He shot a glance through the kitchen window. "Uncle Charlie just about cried when Slade told him you were coming back."

"Eli!" Charlie shouted from somewhere in the back. "Not paying you to chit-chat."

Eli flashed a killer grin before disappearing.

"Cute, yeah?" Slade wiggled her brows.

I nodded, laughing. Cute didn't come close. The guy was fitness model material. Looked nothing like Charlie. No doubt he'd attract a female cult following to the diner.

The cowbell rattled, drawing my attention to the front door and the gorgeous woman storming my way. A breathtaking blonde with a tailored suit, designer heels, and steely blue eyes.

My stomach dropped. So did the stack of menus I had just grabbed.

"Good morning," Slade beamed to the devil at our door.

I dropped to the floor to gather the menus, angered by the tremble in my hands.

"Sit anywhere you'd like."

I lingered on the ground behind the counter, pulling my breaths in a steady rhythm, picturing Tito's face, replaying his words. *In. One, two, three. Out. One, two, three.*

The snap in the woman's voice chilled me to the bone. "I'm not here to eat. I'm here for Tuuli. That is, as soon as she decides to come out from her hiding spot."

I popped up, clutching the menus to my chest like a shield. "Hi, Mom."

"Mom?" Slade stepped closer to me, offering her hand to my mother. "Miss Holt. What a pleasure to meet you."

Slade was privy to every dirty detail about my family. Knew I'd left home to separate myself from that life. She must've sensed my trepidation because she coiled her arm through mine and leaned against me, holding me steady, giving me courage.

My mother shot a quick glance at our joined limbs, then stood taller, "Tuuli. You missed your brother's funeral."

Ice filled my veins. "I know."

"Well?" She lifted her chin, a rare show of courage.

I upped her display of strength and threw in a dose of defiance. "Well, what?"

Mom tugged on the hem of her pink blazer, a nervous habit, reminding me we'd suffered the same conditioning under my father's dominion. "We have a wedding to plan. Enough of this...this...whatever it is you're trying to prove. It's time for you to come home."

"Whisper Springs is my home, Mom. And there isn't going to be a wedding. There never was."

My mother's pale cheeks darkened. "Can we have a word in private?"

Slade's arm tightened around mine. "I'm sorry, Miss Holt. Tuuli's shift just started. As you can see..." she gestured toward the half-full diner, "we're terribly busy. Personal matters need to be handled during breaks. You're welcome to come back later when your daughter isn't on the clock."

Mom's jaw clenched. A telltale sign she was ready to spit venom, a character flaw, according to my father, that had landed Mom in the hospital countless times. She closed her eyes and breathed deep before meeting my glare. "Tuuli. We need to discuss what happened. Your father and I have been worried about you."

I half-laughed, half-snorted. "Worried?" I was about to spew a verbal assault when something eerie dawned on me. A thought that hadn't but should have occurred to me before that moment. "How did you know where to find me? Who told you I worked here?"

Mom's eyes darted back and forth, her angry gaze landing on Slade, then me, then Slade before dropping to the floor.

"How did you know I was here?" I asked again, anger cloaking the shake in my voice.

"It doesn't matter. You belong at home. With us. With your fiancé."

Erik. Of course.

I loved my mom. There was a time, long ago, that we'd been close, that she had been fun and caring, at least when Daddy Dearest wasn't around. But the year I became *a woman*, our dynamic changed. Mom spent more time traveling with Dad, and her doctor, who was also an elder in my father's church, started prescribing more pills for her "condition." I hardly recognized her anymore. I suspected the pills were to blame.

For a moment, a younger version of my mother came back to haunt me, her face softening, her carefree smile almost breaking through. "Please, baby. Get your things. Let's go."

I resisted the urge to hug her, beg her to leave that place, stay with me.

"So I can spread my legs for that sadistic creep and make perfect little babies? No, Mom. I won't ever go back."

She stepped closer, lowering her voice to a growl. "I've protected you all these years." She sounded desperate, her voice panicked, her hands shaking. Someone had sent her, threatened her, most likely. "If you don't come home and marry Erik, I won't be able to shield you from your duty."

Threatened or not, she'd pushed my last button.

"Duty? Duty?" I grabbed my mother's arm and dragged her out of the diner. When clear of the door, I shouted, "I am not a goddamn baby-making machine. Go home. You are not welcome here."

The thought of abandoning her sickened me, but I wasn't strong enough to save us both. Not yet, anyway. I turned to head back inside the safety of The Stop, but not before catching a glimpse of Erik's SUV in the parking lot.

Erik Meyer had never given my mother the time of day. Why would he bring her to me? I couldn't see his face, but I knew he was watching from behind that dark glass. "Why do you stay with them, Mom? I know that you and Dad never officially tied the knot." I ignored her gasp and raised my middle finger in Erik's direction before marching back inside.

"I need a minute," I growled, storming past Slade toward the bathroom. I almost made it to safety before a hand caught my wrist and swung me around.

Tito caged me against the wall, holding me captive with a set of molten eyes. That slow burn I'd fought for weeks spiked into a blaze. I breathed. Tito breathed. He studied my face, warming my weary soul.

I needed to hide and clear my head, but I couldn't break the connection, the silent communication we shared. He was so strong and confident and beautifully terrifying. If I held on tight, absorbed his glare, his energy, maybe, just maybe, I could absorb some of his strength, too. I could be stronger. I could be braver. I could raise my middle finger to my family and not feel riddled with guilt or shame.

Tito's eyes crinkled at the corners before he pressed his lips to my ear and whispered, "I knew there was a beast inside you."

What?

"Good job handling your mother." He kissed my cheek, pushed off the wall, and gave my butt a hard slap. "No hiding. Shake off whatever the hell she said to you. Get back out there, do your job, and don't let those fuckers ruin your day."

With that, Tito turned and sauntered away, leaving me to bask in his ocean of encouragement. I didn't go to the bathroom. I straightened my shoulders, adjusted my apron, and got my ass to work.

Tito

I needed to get my ass back to work. Should have been home, getting shit together for my upcoming excursion with Tucker, or at the mansion, making sure renovations were on schedule. Instead, I made myself comfortable in Slade's office and waited for Tuuli's break.

Halfway through the eleven o'clock news, she stepped through the door, face flushed, shirt stained. More gorgeous than ever.

"Hey," I said, lacking the capacity for anything manlier, like, "Fuck, baby, you look good enough to eat." Or "Bring that sweet smile over here and wrap it around my cock."

Those were the first thoughts that came to mind. But I wouldn't speak words like that to the woman who'd completely shifted my universe. She deserved better. I refrained from verbalizing my feelings, stretched my arms across the back of the couch, and drank her in.

"Hi." Her gaze landed on my chest, then drifted lower. Apparently, her mind was in the gutter right alongside mine. Damn, I loved watching that blush spread over her cheeks. Made every hour I'd spent in the gym or hitting the pavement worth the bloody knuckles and blisters.

"Eyes up here, Bunny," I teased, pointing to my face.

Dear sweet, baby Jesus, her laughter was a shot of adrenaline straight to my ego.

A thousand years of worry seemed to lift from her shoulders. "You're still here."

"Wanted to make sure you were okay."

Her gaze dropped to the floor, her foot bouncing in that cute, nervous tic. "Yeah, my mom. Sorry you had to see that. I hate her."

"No, you don't. You don't have a hateful bone in your body."

"Fine. I love her. But I hate that she wants that life for me."

I wasn't about to engage in a conversation about maternal influence. My mother had wanted a different life for me. Her dreams had sent me into the parochial bowels of hell. "How long is your break?"

"I've got fifteen minutes."

"Walk with me?" I grabbed her hand before she could respond and headed through the back door to avoid the nosey blonde out front.

We headed across the parking lot and down the trail that led to the hidden beach below The Truck Stop's property line. Tuuli didn't speak. Neither did I, distracted by the fit of our hands, the way my calloused palm scraped her soft skin, making me hyperaware of our connection.

I straddled a large driftwood log, and sat, pulling her with me.

The beach was deserted and quiet, the only noise coming from the quiet splash of waves lapping the shore. Across the bay, my uncle's home stood out like a sore thumb. Like The Truck Stop, the Rossi Estate didn't quite fit with the landscape, but it belonged, as much a part of Whisper Springs as the mountains and pines.

"I'm going out of town for a few days on business. I need you to look me in the eye and tell me that you're okay."

Tuuli turned, straddling my thighs, and dusted a finger over my cheek. "I'm more okay than I've been in a very long time."

"You're still having nightmares."

She studied my scar before settling on my eyes. "I don't expect them to go away anytime soon."

"Slade said you could sleep upstairs in their spare bedroom while I'm gone."

A huff. "Tito. I'm a big girl. I can handle bad dreams."

"There's not much you can't handle." I grabbed her ass and scooted her closer, bringing her soft warmth to my hard heat. "What did your mom want today?"

"My womb." There was no hiding the pain that truth caused.

"God, that's so fucked."

She circled her arms around me and dropped her head to my shoulder. Swear to Christ, a fifth chamber grew in my heart just for her. How had I lived without this connection?

"How long will you be gone?"

"A week. Give or take a day."

"What will you be doing?"

"Working with Tucker."

"On the road?"

God, I hated having to say, "It's confidential."

My girl didn't probe. Instead, she sat back, hands on my shoulders and mustered a stern glare. "Promise me something?"

"Yeah, Bunny."

"Be careful. They haven't caught the Rest Area Reaper. The last two attacks happened in Idaho."

I held my laughter at bay, but I couldn't contain my smile. She worried about me. Shit, if she only knew. I wished I could tell her the truth. Tucker was the Reaper. "You have nothing to worry about. You said it yourself, I'm indestructible."

She gnawed her bottom lip, shooting a glance over my shoulder. "I should get back to work."

"Kiss me first."

Tuuli tilted her head, a playful smiling highlighting her face. She scooted higher up my thighs, then leaned forward and fisted my shirt before crushing my mouth with an enthusiastic assault. Her legs curled around my waist, her arms around my neck, and her tongue swept over mine. I absorbed her affections, giving her full rein, and damn did she rise to the occasion, pressing her full weight against me, rolling her hips, grinding, kissing me deep, and slow, and with more passion than any person should be allowed to possess.

I was putty in her hands.

As much as I wanted to roll off the log and sink into her, I refrained. My little bunny had never been allowed full control, and she was blooming with all her freedom. And fuck did it feel good to be a part of that transformation.

Panting and flushed, she broke the kiss and traced the outline of my scar one more time. That ever-crumbling armor I'd once thought unbreakable gained another dent.

Tuuli

We dented the wall. In two places.

Depleted of energy, legs tangled in soft sheets and sweaty man, I stared at the destruction behind the bedpost. The dents were small, easily repaired, tiny blemishes that under the care of the right set of hands, the right tools, would soon blend with the rest of the wall, fit right in, like they had never been a nuisance to begin with.

"What are you thinking about?" A warm hand lay across my stomach, rubbing small circles.

"I'm wondering how sex can be so destructive, and so beautiful all at the same time."

"Like you," he whispered.

"What?"

"Never mind." The pillow rustled beneath his head.

I curled against his solid frame, running my fingers over the ridges of muscle, and breathed deep, savoring the aroma of man and sex.

A low moan vibrated his chest. "I can't get enough of you. The more you give, the more I want."

"I know what you mean." I traced the path of dark hair leading to his thickening arousal, down to the root, then back up. "Is it normal?"

"Don't know. Don't care." He shivered, hips bucking when my fingers traveled lower, teasing. "Fuck normal anyway."

I laughed. Sounded good to me. "Think we should eat?"

"Eventually." He slid a hand down his stomach, then fisted himself, one long, slow stroke, mesmerizing and beautiful for such a simple, sensual act.

A lawn mower roared to life outside.

"What time is it?"

His chest rumbled. "Don't care."

"I should start apartment hunting today before I head to work."

"We decided you were staying with me." Stroke. Stroke.

Gulp. I licked my dry lips. "Yes. Here. In this apartment. Temporarily. You're moving out. I need to find a place too."

"I assumed you'd come with me." All the lust haze disappeared from his voice.

"Tito." I pushed up on my elbow. "That's a big step. I'm young. I need a little independence. Need to learn to stand on my own two feet."

He scrubbed a hand over his face, then turned his head away, chest rising and falling in measured bursts. He swallowed. "Yeah. I know. You're right." With a grumble, he rolled off the bed, shuffled into a pair of sweats, and headed to the living room.

My chest caved.

The front door opened. The lawnmower stopped. Men's voices.

I pulled the sheet up to my chin. The lawnmower started up again. The front door slammed.

Tito stormed back into the room, kicked off his pants, tore the sheet off the bed, and blanketed me with his own naked body.

The smile that greeted me was magic. Pure. Rare. Spellbinding.

"There. Settled. This place is yours as soon as I move out. You've got an apartment. Fully furnished. Close to work. Cheap rent."

"That's not what I had in mind."

Brows pinched, he waited for my argument.

Deflated, I sunk into the mattress. "You missed the whole point. I wanted to do this on my own."

No response. Nothing but sexy hardness and worried eyes.

Jumbled words danced around my head, not one of them connecting with another. He'd been nothing but patient and forgiving with me the past few weeks, and I couldn't find it in my heart to give him grief.

"Thank you," I offered.

A thousand years of worry seemed to melt from his body, his muscles relaxing, eyes softening.

I shifted, inviting him to settle deeper between my thighs. Every inch of my body was sore from our night of sexual indulgence, a pain I welcomed, cherished even. An ache that reminded me I was human, and soft, and desirable.

Tito tucked his arms under my shoulders and sunk into me, one long, slow glide, lighting me up inside, giving me all his power, virility, and need. He trembled, head dropping to my shoulder. "Fuck, Bunny. Jesus fuckin' Christ, you feel good."

Dear, sweet Lord, he felt good, too. I'd never had unprotected sex, but with Tito inside me, nothing between us, no barriers, I wanted nothing more than to continue, to urge him on, to take, and take and take until he came inside me, completing the act the way it was meant to be. Man and woman, making love, procreating.

I stiffened, tightening my thighs around his hips. "A condom." I slapped his butt. "Get a condom."

The idea of pregnancy had always sickened me, a black thundercloud looming over my head. Had I stayed in Rockypoint, childbearing would have been a duty forced upon me. I'd never wanted a family, never wanted to bring a child into a world where The Brotherhood had full reign.

The thought of raising Tito's children, however, filled me with a sense of hope, of purpose, and that scared me, because what if he didn't want the same thing?

"Tito, please," I mumbled into his mouth. "I'm not on the pill."

He offered a reassuring kiss before pulling out, resting his weight on one elbow, and sliding a finger inside me, watching with reverence the way I rolled against his palm. "Would you do it? Get on the pill?"

Arching against him, I breathed, "Yes."

"When I get back, we'll get tested. I've always used condoms, but fuck, I want you with nothing between us."

My heart jetted skyward. We. He said, *We'll get tested.* As in *us*. Together. "I want that too."

He inserted a second finger, teasing me further, driving me mad. "Will you make us an appointment while I'm gone?"

"Yeah. I can do that."

He paused his stroking, face going pale. "They don't have to draw blood for those tests, do they?"

Oh, jeez. Less talking, more rubbing. "Honestly, I don't know. But I'll find out."

"Thank you." He reached across the mattress and yanked the nightstand drawer open. His gaze never left mine while he rolled the latex over his hard length.

I was panting by the time he crawled over me, breathless when he drove inside me, mindless by the time he growled his release and collapsed at my side, sweaty and spent, and holding me tight.

My shift started in two hours. Tito and Tucker were leaving an hour after that. The thought of spending a week alone, sleeping in his bed, alone, made my stomach roll.

I wanted him to stay. Needed him to stay.

If I were selfish enough to ask, there was no doubt he would cancel his trip.

I didn't ask. Instead, I summoned my beast and pushed the worry aside.

Tito

Worry aside, I was not looking forward to the week ahead for too many fucked-up reasons. One? No Tuuli. Two? No naked Tuuli. Three? Shacking-up with Tucker instead of my bunny. Four? Not being able to keep an eye on my girl. The list was endless.

Of course, I would never voice my concerns. Suffering through all the sappy bullshit was pathetic enough, but to expose my belly, so to speak? Not happening. Tuuli thought I was indestructible. I'd let her believe that little fantasy.

Knowing she was staying in my apartment helped to ease some of the anxiety. Even though I'd arranged for extra security at The Stop, I couldn't shake that nagging tingle, warning that she wasn't free and clear of her family.

Roger had no updates to give on the murder investigation. Although, from Tuuli's retelling of the event, the assailants had to be members, or past members, of The Brotherhood. Victims of her father, if my suspicions were correct. She couldn't identify the three men because they'd worn masks. Thank fuck. If she had seen their faces, they never would have let her escape the assault.

As if sensing my agitation, Tuuli traced small circles across my back, her fingers moving in slow, soothing strokes. I closed my eyes, lulled by her sleepy caresses.

"Why don't you have any tattoos?" she whispered, soft and dreamy.

"Mmm," I hummed into the pillow. "Why do you ask?"

"Most people like you have tattoos."

That earned her a slap on the ass. "People like me?"

She rolled onto her back, crossing her arms behind her head. "Big. Scary. Badass."

"Badass, huh?" I asked, pushing up on my elbows to get a better view of those perfect breasts.

"And hot," she quickly added. "Incredibly hot."

I roughed a hand over her smooth stomach, then up to grope a tit. "You've called me scary more than once now. Yet, here you are, naked and exposed, at my mercy. You should be terrified."

"Never." She shook her head. "My beast can sense that your beast will never hurt her. That he'll protect her."

"Ah, Bunny." I rolled on top of her, craving the skin to skin. "Hands down, that is the sweetest thing anyone has ever said to me."

"You didn't answer my question. Why no tattoos?"

"Never felt the need."

"Really?" she asked, brow arched.

"Really."

"That's it?"

She wasn't buying my lie.

"Yep." I tweaked her nipple, hoping to derail her current train of thought.

That sweet little body writhed beneath me. "You're afraid of needles, aren't you?"

Fuck.

"No. Ink is forever. I've never found anything worth putting on my skin forever." Lie. Lie. Lie.

She slapped my hand away from her chest. "You're afraid of needles."

Fuck. I couldn't continue my charade. The girl was too damn cute and too fucking observant.

"Fine." I sat back on my heels, trapping her legs between my knees. "I'm afraid of needles. You happy now? Not so badass, am I?"

Damn, that smile she wore lit the whole room.

"Why do you think you're afraid of them?"

"Not sure. When I was a kid, Mom took me for a check-up. I got a look at the syringes laid out on the tray, and I bolted. They had to chase me down the corridor. I made it into the elevator before a nurse caught me."

Tuuli's rolling laughter made my humiliation worthwhile.

"I fell off my bike when I was seven. Tore my knee open." I tapped the faint scar on my left leg. "My Pops drove me to the emergency room. When they pulled out the needle, I fainted in his arms."

She laughed harder. God, she had a beautiful laugh.

"He never let me live that down." I hung my head in shame. "I can't believe I'm telling you this shit."

She wiped her tear-soaked lashes and sucked in a sharp breath, releasing it slowly, pulling herself together.

I kissed a wet cheek and slapped her hip. "Your turn. What are you afraid of?"

"Thunderstorms," she said without hesitation.

I didn't laugh. I'd experienced her fear firsthand. "Why?"

"My brother and his friends tied me to a tree once." Her breath hitched. That flawless, pale skin broke out in goosebumps.

I knew where the story was headed, but remained silent, stretching next to her and pulling the blankets over us.

"It started to rain. The boys ran into the house." Her eyes glazed as if lost in the memory. "I screamed for Jonas, thinking he'd forgotten about me. He didn't come back. I was freezing and hungry. Erik showed up a long time later with bloody knuckles. He didn't untie me though. He just sat down, no fear of being struck by lightning. He didn't laugh or taunt. Just watched. For hours. And every time the thunder boomed, he'd count, screaming numbers until the lightning flashed, then he'd stop and stare. And when the storm was right overhead, when the boom came, and Erik counted to one, and the lightning struck just across the field, he pulled a hunting knife from behind his back, cut me loose, and told me to run before I turned into a piece of crispy fried chicken."

"Jesus Christ. How old were you?"

"Six."

Fucking psychopath. Fuck. I wanted to kill Erik Meyer.

"The really messed up part?" she continued. "He made me thank him, in front of our parents, he made me stand there and thank him for saving me. Jonas showed up with a bloody nose and a split lip and got whipped for tying me to the tree in the first place."

"Erik kept Jonas away, didn't he?"

Tuuli nodded, curling into me. I pulled her close and combed my fingers through her messy hair. Was I soothing her, or myself? I wasn't sure, because at that point, even with my girl tucked against me, I vibrated with rage, and all I wanted to do was hunt that crazy bastard down and make him bleed.

CHAPTER 10

Tito

"NO OFFENSE, TUCK. But there's a more efficient and effective way to deal with these pestilent bastards."

Tucker chuckled, tightening the knot binding *dangerdawg69*'s hands behind his back. "You mean like shoving their cocks through a meat grinder. One of those old-fashioned hand crank models?"

I grabbed the unconscious fucker's ankles. Tucker took the other end, and we hoisted him, with more muscle than necessary, into the small ditch fifty yards behind where his truck was parked. He wouldn't wake for two hours at least. Not with the shit I'd injected into his neck.

"Wasn't what I had in mind, but I like that idea." I pulled my cap lower and followed Tucker back to the lot. "I've killed men for lesser crimes, you know. Made them disappear."

"We're trying to do good here, remember? Believe me, I want to choke the life out of every one of these child rapists. Gotta choose our battles. We're here to get these girls out of the life. Give them a chance."

We stayed in the shadows. Tucker headed back to the cab of *dangerdawg69*'s truck, while I headed to our unmarked sedan parked closer to the restroom. From my position, I had a full view of the lot. We settled in and waited for the minivan that would deliver our girl.

I tapped my Bluetooth earpiece. "Tell me again why we aren't targeting the pimps?"

"I've been a one-man show until now. Couldn't do it all."

I could.

From my laptop, I entered the chatroom where *dangerdawg69* had arranged his date, alerted the pimp that everything was set, and gave him a description of the rig.

"Right. So, then you've got nothing against me messing with them a bit?"

Tucker laughed. "Define *messing with them*."

"Meat grinder type of shit."

After a long silence, and a few heavy breaths, Tuck said, "What you do on your own time is none of my business."

Good answer.

I watched from a safe distance across the parking lot, while Tucker shifted in his seat and tilted his head. "Blue van. On my left." He flashed his lights twice.

A blue Sienna rolled into sight, headlights flashing in response, and parked two slots down from Tucker. A girl, I guessed not taller than four-ten slunk out the passenger door, wearing jeans and high-heeled boots. A loose-fitting blouse hung off her shoulders, revealing a bare neck and underdeveloped cleavage. Curly white hair covered most of her face. She'd yet to shed her baby fat, and she still carried that awkward pre-teen self-consciousness like a heavy wool blanket.

My stomach rolled at the sight.

Fucking hell. A child. I'd seen dark, disgusting shit in my life. Knew depravity well. Wasn't a stranger to the sex-trade industry.

I'd never been ashamed of my sexual proclivities until I watched that girl, that baby, swallow her fear, choke back her tears, and unwillingly head Tucker's way to trade her body, and her innocence, for a few pieces of green paper that would be snatched from her tiny fingers the moment she returned to that goddamn minivan.

I wanted to grab the piece of shit sitting behind the wheel and flay him, out in the open, for everyone to see.

Did that make me a hypocrite? Damn straight.

Did I give a fuck? Hell, no.

Over our private connection, I listened while Tucker played his part, luring the girl inside the safety of the cab, putting on a show to make it look like she was performing as instructed. I listened to their exchange, the terror in the child's voice, the desperation, and I damn near broke.

When Tucker stuck the needle in her thigh and she fell unconscious against him, he cursed under his breath and mumbled, "Never gets easier."

The rustle of clothing and Tucker's heavy breaths crackled through my earpiece. Then silence. Then, "You're on, Tito."

Hell, yeah. My turn.

I flipped the switch for the police siren and flashed the blue lights mounted on my dash before pulling forward and rolling through the rows of parked semis straight toward the pimp's vehicle. Two women scrambled, half-naked, out of two different cabs on opposite ends of the lot and ran into the woods lining the rest stop.

The blue Toyota tore out of its parking spot and sped toward the freeway on-ramp.

Too easy.

I didn't bother memorizing the license plate. I knew everything I needed to know about the owner. Name. Address. Bank accounts. He had a mother, a sister, and three children with two different women. And he'd not paid a lick of child support in the past seven years. The videos I'd found on Morrison's computer had already been forwarded to the proper authorities, along with the shithead's three addresses, and records of every exchange he'd brokered online over the past five years.

It wasn't meat grinder retribution, but as Aida reminded me time and time again, we were no longer in the murder and maim business. Blah, blah, blah. Atoning for sins, or something like that.

I would never admit to Aida that I enjoyed taking someone down for the sheer pleasure of saving a child's life. I let her believe I was helping Tucker because she'd begged me to join their plight to get these babies off the street. I knew from the beginning she was only trying to get me out of my own head, offering me a new life. What she didn't know was that Tuuli had already taken care of that.

My Bunny. Damn, I needed to get home.

While I provided the distraction with the fake police car, Tucker moved the unconscious girl to our third vehicle. As per our plan, he would drive her back to the Compton Ranch, where she would be well cared for, we would meet up at his parents' home, get a good night's sleep, then head back to Whisper Springs.

I was halfway down the freeway on-ramp when Tucker's voice broke through my reverie. "Tito. Fuck, man. Get your ass back here. We have a problem."

"What's up?" I snapped, cursing myself for failing to turn off the earpiece.

"I've got ten bikers up my ass. Pissed off fuckers by the looks of it."

"Fuck!" I pounded the dash, pulled over, snagged my SIG out of the holder under the seat, and jogged in Tucker's direction, careful to stay in the shadows.

Sure enough, Tucker's truck idled, half pulled out of its parking space, surrounded by a shit ton of angry, leather-clad, Harley-riding motherfuckers.

Fuck me. I just wanted to get home.

When one of the men stepped under the light of the street lamp, I caught the symbol on the back of his vest, a skull and snake. Fucking Satan's Slayers.

Well, shit.

Tuuli

"Shit. Shit. Shit." I apologized profusely and mopped-up the spilled coffee, catching the runoff before it hit my customer's lap.

The man simply lifted his plate and scooted to the safety of the next stool. "No harm, no foul," he said, continuing with the thumb to screen action on his cell like I hadn't almost ruined his dress shirt. Calm and collected.

Unlike me, the bumbling mess.

One week had come and gone. Six days of eight-hour shifts, dinners for one, and worry. One hundred and forty-four hours of no Tito. Two broken glasses, three dropped trays of food, and four jumbled orders.

Good news? The weather had taken a turn for the better. Spring had sprung, evident by the bright leaves decorating the trees and the bright flower baskets hanging from every storefront lining downtown Whisper Springs. Bad news? My heart had seemingly sprung too—one horrendous, unbearable leak.

I missed Tito.

Hard as I tried to stay busy and focused, I couldn't keep that slow leak sealed.

"Hey, Tuuli." Aida's greeting shot a shiver through my limbs. Despite her beauty, the woman terrified me. Maybe because I'd witnessed what she could do to another human on the night we'd been attacked. Maybe because she was strong, where I was meek. Perhaps because she could crush me with little more than a glance.

Tossing my dirtied towel in the sink, I turned to greet Aida. I'd expected her usual disapproving scowl but instead found myself face-to-face with chubby cheeks, pouty, heart-shaped lips, and giant doe eyes.

"Hold her for a sec? I need to pee." Aida shoved the bundle of pink fluff into my arms and dashed around the corner.

Lucia squealed, babbled, and cooed. Clearly, she was conversing with me, and undoubtedly, she was saying, "Hi, Tuuli. My mom is really scary, and I'm happy you're holding me."

I buried my nose in her hair, inhaling her yummy scent, then whispered, "Yes. Your mama is scary, sweet pea."

I cradled Lucia in my arms and plopped my rear onto an empty barstool. Before I could stop myself, I peppered those puffy cheeks with kisses and studied her perfect skin, her tiny fingers, all ten of them, and the double rolls of baby fat around her wrists.

The angel in my arms, so perfect and innocent, so vulnerable and full of potential, smiled up at me, her big eyes bright and full of wonder. My heart swelled, knowing Aida trusted me to care for her daughter, despite my upbringing, knowing what I'd been born into, knowing the baggage I dragged around like shackles.

She trusted me.

In that moment, with that realization, came the snap of strings, untethering me from my morbid family ties. *Snap,*

snap, snap. My soul felt a little lighter, but I also seemed to dangle. When the last strings snapped, would I float, or would I fall?

Slade spun through the double doors like a ballerina on crack and shouted, "Where's that little niece of mine? Hand her over."

I laughed and passed Lucia into the eager arms of her aunt.

Missing the baby's weight, I headed back to work, unable to shake the looming feeling of dread that'd followed me all day.

I could feel it coming. *It* being something terrible, building in the shadows, rolling and swelling like an oncoming thunderstorm.

Life had been going too well. Things had been too easy.

Sure, it'd only been weeks that I'd been living in luxury instead of squalor. Days since Tito had made me feel beautiful and wanted and worthy of a man's attention. In my experience, the good days were few and far between.

I soaked them up like a gluttonous sponge.

I was happy. I was warm. I hadn't suffered a hunger pang in weeks.

I had friends. A job. Tito.

Regardless, I could feel that cold, dark cloud lingering over my shoulder, whispering in my ear, *I'm coming for you.*

When my shift ended, I peeked my head into Slade's office to say goodnight.

Her fingers worked the keyboard, gaze glued to the screen. "Let Roger drive you up the hill. I have to stay late tonight. Payroll."

She looked up from her computer in time to catch my eye roll. Home was only a three-minute walk up the hill. You could see the house from the parking lot.

"Hey." She raised her palms. "I don't like it any more than you do, but those boys of ours want to keep us safe. That's a battle we will never win."

I nodded. "'Night, Slade."

I made my way to the back room, fumbled with my locker, clocked out, and headed out the back door to where Roger Caldwell usually parked.

I thought briefly, and foolishly that maybe that lingering feeling of dread was a bi-product of being tired, or perhaps it was PMS or the fact that I missed Tito.

I dared to let myself believe that maybe good times could indeed stick around.

Naive baby.

Roger's truck sat empty. Perhaps he was stretching his legs. I walked toward the edge of the lot to catch sight of the lake, and that false security shattered in the blink of an eye.

Erik's body cast a dark shadow a split-second before he grabbed my arm. "Tuuli."

His pale skin turned yellow and sinister under the glow of the diner sign. He wore all black, from his combat boots to the beanie covering his head, and not his usual designer gear. No. Erik was dressed for dirty work.

Pinpricks poked at my skin.

"Aren't you going to say hello? Give me a proper greeting?"

Lifting my chin to meet his glare, I asked, "What do you want?"

"I told your father I'd bring you home tonight. I've set the wedding date. We need to make plans. Time for you to come home. You've made your point."

I stepped back. He followed, jerking my arm.

"What point would that be?" I asked.

Erik laughed, clamped his fingers tighter, and dipped his head low. "You got me." His lips parted in a chilling grin.

"I don't fucking know what point you're trying to make. I was just playing nice."

With no warning, he slapped his hand to the back of my neck and fisted my hair. In one sharp breath, I was on the ground, kicking, clawing, struggling to find purchase, to rise to my feet, to fight, scream, breathe, to not collapse in defeat or fear.

To find my beast.

"Ungrateful fucking cunt." Erik dragged me through the gravel toward the dark edge of the lot, the world spinning, a whirl of dark sky, gravel, trees. Doom.

His SUV waited in the shadows, a death trap with jaws open to swallow me whole.

There's a beast inside you.

Rocks tore at my knees, my hips. Fire licked my scalp. But I didn't yield to him. I didn't cower.

"Stop! Let go! No, Erik! Help! Somebody, help!" I screamed, and struggled, and clawed at the hand tangled in my hair.

His grip tightened. He jerked, bending my neck at a sharp angle, forcing me flat to the ground, and clamping his other hand around my throat, squeezing tight.

Evil, steely eyes glared down at me. "Scream again, and I'll shut you up for good."

I couldn't breathe. Shards of light danced in my vision. Still, I kicked, and punched, and scratched. Erik was too strong, too large, too full of hate. My desire to live was no match for his need to dominate. No matter how hard I fought, I would never overpower my lifelong tormentor.

Exhausted, I dropped both hands, palms to the ground, met his glare, and relaxed my body, curling my fingers into the loose dirt.

The vise around my throat loosened.

"Good girl," he growled, leaning foolishly close.

The moment he released my neck, I shoved two handfuls of gravel in his face, aiming for the eyes. He stumbled back. I rolled, pushed to my feet, and ran.

The diner door was so close. I reached for the handle. Pulled. With ungodly force, Erik slammed against me, pinning me to the door, knocking the breath from my lungs. "Where do you think you're going, kiddo?"

I screamed—twisting, thrashing, fighting. Fighting. Fighting. First punching at the door, then punching at his chest.

He grabbed my throat with one hand, this time pulling me off my feet, sliding me up until we were face-to-face. I kicked, unsure where I would strike. He countered with a punch to my gut.

The world blurred. I dangled in his grip, unable to move, unable to curl into the pain. I hung like a tattered rag doll in his strong hold, waiting for the next blow.

Men's voices came from somewhere distant. The pounding of feet. Two men ran past, yelling, "Go. Go."

The cinch around my neck disappeared. I crumbled on the ground. Gasped for air. Blinked through the fog. Tried to make sense of the scene.

More footfalls. "Tuuli. Tuuli. Shit. You okay?"

Tango squatted, hands everywhere, inspecting for injury.

I was far from okay. Angry. Furious. It wasn't fear that made me tremble, though. Murderous urges fueled my cells.

I batted Tango's hands away and scrambled to my feet, searching the lot. Erik's Mercedes was gone.

"You're safe. He's gone."

Roger came our way, phone in hand. He stood next to Tango, heavy breaths, clothes disheveled. "I'm sorry, Tuuli."

He bent at the waist, hands to knees. "I'm so sorry. There was a fight out front, or I would've been here. I would've seen—"

"Stop. Both of you stop!" I shouted. I needed to go home. I needed Tito. "I'm okay. Really. I'm good. I just want to go home."

Tango reached for me. "No, Tuuli, that's not…"

"No!" I raised a palm to shut him up. "Follow me if you have to, but don't coddle. I need to walk."

I ignored the heavy footfalls behind me and made the trek across the lot and up the steep incline, my heart heavy, my mind reeling.

Erik had always been violent. But he'd raised his torment to another level. Something had changed. The dynamic altered. He'd always feared my father too much to leave visible bruises, but now? I pressed my fingers to my throat, then swallowed, testing for damage. Ouch. Aside from the pain, everything seemed to work. No doubt, I'd find ugly marks on my neck in the morning. I cringed but stifled my moan.

I was so tired. So damn fed up with feeling insufficient and helpless. I fought, and he still overpowered me.

I stopped dead, letting my thoughts roll over in my head. I fought back. Dear God, I fought back.

I shook my head, then continued my march up the hill.

The Brotherhood no longer had power over me. I fought back.

Despite my chagrin, a smile tugged at my lips.

Tito

Despite my ire, I couldn't help but smile. Dane had mad skills in the torture and maim department.

"No more. No more," the man begged through bloodied lips.

"From the beginning, motherfucker." Dane Reynolds stuck the tip of his knife into *dangerdawg69*, AKA Matt Child's crotch, piercing the wet denim. "I want names."

Matt had ceased to fight against his binds hours ago. Still, he'd been a hard nut to crack, despite having lost one ear, three teeth, and a shit ton of blood. Toothpicks under the fingernails had finally cracked his armor. Everyone had their breaking point.

"I told you. I didn't get a name. Just an envelope stuffed with cash and a number to call when I had her."

"Why this girl?" Dane growled.

Matt's head hung loosely on his shoulders, rolling from side to side, fighting to stay conscious. "She could've been any girl as long as she fit the description."

"And what would that be?"

"Blonde hair. Blue eyes. Pale skin."

He could've been describing Tuuli. I didn't pay the connection any mind until he said, "And she had to have started her menstrual cycle."

Tuuli's words came back to me. *In The Brotherhood's eyes, the day a girl starts her period, she becomes a woman. She's fair game.* My guts twisted.

I stepped closer to the carnage. "Take off his shirt."

Dane turned his dark eyes to me. "The fuck you say?"

The guy's hair was longer than the last time I'd seen him. His beard was longer, his scowl meaner. He had to be packing at least thirty more pounds of ass-kicking meat on his bones. Dane Reynolds was one scary motherfucker. I kinda liked the guy. I also enjoyed ruffling his feathers.

"I said, take off his fuckin' shirt."

The knife that had been poised to pierce Matt's crotch sliced through the air to land at my throat. "Listen, Freddie

Krueger. Just because I didn't kill you and your pretty boy cousin last time we met doesn't mean we're partners. You're on my turf. I give the goddamn orders."

Dane wouldn't cut me. He had to save face in front of his brothers. Still, I was pissed that I had to spend another day in Montana dealing with Slayer shit when I could've been naked in bed with my girl, so I continued to push his buttons. "Fine. Mr. Reynolds, sir. I'm pretty sure if you were to...oh, I don't know, maybe take off that fat bastard's shirt, you might find some interesting ink. If my suspicions are correct, and they usually are, his skin art will tell you who this fuckin' piece of shit is taking his orders from, and why he's hunting for a specific type of girl."

Dane's nostrils flared. He turned his back to me, ripped open Matt's denim button-up, then used the knife to cut through his wife beater. Sure enough, from the collarbone down, he was covered in black and red ink. Hate symbols. Prison tats. Celtic crosses. Swastikas.

Even with Dane's back to me, I registered the change in his breathing, the shift in his stance, the coiling of his muscles.

Pissed-off biker rage charged the air.

"Goddamnmotherfuckingwhitecocksuckingpieceof shit." His blade sunk through Matt's thigh like a hot knife through butter.

The growled scream barely registered before Dane fisted the guy's hair, yanking his head forward to expose his back, revealing one ugly-ass depiction of a laughing skull set over a jagged swastika. The Brothers of Banshee.

Dane's entire body stiffened before he yelled, "You swallow that racist fucking come when they've got their pink dicks shoved down your throat? You scream that white power propaganda bullshit while you fuck each other's hairy white asses?" He twisted the weapon.

Over the screams, I heard Dane promise to make Matt choke on Slayer cock before they put him to ground.

I honestly didn't know how the guy was still conscious.

Dane continued. "Now, tell me, what are you and your boyfriends doing with these girls?"

The Banshee only smiled a creepy as fuck, bloody smile.

Entertaining as Dane's interrogation tactics were to watch, I really did need to get back to my girl. "Anyone got a pen?"

Three sets of eyes turned my way. The guy standing guard next to me reached inside his cut and pulled out a blue Bic. Skinny. No frills. Perfect. "Thanks," I said, snagging the utensil from his hand. "May I?" I asked Dane.

Brows raised, he stepped away and gestured toward Matt, giving me the go-ahead. I bit down hard on the bottom of the pen, then chewed, crushing the plastic to give it a sharp edge. I stepped in front of a laughing Matt, grabbed his hair, cranking his head back at a sharp angle on his neck, and shoved the chewed end of the ballpoint up his left nostril.

I only had to dig around for a few seconds before Matt yelled, "We're shipping them to Idaho. Brotherhood is paying ten thousand a head for the virgins. Fifteen if they're drug-free and prettied up." Matt's frenzied laugh turned to tears.

"The Brotherhood? You talking about Jeremy Carver?"

"No. Jeremy's not running the girls...his son-in-law runs that show."

My blood ran cold. "Carver doesn't have a son-in-law."

"Semantics. You think Carver's pretty little baby has remained untouched out of respect for Jeremy? Hell no. Erik laid claim to that bitch and her pussy years ago. Meyer's a certified psycho. Every man in The Brotherhood knows not to so much as blink in her direction unless they have a death wish."

I shoved the pen into the fucker's eye, dug around a bit, for fun, and because he'd talked about Tuuli's pussy. When he stopped screaming, I ordered him to continue.

"Rumor has it there's a wedding planned for later this summer. Erik has a shit ton of supporters. Carver's followers are ready for some fresh leadership. Erik has been keeping that sect afloat financially."

"Trafficking blonde-haired, blue-eyed babies," Dane interjected.

"That's only part of the income he's generating for The Brotherhood under Carver's nose."

The conversation continued while I pushed outside to the cool fresh air. Mind reeling. Muscles twitchy. Fucking Erik. Fucking Brotherhood.

Fuck. I needed to get home.

I found Tucker across the lawn, leaning against a gate post, deep in conversation with one of the Slayers. He'd opted to stay outside during the interrogation. Suited me. The country boy needed to keep his hands clean, for Aida and the baby.

"So, you're the Rest Area Reaper," the bald guy said, shaking his head.

Tucker only nodded.

"Guys and I been taking bets on whether the Reaper was a psychopath or a criminal genius."

Dane slammed through the barn door, blood-soaked and brimming with rage. He met my glare, then shifted his attention to Tucker and the bald brother. "We good here?"

Baldy replied, "Yeah, we're good. Prez is on his way."

"Gonna need your intel on the pimp that brought her here," Dane said, more an order than a request.

Fine by me.

I pulled up the files on my cell and hit send. "Check your inbox."

Morrison was as good as dead. Motherfucker, meet meat grinder. Damn if I didn't get a little tingle.

"Where's the girl?" Tucker asked, pushing off the rail to stand straight.

Dane spat. Wiped his brow with the back of his arm. "She's safe."

"No offense," Tucker said, pushing his luck. "But I've witnessed what happens to the girls in your club."

Dane twitched, stepping closer. "She's safe."

"I need a guarantee," Tucker growled, stepping nose to nose with the Slayer, ready to kill for the child.

"She's the Prez's niece. That guarantee enough?"

"Fuck," I grunted, unable to hide my cringe.

Dane pulled a hand-rolled out of his pocket, his glare never leaving Tuck. "How about you fuckers get outta here."

"Not a problem." I slapped a hand on Tucker's back and urged him to back the fuck off. Even I wasn't grisly enough to stick around and watch what the guy inside had coming.

The girl was safe, back with her family.

Matt Child? Well. That fucker was in for a world of hurt.

Tuuli

I hurt. From the top of my head to the tips of my toes. Cracked, but still whole. I hadn't shattered. I was living, breathing, and not at the mercy of any man.

I emerged from the bathroom wrapped in one of Tito's black hoodies and a pair of his boxers. When I came down the hallway, Aida greeted me from the kitchen table, coffee at the ready.

"Hi." She offered me a blue mug along with a rare smile.

I took the warm cup, gripping it with two hands, absorbing the heat. "How did you get in?"

She pulled out a chair and made herself comfortable. "Tito gave me a spare when he moved in."

"Tango told you what happened?"

"He was worried about you."

Her black sweater bore a wet stain over her right shoulder. Odd as it was, that small imperfection put me at ease.

"Where's Lucia?"

"Upstairs." Another grin warmed her icy features. "Rocky is reading to her."

I slunk into the chair opposite Aida, tucking my knees against my chest, my heels hooked on the edge of the seat.

Worried eyes assessed me from across the table.

"I'm okay. I am. Really." I dusted a finger over the darkening bruises on my throat.

"I can see that."

Then why are you here? I wanted to scream. I had always licked my wounds in private. Hide. Hide. Hide. I hated that Aida, of all people, saw me as weak, a victim, but Lord, how I needed to talk. "He's always been violent. A bully. He's never hurt me like that before, though. Something's changed."

She nodded. Paused. Huffed. "I just got off the phone with Tito. He didn't handle the news very well."

"I was going to call him. After my shower."

Aida shifted in her seat. Dark waves fell over her shoulders. She pulled her hair behind her back before straightening her spine and tilting her head. "Listen. I may be out of line, but there are some things I think you deserve to know before this thing between you and Tito progresses."

Her confident mask slipped, revealing a hint of fear. Her eyes glazed, gaze drifting to something over my head before dropping to her hands. "Something happened to Tito before he came to Whisper Springs. He came back different than the guy I grew up with. Broken. Half-dead on the inside." She lifted her chin, blinking her focus back to me. "But the two of you started hanging out, and that spark came back. He's trying to be the old Tito again."

"What happened?"

"That's not my story to tell." *Click, click, click.* Her red nails beat an erratic rhythm against her mug. "What I can tell you, though, is he needs to let go of the shit from his past. He deserves to be happy."

"You think I can make him happy?"

"You do." Aida sighed, gnawing her lower lip. "He's going to storm in here, half-cocked, and hell-bent on going after Erik. That's who he is. He protects the people he loves, by whatever means he deems necessary. He'll do and say some ugly things. That's how he protects himself."

"Aida. I'm not—"

She silenced me with a raised palm. "Just be patient with him. Please. He'll come around. He's stubborn, and tough, and scary as hell. But he's also fragile. He needs to break before he can heal. He's going to fight the change. He'll try to hold his cracks in place. When they start to fall, it will piss him off. That's when he'll hurt you. That's when you'll have to love him the hardest."

I understood more than she could imagine. I struggled to hold my own pieces together. Some days, I wanted to let go, let my pieces fall and shatter.

I'd yet to take a sip of my coffee. Since I hadn't a word to say in response to Aida's confession, I lifted the cup to my lips and forced myself to hold her gaze.

My hands shook. My body hurt. My heart exploded over and over behind my breastbone.

She tilted her head, studying me with a thoughtfulness I never would have expected. "Can I ask you something?"

"Sure."

"The night your brother died. It wasn't your first time, was it?"

I shifted, dropping my feet to the floor. "My first time?"

"Witnessing violence. Murder."

I shook my head. "How did you know?"

She took a sip. Swallowed. "It didn't break you."

Because there wasn't much left of me to break.

"You're so much like this town, Tuuli."

"I don't understand."

"On the outside, Whisper Springs is small. Gorgeous. Picture perfect. But you get to know her, her people, her quirks, you see the secrets she hides. The darkness that gets swept under the rug. My gut tells me there's a novel's worth of dark and gritty hiding behind that meek little mask you wear."

I'd been right to fear Aida. She saw everything.

"I grew up surrounded by hate, and violent, angry, lost men. I've witnessed my share of violence."

"We're not too different, you and I."

I resisted the urge to throw my arms around the scary woman. If she only knew how much her words meant to me. "How's that?"

"We were both born into lives that would crush most. Difference is, my father raised me to fight for my life, take what I wanted. I get the feeling your father taught you to submit for survival, to take what was given, good or bad. Am I wrong about that?"

"I wouldn't call what he did teaching. I was forced to submit. Fighting was never an option. Survival wasn't part of the equation."

"You want to learn to fight?"

"I don't like violence."

"I don't think you understand. I don't mean fight back...I mean fight for your life. To never feel helpless again."

"I would like that." My vision blurred. I swiped at my eyes with the back of my hand.

Aida nodded, waiting for me to gather my composure. "Do you want me to stay until Tito gets back?"

"No."

She pushed from the table. "Will you call if you need help?"

"I don't think Erik will show his face around here. Not tonight anyway."

Aida laughed. God, even her laugh was gorgeous. "I don't mean with Erik. I mean if you need help with Tito."

CHAPTER 11

BILE ROSE IN MY throat. My body burned, rage fueling the fire. I sucked in a hearty dose of oxygen and pushed into the dark apartment.

The space was quiet, save the buzz of the refrigerator's motor. I flipped the switch that lit the room. Nothing out of place. Two empty mugs sat in the sink.

I kicked off my shoes and headed to the bedroom, that damn organ in my chest attempting some high-flying, Cirque du Soleil type shit, dragging my intestines along for the ride.

Soft, steady breaths greeted me. Layer by layer, I peeled off my clothes, biding time, hoping for a shred of calm amidst the chaos buzzing through my head. When I joined my soft bunny between the sheets and pulled her against me, I couldn't tell who trembled harder.

"I fought him, Tito. I fought back," she mumbled into my chest.

Jesus Fucking Christ, I wanted to scream for her. Hunt the fucker down and tear him limb from limb.

Instead, I pulled her closer, and whispered, "That's my girl."

"Don't let go." The words floated up to me, so soft, I thought it'd been my imagination. Tuuli's small body inflated, then deflated before she dragged her fingers up my torso, then curled them around my neck, digging into my flesh. "Don't ever let go."

I struggled to hold her trembling form, fearful that her pain would set me off. She needed assurance, a promise that everything would be okay. I searched in vain for the right words. All I could manage to say was, "He's going to bleed, baby. He'll never hurt you again. I promise."

Despite her shiver, she didn't admonish my threat.

"Where are you hurt?"

She sighed, rolling onto her back. "I have a few scratches. Nothing too bad."

I rolled out of bed, hit the light switch, and threw the covers back. She was bundled in my sweatshirt, drowning in my sweats, but fuck if the sight didn't rearrange my guts.

"I need to see you, baby. Take the clothes off."

She wiggled out of the pants first. Her knees were bandaged, but not enough to hide the bruises. When she lifted the sweatshirt over her head, revealing the marks around her neck, my knees hit the mattress. My soul screamed, battling a level of rage I'd never experienced.

I hadn't been physically ill since I was a child. Used to brag I had a strong constitution. My stomach, however, unaccustomed to my newfound feelings, revolted at the sight of Tuuli, bloody and bruised.

I sucked that shit up, shoved it down deep, and crawled over her, inspecting for more damage. Tuuli watched with feathered breaths, features softening every time I touched her exposed skin.

Scalp to toes, I examined the beauty beneath me, gauging her reactions—winces, gasps, or changes in breathing. She trembled under my touch, blushing, shivering, nipples puckering tight. So responsive. So goddamn brave.

I sat back on my heels, reverence stealing my breath.

Tuuli was changing my landscape. Bulldozing her way through all the bullshit. Clearing a path, allowing light to reach the parts of me that had yet to shrivel under all the rubble.

"You wanna talk about what happened?" I asked, forcing my jaw to relax, bracing for details I might not have the strength to hear.

"No." Weary eyes begged me not to push.

"Okay. When you're ready." I lay beside her once again, curled my arms around her small, naked frame, and buried my nose in her hair, fighting the urge to kiss every battered inch of her body.

We stayed that way, silent and warm, clinging to each other.

"Tito?"

"Yeah?"

"I'm going to learn how to fight."

I wanted to growl my disapproval. Pound my chest and assert my authority. Tuuli had suffered enough under the thumb of male ego. I couldn't tell her *no* any more than I could stop planning Erik's unfortunate, untimely, and if I played my cards right, gruesome death.

Tuuli would never face Erik or anyone from The Brotherhood alone. Telling her so would demean her worth, her desire to protect herself.

I knew that deep down.

Instead of keeping my thoughts to myself, instead of sealing my fucking lips and letting her feel powerful, I kissed her and choked out a response. "You don't need to fight. I'll fight for you, baby."

Tuuli

I couldn't fight any longer. My body ached, deep and hot, buzzing with need. Tito was everywhere, a force of nature, surrounding me, seeping through my flesh and bones.

I'd missed him so much.

I rolled in his arms, bringing us heavy breath to heavy breath.

"I need you," I whispered into his neck, braving a kiss, rolling my hips to bring us closer.

He ground against me in response, a low moan rumbling in his chest. "I need you, too. So fuckin' bad."

He was already hard. His arousal swollen and warm against my skin.

I slid a hand down his torso, then farther still, his skin tightening, muscles tensing under my touch. When I curled my fingers around his hard flesh, his body jerked in response. He sucked a sharp breath through his teeth, and my soul swelled with a rare, heady sense of power.

I pumped the smooth, taut skin.

Tito caught his breath.

I pumped again. He rolled into my touch, one hand cupping my ass and squeezing tight, his other hand fisting my hair.

I stroked him, from base to tip, again and again, high off the thrill, the anticipation, the desire rolling and building inside me. My bruised body ached with new cause, my wounded spirit warming and healing under the sound of his moans, his lustful breaths, his greedy lips.

Wounded, battered, weak Tuuli didn't exist in Tito's embrace, her fragile shell replaced with that of a woman wanted, a woman cherished, a woman worthy, unbreakable in the arms of a man like Tito.

Tito broke the kiss, his hand covering mine to halt my slow pump. Lips parted, chest heaving, eyes dark and possessive, he studied me.

I was heat, and liquid, and needy, my body arching into him, a silent plea for more.

"I need to be in control tonight, Tuuli. I need to be in charge."

I needed him to be in charge, too.

I relaxed, ceding control. Giving myself freely, out of want, not obligation. Out of selfish desire, not stolen will.

"I was scared shitless for you tonight. Out of my fuckin' mind. That asshole touched you. Fuck. He touched you." His voice cracked. "I need to touch you until there's nothing of him left. I need to be the only man touching you. Tell me you understand. Tell me you trust me." He stared, eyes pleading, jaw clenched.

"I trust you."

Faster than the words left my lips, Tito dropped his head and sucked a nipple between his teeth, flicking the bud with rough strokes.

I writhed beneath him, pleasure shooting through me with each tease, every suck, each draw of his tongue across the responsive skin.

He slid a hand down my waist, across my hip, and lower still, until he cupped my sex, applying pressure on the sensitive nub. He toyed, brushing soft strokes across my folds, teasing the entrance, rubbing slow circles with his palm, all the while suckling my breast in slow, aching pulls.

I tried to watch, entranced with the rolls of each carved muscle in his chest, shoulders, and arms, the heavy-lidded glaze of his eyes, the contrast of his large frame over my slight build. I tried to watch, but the pleasure slammed through me like a crashing wave, and I threw my head into the mattress, arching against his mouth, his hands, his heat.

I fisted the sheets at my sides, bucking and trembling under the overload of emotion.

His ministrations traveled down my torso, marking every inch of skin, as promised, with lips, and touches, and nibbles, and raspy exhales. Oh, God. He was undoing me, inch by inch.

Tito moved lower, peppering kisses below my navel, traveling down, down, until he pressed hot, soft lips against my sex, pausing a moment, inhaling, and then diving in, with tongue and teeth and fingers, and I lost my mind, bucking against him, then digging my heels into the mattress, my fingers into his hair.

My body coiled, tense and on the cusp of shattering, my hips rolling, grinding against his mouth. I was a woman possessed, chasing my release, greedy, and strong, and taking what I wanted, fucking the mouth of my lover, demanding he take me over the edge.

When I came, when that moment of all-consuming bliss struck, I arched off the bed. Tito wasn't finished. He cupped my ass, digging into the soft flesh, holding my pussy to his mouth, and he sucked harder, unrelenting, until I cried, rasping, *yes, yes, yes*, tearing his hair, holding him between my thighs while he devoured my pleasure. When I couldn't take anymore, when I tried to back away from his eager mouth, he stilled, pressing his lips to me, his tongue moving in slow pulses, holding me still, holding me together while I rode the wave of tremors.

I slumped—drained and sated and breathless—into the mattress. Tito curled his arms around my waist, laid his cheek against my pelvis, and held me, his head rising and falling with my heavy breaths. He held me until my heart rate slowed, and that vibrant pulse between my thighs dulled to a slow throb.

"Beast," he murmured, sitting back on his heels, gripping my hips, and pulling me closer until my butt rested on his thighs. "You sexy little beast."

He flashed one of his rare smiles. My heart burst. A sharp sting pierced my chest, then spread, warming my veins. Gripping my hips, he positioned me, nestling his thick, hard arousal between my thighs.

"Do me a favor, Bunny. Reach over your head. There's a condom on the nightstand." His gaze remained focused between my legs, where he teased, rubbing his length in slow strokes across my slick and sensitive folds, driving me insane. I wiggled to free myself, but the man only held me tighter.

"Fuck, baby. Hurry, or I'm taking you bare."

I reached over my head, twisting in an effort to reach the nightstand, still coming up two inches short of my goal. I planted one foot on the mattress for leverage and stretched until my fingertips grazed the corner of the foil packet.

Tito groaned.

I pushed harder. Tito's fingers tightened around my waist, but he let me move off his lap long enough to grab the prize.

The world stopped spinning when our eyes met. He'd never looked so beautiful. Cheeks flushed, lips parted, eyes dreamy and drinking me in.

He oozed boyish charm, deep dimples making a rare and brilliant appearance when he whispered, "Damn that was sexy, watching you squirm."

"You did that on purpose." I threw the packet at his chest. It bounced and landed between my legs, the corner scratching my inner thigh. "Ow," I said, giggling.

He gestured at his erection. "Can you blame me?"

And then Tito broke my heart. Tore it wide open. His grin spread wider, and he laughed. He laughed. From his gut. "You should see the way those tits were bouncing. Prettiest thing I've ever seen."

Despite the heaviness of the day, my chest loosened, my spirit soared, and joy filled my hollow parts.

Still chuckling, Tito rolled the condom on and sunk into me, filling me with heat, and pleasure, and gentle bliss. I melted into the bed, absorbing his thrusts, soaking up his kisses, getting lost in the way he loved me with his body.

Tito

Fuck, I loved her body. I loved loving her body. I loved commanding, touching, tasting, smelling, and sinking into her body.

She was my drug. My light. My release, my...peace. The calm to my storm. Tuuli took everything I gave, following my lead, melting into me, clinging, writhing, begging for more. What started slow and easy, fun and playful morphed into frantic, desperate, greedy fucking.

I'd pull away, she'd cling tighter. I'd pound harder, she'd whimper but counter my force.

Inside, Tuuli was liquid silk, tight friction, heavenly torture. Outside, she was sinful temptation. Soft and flawless.

We fucked. We purged. We devoured. We unleashed.

When we collapsed, beat and out of fucking juice, Tuuli curled into me, naked, warm, and limp. I wrapped trembling arms around her, tangled our legs, and buried my nose in her hair. So damn sweet. Even after I'd fucked her raw, she still smelled like an angel.

The clock read 2:58 a.m. I closed my eyes. When I opened them again, the clock read 8:16.

I stretched across the wrinkled sheets, sore and sated, absorbing the sunshine that reached through the small basement window.

On a normal day, I would have already finished my run, and either been at the gym or neck-deep in research.

Instead, I lay completely at peace and willed my morning woody to calm the fuck down. Hard to do when the room smelled of sex and Bunny. Greedy bastard.

Music broke my trance, an uplifting beat that brought ice to my veins. Heavy on the organ, hand claps, and layered harmonies. No. Just no.

I wrestled into a pair of running pants and went in search of my girl, my stomach rumbling when the scent of bacon hit me, body heating when I took in the scene.

Tuuli stood at the kitchen table. God, the way her eyes lit up every time I entered the room? Sucker punch to the chest. Never got old.

"Morning," she sang, head bouncing to the music, hips swaying under the loose-fitting dress she wore. A sheer scarf covered her bruised neck. The pinks and yellows in the fabric brightened the blue in her eyes, and I couldn't help but smile. So beautiful. So clueless to the power she had over me.

I snatched the remote off the counter and muted the volume, too many images pelting my psyche, threatening to let loose demons I wasn't ready to share. Ugly memories that belonged nowhere near my girl.

Tuuli made a pouty face. I kissed it away.

"Is that bacon I smell?"

"It's in the oven." She snatched her purse off the counter and headed toward the door. "There's a breakfast casserole in there, too."

"Wait." A hammer pounded my ribcage. "Where are you going?"

"Church," she replied.

"Are you fuckin' kidding me right now?" I immediately regretted raising my voice.

Her gaze dropped to the floor.

She shook her head, straightened her shoulders, and met my eyes again. "Tito. It's Sunday. I've missed the last few weeks. I really need to go."

"After what happened to you last night, you're just going to walk out of here, alone?"

"I have the Uber app." She held up her new cell and forced a smile.

Un-fuckin-believable. "Are you insane? Uber?"

"I could call a cab if you think that's better?"

"No! Christ! Not the point. So not the point." Was she really that naive? "You were attacked last night, and you're going to stroll out of here like there isn't a maniac out there waiting for another chance to grab you?"

"That's why I called for a ride instead of taking the bus."

Fuck. Fuck. Fuck. The girl made me crazy. "Why didn't you ask me to take you?"

"You were sleeping so sound, and…" Her gaze dropped to her feet. That damn little heel bounced on the floor, her nervous tell.

"And what?"

"I didn't think you'd want to take me. You made it clear how you feel about church." Her shoulders dropped. "Why are you mad?"

I wasn't mad. Was I? Not at Tuuli, anyway. I was angry about the situation. I wanted her time. I needed her time. After last night, she wanted to be with a God who didn't give a shit? Wasn't I enough?

Shit. Now my head was all twisted up. "You know how I feel about church. But...Fuck. Don't you get it?"

"Get what?" she asked, head cocked, eyes worried.

The words slipped free before I considered the consequences. "How I feel about *you*, Tuuli."

Shit.

Every feature on her face brightened, lifting toward the sky like she'd tasted her first kiss of sunshine. "How do you feel?"

Shit.

Shit.

Shit.

Fuck.

"You know, don't you?" Don't make me fucking say it.

She dropped her purse back on the counter and stepped closer, predatory in her approach. "No, Tito. I don't know how you feel."

"You know." I took a step back. The words were there, acid on my tongue. Words I'd never dared entertain.

"Why can't you say it?" She took another step toward me, the bunny stalking the beast. God, her bravery.

After all she'd been through, there was still that goddamn hope in her eyes, that need to be wanted, claimed. She stalked closer still. I retreated, a motherfuckin' coward. They were only words.

Words that would not form.

"Why can't you say it?" she asked, half growling. And then my timid little bunny shocked the shit out of me. With all her might, she shoved at my chest. "Say it. Say how you feel, Tito! Say it!"

I stumbled backward, confounded by her outburst. My heel caught on the rug, and I fell on my ass. Pissed, but embarrassed more than anything, I shouted, "What the fuck, Tuuli?"

Color drained from her face. The fight dissolved from her spirit. She backed away, head down, eyes to the ground.

I rose, nerves vibrating, angry at myself for not being able to tell her what she needed to hear, for being weak, for being less than she deserved.

I fisted my hands at my sides, my nails digging into my palms. I hadn't the wherewithal to fight, the weight on my chest no longer bearable. My body, my heart, my soul, were no longer mine to command. She owned them. She owned me. Why couldn't I verbalize what was so blatantly obvious?

"I'm sorry I pushed you," Tuuli spoke to the floor. Stopped, straightened her shoulders, and met my glare. "I need to go. I'll see you later."

She stared for a heartbeat longer, waiting for me to speak. When I didn't, she turned and headed for the door.

She couldn't leave. She couldn't walk away. "Don't go."

"Why?" she asked, one hand on the doorknob.

I closed the distance between us, pressing my chest to her back, and slamming a palm against the door. "I'm addicted to you. I'm obsessed with you. You're all I think about."

Her breath hitched.

"Actions speak louder than words, Bunny." I bent and whispered in her ear, "What have my actions told you?"

Tuuli sucked in a sharp breath, her head falling back against my chest. She turned, circled her arms around my neck, and pulled me close, smashing her lips to mine. She kissed the ever-loving fuck out of my mouth, decimating my unease, igniting instinct, smothering that cold, black lump in my chest with her warm, bright life.

I coiled my arms around her hips, lifting. Her legs locked around my waist. Her tiny body writhed against me, rubbing me wrong in all the right places.

Hell. Sweet fucking hell.

Too soon, she ended the assault. I struggled to breathe. Tuuli planted her hands on my shoulders, stared at me long and hard, smiled, then shimmied free of my embrace. She opened the door.

"Tuuli," I managed to groan. "Don't."

Over her shoulder, she argued, "I need to go to church, Tito."

Actions speak louder than words, I reminded myself. Fuck. "You're not going alone."

She stopped, halfway over the threshold.

I didn't have the heart to chastise her defiance. I was proud of her for fighting. For standing up for herself, even if I didn't agree.

Erik was out there, somewhere, biding his time. I couldn't let her go anywhere alone.

So, for the crazy little woman who'd brought me back to life, I broke one of my cardinal rules.

I sucked in a sharp breath, and said, "Just wait, please. Let me change. I'm going with you."

Tuuli

"Are you coming in with me?" I stood next to his window, arms at my sides, heart in my throat.

"I'll wait in the car." Tito eyed the steeple, the muscles in his jaw working overtime.

"You do know there are three different entrances into the building, right? You can't watch them all." Low blow, playing on his protective instincts, but he'd brought me this far. A little extra nudge wouldn't hurt.

"Fuck." His face reddened, then paled. He studied the building, gnawing on his lip.

"I'm going in." Walking away was hard, but if I waited, I would cave. He seemed so vulnerable, and I hated knowing he was doing something so out of character just for me.

I started across the parking lot, forcing my smile, scanning for signs of Erik, or any of my family for that matter.

Halfway to the entrance, a warm hand cupped mine from behind. Tito laced our fingers and squeezed tight. Painfully tight. I pushed through the discomfort, aware of his struggle, sensing how hard it was for him to walk through those church doors, remembering how difficult it had been my first time.

My stomach knotted. Maybe I'd pushed him too hard. Would he regret coming along and decide I wasn't worth the trouble?

I glanced up and shivered at the hard set of his features, the haunting sweep of his gaze. He seemed to study every face we passed, assessing every threat.

His body stiffened with each step closer to the building, his fingers tightening around mine. His silence was deafening. Nauseating.

Two feet from the doors, I pulled Tito aside. I'd lost all steam. I studied his shoes and struggled to force the words from my head to my tongue.

"What's wrong?" Tito stepped in front of me, then tapped under my chin, urging me to look up. "You okay?"

"You don't have to do this. It's okay. We can go home. I never should've pushed the issue."

"Oh, baby." He dropped his forehead to mine. "I'm proud of you for pushing. Don't back down now. We're almost there."

"I can tell you don't want to go in there."

He lifted our joined hands. "See this?"

I nodded.

"I've never held hands with a woman. Ever." With his free hand, he cupped my jaw, his thumb tapping a soft rhythm on my cheek. "I'm holding your hand right now because I need *your* strength. You'll help me tough this out. We're doing this together, me and you. Okay, Bunny?"

Together. God, how I loved that word. "Bunny and the Beast."

He laughed before landing a soft kiss on my nose. I'd never felt so cherished. "Yeah. Bunny and the Beast. I like that."

He stepped back and sighed. "Church is important to you. You're important to me. So, I'll deal. Got me?"

I nodded, silenced by his tenderness, his perfect words.

"Just don't let go, and I promise not to freak on you. Sound good?"

"Yeah. That's good," I whispered.

Hand in hand, we walked under the stained-glass image of Jesus and found a spot in the back row. Pastor Davies stepped behind the pulpit. His beard was longer, but well-kept. He dressed casually, welcoming even, in khaki slacks, a pale green button-down, and his signature black Chucks.

Tito shot me a puzzled look. "That's the minister?"

"Pastor."

"Hmm," was his only response.

Tito barely moved for the next forty minutes, tension emanating off his body like a radiant heater. My heart broke, knowing my strong man, the man built of confidence and power, sat next to me, struggling, and out of sorts, in the one place I found comfort.

When the sermon ended and the band took their place on stage, I nudged Tito and nodded toward the exit, hoping to avoid the after-service chaos. "Let's go," I whispered. "I'm starving. Can we grab something to eat before I head to work?"

Without looking my way, Tito led me outside. It wasn't until I snapped my seatbelt into place that he took a cleansing breath. I wondered if he'd ever shown his vulnerable side before. My chest constricted at the thought.

"Thank you," I blurted.

With a huff, Tito roughed a hand through his hair and said, "You're welcome." Fiery eyes met mine. He opened his mouth to speak, then stared. I couldn't tell if he was angry, frustrated, or relieved. I couldn't read him at all. He then reached over and tangled his strong fingers in my hair, pulling tight at the nape, forcing me to keep eye contact.

I couldn't bear to look at him, yet I couldn't tear my gaze away from the stormy man. He studied my face, caressed the bruise on my neck, then met my eyes.

With a low, throaty gravel, he said, "You look beautiful today." He released my hair, rubbed his thumb over my bottom lip, licked his own, and whispered, "So damn beautiful," before starting the car, and pulling away.

Actions speak louder than words.

Heat splashed my cheeks. My stomach growled. Tito laughed. Loud and deep and genuine, decimating any lingering tension between us.

"I'll make you lunch at home." His gaze raked the length of me, his dimple coming out to play. "Then I'm having you for dessert."

CHAPTER 12

WARM LIPS AND A scratchy beard dragged across my abdomen, leaving prickly tingles before moving lower and lingering on the sweet spot between my thighs. A sharp nip forced a squeal from my lips. A deep chuckle rumbled from between my legs. The room was pitch black, but I could feel Tito's hot breath on my bare skin, his strong hands on my hips.

My entire body ached from exertion as well as lack of sleep. Tito had been insatiable since our tiff last Sunday. We hadn't spoken about my outburst, how I'd pushed him, or the aftermath, but we'd communicated our apologies in other ways.

Tito's sex drive was voracious, but he was never selfish. What he took from my body, he gave back tenfold. And while I couldn't get enough of him, night after night of mindless bliss had me worn. I had zero energy to spend. I squeezed my thighs together, tightening them around his solid shoulders. "Tito. I can't. I'm so tired. Can we sleep a little longer, please?"

"No more sleeping." He kissed my thigh and pushed off the bed. "Don't worry; I'm not ready for another go. My dick needs a break, you insatiable beast. Get up. We're going for a run."

"Run? It's still dark." I wrestled a mess of hair off my face. "What time is it?"

"Five." He grabbed my big toe and gave it a tug. "Come on; you'll thank me later."

I rolled over with a moan, my mind already halfway back to dreamland.

A sharp sting bit my butt cheek. "You can get yourself up, or a cold shower can do the trick. Your choice."

"Okay. Okay." I pushed off the mattress.

Tito offered a hand to help me stand. "Your clothes are here." He patted the end of the bed. "We're leaving in five."

I slipped into the outfit he laid out for me, fumbling through the dark. I'd never bought workout clothes for myself, and I wondered when he'd had time to go shopping. He hadn't left my side since the night of the attack.

Lately, I'd find gifts hiding in plain sight. New clothes hanging in the closet. My favorite candy bars in the bottom of my purse. New perfume on the bathroom shelf. I'd thank him, and he would merely shrug. No big deal.

When I made my way to the living room, Tito waited in his signature dark pants, black running shoes, and grim reaper hoodie. I looked down at myself and laughed. We matched.

"Here, put this on. It's chilly out." He offered me a pullover hoodie, that surprise, surprise, was black like the one he wore.

I pulled the cloak over my head and grumbled, "Okay, Grim. Let's do this."

"Grim." Laughing, he ducked to my level and planted a kiss on my dry, worn lips. "If you only knew."

When we stepped outside, the crisp morning air shocked the sleep haze from my system. We started at a slow pace, toward the city beach, then followed the running trail that stretched around the north side of Lake Willow and along the river toward Hollow Falls.

I did my best to keep up but slowed to walk on several occasions. Walking, I could do. Lord knows I'd done plenty of hiking over the past months. Running, though? My legs were lead weights.

Tito didn't complain when I needed a break, didn't chastise, only stayed by my side, reminding me to breathe, checking often to make sure I was okay.

I wanted to be strong for him. I wanted to keep up, even though my insides felt like boiled pudding and my legs trembled like a toddler wearing her mama's heels. We came around a bend alongside Ravendale Park and I cried for joy when Tito stopped at a bench that overlooked the river.

We stretched for a minute, then he wrapped an arm around my shoulders and turned me to face the way we'd come. Blinding light peeked over the mountains in the distance. The scene was beautiful and breathtaking but had nothing on the intensity of the man standing next to me.

I dropped to my butt on the damp running path and leaned back on my arms, taking in the bright blue sky, the green and golden hues of the landscape, and waited on the warm sun at my front to chase away the dark sky lingering at my back.

Tito sat next to me, forearms resting on his bent knees. The world was quiet, aside from the rush of the river and the chatter of birds calling each other to rise. I watched Tito watching the sunrise. He gnawed on his lower lip, fists clenching and unclenching. I sensed a shift in his mood and my stomach lurched.

I ached to know his thoughts.

Drawn to him, I reached up and dusted a fingertip across the puckered skin on his face, tracing the length of his disfigurement. "Tell me about the fire."

His chest rose and fell. His gaze sliced toward me, never landing, and focused again on the newborn sunlight rolling toward us like a swelling wave.

I dropped my arm and waited, chest concave, for an answer. When he didn't speak, I swallowed my apprehension. "Why don't you like going to church?"

A huff. Tito dropped his head back on his shoulders, clearly frustrated.

Again, my stomach lurched, then flipped.

I shouldn't have pushed. Eyes down, lips sealed. That's how men liked their women. I shouldn't have pushed, but I did.

"Are you ever going to open up to me?"

Silence.

And in that quietude, I found anger, and courage, and clarity.

"We're never going to work if—"

In a blur of heavy breath and angry eyes, I landed flat on my back, caged between a pair of trembling arms. "We're never going to work if what? If I don't tell you everything? Jesus Christ. Is this how it's gonna be between us?"

"No," came a weak reply from a pathetic voice that couldn't have been mine, so pitiful even Tito cringed.

"You wanna know what keeps me awake at night?" His face softened. "I worry that we'll never work if I *do* tell you everything. My secrets will hurt you. My truths will be the end of us. So, tell me, what am I supposed to do?"

Tito

"You're supposed to trust me." Her bottom lip quivered. Her gaze held steady. "I'm not a child, Tito. I can handle the truth. You should know that by now."

I did know. She'd proven her strength time and time again. "Tuuli. My past, my truths? They'll weigh too heavy on your conscience." She was light, where I was darkness. She valued forgiveness, where retribution was my sustenance. She was grace. I was...Grim. A reaper.

I wanted her to know me. All the ugly. All the pain. But to share my stories would extinguish her light. Dull the shine in her eyes.

Truth be told, I was afraid. Terrified of extinguishing her spark, of never enjoying the blush that dotted her cheeks when we touched, or never hearing that small gasp every time I pulled her close, or of never feeling her shudder beneath me.

I was afraid.

I was the weak link in our...our...fuck...relationship.

I should have stayed away.

Vulnerability was painful. Made a man weak.

She lifted a hand, touched my face, smiled up at me. "Never mind. I'm sorry I asked."

God. Now she was apologizing for my deficiencies. "I'm fucked up. I'm not a good person. I..."

Murder people.

"Your sins are no greater than mine. You saw past my wrongs. Why wouldn't I do the same for you?"

She waited for a response. I had nothing to give. Coward.

"Okay." She pushed at my chest. "Let me up."

Tuuli was shutting down.

I pushed to my feet. Offered a hand to help her stand.

"We should head back. I need to get to work." She searched my face again, a small flicker of hope still in her eyes.

Say something. Anything. Fucking coward.

Her posture changed, making her smaller somehow. Tuuli turned and headed toward home. I followed two paces behind, my throat, my ticker, tightening with every inhale and exhale.

In. *One, two, three, four.* Out. *One, two, three, four.*

My brave, angry girl ran all the way home, slowing only once.

She showered. I fried eggs. She dressed. I buttered her toast. She fixed her hair. I set the table. The silence, the unspoken words, bounced off the walls, gaining speed, building, rolling, electrifying the air around us.

I waited at the table. Tuuli emerged from the bathroom.

"I made breakfast."

"I'm not hungry."

She headed for the door. I tossed her plate in the sink.

"I'll drive you down."

"Tango is waiting for me outside. He'll drop me off."

Ouch.

I watched, tongue-tied and dizzy, as she slipped into her Docs, then bent to tie her laces.

True, her gaze hit—with laser precision—every point of her attention, avoiding me with steel-spined resolve, but never once did it drop to the floor in submission or fear. Not one time.

As much as I wanted her eyes on me, as much as I needed her to cry, or scream, or yell, and tell me I was being a jackass, or to fall into my arms and tell me everything was going to be okay, I was proud of how far she'd come.

She wasn't only breaking free of her family binds. She was growing. The air around her shifted, crackling with energy, alive with the promise of an oncoming storm. I hated that she was pulling away. But I loved that she was finding her strength. Her voice. Her beast.

The ache in my gut settled deeper.

"Tuuli. I'm—"

"Sorry." She stood straight, arms at her sides, heel bouncing. "I know."

I stepped closer. She chewed her bottom lip.

Closer still, her eyes found mine. I reached for her, she stiffened, sighed, then fell against me, mumbling into my shirt. "When are you moving into your condo?"

Goddamn that hurt. "Are you eager to be rid of me?"

"No. I just..."

"Need space." I squeezed her tight. "I get it. Space will be good." Lie. Lie. Lie.

"That's not it. I just...I don't know. It's hard enough knowing you won't be here. I want to get the leaving part over with."

Bullshit. "It doesn't have to be this way."

"It does. I don't expect you to understand."

I understood. She needed things I couldn't give. "I'll have my shit out of here by this afternoon."

Her eyes liquefied. "I gotta go."

How could I let her go? She belonged right where she was. Against my chest. "Are we good?"

Warm lips pressed against my neck. "We're good."

"Can I pick you up after your shift?"

"Yeah. I'd like that."

"Good. So, it's a date."

She tilted her head back to meet my gaze. "Yeah. I like that. A date."

I kissed her hard, our goodbye settling in my body like the early stages of the flu.

I was moving out, but I wasn't letting her go. I was merely stepping back, giving her room to grow. That's what I told myself, anyway. Every second felt wrong. Every word, every action, off. Everything except for the kiss.

She pulled away, and whispered, "See you tonight," then forced a smile.

I should've begged her to stay. I should've spilled my truths. Instead, I opened the door and moved aside. A coward.

I let her walk away.

Tuuli

I walked away, the weight of his stare a gale-force wind at my back.

When I climbed into Tango's Rover, Rocky shouted a hello from the back seat. I forced the emotion from my voice and turned to address the little lady-killer.

"Good morning, Rocky. All ready for school?"

He held a football in one hand and a juice box in the other. The boy was all green eyes and cheesy grin. "Yep," he said, his legs kicking up and down. "We have a field trip today."

"Yeah? Where ya going?"

"To see the fish hatch."

"The fish hatchery," Tango chimed in.

"We get to take the school bus and have a picnic."

"Wow. That's so cool."

"I like fishing. I have two poles. Uncle Tuck taught me. Do you like fishing?"

"I do like fishing. My brother taught me how when I was—"

My throat clogged tight. My eyes burned, brimming with moisture. My head spun with a tidal wave of memories. Jonas had been decent, once upon a time. Like the summer he'd taught me to fish. We had spent most our days down by the dirty river, under the shade of the river birch trees. Jonas packed sandwiches, soda, and chips. I carried the backpack;

he carried the poles. He mostly ignored me, but he would always let me listen to his iPod, and I used to think that was pretty awesome. He never told his friends about our secret fishing hole.

One tear rolled down my face, then another, catching on my lip.

Tango cleared his throat and said, "Hey Rockster, I don't think Tuuli has heard you sing the 'Nifty Fifty' song yet," effectively changing the subject.

I wanted to hug him.

From the back seat, Rocky belted out lyrics, "Fifty, nifty, United States, from the thirteen…"

Tango offered me a sympathetic smile. I mouthed *thank you* to him and released a long breath, blinking the swelling tears from my eyes. Maybe I missed my brother after all. Parts of him, anyway.

We reached The Stop minutes later. Rocky was still singing. I hopped out of the car, shouted a thank you to Tango, and waved goodbye to Rocky. "Have fun with the fish."

When I walked through the front door, Officer Caldwell stood at the counter, arms folded over his chest. "Morning, sunshine."

"Good morning, Roger."

He cleared his throat. "Can I have a minute?"

"Sure. Everything okay?"

"Yeah. Yeah. Slade said we can use her office."

I followed him down the hall and into the private room.

He closed the door behind us, hooked his thumbs in his belt, and waited for me to sit.

Roger was a good-looking man. Especially in uniform. Average height. Athletic physique. Clean cut. He wore his dark blond hair trimmed close to his scalp, and worry wrinkles framed a wise set of eyes.

A freight train rumbled through my chest. "Did you find the men who killed my brother?"

"No. But we will. I promise. And I've got everyone looking for Erik Meyer, too. But that's not what I wanted to talk to you about." Two heavy steps and he was in front of me, squatting to meet me at eye level. "This is officially off the record. Understand?"

I nodded.

"I need to know if Tito's been acting out of character."

"Why?"

"Considering the amount of money he's paying the men to keep an eye on you, and the way he blew up the night Erik attacked you—"

"Wait. What do you mean he blew up? What happened?"

"Fuck." His head dropped low, his hand lading on my thigh. "Fuck." Roger stood and paced the room, arms crossed, scratching his jaw. "I just assumed you knew. God, I'm sorry."

"Knew what?"

Roger stared at the floor, gnawing his bottom lip, contemplating his next move, no doubt.

"Fuck it. You deserve to know," he said, stopping again in front of me. "That night, Moretti had Tango and me meet him and Tucker here at the diner the second they got back to town. Wanted us to fill him in about what happened and explain how Erik was able to get anywhere near you. Guy goes ballistic. Starts tearing the place apart. Throwing shit. Breaking dishes. Took three of us to drag him out. Almost an hour to talk him down. He was rambling on about murdering Erik, going after your father."

Roger's story made no sense. Tito had been so sweet and caring that night. "He was just upset. He wouldn't...he's not..." I couldn't finish my thought. I remembered his words after I'd confessed what I knew about my father.

I'm going to kill Jeremy Carver and burn that church to the ground.

I blinked up at Roger.

"Tuuli. I like you, and the last thing I want to do is interfere. It's just...damn. He was lost in his own head. Scared the shit out of me, if I'm honest. Bothered me so much, I decided to research the guy."

"And?"

"Nothing. There's nothing on him. Like he never existed before he came to Whisper Springs. Just be careful. Okay? You have my number. Call if you need anything."

Mind reeling, I stared at the handsome cop. His worried eyes, his unsure stance, the heavy weight on his shoulders. It unsettled him to share the information. He was loyal to Tango, making him loyal to Tito and Tucker. He risked that relationship because he was worried about me. *Me.*

"Thank you, Roger. I'll be careful. And I promise I'll call if I need you for anything."

He let out a long breath. Nodded. Held my gaze.

"And I won't say anything to Tito about our conversation."

"Appreciate that." He gave me a crooked smile and turned to leave.

I took a moment to absorb the weight of our conversation, recalling the way Tito had checked-out when he was hitting the heavy bag on our first date. Like a different soul had occupied his body. Yes, he was scary, and big, and dangerous, but I'd never feared for my safety. He'd never been anything but gentle with me. I shook off the nerves and busied myself with work.

With every hour that passed, every thought and memory unraveling from my complex tapestry, every roll, rise, and dip of my emotions, my future slowly lay itself at my feet. My path had always been dark, shrouded by the gnarled, tangled pieces of my life. That was no longer the case. I could see now, with newfound clarity, what lay ahead for me. I was done living under the thumb of Jeremy Carver. Tired of hiding in the shadows. So over being afraid.

Tito's words came back to haunt me. *I'm going to kill Jeremy Carver and burn that church to the ground.* What a terrifying statement. I needed to know him better. I deserved to know the whole Tito Moretti. Every ugly detail.

An hour before my shift ended, I texted Tito and canceled our date, told him I needed to be alone. Then, I called one of the people I feared most in the world, one person who could give me the tools I needed to shed the pathetic skin I'd been living in. Much to my surprise, she agreed to help.

When my shift ended, I stepped outside, physically tired, emotionally numb, but clear-headed and one hundred percent committed to taking control of my life.

Until I heard, "Bunny."

Oh, my. That voice.

Tito leaned against the hood of his car, legs crossed at the ankles, arms folded over his massive chest. He wore jeans and boots, and a brown V-neck sweater that enhanced his lean physique. The scowl he wore, although meant to be threatening, only complemented his outfit.

I stopped in my tracks and admired the brooding man, then mimicked his pose, crossing my arms. The pull between us was a force of nature, and my legs strained to stay in place.

I studied him, studying me. The man was not happy, which I assumed was because I'd broken our date. But it was not my job to make him happy. And what a great feeling to let that burden go.

Neither of us moved for what seemed an eternity. Just as I was ready to crack, Tito shook his head, scrubbed a hand over his face, and came my way, amped like a fighter about to take the ring. I stood my ground. My body trembled in fear or anticipation...I wasn't sure.

Before he reached the halfway point between us, I dropped my arms and sprinted his way. A puppet to her master, at the mercy of invisible strings. A smile cracked his stoic face, and I launched myself against that warm, inviting chest, circled my arms around his thick neck, and before he could take control, I smashed my mouth to his, curled my legs around his waist, and let him know just how much I'd missed him.

Tito

Hell, I'd missed her. It'd only been eight hours. Eight goddamn, miserable hours.

The girl was lighter than shit, but when she threw herself at me with wrecking-ball force, my world righted itself. When she kissed me? Sweet Jesus. Hands, lips, tits, and moans. I forgot why I'd come.

I managed to get us back to my car and prop her ass on the hood.

She smelled like bleach and French fries. Tasted like minty lip balm. Damn, I wanted to ravage and dirty her, clean her up, then start all over again. I broke the lip-lock, then moved down to her ear, her neck, licking, biting, and marking that salty skin. Her fingers curled into my hair, pulling tight.

I grabbed her hips, yanking her harder against me, grinding my erection against that perfect spot between her legs. A ridiculous, sexy noise rose from her throat, setting me on fire.

"In the car, now. Or I'm taking you right here for the world to see."

Tuuli leaned back on her arms, chest heaving, lips swollen, taking me in—my eyes, my scar, my chest. When she raised her gaze again to mine, she mumbled, "Yeah, hell, why not?" and pushed me away.

That damn little bunny opened my car door, crawled behind the passenger seat, kicked off her shoes, then shimmied out of her khakis.

Fuck. Yes. I wiped the moisture off my mouth with the back of my hand.

The back seat of my Mustang was cramped as hell, but I managed to sit and work my jeans down my hips. The second my cock sprang free, that feisty little bunny straddled me. She grabbed the back of the seat, lifted her ass, and slid that slick, tight pussy down the length of me.

"Tuuli. Shit. God, I missed you today."

She bit my neck, rocking her hips.

"Ah. Fuck."

Frenzied and furious, she rode me, like we were running out of time, like if we stopped, the world would end. And damn, right then, the world could've imploded, and I wouldn't have noticed. She was Heaven and Hell, all rolled into one tempestuous little package. Writhing, moaning, fucking, taking what she wanted, mindless to the fact I was trying to keep up, clueless to the damage she was doing, breaking me from the inside out.

Her tits bounced beneath her shirt. I wanted them. But there was no time, no space to rid her of her clothes, and all I could do was curl my fingers into her bare ass and take her assault. I laid my head back and watched my girl chase her pleasure. Eyes closed, face pink, lips swollen and parted. We were as close as two people could be, but Tuuli was gone, lost in her head, in her self-indulgence. So consumed in her own pleasure, I may as well have not existed. She was using me, and fuck that hurt.

Despite my wounded ego, I was proud. My goddamn little bunny wasn't a bunny at all. She was a beast.

She slammed her hands to the ceiling, pushing her body harder against me, rocking her hips, finding the friction she needed. Her head fell back, and she cried, "Oh, God. Shit, shit, shit." The force of her orgasm hit hard, her body curling forward, her thighs slamming against my hips, her core squeezing my cock in tight pulses.

Her neck was exposed. I buried my face there, shouting profanities through my own release.

I clung to her, catching my breath until she pushed me back against the seat and rested her ass on my thighs.

Our eyes locked, neither of us speaking. We breathed, still connected, as close as two people could be, but I'd never felt such distance.

"You broke our date," I growled.

"I had to."

"Why?"

Stormy eyes met mine. A tear slipped free. "What did you do in New York? Who were you?"

A dull ache rose in my chest. "Tuuli. Not now. Please."

"When, Tito?"

"I'm not ready. Please. I just...fuck. Not now."

"How do you feel about me?"

"You know."

She climbed off my lap, leaving my dick cold in the breeze. I didn't care. A storm was raging in that perfect little head of hers. Those eyes hid nothing. "Tuuli."

"Just shut up, Tito. Shut up and drive me home." She tugged her panties up her legs and started on her pants.

What the hell?

I opened my mouth to speak, but the words wouldn't come. Instead, I tucked my junk back where it belonged and climbed out of the car. How did things turn to shit so fast? Fuck. A simple answer was all she wanted, and I gave her nothing. Not a goddamn thing.

By the time I made my way to the driver's seat, she was tying her shoes.

I drove up the hill, opened the door, and helped her out of the car.

She stormed to the door of my...her apartment, slipped the key in the lock, then turned, chin up, eyes down.

My guts twisted.

She was giving up. On me.

I caressed the soft skin on her cheek, cupped her face, and urged her to look up. "Let me come in."

Her face crumpled and she dropped her forehead to my chest, shaking her head no.

"Why?"

Her chest rose and fell, she stepped back, tears flowing full stream. "Why?" She swiped her face with the back of her hand. "Because I love you, Tito. I love you so much."

I love you.

Her words slammed into me, hard and swift. My insides recoiled, protesting.

"I've given you all of me. Everything. I can't settle for anything less than all of you. I deserve to know who you are." Throwing her arms out wide, she continued, "I can't pretend we're a happy couple when I don't know you at all. I deserve one hundred percent of you. I won't take anything less."

I backed away, scrambling to find the proper response. Something. Anything to keep her from giving up, from ending us. "Please, baby. Just let me come in. Let me catch my breath. Let me hold you."

Her head fell back on her shoulders and she screamed, "No. God!"

The world around me blurred.

"Did you hear what I just said to you?" Small fists pounded my chest. "I just told you I love you. I love you. I love you. I love you! Don't you have anything to say?"

So much. So much.

"It isn't fair to me. It isn't fair that I can't know you. Do you understand?"

"You know me, Tuuli." I fell to my knees, the weight of her words, the force of her emotion too much for me to bear. "Better than anyone. Please, don't do this right now."

She backed against the door, her trembling fingers curling around the handle. "I love you, Tito. I always will. Nothing will change that. But I won't share a bed with you. I can't keep giving you my body and soul when I'm only getting tattered pieces in return."

If I could just hold her. If she would just let me hold her, everything would be okay.

I reached for her. She swatted my hand away.

"I'm not giving up on you, or us. But I can't give up on me, either. Go home to your castle. Figure out what's important to you. I'll be here when you're ready."

The door opened. My girl disappeared. The click of the lock sliding into place rang like a church bell between my ears.

I stared at the motherfucking door for ages, willing her to open it back up, invite me inside.

I waited, unmoving until my legs fell asleep beneath me. The door never budged.

I'd been so wrong. That girl wasn't a timid little bunny. She wasn't a beast either. She was a Tempest. A fucking force of nature. Coming in slow and steady, surprising, refreshing, caressing me with her brisk wind, then striking hard with everything she had, tearing my world apart from the roots, and leaving me in total devastation.

CHAPTER 13

Tito

"DON'T BE MAD, BUT I need you to come to the mansion," Aida cooed into the phone.

I held back a chuckle. In the past, whenever she opened a convo with the words, *don't be mad*, it was code for *grab a mop and bucket* because she'd riled another shitstorm and she needed me to mop up the mess.

I didn't miss those days.

Through the computer screen, I watched her tuck a blanket tighter around her sleeping daughter.

"I'm already here. Been watching you girls for an hour now." Half-truth. I'd been watching them for two weeks.

"Fucker," she mumbled, then looked up to the camera and flipped me the bird. "Are you seeing this?" She pointed over her shoulder to the gym. "It's amazing. Tits, I swear, I never would've guessed the little mouse was such a beast."

Beast was right. She'd ripped me to shreds with words sharper than claws.

Through the other screen, I watched Tuuli attack a heavy bag like she wanted to shred the thing. Her form was off. Her breathing all wrong. But the little warrior was on a mission, releasing a shit ton of bottled rage.

Aida looked so animated through the screen. I hardly recognized my best friend anymore. She'd yet to shed all her baby weight, but damn, did she rock those curves. If she wore makeup at all, it was barely noticeable, and she looked fresh-faced, younger, and happier than I ever would've thought possible. One thing that hadn't changed? That damn devilish glint in her big brown eyes.

"What do you think you're doing?"

"I'm teaching the little mouse to fight." Aida's eyes widened. "I can't wait to introduce her to my knives."

Aida and her damn knives. I swallowed a profanity. While I was happier than hell to have Tuuli in my sights, the purpose for her visits to the mansion didn't sit right. "No. No blades. Jesus, Princess. Are you trying to get her killed?"

"Hell, no. I'm empowering her. That girl has been made to feel inferior her whole damn life. It's fucking pathetic."

"And you think you can turn her into a miniature Ronda Rousey with a few training sessions? She'll get herself killed. She doesn't like violence. She doesn't have the heart to hurt another human being."

"That was before."

"Before what?"

"Before she stood helpless, watching three men rape and murder her brother. Before she was attacked by a fucking psycho twat five times her size."

Goddamn, I hated when Aida was right. Tuuli needed to learn how to defend herself. But it should've been me teaching her those survival skills. "Why are you doing this?"

"Because I can." She winked. "And because she asked for my help. How could I say no?"

"Bullshit." I raked a hand through my hair. "You're meddling. Fuck's sake, Princess, stay out of my business, and leave my girl alone."

Aida moved directly under the camera and showed me her angry face, one hand fisted on her hip. "Whatever you did to muck things up between the two of you, fix it. You've been a miserable fuck for weeks."

Three weeks and four days to be exact.

"Not your goddamn business." I ended the call, blowing steady breaths through my nose.

Aida walked back into the gym and cranked the volume. Eminem blasted through the speakers. I stared at the security feed and watched my two favorite women walk through basic self-defense moves.

Another hour passed before Aida jogged to the adjacent room, then came back carrying a screaming Lucia. The ladies exchanged words. Tuuli pulled a sweatshirt over her head, then headed outside.

Tuuli and I hadn't spoken since the night I moved into my condo, leaving my heart and guts at her apartment door. I had, however, kept a close eye on her, from the shadows anyway. Erik was still off-radar, but I was doing everything in my power to flush him out. The guy was a ghost. And I wasn't taking my eyes off Tuuli. Not while Erik Meyer was still breathing.

Every passing day had been more excruciating.

I needed to soothe my ache.

I needed my girl.

Watching from the shadows no longer sufficed.

I caught up with her halfway across the lawn.

"Hey, Bunny."

She whipped around to face me, eyes bright, cheeks rosy. "Tito."

Dear God, that blush.

Her gaze dropped to her Adidas. "Aida said you wouldn't be here."

I tapped a finger under her chin until those blue beauties lifted. "That a bad thing, me being here?"

After a long pause, she mumbled, "No. Not bad." She took a step back, swallowed, straightened her shoulders. "You working?"

Damn, I wanted to calm the shake in her voice. Preferably with my lips. "Been here all morning." I rubbed at that obnoxious ache in my chest.

"You look exhausted."

Because I hadn't slept in weeks. "I'm good."

"How was your trip with Tucker?"

"It was good. Very good." God, I wished I could tell her that we'd pulled two girls off the streets.

She stared long and hard, thoughts spinning. I stared right back, absorbing the attention, hoping like hell she wasn't searching for words to send me away, but bracing for them nonetheless.

She blinked. Cleared her throat. "Listen. Um. Aida drove. But..." She tapped her heel against the overgrown grass. "Would you give me a ride home?"

She may as well have handed me the world. "Let me grab my keys."

Pride kept me from crumbling into an emotional mess at her feet and begging her to come home with me. Instead, I jogged back around the house, locked up, sent Aida a quick text, and met Tuuli at my car where she stood staring at the lake. When I approached, she sucked in a breath. "It's beautiful here."

I followed her gaze to the willow tree standing alone on the shoreline.

Over her shoulder, she gave me a sad smile. "That tree needs a swing, don't you think?"

I nodded. Opened my mouth to speak. Nothing. Fucking desert in my throat.

"I used to love swinging. We had a huge maple in our backyard when I was a girl. I begged my dad to hang a swing from the tree. He never did. One day, Jonas climbed the tree and tied a rope around the branch, then tied an old tire to the end. I had so much fun that day. The next morning, I ran outside to play on my swing. It was gone. Jonas had a black eye, and he didn't talk to me for over a month.

She turned to face me. Even lost in her sad memories, she took my breath away. So fucking beautiful.

I cleared my throat. "A swing would be perfect. The kids will love it. I'll talk to the contractor."

Her entire face lit up. Holy fucking shit. That smile. Dagger to the heart.

My chest cracked wide open. Swear to Christ, I winced from the pain.

Tuuli

The pain was unbearable. He was so close—an arm's length at best—yet lightyears away. I wanted to touch him. Hold him. Kiss him. I needed him to tell me everything was okay. I needed him to need me, to be so desperate for me that he would break down, tell me everything, give me all of him. I needed him to trust that I could handle his burdens.

I focused on that damn willow tree because if I looked at Tito, I would break. Under his intense heat, my resolve shriveled and dried, flaking off, layer by layer, floating away in the warm spring breeze.

"Tuuli."

His breath blew my hair. His heat enveloped me.

Like a puppet on a string, I leaned into him.

"Can I kiss you?"

Yes. Kiss me, please, I wanted to beg. Instead, I turned in his arms and cupped his face. "Tell me something I don't know about you. Something big."

Angry eyes searched mine, begging me to take my question back. Aida's words played on repeat in my head. *He needs to break before he can heal.* I couldn't back down.

His lids slammed shut, then opened, gaze focused over my shoulder.

"Please," I whispered. "One thing so I can kiss you." I inched closer. "I need to kiss you."

I feared he would pull away. Instead, on a deep inhale, he cupped the back of my neck, squeezing tight, like he was afraid I'd run if he didn't hold me in place. His strong jaw tensed. "I was molested by my priest when I was a child." He sucked in a sharp breath. Blew it out. "You wanted to know why I don't like church. That's why."

Oh, God. Oh. God. No wonder he'd wanted to kill my father. I struggled to keep my tears at bay. Sympathy was the last thing he needed. I rose high on my toes, pulled his face down to mine, and brushed my lips in a soft stroke against his mouth, savoring the fullness, the scratch of his stubble, inviting him to take the lead.

He didn't kiss me back, though. His grip tightened and he only stared, working his jaw, arms trembling. He wanted to say more. To share his secrets. He wanted *us*, his internal battle evident in the depth of his glare, the wariness, the pain.

Tito had given enough for one day. I wouldn't push further.

I kissed him again, a quick peck on the corner of his mouth. "Thank you."

His face crumpled.

My heart bled, but I walked away and let myself into his car.

Shoulders hunched, he stared at the water. I waited, palms sweaty, pulse racing.

He wiped at his face with the back of his hand, then turned my way. When our eyes met, he smirked and shook his head, all vulnerability gone.

We didn't talk on the drive home. Thrasher metal blasted through the speakers, stifling any chance for conversation. I was okay with that. He'd given what I'd asked, a gesture that meant everything. A small victory. A baby step forward.

When we reached the house, he walked me down the steps. I slid the key into the lock, then turned to face my beast.

Saying goodbye sucked. I wanted to invite him in. I wanted to tear at his clothes and lose myself in the dips and valleys of his physique. *I want. I want.* I wanted him. All of him. Not just his body. His troubles, too. And that was the very reason I couldn't act on my selfish urges.

"Thank you for driving me home," I mumbled.

He lifted a hand to my cheek and brushed his knuckles across my skin. His touch, so soft and tender, reached every unreachable inch of my body. I closed my eyes, absorbing the sensation, welcoming the ache, inhaling his scent, and holding it in my lungs, greedy for more.

When I looked up, he was staring at my mouth, eyes tortured, bottom lip tucked between his teeth. My entire body flooded with heat. The thump, thump, thump in my chest moved to my abdomen, then lower.

"I miss you so goddamn much," he rasped, voice thick and sticky.

In a moment of weakness, I blurted, "I wouldn't mind if you kissed me again."

A sad smile graced his face. "No. Not until I've earned it."

God, my soul. My soul. It ached. It bled. What was I doing? To him. To us?

We held each other, his cheek on my head, my ear to his chest, his heartbeat steady and strong. With a sigh, he let me go. "Lock the door behind you."

"I will."

"Goodnight, Bunny." He took a slow step back.

Why did saying goodbye feel so wrong? "Tito."

"Yeah?" Another reluctant step.

"Are you going for a run in the morning?"

"Always do."

"Can I join you?"

"Fuck, yeah." He jogged up two steps. Stopped. Turned to look at me. "Hell, yes." Two more steps, he shouted over his shoulder, "Yes." He reached the landing. "I'll be here at six."

He disappeared, then came right back into view. Hands on hips, he ordered, "Lock the door." Then he waited.

I retreated inside. Engaged the locks. Then fumbled for my phone and shot him a text.

Locked. G'nite.

My phone buzzed with a reply.

Nite, Bunny.

I waited for the roar of his engine and the crunch of his tires to reply.

I miss u, too.

I fell into bed early and slept like a baby.

Tito

I hadn't slept more than two hours on and off since moving into the penthouse. Then again, I hadn't slept a full night in twenty years. Only difference, really, was that now, a blue-eyed pixie kept me from dreamland rather than the red-eyed demons that've haunted me for years.

I fell out of bed at five. Arrived at Tuuli's apartment at five-thirty. Waited in my car until five-forty-five. Banged on her door.

She opened seconds later with a mile-wide grin, a bouncy knot of hair on top of her head, and my fucking sweatshirt hanging to her knees. She was drowning in the thing. Hell, if the sight didn't turn me on.

"Morning, Grim." She rose on her toes, kissed my chin, then studied my face with a pout. "You sleep last night?"

"Yeah." Not a bit.

Brows furrowed, she chastised, "You're lying."

Sleep wasn't important. Time with my girl was life or death. "Doesn't matter. You ready? We gotta go if we wanna catch that sunrise again."

"Tito." She dropped back on her heels and pulled me inside.

"Bunny. Run. Remember?"

"No." She continued dragging me down the hall, then kicked the bedroom door open. The bed was unmade, and the room smelled of sweet, warm, vanilla-scented woman. I took a deep breath, eyeing the wrinkled sheets, picturing her naked on that pillow-top queen size. A fresh wave of energy warmed my weary muscles. Warmed other places, too.

Fuck. "This isn't a good idea."

"Sit," she ordered, pointing at the mattress.

"I can't."

She grabbed my shoulders, turned me around, then pushed until my ass landed on the bed. "You can. You will."

Bossy Tuuli was hot, fraying my already jagged nerves. No way in hell would I catch a wink of sleep. But I liked her determination. She wore it well.

"You need sleep." She grabbed the hem of my shirt and tugged, trying to pull the damn thing over my head. "You've got stacks of bags under your eyes."

"I'm fine," I said, putting zero effort into my argument, raising my arms to help.

"You're not." My tee flew across the room. "Fifteen minutes. Just give it fifteen minutes. A power nap. Then, we'll go chase the sunrise."

I had no intention of winning the argument. But still, I played along. "On one condition."

An eye roll. "What?"

"You lay down, too. Let me hold you."

Sweet hell, that blush.

"That was the plan."

"Okay, then." I toed off my shoes. "You should've said that in the first place."

Tuuli kicked off her Adidas, removed her sweatshirt, pulled back the blankets, and waited for me to settle between the sheets. Then, she snuggled close, wrapped her arms around me, and with those delicate fingers, started a slow stroke across my back. I nestled my head against her chest, her heartbeat a soothing rhythm, a lullaby. Her touch was entrancing. Her scent, intoxicating.

As I fought my weary lids, I curled an arm around her waist, hugging tight, and wondered if that was the closest I would ever get to Heaven.

When I opened my eyes, my angel was gone.

2:47.

I'd slept over eight hours. Not one goddamn dream.

Tuuli

"You day-dreaming again, Toodaloo?" For the third time since my shift had started, Charlie rapped his knuckles on my head, shocking me out of my trance.

"Jeez. Sorry. My head is all over the place today." I shook the funky vibe away and snatched the stack of folded towels out of Charlie's hand.

Somehow, I had managed to make it through seven-and-a-half hours of a packed house without dropping any dishes or spilling any coffee. Every time the cowbell rattled, my heart jumped into my throat. Every time I looked to see who had entered and it wasn't Tito, my chest deflated.

"You miss him, don't you?" Tango's thick, raspy voice shook me out of another reverie.

"Where'd you come from?" I squeaked.

He hooked an arm around my shoulder and steered me toward the end of the hall, smiling down at me with a crooked grin and those exotic, hypnotizing eyes. Seriously, those green babies should come with a warning: Weapon of Mass Destruction.

"I do. I miss him more than I want to," I confessed.

"He misses you, too."

Tango Rossi was one of those rare beauties, so perfect that you wanted to stare, but much like looking at the sun, if you ogled too long, you would go blind. So, with great effort, I held his gaze. "I'm trying to do the right thing. Trying to be a strong independent woman and all that. But...gah...I don't feel right. Nothing feels right."

Tango threw his head back and mumbled something to

the ceiling, in Spanish I think, before grabbing my shoulders and shaking me. "That's exactly what he said."

"Why is this so hard?"

"Because nothing worth fighting for is easy." He leaned back against the wall, arms crossed, head cocked. "Want my advice?"

"Sure." I hugged the towels to my chest.

"Stick to your guns. Don't give in. But don't give up, either. He'll come around."

"How do you know?"

"Because you're a woman worth fighting for." He shot me a dreamy-eyed wink, pushed off the wall, and sauntered away, leaving his words behind to seep through my skin, my blood, my soul.

Because you're a woman worth fighting for.

He said woman. Not girl. Not brat. Not bitch. Woman.

I was worth fighting for. I had to believe that truth, for nobody else but me.

I headed back to the dining room with a bouncier spring in my step. A new customer was seated at one of my tables. A little on the short side, but thick on bulk. Messy black hair. Colorful ink covering his arms.

"Hi, there." I smiled at the guy. "What can I get for you?"

His leg bounced incessantly. His thumb rapped a nervous beat on the table.

"Hey. Hi." He glanced around, then leaned toward me. "Tuuli Holt?"

My stomach twisted. Throat shriveled. "Mmm...hmm."

I looked over my shoulder. Slade was behind the counter, chatting with one of our regulars. Tango was nowhere to be found, and...Oh. Good. Andrew, one of the new security guards, was seated at the corner table, attention focused on me. I sucked in a calming breath.

"Hey, Tuuli." He smiled. A warm, friendly smile, then offered a hand. "I'm Miguel. A friend of your brother's."

Every organ in my body dropped an inch. I swallowed a whimper. "Hi."

"Hey. Listen." He scratched his head. "I'm really sorry to hear about what happened."

"Oh. Thanks? I'm sorry. How do you...I mean, how *did* you know Jonas?"

"We met in Seattle. Did some business together."

"Oh." Business. I could only imagine. I didn't ask for details.

"You have a minute? If you're busy, maybe we can talk after your shift?" Miguel's voice was soft, kind, and carried a slight accent.

"Now is fine. Do you want a drink or anything?"

"No. Nothing. Thanks. Can you sit?"

"Sure." I fell into the seat across from him. "Is everything okay?"

Miguel reached into his backpack, retrieved a manila envelope, and slid it across the table. "Jonas gave this to me a year ago. Said if anything ever happened to him, I was to give it to his sister, Tuuli Holt. I'm sorry it took me so long. I only heard about his passing two weeks ago. Had to do some digging to find you."

The envelope was heavy and thick. On the front, in Jonas's messy handwriting, was my name, and nothing else.

"What is it?"

"I don't know." He started to scoot out of his seat.

"Wait." I slapped a hand on his wrist. "Where are you going?"

"Home. My job is done."

"Your job? I'm so confused."

He huffed, sat back down, stared out the window, then reached across the table and tapped the envelope. "Your brother wasn't who he pretended to be." His gaze dropped to the envelope, then bounced back to me. "Whatever is in there? He said it was imperative that you have it. That's all I know. That's all I can tell you. He paid me a lot of money to deliver this package, but even if he hadn't..." His eyes slammed shut and he shook the thought away before grabbing my wrist and squeezing tight. "I owe him my life, and I could never let him down."

Startled by his intensity, I jerked my hand away, not out of fear, or pain, but the hurt behind his eyes, the agony in his voice. Miguel then hurried out of his chair, and without glancing back, slipped through the door and into the dark night.

Rubbing my wrist, I stared at the package in my hand, vaguely aware of a commotion outside. Men's voices. Shouting.

Jonas had spent most of his life ignoring me. Why would he do this? I flicked the corner of the envelope with my thumbnail, debating whether to open the thing immediately or wait for privacy.

The cowbell rattled.

I tugged at one corner of the seal.

Footsteps. The cowbell.

Flick. Flick. Flick. To open, or not to open?

Slade ran by, shouting, "Goddammit, Tito!"

My heart jumped to my throat, and I looked outside. Miguel lay on the ground, his face bloody. Tito crouched over him, fist raised to strike. Tango dove, hooking an arm around Tito's chest, tackling him backward to the ground.

The kid at table three yelled, "Cool," his face pressed to the glass while his mother watched in horror.

Tito wrestled Tango, eyes dark like death, a beast, but not *my* beast.

I wanted to vomit.

Refusing to watch, I made my way toward the kitchen, then down the back hall where it was quiet and there was zero testosterone. I slid down, down, down, landing hard on my ass, then turned the envelope over and over, contemplating its contents.

"What did he want?" A large, bloodied hand ripped the envelope from my grasp. "What is this?"

I followed the fingers, the hand, and then the arm that led to a thick neck, and a red, angry face.

"Tito, don't."

Ignoring me, he ripped the top of the envelope. Vile anger heated my insides, forcing me to my feet. "What are you doing?" I yelled, snatching the paper and clutching it to my chest. "That's mine."

Heavy breaths hit my face. His chest rose and fell in large sweeps. Fingers curled around my arm, and despite my protests, he pulled me down the hall.

"Ouch. Stop."

His fingers loosened, but his gait didn't falter until he pulled me into Slade's office and kicked the door shut behind us.

Miguel sat on the couch. Andrew towered over him, gun at the ready. Tango stood in the corner, phone to his ear.

"You know this guy?" Tito asked, pointing toward the man on the couch, all heavy breaths and haunted eyes.

"He said he knew my brother. Jonas wanted me to have this." I shoved the envelope against his chest, harder than necessary.

His hand slapped over mine. "You don't know him?"

"No."

He slipped the package from under my hand and dropped the contents onto Slade's desk. A pile of paper. Two crisp, clean stacks of hundred-dollar bills. A small, clear plastic box containing memory cards and flash drives.

I scooted closer, pushed Tito out of my way, and rifled through the papers, landing on a newspaper clipping. The headline read: *Eileen Grady's Disappearance Remains a Mystery. Family Distraught. Pregnant Teen Believed Dead.*

The article was torn from a Chicago newspaper dated twenty-one years earlier. The face in the photo could've been mine. The girl was clearly pregnant. But the scowl she wore? I knew that grimace well. My mother.

"Tito?" I handed him the clipping, my icy fingers trembling. "What is this?"

I picked up the next paper in the stack. A birth certificate. Mine. The one beneath it belonged to Jonas. Another. Eileen Grady. And another. Ingrid Holt.

Tito scooted around the desk and sunk into Slade's chair. His fingers floated across the keyboard, brows drawn tight, jaw set tighter.

I picked up another clipping. "Suspect in Eileen Grady Kidnapping Found Dead."

Tito cleared his throat. "Shit."

"Tito?" My hands trembled. Mind reeled.

"He's not your father. That's why there are no records. That's why your mother doesn't share his name. It's all a fuckin' ruse." His eyes found mine, then bounced back to the screen. "Jeremy Carver was incarcerated in Missouri when Eileen Grady, who is clearly your mother, disappeared from her after-school job in Chicago. She was four months pregnant."

"No. That's ridiculous." The room blurred, my bones turning liquid.

In a blink, Tango was at my side, holding me steady.

"Carver likes boys, Tuuli. Think about it. You ever see your parents together? They ever share a bedroom? Kiss?

Touch? Hell, have you ever seen them fuckin' smile at each other?"

"No." I hadn't. Except for public appearances, the two of them were never together. I couldn't remember a time Jeremy spent the night at the house. Sure, he'd show up for meals because one thing my mother did well was cook. He'd also show up for punishments. Other than that, well, I had no clue where he laid his head at night.

Tito turned back to the computer. "Ingrid Holt died forty years ago. Your mother took her name. Her social security number."

I watched in horror as his fingers battered the keyboard, his eyes scanned the screen, and a wall fell around him. Much like when he'd attacked the punching bag, he zoned out, the Tito I knew disappeared, and a man possessed took his place.

A disturbing silence blanketed the room. My stomach rolled, head buzzed.

"Tito. What's hap—"

"Take her home, T," Tito blurted without so much as a glance my way.

"No," I protested. "This is my life—"

"Now, Tango!" he yelled, slamming a fist on the desk.

Tango hugged me closer, his voice low, a forced calm that wasn't necessary, but appreciated. "Come on, Tuuli. Let's leave him to it." He scooted me out the door. It wasn't until we reached his car that he offered a sympathetic grin. "It's better to steer clear of Tito when he's working."

CHAPTER 14

Tuuli

MY REFLECTION TAUNTED ME. I pursed my lips, turning my face this way then that, checking my teeth, the blade of my nose, the slant of my forehead. There was no denying I shared DNA with the woman who called herself Ingrid Holt. Same eyes. Same platinum hair. Same pert nose. Pouty lips. Porcelain skin. Petite frame.

I was the woman's daughter, without a doubt. But who was Ingrid? Who was Eileen Grady?

What about my real father? Did he even know I existed? Would he have liked me? Hugged me? Driven me to school?

Slumping against the wall, I lowered my butt to the linoleum, the truths of my life settling into place with palpable *click, click, clicks*—Jeremy Carver was not my father. I was not the offspring of a hateful, abusive, child rapist. My whole existence, every vile detail, was a lie.

A soft rap hit the door. "Bunny. You in there?"

Wasn't fair, really, how the warm, worried tone of Tito's voice melted the icy wall I'd spent all night constructing. "How did you get in?"

"I still have my key. You didn't answer when I rang the doorbell."

I hadn't heard the doorbell through the buzzing in my head, lost in my bubble of self-reflection.

"Can I come in?"

My insides vibrated, warming in anticipation. "I s'pose."

The door swung open. Dark, scary, hooded Tito stepped across the threshold, eyes softening when they landed on me. "You haven't returned my calls."

"Haven't felt like talking." I forced spite into my words, though they sounded anything but mean. I tried to be angry, had every right to be livid, yet an air of liberation surrounded me, leaving me in an obnoxious state of bliss.

"Fair enough." He joined me on the floor, shoulder to shoulder.

Fighting the urge to snuggle against him, I hugged my legs and rested my pounding head on my knees. "Where's Miguel?"

"On his way home," Tito said, voice laden with worry, and maybe regret.

"You didn't hurt him again, did you?"

"No. Hell, no." He inspected the bandage on his right hand, stretching then fisting his fingers, swelling evident even under the white gauze.

"You do that often? Beat up strangers for no good reason?"

"He grabbed you." His offending hand landed on my knee. "I confronted him outside. He swung first. We talked it out after you left. There isn't much more to explain."

Men. Neanderthals. All of them.

"Did you check out the files?"

"Yeah." His breaths quickened, his hand leaving my knee to scratch his jaw.

"And?"

A low groan rose from his throat. "Your brother collected enough evidence to put Jeremy Carver away for life."

"Evidence?"

"Videos. Some of them dated ten years back."

The temperature dropped twenty degrees, forcing a shiver. "The boys."

"Yes. Boys." Tito choked on his words, blanching.

"Oh, God." I laced my fingers between his, my gut churning like a simmering pot of mud. "Please, tell me you didn't watch."

He didn't answer, not verbally, but his whole body stiffened, shifting the air around us. "That's not all."

My nerves couldn't take any more.

"He collected files on Erik Meyer, too. Recent transactions. Buying and selling children."

"Stop." I hugged my legs tighter. "I can't hear any more. Not tonight."

A warm arm came around me. Soft lips pressed against my head, lingering before he released a sigh. "Tucker has friends in the FBI. They're meeting in the next day or two. Hell is going to rain down on that damn church, Tuuli. Your brother did a good thing."

"He's not my brother." I wasn't sure if that truth made me happy or sad.

"God, baby." Like I weighed nothing, he pulled me across his lap, warming me with strong arms and the heady scent of his body wash. "This has got to be hard. What can I do?"

Tito never had to do anything but be present to make me feel better. A weakness on my part, or perhaps one of his super-strengths. "My whole life, Jeremy told me I was nothing. My only worth, my only purpose, was to make babies and to serve The Brotherhood. I never loved that man. But I always wondered why he hated me so much."

"You deserved better." He kissed my head. "So much better."

Gah, this man.

Shifting, I straddled his thighs and pushed the hood off his head. His raw beauty stole my breath, and for a moment, I could only stare, struck dumb by the empathy lighting his hard features.

He moaned. "It kills me to see you hurting."

The heat of him between my legs was almost too much to bear. I raised a finger to his scar, tracing the outline. "Oh, Grim. Don't you see? I'm not hurting. I'm not sad. I'm free."

His hazel eyes widened, glassy and full of awe as if he'd discovered the eighth wonder of the world, as if he were proud. "There's my brave, beautiful girl."

He stroked my hair, smoothing the strands between his fingers. His gaze moved from my shoulder to my chest, then traveled in a slow, appreciative gander up my neck, pausing for a moment on my lips before settling, eye to eye, like a weary traveler who'd just returned home. "Can I kiss you?"

His pulse beat under my palms.

A kiss. What harm could it do?

I leaned closer, craving a taste, the full, soft flesh, the scratch of his stubble.

His minty breath drew me closer. "Please. One kiss."

Temptation was a terrible, deceitful entity. I couldn't give in. "Tell me something I don't know about you. Something big."

Groaning, he curled his fingers, gripping my butt cheeks.

I ached. God, how I ached, missing his skin, his strength, his heavy breaths and heady moans.

It was obvious he didn't want to talk, so I upped the ante. "One confession. Two kisses."

His head fell against the wall, rolling to the side. "The house fire I told you about."

"Mmhmm," I hummed, biting my bottom lip to keep from kissing the scar on his face.

"It was my fault. People died because of me."

Before I could react, or respond, or register the weight of his words, Tito slammed his hand to the back of my head and stole those two promised kisses, the first fast and desperate, the second, slow, needy, relentless, begging. *No more questions. Please. I've got nothing left to give.*

Ages of pain seeped through that kiss.

I absorbed his brutal emotion, curling around him, melting against his tense muscles. He trembled beneath me. I tightened my grip.

On a gruff moan, he buried his face in my neck. "God, Tuuli." A deep inhale. His arms snaked around me, fingers holding tight. "I've never said that out loud."

Then my beastly man sucked in a hitched breath, and I knew he was fighting to hold his emotion at bay.

He'd allowed me another glimpse of a heavily guarded soul, a costly confession.

I leaned back, tapping his chin like he often did to me, urging him to meet my eyes. "There's my brave, untouchable man."

I kissed him again. Because I could. Because he needed me.

His gaze aimed somewhere over my shoulder, unfocused and solemn. Then he smiled. "That was three kisses."

"I've missed your lips."

His face crumpled, agonized before his mask fell back into place. "Can I stay for a while?"

I wanted nothing more, despite trying so hard to hold my ground. "Would you? Until I fall asleep?"

"Shit, Bunny. Of course. Anything. Anything for more time with you."

I woke three times that night. The last, around three a.m. Tito lay on his back, one hand behind his head, the other lying across his chest, thick eyelids fanned over his olive skin. Sleeping like a baby.

Tito

I'd never slept so good in my life.

Shortly after four-thirty, I kissed my bunny, slipped out of bed, and drove home, anxious to hit the open road. I changed into my running gear and fell quietly into the zone, losing myself in the steady rhythm of heavy breaths, the punch of rubber against wet pavement, and the deafening swoosh, swoosh, swoosh between my ears.

I ran until the sun winked at me over the horizon, then headed back. After a long shower, I stood at my bedroom window. The lake was still, an eerie shade of blue, daunting, like something deadly lurked just below the surface. Overhead, a cloud loomed, black and pregnant with threats of doom, sending an icy chill to my marrow.

I turned to face my rumpled bed. It too haunted me. Large, empty, cold. I'd wanted room to breathe. But, hell, the whole space I occupied, despite its luxury, shrunk around me, and I longed for the small basement apartment, more accurately, the woman I'd left sleeping there, the beauty who'd breathed life back into my soulless carcass.

I was so fucked. Fucked for her. Fucked for caring. Fucked for letting someone in, for wanting so goddamn bad to share my life with Tuuli. Fucked because I knew what I needed to do to be with her, and what if I wasn't capable?

Son, I love you. Come with me. Everything will be okay.

My cell buzzed. Tango's mug filled the screen.

I tapped accept, shaking the voice from my head. "Hey, pretty boy."

"Morning, Grim."

"Grim? Really?"

A fat bumblebee banged against the window, bouncing twice before falling out of sight.

Tango chuckled. "If the shoe fits."

"Have you heard from Tuck?" I asked, rifling through the closet for a clean shirt.

"I did. Things are in motion." He yawned into the receiver. "Tito. I'm proud of you, man."

"For what?"

"For doing the right thing. Handing that intel over, rather than going after Carver yourself."

The black cloud followed me into the bathroom, dulling the white tiles. "I want to rip that sick fucker to shreds, Tango. I almost made a trip out there last night."

"What stopped you?"

I stared at my reflection, roughing a hand over my jaw. I needed a shave, but Tuuli seemed to like the rough texture, and damn how I wanted her to keep on liking me. "A goddamn little bunny. That's what stopped me."

"She's no bunny. Haven't you figured that out by now?"

Yeah. I had.

"Anything new on Erik?"

"Guy's a ghost. Cell's inactive. No online activity. Bank accounts haven't been touched. Got eyes on his parents, as well as anyone he's ever so much as blinked at. Fucker is smart, I'll give him that," I said, heading back into the bedroom.

"We'll get him. Feds are involved now. He'll turn up one way or another."

I looked at the clock. "I know, T. He will." And fuck, I hoped I'd be the one to find him first. "I gotta go. Talk to ya later."

I ended the call, dropped my ass to the mattress, and shoved my feet into a pair of black socks. Jeans next. Then boots.

Sunday. Fuck. Nausea rolled through me.

I love you, son.

Three deep breaths and I pushed to my feet, forcing the voices away, focusing on Tuuli. One goddamn hour. I could handle one hour. Fuck. Fuck. Fuck. I wiped sweat from my brow and forced one foot in front of the other, anxious as fuck, but grateful for another day. I had to seize every opportunity, make every moment with her count. I had to show her what I couldn't verbalize. I had to let her know that she was worth fighting for.

Tuuli

You're a woman worth fighting for.

My new mantra.

I studied my reflection, smiling, read the note Tito had left on the mirror, then made my way outside.

Birds celebrated the blue sky and bright sunshine with noisy songs, and the trees seemed to stand taller, arms raised in gratitude. I wanted to join them.

Nose to the sky, I inhaled, welcoming the burst of cool morning air into my lungs, allowing the fragrant new blooms to bombard my senses.

When I brought my gaze back down to Earth, the formidable figure standing in wait knocked all that fresh oxygen clean out of my system.

Tito leaned against his Mustang, one booted foot crossed over the other. He wore a light silver dress shirt tucked into a pair of dark jeans. Both hands were shoved into his front pockets, and when I caught his appreciative gaze, the smile that broke loose across his scruffy face made my heart burst with a thousand tiny explosions.

He quickly set his expression back to stern, then came my way, hands fisted at his sides, strides unhurried. Even without his signature cloak, the man was beautifully intimidating—a thousand feet tall, a mile wide, and unfaltering in his brutal confidence.

Thump. Thump. Thump. The banging in my chest was painful.

My guts begged me to run to him. My feet remained glued to the ground.

"Goddamn, you give the sunshine a run for its money." His arms coiled around me, pinning mine to my sides with a hug so tight I feared my infrastructure would crumble. I was left hanging, my feet dangling at his shins while he swung me around once, kissed my cheek, then lowered me back to the ground.

"I missed you," he whispered, lacing our fingers and leading me to the passenger side of the car.

I'd missed him, too.

He waited for me to settle into the leather seat before closing the door.

I had no words. No breath. Not one coherent thought other than, *I love this man.*

He backed out of the driveway, lips pressed tight, knuckles white.

The thought of him as a helpless child at the hands of a monster who called himself a priest made my eyes well.

Tito shot me a quick glance, then focused ahead. "Hey. You okay?"

"You're taking me to church."

"I am."

"Why?"

His eyes never left the road. "Because you're my girl."

"But you hate church. And I understand why you don't want to go, and I would never want you to feel like you have to do this. Ever."

"I'll deal. Don't worry about me."

I couldn't swallow past the gooey ball of emotion stuck mid-esophagus, choking me, causing my eyes to fill with pesky liquid.

I love this man.

He loves me, too.

I managed to croak a pathetic thank you, then focused my attention out the window because if I let those tears fall, every other part of me would crumble to dust.

The church service was beautiful, even more so with Tito by my side. He held my hand for an hour and ten minutes, not letting go until I was safely tucked back into his car. Yes, he was tense, and yes, I could tell his mind had been elsewhere through most of the sermon. But he was with me. He was there, for me.

"Thank you."

"For what?"

"For last night. For this morning." For always being there. For knowing when I needed him, I left unsaid.

Actions speak louder than words.

Tito's actions were a roadmap leading straight to the wild, bleeding heart hidden deep in his battered soul.

I wanted to ask him, *why me?* I wanted to ask about his childhood. His parents. I wanted to know what happened to the priest who abused him. I wanted to know what made him tick.

His hands tightened around the steering wheel like he could read my mind, like he was bracing for more questions, more demands. A kiss for a secret. A confession for my time. A truth for my heart.

I had no doubt he would do his best to meet any ultimatum I threw his way.

I wouldn't push. *Not today.* Maybe never again. I was a woman worth fighting for, but Tito was worth fighting for, too. As much as I was. Maybe more. Maybe no one had ever fought for him. He'd fought for me since the day we met.

He has to break before he can heal.

I was no longer wholly convinced that was the case.

I wanted Tito. The whole of him. The parts of him. Whatever he could offer.

So, I didn't ask him any of the things I wanted to know. Instead, I said, "You are so fucking beautiful."

His face broke into an infectious grin. "Did you just say fuckin'?"

There was nothing more gut-wrenching in the world than Tito's smile.

Tito

Damn. That smile would be the death of me. And when she laughed? I could touch the fucking moon.

When we pulled onto the street, she cleared her throat and announced, "I'm going to sign up for classes this fall at the community college. I've already talked to Slade about it. She told me she'd work around my school schedule, so I can work as little or as much as I need."

Tuuli surrounded by horny college assholes. Fuck. That damn organ in my chest beat with the force of a jackhammer. I wanted to drag her to my castle and lock her away, keep her all to myself. Instead, I smiled and said, "I'm proud of you."

Swear to Christ, her face turned twenty different shades of red.

I drove her home and waited on the couch while she changed. When she came out of the bedroom, rocking those rosy cheeks, and swaying hips, I wasted no time.

"Can I kiss you?"

"Yes," she complied, too fast, and too damn breathless.

"No," I chided, motioning her to come closer. "That's not how it works anymore."

Her brows pinched "What?"

"The game we've been playing."

"Oh." A lazy grin appeared and she moved closer, stopping when she stood between my spread legs.

"Can I kiss you?" I asked again.

"Tell me something I don't know about you. Something big."

"I never went to college," I confessed, and continued before losing courage. "When you go, I'm afraid you'll meet someone new. Someone who'll give you more than I can, someone who isn't fighting demons from their past."

All the joy drained from her face and she gripped my chin, fast and hard like a mother scolding a child. "I don't care about your past. I know what kind of man you are now, and that's all that matters to me." She pinched harder, moving to straddle my thighs, holding my gaze with fierce resolve. "I want you, Tito Moretti. And I take back what I said before, about needing all of you. I was wrong." She pinched her lips together, swallowing, searching my eyes. "If you can only give me parts, that's more than I could ever ask for. Because even the smallest piece of you is more precious than the whole of anyone I've ever known."

Until that moment, words meant little to me. Until she spoke up with that strong, unwavering voice, her head held high, her eyes locked on mine, not once hiding or retreating, words had never held any power.

Right then? Fuuuuuck.

Tuuli's words sliced my resolve to shreds. Everything, every damn, hard-headed, bullshit idea I'd had about love, and forever, and sharing a life with someone was swept up in the storm of her blue eyes, tossed in the turbulent gusts of her spirit, and spit back at my feet, lifeless, powerless.

All at once, I was angry and desperate. Gutted. I rolled us over, pinning her beneath me.

Arms trembling, I hovered, inches from her face. "You can't take those words back once you say them. Do you understand? I've given you space. I've done my best to stay away because that's what you asked. But if you say those words, if you say you're ready to take me as I am, whatever parts I'm capable of giving, you have to mean them. Because if you walk away..." The bullshit that had collected and hardened over the years, the wall of devastation and rage I'd built, that wall exploded, and fuck was it painful, and fuck, I didn't want her see me break but damn if I didn't fall into her chest and lose my shit.

"I won't survive that devastation, baby. I won't. So, mean it when you say those words to me."

Tuuli didn't speak. She raised her mouth to mine. With lips, and body, and whispered promises, she sealed our fucking fate.

CHAPTER 15

Tito

"YOU STAYING AWHILE?" Tuuli asked, tying her apron around her waist.

"No. Headed to the mansion. Got some things to take care of. See you tonight?" I hated every inch between us.

"See you tonight, Grim," she said, heel bouncing on the floor, chin down, eyes soft and lifted to mine.

"Bye, Bunny."

She stood at the counter, face flushed, smile shy and appreciative, drawing my attention again to those gorgeous lips.

I wanted her mouth, so damn bad.

My ticker kicked. I really needed to go. But damn, she deserved a better goodbye than what I'd offered.

"I need to kiss you," I said, stepping close enough to feel her body buzz. "Hurry. Ask me."

"Ask you?" Her brows quirked in confusion and she leaned back against the counter as if she needed the solidity. Then those big blue eyes smiled up at me. "Tell me something I don't know about you. Something big."

I attacked. An anaconda securing its next meal, coiling my arms, lifting her high. Lips to her ear, I whispered, "I once hacked the Department of Defense." I took that mouth the way she deserved, the way I needed, and gave her a goodbye she would never forget.

Her arms snapped around my neck. Her body arched. She whimpered, a fucking sexy low moan that shot adrenaline straight to my cock. Fuck. The girl kissed like she wanted to crawl inside my skin and settle there.

I lowered her back to the ground, bending to keep our connection. She didn't break the lip lock. I cursed into her mouth and pulled away. And then that damn little bunny curled her fingers around the waistband of my jeans and pulled me closer like she wasn't ready to let go. And I wanted—needed—more than anything to drag her away and get lost for months in that sweet little body.

Her chest rose and fell, moist lips parting. "See you tonight. Don't be late." Then she released me, turned, and sauntered through the swinging double doors like she hadn't just taunted a starving beast.

Goddamn.

I couldn't help the cheesy-as-fuck grin that accompanied me through the dining room, out the doors, and across the lot to my car.

A grin that disappeared the moment I spied a like-minded monster, straddling a mean ass Harley, having words with Tango.

I reached them in time to hear Dane say, "Voltolini is dead. The deal he made with my brothers is null and void. We're taking Banshee territory. I'm only relaying this information out of respect. For now, Whisper Springs will remain neutral, but we will pass through when necessary."

Tango looked ready to murder, head cocked, fists clenched tight. "No fucking way. You're not bringing Slayer shit through my town."

"You ain't got a choice, pretty boy," Dane countered, looking nothing but relaxed. "No cartel army to back you up this time."

"Reynolds." I raised my chin to the bearded biker.

He didn't take his eyes off Tango, but grunted back, "Moretti."

Tango dropped his head, defeated, then scrubbed a hand through his hair. "That all you come here for?"

Dane tugged a hand-rolled out of his cut and lit the bastard, making Tango wait while he enjoyed a drag. "Christian Brotherhood of Faith is holding a week-long rally."

"We're aware."

"Banshees are attending. We're striking in two days."

"Jesus Fucking Christ." Tango paced. Spit. "You're gonna start a war."

"They started the war when they stole one of ours."

"Payback. For the girl." I knew retribution was coming. Hadn't expected it to take so long.

"I'm not okay with this," Tango added, his opinion falling on deaf ears.

Dane stared at my cousin like he was nothing more than a gnat. "You don't get a say."

Guy was right. We no longer had Voltolini to back us up. We were nothing against the Satan's Slayers.

Still, I could see Tango's gears grinding, so I stepped in. "That all?"

"No." Dane's glare finally met mine. "Found your boy."

My BPM spiked. "Erik Meyer?"

He blew a smoke ring. "Banshees have been giving him shelter."

My palms twitched. "Where is he now?"

"North of town. About forty-five minutes out. Off the grid. He's attending the rally. Word is, Carver is stepping down; Erik's taking the throne. I figured you might enjoy watching us bury him before that happens."

No hesitation. "I'm in."

Dane nodded. "We leave now."

"Not a problem."

He dropped his smoke, leaving it to burn, and threw a leg over his bike. "Hope you can keep up."

"Tito." Tango toed dirt over the smoking butt. "You have no reason to go. Slayers aren't gonna let him live. Keep your hands clean."

Fuck that shit. Erik Meyer put hands on my girl. The monster in the crisp, clean suit hurt children. Bastard was gonna bleed. "Clean hands are for pretty boys."

Dane snorted.

I wasted no time on goodbyes. Dane's ride rumbled. I jogged to my car, ignoring the *fucks* coming from Tango, pulled up my killer playlist, and readied for war, the darkness already descending.

Tuuli

The darkness descended like an omen, closing around me, its whispered warnings stealing my breath as I watched the live feed through the television screen.

"Jeremy Carver, leader of The Christian Brotherhood of Faith Church, was found dead this morning at his Rockypoint home."

The reporter stood at the guarded entrance to The Christian Brotherhood of Faith Compound.

"One eye-witness stated, and I quote, 'It was gruesome and inhumane, and I can't imagine what kind of monster would do this to another human being.'" The reporter then continued, "Authorities have seized the one-hundred-acre compound."

I muted the sound. In the background, past the main field, red lights flashed. My mom's house was on the other side of that field.

My mother. Oh, God. She had to be okay. They hadn't mentioned her once in any of the reports.

I dialed her number again. No answer.

I texted again. No response.

I sunk deeper into the sofa cushions, shivering despite the warm temperature.

Where was Tito?

I dialed his cell for the tenth time. Nothing. I see-sawed between worry and anger. He hadn't met me at the diner the night before. No phone call. No text.

A knock sent me flying off the couch and sprinting toward the door in hopes that a pair of strong arms and stormy eyes waited on the other side.

Slade greeted me, still in her uniform. "Hey."

"Hi," I said, breathless, anxious. "What's up?"

"You watchin' the news?"

I nodded, thankful for the distraction. "Im worried about my mom. She isn't answering her phone."

"Well." She pushed past me, not waiting for an invitation. "You don't have to worry alone." Like she knew my soul, Slade pulled me against her, hugging tight and fierce, giving exactly what I needed.

God, she was an awesome boss. And landlord.

And friend.

"My life is such an ugly, embarrassing mess," I mumbled into her shirt.

She didn't respond. But she did drop her arms and scoot me toward the kitchen, where she proceeded to make us each a mug of coffee.

I fell into the chair.

She scooted into the seat opposite mine. "Let me tell you about ugly and embarrassing..."

The coffee warmed my insides, while Slade spilled her guts across the small kitchen table. She gave me the details of her upbringing, and how she came to own the diner at such a young age, how Tango had broken her heart years ago, and the desperate things she had done to protect Rocky. She spoke mostly about forgiveness and fighting for the people you love.

There was no judgment. No pity. I spilled my secrets, too. The abuse. The boys. I showed her my tattoo. Told her the truths Jonas had unearthed about my mother and her kidnapping.

"I'm sorry." Slade reached a hand across the table, covering mine, and giving it a squeeze. "Have you talked to your mother about any of this?"

"I can't get ahold of her. I've been calling and calling. Leaving messages," I said, choking back a sob. "She's probably still mad that I kicked her out of the diner."

Now that Jeremy was dead, I feared she would be fair game to the men of the church. I had to tamper those thoughts or I'd lose my mind.

"I need to know if she's okay."

Slade glanced at the television. "By the looks of things, nobody is getting anywhere near that property for a while." She snapped her head my direction, eyes big and bright. "I bet Tito could track her phone."

My stomach sank. "I don't know where he is. He hasn't answered my calls either."

"Oh," she said, slumping into her chair. "Tango was up pacing all night. Said Tito was being a jackass but wouldn't give me details." Slade chewed her thumbnail, then smacked the table. "What about Roger? He might know something."

Why hadn't I thought of that?

I tapped my cell and pulled up the one number I never thought I'd have to call.

Roger Caldwell answered immediately. "Tuuli."

My voice broke, "Roger."

"Everything okay? Did he hurt you?"

Punch to the gut. "No. God, no." Why would he ask that?

He cleared his throat. A child laughed in the background. A squeal. More giggles.

"I'm sorry to bother you so late. It's just—"

"You're watching the news," he cut in, his voice apologetic.

"I'm worried about my mom. She isn't answering my calls. I was hoping you knew someone, or maybe you could...I don't know."

"I'll see what I can find out. I've got buddies at the Rockypoint Precinct. Hold tight, though. They've got their hands full right now. I might not know anything until morning."

Morning was too far away, but what choice did I have?

"Thank you, Roger."

I had nothing left to do but wait.

Tito

I should have waited longer. My head was still fucked, lost to chaos, the adrenaline high. I should have stayed away. But I needed my girl.

The Stop was bustling. Alive with animated chatter, humming with energy.

I searched the room. A sticky-faced toddler occupied my usual table, finger painting the formica in shades of oatmeal and orange juice.

Margie threw a, "Morning, Tito," over her shoulder as she passed, balancing three plates.

"Tuuli?" I asked.

"On her break." She tilted her head toward the back.

I couldn't get to her fast enough. Like some addict suffering withdrawals, I'd been edgy, and irritable, nauseous, and every muscle in my body ached, jonesing for my Tuuli fix.

Slade's office was the first door I passed. Hand poised to knock, I paused when I heard muffled voices. Angry voices. Slade's being the loudest. "Well, Dane doesn't like you. Let me talk to him. I'll make sure he keeps the Slayers out of town."

Followed by a, "Fuck that shit. You're not going anywhere near the psychopath."

I backed away and headed for the break room, breathing deep, my nerves snapping like a million live wires. Through the half-open door, I had a straight shot of the view inside. All five-foot-nothing of my bunny leaned against the sink, raised on her toes to get a good look in the mirror. My head spun. Chest thumped. All the weight, all the goddamn darkness, all the mayhem spinning through my head faded, and I took a long overdue breath, a much-needed pause, and like a goddamn stalker, I watched from the shadows.

Tuuli studied her reflection, scrutinizing her red-rimmed, swollen eyes. Fuck. She'd been crying.

Did I cause those tears?

I sure as hell didn't want to be the cause of her pain, but I'd be a liar if I didn't acknowledge the morbid swell in my ego thinking that someone would cry over my sorry ass.

Her brows pinched. She picked up her phone and looked at the screen. Bit her lip. Cocked her hip. Tapped a message with her thumb.

My cell vibrated in my pocket. I stepped away from the door to read the screen.

Plz let me know UR ok.

I had ignored her calls and texts. Jackass move, but I couldn't have an angel in my head when I had butchery on my mind.

Last night had been a cluster fuck.

Erik hadn't been where Dane had said he would be. But we'd found something worse. Much worse. And where Dane had seemed to have no problem stomaching the scene we'd interrupted, I'd lost my fucking mind. Took three Slayers to pull me out of that cabin, but not before I'd fed one sick pedophile his own cock.

I looked down at my trembling hands. The swollen, gnarled knuckles. Ruined, sinful, dirty hands. Why were they shaking?

Dark images flashed through my mind. Children's tears. Vacant stares. Hollow souls. Wrinkled, old eaters of innocence. So much skin.

I love you son. You love me, too, don't you?

Darkness slithered, closing in. I couldn't get swallowed again. I needed light.

I shoved into the room, greeted with a gasp. Her phone clattered in the sink. Everything numbed.

Stalking closer, I made sure I had her full attention.

My chest ached, stretched to its limit. Palms twitchy, throat dry. I breached her personal space, making it my own, and let the words loose, giving her my soul, whispering, "I need you. I'm broken, and I need you to fix me." I swallowed her response with a kiss, stealing her beauty, her peace, cleansing my dirty spirit the only way I knew how.

Mouth to mouth, I walked her backward until there was nowhere to go, then slapped my palms to the wall above her head, pressing close, allowing no room for escape or pause.

The little bunny kissed me back, clawing my chest, curling her fingers around my neck, crawling up my body like a goddamn monkey, clinging with arms and legs. Feeding my soul with lips and moans. Washing away all the damn ugly.

Darkness loomed at my back while my beast roared for release. I tugged at Tuuli's shirt, pulling it above her head, her arms rising with it, and I held her there, pinned against the cold brick wall, taking my fill.

The room was quiet, the urgency a deafening, primal roar. I released her arms and reached behind my waist to unhook her legs.

She fought me, and damn if my rock-hard cock didn't do a painful happy dance. I broke the kiss and gripped her warm cheeks, holding her face a hairsbreadth from mine. "I need those pants off. Now."

"No. Not here. We—"

"Off. Now."

It took her all of two seconds to kick off the shoes and wiggle out of her khakis. Two heartbeats more, and she'd freed my cock, gripped it with her small fingers, and started slow and steady, stroking away the ache.

Her cheeks blazed a brilliant shade of red. "We don't have much time."

No, we did not, especially with her hands on my dick. I grabbed her thighs and hoisted her to my waist. When she gripped my shoulders, locked those creamy legs around my ass, and skin met skin, my control slipped, and I shoved into her with one hard thrust, sinking deep.

Fuck, she was so goddamn light in my arms. I hated that she trusted me when I was so dangerous, but fuck, I loved that she gave herself so freely, so carelessly.

All I wanted, all I needed, was pinned, half-naked, between me and the wall. Sweet hell, how I wanted to love her, and protect her, and trust her with every one of my broken pieces. I slipped into my dark place and lacking the strength to fight him off, let the monster free. With each roll of my hips, I gave her everything. All my hurt, all my pain, every fucking regret, every God-forsaken, soiled, dirty piece of my past.

"Why do you want me? I'm gonna destroy you. Like everything in my life, I'll ruin you."

Tuuli

Ruin me. Destroy me. Tear me to shreds. Bring it on.

Yes, he held my heart in his powerful fist. Yes, he had the power to crush that tiny organ to dust. Didn't matter. Because I knew every time I shattered, he would collect all the pieces and put me back together.

My back slammed against the brick, again and again. His thrusts were violent, breaths ragged, words filthy.

We were not making love. Not even close. Tito was purging. Hurting. He was angry and raw, and I was merely the punching bag absorbing his blows.

I didn't cry out. I didn't stop him. I hated his pain, but I loved that he used me to purge. My back burned, but I wanted more. I wanted all his unbridled, honest emotion.

Strong fingers dug into my ass. I bit my lip to silence the scream. He slapped the wall above my head with his free hand before gripping the hair at my nape and pulling, forcing my head back, exposing my neck. He buried his face there, his breaths a thunderous roar in my ear.

His body tensed, then trembled, and with brutal thrusts he came, crushing me with his hips, clinging to me like I was his last tether to Earth. He breathed, and squeezed, and vibrated against me.

It was then I noticed the bruises. The cut lip. The dark circles under his eyes.

His unshaved mug, hot and scratchy, was a balm beneath my fingertips. I held him face-to-face, asking without words, *what just happened?*

I'd never seen eyes so dark and hollow. The Tito I knew wasn't the man staring back at me. I traced the deep lines across his forehead. He gave nothing.

"Tito." I kissed the corner of his mouth. "Come back to me, please."

He blinked, jaw muscles working under my hands. "Did I hurt you?" He dropped me like I'd scorched him, then held me at arms' length, stormy eyes inspecting me.

I shook my head.

"Fuck. Fuck!" Tito turned his back, yanking his jeans over his ass, then grabbed a wad of paper towels. He cleaned between my legs with gentle strokes and trembling hands, then helped me step into my clothes while I steadied myself on his shoulders.

So many questions. So many things I wanted to say. The words gathered so fast, they clogged my throat before making their exit.

"Tuuli..." He backed away, gaze dropping to the ground. "I—"

"What happened?" I interrupted, grabbing his wrists to halt his retreat. "Where'd you go just now?"

Agony shaded his features, tearing my guts out. "I never should've come here. Not when my head is such a mess."

"Don't say that. Please. You can always come to me."

"You weren't safe." He dragged swollen hands through his hair. "Fuck. I could've hurt you."

"But you didn't."

He gnawed his bottom lip, then paced the room, hands to hips. Back and forth. Breathing deep.

"Tito. You're scaring me."

He stopped. Dropped his hands, his shoulders, his chin. Three deep breaths and his eyes met mine. "Can I kiss you?"

He didn't want a kiss. He wanted to talk. Confess. Our game was the only way he knew how.

I played along. "Tell me something I don't know about you. Something big."

Another deep breath. Tito nodded as if he needed to convince himself to speak, then lifted those dark eyes to mine, holding me captive. "When I was eleven, I killed the priest who raped me."

The Earth slipped away. I stumbled backward, the brick wall catching my fall. "What?"

I'll kill Jeremy Carver and burn that church to the ground.

The room spun. A sharp pain twisted my insides.

Jeremy Carver found dead. Gruesome and inhumane.

"Bunny. Say something." He reached for me.

I slapped his hand away.

A priest? He killed a priest? God, he'd tried to warn me, that morning on the running trail. *My secrets will hurt you. My truths will be the end of us.*

"Baby. Don't shut down on me," he begged. "You said you wanted every dirty piece of me, remember?"

Oh, God. Oh. God. His bruises. His torn-up hands. No. No, no, no. "You killed Jeremy."

His head snapped up. "What?"

"Was it you?" A vicious rumble started in my chest, rising, rising. Spilling over.

"Jesus, Tuuli. No." He shook his head, backing away. "You can't think I'd—"

My palm met his cheek, the crack loud and grotesque. "You killed Jeremy Carver!" I screamed, releasing all the ugly, vile emotions I'd stockpiled, regretting my outburst the second I made contact.

His head jerked to the left. The air turned frigid.

Oh, God. I wanted to scream and cry. Throw punches. Make him hurt like I hurt because he was killing me. Why would he go after Jeremy? Why would he risk everything? Risk us? Why?

Tito dragged his tongue along his lower lip, chest rising and falling, fist clenched. I waited, razor-spiked blood pounding through my skull, the air roaring between us, thunderous and devastating.

"Tito," I whispered, hating the disconnect, desperate to understand his motives. "Why?"

He turned, dark eyes aimed over my head and moved past me, dragging all my oxygen with him. I couldn't watch. I couldn't look away. I couldn't wait for him to leave. I couldn't let him go.

He reached the door. His body coiled.

With a roar so loud, guttural, and pained I felt it in my toes, he threw his fist through the heavy wood, effectively leaving a hole in my chest.

Then he was gone.

CHAPTER 16

Tito

"GET UP." A BLACK painted toenail dug into my ribs.

"Nah, I'm good." My words slurred, the right side of my face numb and uncooperative. I could always count on Aida for a good fist-to-face therapy session. Princess had a deadly left hook and a knack for knocking demons loose.

I stretched on my back, the training mat a perfect cushion to lay my head and lick my wounds.

Aida stood over me, ignoring my glare, then planted a bare foot on my chest. "So, you confess to killing a priest, but when Tuuli asks if you murdered that Carver fucker, you get butt-hurt and put a hole through the wall?"

"Something like that."

"Fucking idiot." She made a tsk sound, cocking her head. "Have you talked to her yet?"

"No."

"Why?"

Good question. "It's better this way."

"Oh, grow a pair, will ya?" She dug her heel into my chest, shaking me. "Stop being a whiny bitch."

"Get off me," I growled, shoving at her shin.

"No." The pressure on my torso increased.

"Princess. I'm not in the mood."

"Don't care."

Aida knew damn well I could take her down with a flick of my wrist, but she pushed anyway, confident, and rightly so, that I'd never do a fucking thing to hurt her.

"Go to her now and make things right." She slid her foot to my throat and slowly shifted her weight, a reminder that she could end my life were she so inclined.

"You two about done?" Tucker's deep voice boomed through the room. "Mom and Dad will be here soon."

Lucia squealed in her papa's arms, bouncing and pumping her fists when she spied her mother.

I almost laughed at the sight of Tucker and the baby. He wore khaki utility shorts and a faded Toby Keith concert tee. Lucia donned beige leggings with the same damn shirt as her pops but in mini size. Both of them wore baseball caps with the Slade Trucking logo on the front.

Aida dropped low, her knees bracing my shoulders, her full ass resting on my gut, then gripped my chin and pinched hard, cutting me down with her cold, hard death stare. "She loves you, Tits. She's no stranger to violence and death. Tell her who you are." She fell forward, dropped a kiss on my forehead, and hopped to her feet. "Give her a chance to decide if she can live with your past or not."

It was the *not* that scared the shit out of me. I stared at the ceiling, fighting a shiver.

What if the church girl couldn't live with a reaper?

I poked at the sore spot on my lip, rolled to my stomach, and pushed to hands and knees.

Tucker surrendered the baby to Aida, kissed them both, and watched with a dumbass smile on his face as they disappeared down the hall.

He turned to me, wearing a judgmental glare. "You look like shit. And I don't mean the bruises on your face."

I huffed. "Been a rough couple of nights."

"I know." Hands to hips, he dropped his head. "You need to go home. Get some sleep. Get your head on straight."

My head was fucking fine. My heart? An entirely different story.

I snagged my shoes and car keys off the floor.

"Tito…"

"Yeah?" I asked over my shoulder, hand on the doorknob.

"She your forever girl?"

Six months ago, I would've laughed at such a ridiculous question. Now? No hesitation. "Yes."

Tucker laughed. "Then it's only right she knows. About your past, and about everything we're doing here." He gestured around the room.

"You okay with that?" Tucker's *everything* was nothing compared to my *everything*. Yeah, he had a history, but his list of dirty deeds was minute compared to the sins I'd racked up over the years.

He merely shrugged. "I've got a soft spot for that girl. We all do."

My ticker hammered my ribcage. "What if I tell her everything and she runs?"

Bastard shot me a cocky grin. "You already know the answer to that question."

I did. If she ran, I'd give chase. I'd found my heartbeat. Even if I wanted, I couldn't let her go.

Tuuli

I couldn't let him go. Even if I wanted. Even after his confession.

I wasn't angry. I wasn't hurt. Oddly, I wasn't confused, either. He had killed his abuser. Was it self-defense? Or premeditated? Either way, he'd taken human life, and I should've been frightened. Only, I wasn't scared. I was curious. And if I were being honest with myself, I wasn't surprised.

I thought of the night Rafael Turner had taken Aida and me to that awful hotel room. I had seen the bloodbath. I remembered the look in Tito's eyes as he stood amidst the overturned furniture, the gore, and Rafael's lifeless body. He was stoic and calm. We'd made eye contact, briefly, as Tango had carried me out of the room. I'd known Tito was dangerous then. I'd known all along. I'd liked that about him, his fearlessness, fierceness. His willingness to do what needed to be done, no matter the depravity.

I understood why he didn't want to tell me his secrets. I loved that he wanted to protect me from his sins.

My entire life, I'd witnessed vile, unforgivable acts, and stood silent out of fear and shame. Understandable when I'd been a child. But I was no longer a child. I had no excuse for not speaking out. For not ending Jeremy Carver's abuse. No excuse.

True, I would wear a heavy blanket of guilt for the rest of my days. Such was human nature. Tito, too, wore his own shackles of remorse. I understood. More than most.

Difference was, I understood that I was forgiven. Tito did not. How could anyone with a conscience carry such a burden and not collapse under its weight?

A loud *bang, bang, bang* made me jump. Tito. No one else knocked with such authority. I smiled despite my nerves and took three steadying breaths before opening the door.

Tito stood stone still. Dear Lord, those eyes. Dark and stormy, threatening and promising all at once. "I'm an idiot."

I sighed, my heart battering my chest like I'd run a marathon.

Warm hands gripped my hips. Weary, pleading eyes captured my soul. "Can I kiss you?"

Tears threatened and I curled my lips between my teeth, fighting for composure.

He pressed closer, his arms curling around my waist. I circled mine around his neck, marveling in his solid stature, leaning closer, trusting he would bear my weight.

"Tell me something I don't know about you. Something big."

He walked me backward, kicked the door closed, and pressed his lips to my ear. "The priest? He used the words you want to hear. Those three words you deserve. He used them every time he hurt me." His breath hitched, fingers digging into my flesh. "Those words that are supposed to be precious? He ruined them. Made them ugly and disgusting." His arms tightened, holding me upright, predicting correctly that I would buckle with his confession. "And Bunny, what I feel for you is infinite, it's solid, it's painful, and I'm afraid to ruin it with those words."

Burying my face in his shirt, I let the tears fall. Tito soothed me with tender kisses.

"I wish you wouldn't cry, Bunny."

I looked up to find his eyes wet with threatening tears.

"A million lifetimes have passed since then."

"Why?" I asked, choking on the emotion. "Why did you kill him?"

"So he couldn't hurt anyone else," was his candid answer. A truth I believed to my soul because that was the stripped down, bare bones, unpretentious man who I knew and loved. A protector.

"You were a child." I thought of all the boys who had passed through Jeremy's office. All the lives he'd destroyed.

All the abuse I could have prevented had I only been brave enough, strong enough to speak up. To tell someone, anyone.

I hadn't been strong enough. But Tito had.

"Is that why you killed Jeremy? So he couldn't hurt anyone else?"

His arms fell to his sides and he stumbled back a step, eyes darkening.

"I didn't do it. And I can't tell you how much it kills me that you assumed..." Gaze aimed over my shoulder, he dropped his chin, shook his head. Huffed. "Six months ago, I wouldn't have hesitated to take him out. Only I wouldn't have left any evidence."

Oh, God. What did that mean? "And now?" I asked, unsure if I wanted clarification.

"Now? Now I have this bright blinding light challenging my dark urges, chasing them into the shadows. I've done horrible things. I've earned my place in Hell. And I wanted to drag as many sick bastards as I could down with me. But since the night Tango carried you out of that bloody hotel room, and you looked at me like you could see right through me, I haven't needed to...Fuck." He scrubbed his face, then dropped his hands. "I just want to be worthy. I need..." He cupped my face, those strong fingers trembling, and pressed his forehead to mine. "I need you to have a little faith in me." His lips met my fevered skin, and moments passed before he pulled away. "I need to show you something. Can we go for a drive?"

I could've denied Tito. I could've walked away. Started over. Free from The Brotherhood. Free from Tito's demons. He was offering me two choices: take my hand, accept me for who I am and never look back, or walk away, free and clear of all the ugliness. When I stared into those pleading, weary eyes, my whole body warmed, my soul sang, and I knew there was no choice. Tito was the only home I'd ever need.

I slid my hands down his body and laced our fingers. "Let's go."

The smile that cracked his face was hands-down the most beautiful sight I'd ever seen.

Tito

What a beautiful thing to watch Tuuli put the pieces together, her wide eyes sharpening, then filling with tears. "The Rest Area Reaper?" she asked, never breaking her gaze from the images of the little girl on the screen.

A response wasn't necessary. My brave beauty had figured it out.

"You and Tucker?"

I nodded, gnawing a rut across my bottom lip.

She smiled, watching the screen, nails tapping an erratic rhythm on the stainless-steel desktop, heels bouncing against the cement floor. After excruciating minutes, she turned to me. "This is where you were the night Jeremy was killed?"

"Yes."

The screen cast a soft, eerie glow across her face, sharpening her angelic features. I gripped the sides of my chair to keep from pulling her into my lap.

"The mansion isn't for troubled teens, is it?"

"Not exactly."

"Those weren't business trips you took with Tucker. You were rescuing girls."

"Right."

Dropping her hands to her lap, she turned to face me. "Why didn't you tell me?"

"It wasn't my secret to tell."

Tuuli slumped into her chair, head falling back, fingers linked across her stomach. She swiveled her chair side to side and seemed to contemplate the ceiling. I waited, palms sweaty, gut churning, while she processed.

"Rest Area Reaper," she mumbled.

I sunk deeper into my own seat. "Fuckin' hate that name."

She shrugged. "It's fitting."

"It would be fitting if I was allowed to send those pedophiles to Hell," I grumbled, before contemplating the weight of my words.

Her head snapped up, eyes worried. "Do you want to?"

My intestines knotted tighter, vicious heat coiling through me. "I won't lie. I want nothing more than to make them suffer before burying them."

"Have you?" she asked, spine straightening.

"No."

"There've been others though, haven't there? The priest wasn't the only person you've killed."

Fuck. I didn't want to have this conversation. "There have been others. It was my job."

"For Aida's father?"

My ticker stopped, hackles raised. "What do you know about Aida's father?"

"That night, in the hotel, I heard Rafael talking to Aida. They talked about Luciano Voltolini."

I pretended to be amused, although my calm demeanor was nanoseconds from snapping. "I suppose you heard a lot of things that night."

She leaned forward, elbows to knees, head tilted to hold my glare. "Yes."

She'd kept the information to herself all this time.

Breathe in. *One, two, three.* Out. *One, two, three.* "So, you know who Voltolini was?"

"Everybody does," she replied. I lost her to thought for a brief moment before she scooted closer, landing her hands on my knees. "Rafael told Aida that the devil came for his family. Took them out one by one. That he was the only Marcovic left."

I swallowed a thick lump of disgust and loathing. Where the fuck was she going with this?

"The devil was you, Tito. Wasn't it?"

And there it was, the Haymaker. One swift, no-holds-barred punch. The little bunny hit me with everything she had. No more secrets. No more reveals. She'd chipped away the last layer, leaving me raw. "They were bad people, Tuuli. The worst kind."

Fuck. Fuck. Fuck. I broke out in a cold sweat. She wanted the real me. Well, there I was, sliced open, dripping all my ugly truths at her feet. "Voltolini ordered them dead. Those were his last words to me or anyone. I had to honor them."

"Why?"

"Because I owed him my life."

"Why?" She scooted closer still, no fear in her voice, no pleading in her eyes. No judgment. Only curiosity.

"Because he saved my life. Took care of everything after I choked that fuckin' pedophile priest to death on his office floor. Luciano cleaned the mess. Made the evidence disappear. Took me under his wing. Taught me to channel my anger."

"When was the last time you killed someone?"

God. Hadn't she had enough? "Rafael Turner."

"And the last time you wanted to kill someone?" she asked, unrelenting.

I pointed to the security feed. "When I found that girl with..." I couldn't continue, my nerves already stretched beyond their limit. "I beat those fuckers to near death, but I stopped."

"Why did you stop?"

I tapped at my temple. "You. Your voice in my head."

She seemed to like that answer, her fingers curling into my flesh in response.

Still, she continued, "That's not the only reason though, is it?"

I'd reached my breaking point. "No. Goddamn, Tuuli. No." I pushed away from her, my chair slamming against the wall behind me.

"Why did you stop, Tito?"

"Fuck!" I yelled, digging my palms into my temples. "I'm tired. Tired of it all. The voices in my head, the ghosts, the goddamn shame." Moisture rolled down my face. I let it fall, not ready to acknowledge my weakness. "The rage. The anger. I don't want it anymore."

Finally, she leaned back, granting a reprieve. Silence hung between us, gritty and chafing, the only sound, our heavy breaths—mine, wet and burdened, and hers, slow and controlled.

"I have a confession to make." She rested one elbow on the armrest, planting her chin in her palm.

"Yeah? What's that?" Why was my voice so goddamn raw?

"When I heard that Jeremy had been murdered, I was happy. I was so relieved that, for a brief moment, I wanted to laugh and dance around the apartment. How messed up is that? What kind of monster does that make me?" Her gaze dropped to the floor and I hoped to God it wasn't in shame.

I cleared the grit from my throat. "It makes you human."

Another long silence.

"I'm sorry about the other day in the break room."

She nodded, lifting her eyes to mine. "I know. Me, too."

"Finding that girl..." I pointed to the screen. The security feed from the kitchen showed the twelve-year-old we'd found in the cabin where Erik was supposed to be hiding. The child was currently baking chocolate chip cookies with Tucker's mother. "It took me to a dark place. Weighed me down with anger, and guilt, and pent-up energy, and the only thing I could think about was getting to you. I knew you'd wash the filth away."

"Tito," she sighed, rising from her seat and stepping between my knees.

"I get it now. I understand why you go to church." I curled my arms around her small waist, hugging her close, burying my face in her chest. "You're my church, Bunny."

"No." She leaned back and cupped my jaw. "Don't say that. I'm just a girl, every bit as broken as the boy she loves."

That word again. Love.

I love you, son.

I fought a shiver and choked on the rising bile. Fuck. If anyone deserved those words, it was my girl.

Someday, I would give them to her. Someday, I would be strong enough.

"Tell me I haven't lost you. Tell me you can live with my sins."

Tilting my face upward, she stroked her thumbs under my wet eyes. "I told you before; I know who you are *now*. That's what matters. Just please don't lie to me. Don't hide things. I need the truth. I need you to understand that I'm strong enough to deal with whatever life throws at us. Whatever comes our way, we'll work through it, okay?"

I nodded, pulling her down for a kiss. Expressing through touch what I couldn't give with words and trusting that she understood exactly how much I loved her.

Tuuli

Tito loved me. Not a doubt in my mind. He couldn't form those three simple syllables, but what were words, anyway? Sounds strung together, an archaic form of communication. Words couldn't be trusted. Words were too easily manipulated, practiced, weapons wielded, too often spewed with little thought.

Tito loved me. I knew because although he wasn't able to verbalize, I saw the truth in his eyes, the way they changed when they fell on me—softened, but sharpened, piercing and curious, and brimming with want.

Oddly, after his confession of murder, when I should have been scared, I couldn't help but feel closer to him. Safer by his side.

Sure, my morbid sense of comfort was likely because of my upbringing. The violence, the threats, the manipulation. The abuse. I'd been surrounded by dangerous men, deadly men. Men who fed off my fear, men who wielded their self-imposed power like a judge's gavel.

But my Grim? Even at his scariest, he held me at his side, never at his feet. He imposed his power only to shield me, never to control. He used his strength only to lift me high, never to beat me down.

I knew, without a doubt, that Tito Moretti, my Grim, loved me. Rare, unconditional, and undeniable love. The kind of love you risked deep-rooted morals to hold close, knowing that with time and heartache, trials and adventures, extreme highs and vicious lows, only grew stronger and more precious.

Walking away would never be an option, no matter his sins.

He leaned back, hands clasped behind his neck, his beautiful face on full display, contemplative scowl deepening his worry wrinkles. "Tell me what you're thinking."

A flurry of palpitations erupted in my chest. I studied those exotic eyes, the wrinkles framing them, the thick lashes, the way they held me captive, making my pulse race like I was at the precipice, teetering, a tiny nudge from falling, falling, falling toward something blinding, and breathtaking, and brilliant.

I made myself comfortable in his lap, hooking my arms around his waist, resting my head on his shoulder. "I'm thinking that from the very first time I laid eyes on you, Tito Moretti, I knew you were going to rip my world apart, tear out my heart, rearrange my guts, frighten me, and challenge me all in one fell swoop. But what I didn't know was that you were going to lift me so high I couldn't see the Earth below."

His chest vibrated. "What do you see now?"

"Possibilities."

"Do you see me?" he asked, one hand cupping my butt, the other, my chin.

I arched my neck to find a smile. "I see nothing but you."

His brows lifted along with the left corner of his mouth. "Do you like what you see?"

"I love what I see." I roughed my fingers through the scratchy hair on his jaw. Then asked, "What do you see?"

"I see us." He dropped a chaste kiss on my nose. "You and me against the world."

"Thank you for telling me the truth," I settled back against his chest.

His arm tightened, pulling me closer. "Thank you for not leaving."

I enjoyed the steady beat of his heart for several minutes, the lulling rise and fall of his chest. "I'm worried about my mom."

Tito shifted, clearing his throat.

"I talked to Roger today. Nobody's seen or heard from her since the morning before Jeremy died."

"Tuck told me." Tito lifted me off his lap, his spine cracking as he rose to stand. "I've put feelers out. FBI is involved now. She'll turn up."

I had to believe him because the alternative was more than my soul could handle.

"We should go," he said, bending to kiss me.

I glanced at the computer screen one last time, my heart breaking all over again. It wasn't fair that Erik was free to bully and terrorize. I hated that my silence over the years allowed more children to be hurt. I couldn't change the past. But I could atone.

"I want to help." I dusted a finger over the child's image. "I want to help care for these girls, Tito."

"Yeah?" He snagged his keys off the desk, then his wallet.

"Yes."

"We can talk to Aida and Tucker tomorrow." He grabbed my hand and led me outside. "That would be great, Bunny. We'd love having you here."

He opened the car door and waited for me to settle before closing it again. When he was comfortable in his own seat, he said, "Can I take you to my place tonight? Something I wanna show you."

Again, the fluttering in my chest. "Sure."

He navigated the long, private drive and hit the main highway leading back toward The Stop. Windows down, bass booming, we drove. I watched Tito, watching the road. Thumbs tapping. Lips moving to the lyrics. He glanced my way, a devilish, mind-numbing smirk on his face. I couldn't remember ever being happier. Together, Tito and I would beat the darkness. We would escape the spindly fingers of our past.

In the far distance, black clouds crept over the treetops.

"Looks like a storm is coming," Tito mused, glancing my way before focusing back on the path ahead.

His words cut through me like a warning.

I should have heeded that warning.

CHAPTER 17

Tuuli

THE WIND CAME FIRST, pushing the evergreens to their limit like a drill sergeant dance instructor, limbs bending and stretching beyond their breaking point. The rain followed close behind, hitching a ride on ominous black clouds, then cutting loose to flood the streets.

By the time the power went out, our last customer had fled for the safety of home. Before the first lightning strike lit the sky, we'd locked the diner up tight and called it a night.

I stood in the dark hallway, the centermost point of the building, far from any windows or doors, and listened, Tito's footsteps growing closer, my pulse racing faster with each patter of rain on the roof.

Warm, rough fingers sliced between my own before offering a reassuring squeeze. "The car is parked right outside the door. Two steps and you're in."

He led me toward the back exit, hand in hand, feeling our way through the dark. The diner seemed to shudder, sensitive to the electric, angry storm outside. My chest rattled, too, responding to both the man at my side and the lingering threat beyond the walls.

Tito's cell buzzed and he stopped to tug the phone out of his back pocket, the screen illuminating his face. His eyes met mine briefly before he answered. "Dane. This better be good news."

Eyebrows knitted, he scratched his beard, shot me another glance, then ordered me to stay put while he disappeared into the kitchen. His muffled voice rang angry through the dark, empty hall.

Minutes later, he shoved through the swinging doors and grumbled, "Change of plans."

Icy chills ripped through my skin and bones. "What's wrong?"

Joining our hands, he stepped close to me and drew a deep breath. "Erik's been spotted in town."

"Good." The weight of a thousand worries left my shoulders. I searched my handbag for my own cell, rifling through wads of paper, candy wrappers, tubes of lip gloss, and, gross, something soft and sticky. "Let's call Roger."

"We can't," he snapped, clamping his fingers around my wrist.

I paused my retrieval, dropping my phone back into the bottomless pit. "Why?"

"Because there are people who want Erik more than we do."

"Who?"

"Bad people."

My stomach protested, threatening to expel my lunch. "So, what do we do?"

"You are going to wait with Tango and Slade." He pulled me close, sliding a hand to my neck and curling his fingers in my hair. A long sigh. "I'll drive you up the hill, then I'm meeting a couple of men back down here."

I jerked free of his grip. Nothing about his idea sounded like a good plan. "And then what?"

He headed toward the exit. "Then, I help them grab Erik. I come pick you up. We have our date." The restraint in his voice was obvious. He didn't like the plan any more than I did.

Thunder struck. Rolling and rumbling, wreaking havoc through every cell in my body, quieting any protest.

Tito stepped ahead to push open the door, then looked over his shoulder. "Ready?"

No. I was not ready. I'd lived with monsters my whole life, yet I was terrified of a little storm.

"I could just stay here. Wait for you to get back. Lock myself in the office."

He chuckled, low and rumbly like the storm outside, only sexy. "Not an option, Bunny." He dropped a warm, wet kiss on my mouth, rendering me breathless, boneless, fearless. "It's safer at the house. Besides, Rocky already has the flashlights charged, and he's waiting for you before he starts with the ghost stories."

He pushed the door open. A gust of wet wind hit my face. Tito dropped my hand and shoved me out of the way with such force, I stumbled and landed on my ass, my purse flying.

With a sickening crack, Tito flew back, his head slamming into the wall behind him. He crumpled to the ground. Before I could react, a large figure blocked the doorway, then stepped over Tito like he was nothing more than a dust bunny.

I scrambled backward, deeper into the dark.

Another figure came through the door.

Heavy boots squeaked on the tile floor. Coming closer. His face was hidden in the dark, but there was no mistaking Erik's voice. "Riley. Kill that fucker."

My lungs seized, my throat closed.

"Tuuli," Tito mumbled. "Run."

Erik stalked closer. The roar between my ears grew louder.

I scrambled to my feet, slipping twice before finding my footing.

"Don't run. You'll only make it harder on yourself."

I didn't want to leave Tito, but I knew Erik. He hated losing, and if I ran, he'd chase, giving Tito a fighting chance.

Rain pounded the roof and windows, distorting sound in the dark hallway. Step by step, I moved back, feeling my way along the wall until I reached the corner. I was certain Erik could hear my desperate breaths, the loud boom, boom, boom in my chest.

"Come here, kid. Don't make this harder than it has to be."

I turned and sprinted down the hall, through the diner, smashing into the front door, my hand shaking so hard I struggled to turn the lock. The sky lit up, brightening the room. On impulse, I counted. *One, two, three, four, five.* Boom.

The door rattled against my hand. Oh, God. The storm, or Erik? I didn't know which was worse.

There's a beast inside you.

I pushed, first through my fear, then the exit, the wind jerking the door out of my grip.

I ran. Into the dark storm. I ran across the flooded lot, the water slowing me down. I lifted my legs higher, pumping my thighs until they burned.

Erik was behind me. His splashes louder, growing closer. I didn't dare look back. Only forward.

My clothes weighed a ton, sticking to my skin. The wind was against me, challenging my escape. I hit the base of the hill, thankful to be out of the puddle. I couldn't breathe, I couldn't see, but I forced one foot in front of the other.

Twice I slipped. Twice I pushed to my feet and continued.

Three more strides and I would've hit the crest of the hill. Three more steps, and maybe Tango or Slade would've heard my screams.

A mountain of wet, hard, angry muscle crashed over me, knocking me to the ground. His chest pinned my head to the wet grass, and the steady stream of water covered my face. A heavy hand splayed over the back of my head, grinding me deeper into the wet soil, suffocating, crushing.

His weight disappeared and I lifted my face, sucking in precious oxygen, coughing and sputtering rain and mud.

Allowing no time to recover, Erik flipped me to my back and laid his weight over me, pinning my legs between his own, fisting my wet hair, holding me at his mercy.

I couldn't see his face through the sheets of rain, but the rage in his voice was palpable. "You should've married me. The Brotherhood would be mine. You'd be a fucking queen."

He spit in my face, hopped to his feet, grabbed my ankle, and shouted, "You ruined everything. Useless, fucking bitch." Then he turned to drag me down the hill, back toward The Stop.

I kicked, clawed, and twisted. The wind and rain drowned my screams. I was wet. I was mud. I was dirt. Blood. Torn clothes. I was angry. I was a beast.

True, my beast was no match for Erik's strength, but I was never again going to be his victim. Never again would I concede or submit. I would fight until my last breath.

I lost my shirt halfway down the hill, along with several fingernails, and I was sure, too much skin. Still, I fought.

Erik stopped when we reached the parking lot, dropped my leg, and squatted. "You know..."

I didn't wait for him to finish. I swung my leg. My boot connected with his face, knocking him sideways, but not down.

I kicked again. Then twisted, pushing to my feet. Something struck my head, knocking me back to my knees. The world spun. My vision blurred.

Like I was nothing more than a winter jacket, Erik threw me over his shoulder, knocking the air from my lungs. I struggled to stay conscious.

He carried me back into the dark diner. Lightning brightened the sky, and I counted. *One, two, three.* Boom.

A laugh bubbled from my chest. I was about to die, and still, I was scared of the storm.

"What's so fucking funny?" Erik dropped me to my feet. My legs gave out and I slumped to the floor.

Wiping hair off my face, I lifted my chin. "I'm not scared of you."

"What?"

"You're going to kill me, and I'm not scared."

A smile evident in his voice, he snapped, "I'm not going to kill you, stupid kid."

"No?"

The bully squatted out of striking distance. "Fuck, no. Our arranged marriage was bullshit. Jeremy promised to make me his successor when you and I tied the knot, but really, he only wanted to keep me around 'cause I played his game better than anyone. I was his favorite fucking toy. Sick fucker thought he was using me? I was using him, keeping him busy with his perversions while I built my own empire behind his back. He's dead now. Feds are crawling all over the place. Time to move out of Idaho. Besides, got more lucrative dealings in the works."

"So why are you here, then? I don't matter anymore."

"Oh, this is the fun part. Found a buyer in Texas. Rich fucker. Likes his girls small and young. But when I told him you were Carver's daughter, he paid top dollar. Said he's known you since you were a baby, always had an eye on you. Didn't even matter that you're legal now. He said you still look young enough."

"You sold me?"

"I sold you. Get up." He nudged my shoulder. "Need to get on the road. It's a long drive."

So many emotions, so many thoughts tumbled through me, I couldn't make sense of anything other than defiance. "I'm not going anywhere."

"Afraid you don't have much of a choice."

I mimicked his growl, "'Afraid you're gonna have to kill me."

That earned me a slap.

He fisted my hair. Grunting, he rose to his feet and dragged me across the checkered tile floor, my thrashing nothing more than an annoyance.

When he pushed through the double doors, he froze, his fingers loosening. "What the fuck?"

I twisted and turned to look.

Despite the dire situation, the violent, morbid scene, I smiled.

Tito

She smiled. Fucking smiled. Despite the cuts, bruises, and blood, and even with her muddy, mangled hair, I'd never seen anyone, or anything, more beautiful.

"Tuuli. You okay?" The words left me on a choked groan.

Laughter bubbled from her throat. Yeah, she looked like a mad woman. Yeah, she was on her hands and knees, a dead man's fingers twisted in her hair, holding her at his mercy, but she didn't cower, she didn't cry. She laughed.

Ignoring Tuuli, Erik asked, "Where's Riley?"

I stretched my bloody knuckles, itching to rile the guy. "Which parts of him?"

"What'd you do?"

"I did what needed to be done."

The sky lit up outside, throwing another blinding flash through the diner, distorting Erik's features, exposing the demon inside.

Tuuli's eyes widened and her lips moved, counting, *one, two*. Boom.

My bunny laughed harder. Girl was losing her shit. I had to get the situation under control.

Erik crouched, pushing her head to the floor. "Don't fucking move," he ordered, untangling his fingers from her hair and stroking her head like she was a goddamn dog.

Took every ounce of control I had not to end him where he stood.

I stayed put and attempted to draw his attention away from Tuuli. "I told you, lay hands on my girl again, you'll be fishing your fingers outta the lake."

He rose to his full height, turned to me, and replied, "Told you, she was mine before she was born."

"Yeah? Explain how that works, how you think you can own any girl?"

"Bitch was bought and sold while she was still in her mama's fat belly. Now that Jeremy's dead, I own Mommy, too. Lots of men willing to pay top dollar for that pussy. I'll give every one of them a whack at her, soon as I'm finished taking my fill."

So, Erik had Tuuli's mother.

Through my periphery, I watched Tuuli crawl backward, rise, then slip through the kitchen doors, quiet as a mouse.

That's my girl. Hide.

"I have it on good authority you don't like pussy. I've seen the videos. You and Jeremy."

Idiot came at me. No plan of action. Pure hatred. Pure adrenaline. His first strike was clumsy, slowed by the weight of his wet clothes no doubt. The second hit home because I'd allowed it, giving him a sliver of hope, but I didn't strike back, not yet. Instead, I moved deeper into the hallway, drawing him farther away from Tuuli.

"You're fucking dead," Erik sputtered, coming at me again.

The dim lighting from the exit signs offered little aid. Bad for Erik, good for me. I'd always worked better in the dark. The pale giant came at me again and I struck him in the solar plexus, only enough to knock the wind out of his sails, and he stumbled backward. I struck again, a chin tap, holding back. I wanted him conscious but hurting.

His nose was my next target. I only struck hard enough to break the cartilage. Let him know I wasn't fucking around. His hands whipped to his face, leaving his midsection wide open. I took another shot, landing a body blow. The piece of shit crumpled, landing right where I wanted him, at my feet. At my fucking mercy.

The light flickered. Came on. Went dark again.

Tuuli pushed through the door holding Charlie's rifle to her goddamn shoulder. "Where's my mom?"

Erik looked up, pure, murderous hatred rolling off him in waves. "I should've killed you the night I ended Jonas." He wheezed through his pain. "I should've fucked your ass and slit your throat."

Her gasp echoed, bouncing off the brick walls. "It was you?"

Fuck. Fuck. The situation was turning to shit. "Tuuli. Put the gun down."

"Back off, Tito," Tuuli ordered, voice booming, gun aimed at Erik's midsection.

"Where is my mom?" she asked again, deep and threatening.

"Won't matter." Two deep breaths. "By the time you find her, there'll be nothing left to save."

Crack! The butt of the rifle hit Erik's forehead. He screamed, loud and shrill, arms raised to shield his head.

His cries turned to laughter. Crazed. "The Banshees have her. Jesus Christ. I'll fucking kill you."

"Not if I kill you first." She raised the gun again to her shoulder, aimed, and took a deep breath.

"Tuuli. Don't do this."

"He'll never stop hurting people."

I didn't recognize her voice anymore.

"Tuuli. Listen. Trust me. Don't do this."

She stepped closer, gun aimed at Erik's head.

I had to stop her. I would not lose Tuuli to my demons.

Pulse racing, head pounding, I asked, "Can I kiss you?"

"Are you fucking kidding me?" Erik screamed.

"Ignore him," I ordered, throwing extra grit into my voice, hoping she'd submit one last time. "Look at me."

Her head aimed my direction.

"Can I kiss you?"

My sweet angel complied. "Tell me something I don't know about you. Something big."

Fuck, I loved how much she trusted me.

"I love a girl. I love her so fuckin' deep and true, she's part of my DNA." God, it hurt to say those words. A beautiful, cleansing, steel wool to the veins kind of pain. "So, you see, you have to put the gun down. You have to let me handle this, you have to trust me, 'cause I can't lose the woman I love." I took careful steps in her direction. "I can't let you fall victim to the demons I battle. They want you, baby. I can feel them, they're everywhere—in the dark, in the shadows, just waiting for you to cross that line, take that shot. You do that, they're in. Those demons are in your head for good, and I know you don't want that."

"If I kill him, then you won't have to." Her voice trembled, betraying her motives.

Fuck. She was protecting me. Fighting for a soul that was long ago damned.

"I love you," I said, giving her the facts, straight and true, hating the words, but feeling the sentiment to my marrow. "Listen to me. Neither one of us is killing Erik. Where's that faith, Bunny? I've got this under control. He's never going to hurt another child. He's never going to hurt you again. I promise."

"How can you promise?"

I grabbed my phone out of my back pocket. Swiped. Sent the text. "In about two seconds, some men are gonna come in here. They're with me. Don't shoot."

Flashlights preceded the heavy stomp of boots.

Dane's voice cut through the darkness. "Took you long enough. I was beginning to think he got the jump on you."

"Riley secure?" I asked, positioning myself between the bikers and my half-naked girl.

"Fucker's not goin' anywhere." He aimed the light on Erik. "What's the holdup?"

"Tuuli here is deciding whether or not she wants her piece of him, too."

"Tuuli. Nice name." Dane lowered his light, tucking it under his arm, before leaning to the left to look around me. "Listen, baby. I understand you've got good reason to take this fucker out. Can't say I blame you. Thing is, I promised to bring him to my pres. That's a promise I can't break. I can assure you, this twat ain't gonna live to see next week. But he can't die today. He needs to answer for what he's done. I can promise you, though, he will suffer." The big biker stepped up to Erik and leaned his shoulder against the wall. "Tell you what. You put that gun down, I'll throw in a little extra torture, just for you. Sound good?"

Erik laughed again, maniacal, desperate. "Shoot me, Tuuli. Shoot me, you fucking cunt. Fucking traitor. You don't deserve that mark you wear. I shoulda cut that tat off your back and then fucked your ass. Fucking cunt. Shoot me. Shoot me!"

Dane shut him down with a steel-toe to the jaw. Shot me a nod.

Tuuli sobbed, the gun bobbing in her hand. I stepped closer, voice low. "Baby. Give me the gun."

She lowered her arms. "He made me watch."

"I know." I stepped closer, laying a hand over her shoulder.

"He has my mom."

"We'll get her back. You have to trust me. Let me take you home." I slid my hand down her arm, over her hand, over the gun, and gripped the metal tight. "That's it. Let go."

Dane and his crew moved in behind me, not wasting a beat. Slow and steady, I moved between Tuuli and the Slayers, blocking her view. The less she saw of them, the better.

"It's over." I cupped the back of her head, pulling her against my chest, and dropped a kiss on her wet hair. Her fingers slipped off the gun, her hand falling to her side.

Over my shoulder, Dane asked, "We good to go?"

"Yeah. Go." God, her skin was cold.

"Wait." Tuuli jerked away from me. "My mom."

"Fuck, Moretti. Gotta get this show on the road. Long drive. Long fuckin' night."

"Dane," I warned.

He huffed expletives. Someone grunted. I didn't turn around.

Erik screamed, the sound much like the wails of the children I'd watched him break on those damn recordings.

Dane's voice rose behind me, full of lethal warning. "Where's Tuuli's mom?"

"You'll never find her...ow. Fuck."

Unholy, fleshy, gurgled noises rose from the floor.

Tuuli buried her face in my chest, covering her ears.

"I'll only ask one more time. Where. The fuck. Is. The bitch?"

Had to give Erik credit. The psychopath could take a beating. He sobbed. Screamed. Laughed, then yelled, "Over the fucking rainbow, assholes. She's over the fucking rainbow."

More screams. Then silence.

"Guy passed out. Sorry," Dane grunted, his leather creaking as he rose to stand. "Don't have time for this shit. Gotta hit the road."

"No. No. No." Tuuli tried to pull out of my arms. "Tito. My mom."

Fuck. I was helpless to do anything but hold her tight and keep her from pissing off Dane. "Shh. It's okay. I'll find her. I'll find her for you." I stroked her hair and whispered in her ear. "Breathe, baby. Breathe."

Tuuli

I couldn't breathe. The air around us was thick with brutality and dripping with incitement. I pulled away from Tito, hoping to reach Erik, beat the truth from his vile flesh. Punish him for all the wrongs he'd committed.

Tito braced an arm around my waist, hoisting me off my feet. Holding me steady while I fought.

"Tuuli. You can't. They'll kill you, too. They're Slayers."

His words struck their intended target. I stilled, giving in to his unyielding hold on me. Slayers. I'd heard Jeremy and Jonas talk about the motorcycle club. Enemies of The Brotherhood. One of many.

"I promise. I won't stop until I find her." His rough, ragged voice drained the fight from my bones.

I believed him. He would find her. He wouldn't stop until she was home.

My hands trembled. The rest of my body followed suit, crashing from the adrenaline rush.

"I need air. I feel sick." I jerked out of Tito's grip and bolted for the front door.

The sky lit with a blinding flash, followed immediately by an earth-shaking rumble. The storm was right over us.

I pushed through the door, the cowbell clunking its greeting, and sucked in a large dose of air, daring the storm to do its damage. Take me. Hurt me. Punish me. I stayed under the awning, back pressed against the white brick, and I watched lightning dance across the lake. No longer fearful.

My storm was over.

Erik was over.

Jeremy was gone.

The Brotherhood, soon, would be over.

I fell to my knees on the cold, wet cement. Every inch of my body screamed in protest. I screamed out loud through the pain at the storm. At God. I screamed for my mom. For Jonas. For wasted lives. I screamed until my voice gave out. Until I was empty. Until there was nothing left to purge.

Depleted, I dropped my hands and my head to the ground. I cried, and I prayed. For forgiveness. For strength. For my mother.

A warm arm draped over my shoulder. Another wrapped around my chest. Tito lifted me to my feet. Made sure I was steady, then wiped the wet strands of hair off my face. "You good now?"

I nodded, finding peace and solace in those worried eyes. He yanked his shirt over his head, placed it over mine, and helped me pull my arms through the sleeves.

"You're bleeding everywhere. Need to get you cleaned up."

He guided me back through the diner. Two men held flashlights aimed on Erik. One bald, one with long, black hair. Both of them huge. The man Tito called Dane, whose face was hidden behind a long, unkempt beard, was tugging Erik down the hallway by his hair, hands secured behind his back, ankles tied together.

Erik's eyes popped open, searching blindly. "Tuuli. Tuuli. Please. Don't let them take me. Tuuli. Help me. Tuuli."

"What are they going to do to him?" I whispered, unsure if I wanted the answer.

"Whatever it is, it won't be enough."

A hard shiver ran through me. More violence. More murder.

We followed them down the hall. Erik fought against his binds, bucking and twisting. The bald man laughed, swung his flashlight, and Erik went still.

"Stay here." Tito braced my shoulders. Kissed my forehead. "I'll be right back."

I caught the door before it swung shut and watched him follow behind the bikers, all dressed in black leather. Physically, Tito was not as tall and not as big as the other men. But in their space, he was every bit as fearsome. More so even. They stepped away when he approached, as if in respect, or fear. I couldn't be sure. It was dark. I was probably in shock.

As they paused to talk, I allowed myself one last look at the man who had tortured me and made me live in fear. I remembered the boy, the bully. I remembered the threats. The promises. His secret hideouts.

I hated that I wanted him dead. That knowing he would suffer gave me pleasure. I hated that he'd turned me into a monster.

Somewhere over the rainbow. A memory tickled my nerves.

I waited for a painful beat before following Tito outside. He didn't notice. He didn't hear me approach because he was bent over Erik with a hunting knife in his hand. And he was cutting. And although I couldn't see the blood. I heard the sound, the screams.

Over the rainbow.

Somewhere over the rainbow.

I knew where he'd sent my mom.

I knew where to find her.

I needed to tell Tito. We needed to leave before it was too late, before she disappeared. I stepped closer, then paused when I heard him say, "I told you if you touched my girl again, you'd be fishing your fingers outta the lake."

One of the bikers said, "Fuck. That's fucked up."

"I always keep my promises," Tito growled, bending low to Erik's ear.

I was done. Done. Done. No time to hide or move out of the way. I vomited. Right there. All over my shoes.

"Tuuli," Tito grunted over his shoulder, not a lick of apology in his voice. "Shit, you were supposed to stay inside."

He rose and came my way. Face and hands bloody.

"Don't." I backed away. "I can't do this. I can't do this anymore."

So much blood.

He continued anyway, eyes wild.

"Stop, Tito," I pleaded, desperate for a moment alone. To clear my head, to come up with a plan. "You're a mess. Just give me your keys. I'll wait in the car."

He paused, hands to hips, bare chest rising and falling, water sluicing down every ridge of muscle. Tilting his head, he blinked the darkness away, and whispered, "Tuuli."

"Just give me the keys." I held out my palm.

Eyes worried and body taut, he tugged his car keys out of his front pocket.

I snatched them from his fingers and ran into the diner to grab my purse. Without looking back, I tucked myself into the driver's seat. Fired the engine. And drove into the night.

Tito

The night sky collapsed around me. Falling. Falling. Crimson stained drops. Drip. Drip. Drip. I watched until my headlights disappeared, dragging my guts behind.

She wasn't supposed to come outside. She wasn't supposed to witness my final act of savagery.

Fuck.

I scooped Erik's bloody digits off the ground.

"The hell you gonna do with those?" Baldy asked, sneering at the mangled flesh in my hand. "Make a necklace?"

"Nah. Fish food."

I didn't regret taking my two pounds of flesh. Men said desperate things when death came knocking. Erik, however, knowing he was on his way to a miserable, bloody end, had only laughed, telling me, "I had her first. My fingers were inside her first. You'll think of me every time you touch her. I win."

He'd practically begged me to follow through on my promise. I didn't regret taking his fingers. I regretted the look on Tuuli's face.

"Sick fucker." The bald man laughed. Wasn't sure if he meant me or Erik. Didn't fucking care. I'd made a promise. I kept my promises.

"We good?" Dane asked.

I nodded. "All good."

"See ya on the flip side."

I waved him off, waited for the men to make their exit, then drudged through the rain, across the lot, and down the steep incline to the beach.

The storm was farther away now, lighting the sky behind the mountains in the distance.

I stood ankle-deep in the black water. I wasn't a praying man. Far from it. But I was beginning to believe there was a higher power pulling my strings, guiding me toward redemption, deserved or not.

Death's claws no longer pierced my blood and bones, her grip loosening, surrendering my destiny to the woman more deserving of my soul. Tuuli led me out of the dark. I never wanted to go back, and I feared if she didn't return, if I'd broken her for good, I'd fall deeper into that vile pit and give myself wholly, completely, forever to Lady Death.

I tossed the bloody appendages one by one, trusting the current to carry them far away, waded deeper into the murky water, then deeper still, until my lungs constricted and my muscles locked tight. I sucked in oxygen and submerged myself completely, the cold bite consuming me, washing me clean.

When I came up for air, Tango waited on the shore. "The fuck'd you do now?"

I only laughed, lifting heavy, water-logged legs toward the shore. "Great timing, cousin. Great fuckin' timing."

After we'd cleaned the diner, leaving no trace of Erik, Riley, or the Slayers, Tango let me into Tuuli's apartment. I showered, slid between her sheets, and sent a text.

Bunny. Come home.

I waited three hours. No response.

She would come back.

I love a girl.

No response.

Fuck. What a fucking day.

I loved her. She loved me.

I laid back on her pillow, phone in hand, and engaged the tracking app connected to my car.

She would come back.

CHAPTER 18

Tito

"SHE CALL YOU YET?" Tango dropped to his ass in front of me, finally dropping the football he'd been spinning on his finger for the past five minutes.

"No," I grumbled, choking on the bitter taste of anxiety.

He laid back in the grass, using the pigskin to prop his head. "But you know where she is."

"Of course I do." I'd pulled out all the stops to keep tabs. Traced her debit card. Her phone. My car. I'd even breeched Roger Caldwell's privacy, knowing he was in constant contact with my girl. I owed that man. Owed him big.

"And?" He arched one brow, arms folded across his chest, waiting for my full confession. "It's been three weeks. Why haven't you gone after her?"

"Sometimes people gotta work shit out on their own." I didn't mention the fact that her last and only text had said, "Have a little faith in me."

Easier said than done.

Fucking sucked. But I'd give her all the time she needed to clear the shit in her head. Come back ready to move forward. Hopefully with me at her side. And she was coming back. That I knew. The little green dot on my cell phone app told me she was close. What I didn't know was whether she was coming back to stay or say goodbye.

Fuck. Why was I so goddamn nervous?

"She called Slade this morning." He studied my face for a reaction. When I gave none, he continued, "But you knew that already. Didn't you?"

I shrugged.

"She found her mother. You knew that, too."

His words cut deep, but my chest swelled with pride, regardless. Tuuli had done that good deed all on her own. Hurt like a son of a bitch knowing she'd gone to Roger and the Feds for help instead of me, but those wounds were superficial. The endgame was all that mattered, and my little bunny had come out the victor.

Tuuli had slain her final beast.

"Is it ready? Is it ready?" Rocky barreled our way, stick in one hand, bucket of lake water in the other.

I tugged one last time on the ropes, checking my handiwork, then stepped back. "What do ya think? She look ready?"

He nodded, wide, green eyes blinking up at me. "Will I go high?"

"To the sky," Tango threw in.

Rocky dropped his gear.

I grabbed his hips and hoisted him into the seat. "Ready?"

"Go high, Tito."

I gave him a big push and the little guy squealed.

Slade and Aida made their way across the lawn, opposites in build, but equals in beauty. Slade wore a faded T-shirt that hugged her tits, and cutoff shorts that showed off long, lean legs. Aida wore a faded pair of overalls over a tank top that barely covered her ample chest and a pair of well-worn work boots.

I couldn't hold back a grin, or a laugh. Shit. Seemed like only yesterday Aida wouldn't be caught dead in anything other than designer heels, and now she sauntered my way with dirt on her face and a smile that would bring the devil to his knees.

"Yay! It's done." Slade jogged to my side and took over pushing her son. "Hold on tight, babylove."

Aida pulled me in for a hug. "Guess what?"

"What?" I leaned back and wiped at a smudge on her cheek.

"I just signed the last check. The contractors will be out of here tomorrow."

"God, Princess. I'm so fuckin' proud of you."

She grabbed my hand and walked me toward the shoreline. "We're gonna do something good here, Tits. Can't you feel it?"

"You're an amazing woman. I don't tell you that enough. But you are."

Aida was either sunburned or she'd grown a heart because those cheeks of hers blazed. "You've never told me that."

"Well. I'm telling you now."

"Thank you," was her simple reply.

We walked for a bit along the small stretch of beach until we reached the edge of the property. Aida stopped and plopped her ass in the sand. I followed suit.

"Can you believe where we ended up?" she asked, shielding her eyes from the early afternoon sun.

I shook my head.

"Ever think about going back?" She picked up a stick and drew swirly patterns in the sand.

"Not a chance in hell." I leaned back on my arms, raised my face to the sky, and sucked in the clean, untainted air. "You?"

"No." She shook her head. "Hell, no."

Aida turned to look at me, a question in her eyes. She reached up and traced a finger over my scar. "You know what happened to my dad was not your fault, right?"

My ticker dropped to my gut. "It was my fault. I led those fuckers straight to him."

Aida grabbed my chin and pinched hard. "It's not your fault."

"No offense, Princess, but you weren't there. You can't say that."

She looked over her shoulder, then back to me, eyes narrowed. "Tucker found my mother. A few months back."

"What the fuck? Why haven't you told me?"

"I wasn't sure what I wanted to do with that information. He said she had good reason for staying out of my life and that he would tell me more when I was ready."

"Well? Are you ready?" Fuck. How was she so calm? She'd spent her whole life wondering who her mother was and why her father had refused to talk about the woman who had given birth to his only child.

Aida cocked her head to the side, offering a crooked grin. "I'm happy. I don't need to know. She's alive. She's safe. That's enough for me." Her eyes focused over my shoulder. She opened her mouth to speak. Then snapped it shut.

"Aida, what is it?"

"I have my suspicions, Tito." She reached into her pocket and pulled out a wrinkled piece of paper with a Georgia address written in black ink. "I think you'll find the closure you need if you check this out. If my gut instinct is right, you'll see you're holding on to misplaced guilt."

I tucked the paper into my pocket, met her soppy gaze, and wiped moisture off her cheek. I didn't have to ask to know she was talking about her father. If she suspected Voltolini was alive, then he was alive. Aida's gut was never wrong.

"Is this something you need me to dig into?"

"No. This is for you." She offered a sad smile and studied my reaction before turning her attention to the shoreline.

The truth wouldn't matter. I had stewed in guilt for so long, I reeked of it. Knowing whether or not Luciano had survived the fire wouldn't change anything. Too many others had died.

I studied the scenery. Soon, Lake Willow would be alive with boats of all shapes and sizes. Water skiers. Jet skis. For the time being, the water was quiet and still, small waves licking the shore. I envied the stillness.

"Hurts, doesn't it?" Aida's voice broke my reverie.

"What?" I asked.

"Love."

God, the woman always knew right where to hit me. I dropped my head. "I miss her so goddamn much."

"She'll be back. You're doing a good thing, letting her work this out on her own." Aida patted my back, then hopped to her feet. "I gotta go inside. Feed Lucia. Lunch will be ready soon. Lettie's making a feast."

Tucker's mom had settled into the mansion like she'd lived there all along. She was going to be amazing with the kids.

I sat in the sand, listening to Rocky's laughter, an ache settling in my gut. My father and I had once been close like Tango and Rocky until the night Luciano had covered my crime. After that, neither one of my parents had been able to look me in the eye again. Shame. Guilt. Disgust. Fear. Whatever the reason, our relationship had suffered because I'd killed a man. I'd ended an untouchable man's life so he couldn't fuck up another kid.

I had no regrets. My path, no matter how vile, had led me to Tuuli. If my actions also took her away from me, so be it. At least I'd known for a little while that I still had a beating heart in my stone-cold chest.

I had Aida. I had a family. I was an uncle by default to Lucia and Rocky. And I would only give them the best of me. The me who had been uncovered by the tempest that was Tuuli Holt.

"Tito. Come on. Lunch is ready," Rocky bellowed, mere seconds before slamming into my back and circling his arms around my neck.

Yeah. Shit was good in Whisper Springs.

I pushed to my feet, hoisted the little monkey higher up my back, and hooked my arms under his legs, bouncing him hard as I jogged across the lawn. We had almost reached the door when the familiar rumble of an engine drew my attention to the driveway.

Fuck me.

My Mustang.

Dirty as shit. Gospel music thumping out the rolled-down windows.

I swung Rocky around to my front and set him on his feet. "Hey, little man. Go inside, get washed up. I'll be right there."

"Hurry. I'll save you a seat."

I reached the driver's side door before the car completely stopped.

The smile that greeted me was so goddamn beautiful, so fucking serene, I knew all my worry had been for nothing.

"Bunny."

Tuuli

"Grim."

Sweet Jesus. The man was a sight. Rumpled hair. Overgrown facial fur. Firestorm blazing in his tired eyes. Before I could set the brake, he jerked the door open, unhooked my seatbelt, and pulled me against his thick chest, choking me with a hug so tight and full of gratitude I feared my head might pop.

Face buried in his shirt, I savored the aroma of sweat and sunshine.

His words came fast and furious.

"Fuck. I love you so fuckin' much, Bunny." Kiss, kiss.

"I thought I lost you." Nuzzle, nuzzle.

"Couldn't fuckin' breathe." Nibble, nibble.

"I love you." Emotion choked him, his voice breaking, his hold tightening.

He loved me.

I had so much to tell him. So many things I needed to say, but I couldn't speak past the lump in my throat. And that was fine. We had time. We had forever.

So, I stayed between his strong arms, breathing him in, memorizing the rhythm of the thump, thump, thump in his chest.

I was home. I was where I belonged. I was his bunny; he was my beast. He was safety. Protector, lover, friend, fighter, my rock, my home. My beautifully broken, perfect man.

He showed no sign of letting me go, so I mumbled into his shirt. "Can I kiss you?"

His whole body rumbled with a chuckle. Into my hair, he mumbled, "Tell me something I don't know about you. Something big."

I smiled, unable to contain my joy. "I found my mom."

A rush of air blew my hair. His hands dropped to my hips, rendering me weightless before I landed on the hood of his car. "Baby. That's..." He dropped his head. Laughed.

Lifted his eyes to mine. "I know. I knew the whole time. I'm so proud of you."

He knew. He'd kept tabs. I expected nothing less. "Thank you for not coming after me."

"You have no idea how hard it was for me to stay here, waiting."

I had a very good idea. Every day I was gone, I struggled not to hop in his car and hightail it back to Whisper Springs. "I needed to go alone, Tito. My mom and I...we needed that time."

He nodded, eyes darting from my eyes to my lips, and back up again. "Is she okay? Are you okay?"

"I took her home, Tito. To her family. Her real family. I met them. Both of my grandparents are alive. They're still married. They're wonderful people. I have aunts and cousins. We cried a lot. Mom was overwhelmed. She's going to stay. We found her a good doctor to help her work through all of this."

He dropped his forehead to mine. "God. I could've helped, too."

"I know. But my mom, she's been through so much. Worse than I have. It would've been hard having you there. Having any man there."

His chest rose and fell. "I want to hear everything. When you're ready."

"Erik's parents took her from the hotel where she worked with her boyfriend." A shiver tore through me. "My father."

"Michael Foster," he added. He'd read every file he could find on my mother's disappearance. "Did you meet him?"

"No. But he knows we're alive. He's been in contact with the Feds, and he knows how to find me when he's ready. He blames himself for what happened. Thinks he should've been there to protect her."

"What happened? How'd they snatch her from a busy hotel?" Tito brushed soothing strokes up and down my arms.

"The day they checked out, Erik's mother said she lost her wedding ring and asked if my mom could help her find it. Of course, Mom goes into their room to help. Next thing she knows, she wakes up in a strange bed in another state."

"She must've been terrified."

"They threatened her life, her parents. After I was born, they used me to keep her quiet. Said I'd suffer at the hands of every member of The Brotherhood if she ever tried to leave or told anyone who she was."

Tito cleared his throat, his restraint evident in the tight set of his jaw. "Your mom isn't the first girl they'd abducted, I suspect."

I shook my head, my gut tightening. "Jonas's mother was their first. She'd tried to leave. When they caught her, each male member of The Brotherhood was allowed to punish her however they saw fit. Then she disappeared." I pinched my eyes shut, halting the tears. "Jeremy showed my mom pictures of what they'd done to Jonas's mom. He reminded her every day of what would happen if she tried to leave."

"So, your mom raised Jonas as her own."

"They gave her no choice. Sixteen years old, forced to raise another woman's child. Scared for her own life."

I continued to fill Tito in on the past weeks. He listened. He wiped my tears when I cried. I clung to him, grateful for those solid arms.

"I'm sorry I stole your car," I said, wiping the last tear with the back of my hand.

"You didn't steal it. I gave you the keys, remember?" He flashed his playful grin. "Now, can we stop talking and get to the kissing?"

I hooked my fingers around his neck and pulled him down, meeting him halfway with a clumsy, hungry kiss. A kiss I felt from the roots of my hair to the tips of my toes.

"Toodaloo!" Rocky bellowed from the front door, interrupting our reunion. "You're here. Did you see the swing?"

"Swing?" I pushed Tito away and stretched to see around his massive chest.

"Yeah!" Rocky took off at a sprint toward the beach, squealing, "I helped build it!"

I followed the little man's trajectory. Sure enough, hanging from the willow tree was a simple, yet beautiful, handmade swing. Tito gripped my hips and buried his face in my neck. "I wasn't done with the kissing."

"Get off, you beast. There's a swing!" I shoved a groaning Tito away and hopped down to run, my inner child breaking free.

I thought I'd have to fight Rocky for a turn, but the little lady killer stood in wait, and when I reached him, he said, "Get on. I'll push you."

As I wiggled my butt into the seat, he warned, "Be careful. It goes really high."

Oh, Lord. He was already protective like his father and uncles.

"I'll be careful."

Rocky gave me a shove. I barely moved. He pushed again, putting his full weight into the motion. I helped with a leg pump.

"Stand back, Rockster," Tito's gruff voice commanded. The swing jerked to a halt. "This girl's gonna fly." Tito pulled me back, then gave a hard shove. My body jetted toward the lake, then up toward the blue sky.

My stomach fell on the backswing, and when Tito pushed again, my insides fluttered and laughter erupted from my gut. Tito stepped aside and stood, arms crossed, watching me with his gorgeous smirk. Rocky stood at his side, mimicking the pose. The two of them were talking, but I couldn't hear their words through the whooshes of air.

It wasn't until Tango joined us that I stopped pumping my legs so I could slow enough to stop. My entire body buzzed. My head swam. My stomach seemed to float. Tito stepped to my side and helped me stop completely. I wasn't ready to get off yet.

"My turn! My turn!" Rocky hopped on the balls of his feet.

Tango hoisted the little boy atop his shoulders in one swift move. "Lunch first, little man." He shot me a wink. "Happy you're back, Tuuli. Everyone's inside. Come and eat."

"Nope." Tito threw an arm around my waist and hoisted me off the swing, not letting my feet touch the ground. "Bunny and I have a date."

"We do?"

"We do."

The world spun and I landed over his shoulder with an embarrassing "Oomph."

"Tell everyone we said goodbye," he shouted.

Tango only laughed.

Rocky yelled, "Bye Toodaloo!"

"Tito. Wait—"

His large hand landed hard on my rump, silencing any protest.

"Ow!" I laughed, stretching my arm to slap him back, his hard muscle offering no give.

We reached the car. Tito crouched to lower me to my feet. Before I could gain my bearings, warm hands cupped my jaw, tilting my face to the perfect angle for a lip-lock, giving me a taste of the mouth I'd missed so much.

Tito was all muscle, tongue, and heavenly noises, walking me backward until my butt hit the Mustang, never once relenting, using every available body part to work me into a frenzy.

The sun beat down on our fused bodies, warming my skin, but sweet Lord, my insides were molten. The air we shared, ripe with the aroma of fresh cut grass, pine trees, and sweaty sunbaked skin, only added fuel to my fire.

Days of driving had made me weary. One touch from my Grim and every stiff muscle sparked with new energy. My soul buzzed with joy and hope, every cell in my body felt bubbly and free.

Oh, thank you, Jesus. I was free.

Tito

We were free. Free from her tormentors. Free of my demons. Free to move on, start fresh. Start building our life together.

We rode the elevator hand in hand, anticipation a living, breathing entity, plucking my nerves with spindly fingers. Tuuli hadn't been to the penthouse since I'd made it mine. Aside from my office, I'd only bought furniture for the bedroom, hoping that someday she would call the space her home, too, and then we could decorate together, a touch of Tuuli here, a hint of me there. I couldn't wait.

We stepped inside, my palms sweaty.

"No furniture?" she asked, toeing off her shoes.

Not yet, little beast. "I'll get around to it. Hungry?"

"A little." She sauntered around the kitchen island, running her fingers across the smooth granite, a contemplative purse to her lips. The pink T-shirt dress she wore reached mid-thigh and that creamy skin did a number on my libido. She paused, her left heel bouncing on the floor.

Damn, I'd missed her nervous tics "What is it?"

"I start classes soon."

"I know." I shifted, fighting an erection. "I can't wait to help you study."

"Between work and school, I'll barely have time to eat and sleep."

My insides shifted something fierce, my boner no longer an issue. "You're worried about us?"

Those electric eyes flashed, then softened, shoulders dropping. "No." She moved around the counter and grabbed my hand. "I'm not worried about us at all. You're the only constant, the only part of my life I have no doubts about."

Thank fuck. "What is it then?"

Stepping closer still, she tilted her head, studying my face. "I had a lot of time to think on my drive home. About us. About my future." Wrinkles formed on her small forehead. "We've been through so much." Her grip on my hand tightened. "Each of us. On our own. Together."

"What are you trying to say?"

"I'm going to start seeing a therapist. Everything that's bouncing around in here." She stepped back and tapped her head. "It's too much. I can't sort it on my own."

A rush of air left my lungs. God, my girl. So much stronger than me in every way that counted.

She blinked up at me, shy but determined. "I think you should see someone, too."

"You're all the therapy I need." I flashed a playful grin, then an eyebrow wiggle, raking my gaze up and down the length of her tight little body.

"Tito. Please. I'm serious."

So was I. "I'll think about it." I'd never considered a shrink, but hell, anything to make my bunny happy.

"Thank you," she sighed, those lines in her forehead disappearing.

The smile she flashed warmed me in all the right places. I wanted more. "Come upstairs. I want to show you something."

We ascended the steps two-by-two, bypassed my bedroom, and hit the stairs leading to the rooftop deck. When we reached the glass slider, I blocked her view. "Close your eyes. Don't open until I say so."

Heel bouncing, hips shaking, she squeezed her eyes closed.

I led her across the deck. Settled her into position. Stole a kiss. Whispered, "You can look now." I nodded over my shoulder and stepped out of the way.

Her eyes lit up, putting the blue sky at her back to shame.

Suspended from an overhanging beam, a double swing constructed of rope and cedar dangled between the hot tub and a cluster of potted plants. Tuuli stepped closer, brushing her fingers over the carved letters on the seat. BUNNY on her side. BEAST on mine.

"It's beautiful," she murmured, head dropping low. "I can't believe you did this." She gripped the ropes, sliding her hands up their length before turning to sit. Closing her eyes against the warm breeze and bright sun, she lifted her face, angelic, and so fucking beautiful, my breath hitched. "C'mon. What're you waiting for?"

I claimed my side of the swing, gripping the rope tight, my hand above hers, fingers touching. My feet rested firmly on the ground. Hers dangled, toes dusting the Ipe decking.

With a slow push, I got us moving. Soon, we soared. Tuuli's laughter pierced me, arrow after arrow through the chest. On the upswing, we seemed to float over the lake. The backswing made my stomach drop, forcing nervous laughter from my own chest.

Fuck. I felt like a fucking kid again. A boy with no weight on his chest. No demons to darken his soul. No worries to steal his whimsy.

When we finally slowed to a stop, Tuuli rested her cheek on the rope, liquid eyes staring up at me, a lazy grin highlighting perfect, rosy cheeks.

"That was fun," I admitted, head spinning, heart racing.

"Thank you." She leaned forward, lips dusting mine, and whispered, "I fucking love you, Tito Moretti."

A series of explosions erupted in my chest. "You just said fuckin' again."

With a shrug, she teased, "You bring out the best in me."

God, the things I wanted to do with her not-so-dirty mouth. "I really need to kiss you now."

"I need to do more than kiss you, but I've been driving for days. I need a shower."

Damn, that devilish glint in her eyes.

I leaned forward, intent on ravaging that mouth despite her plea. Tuuli shoved me away, hopped off the swing, then dashed around the hot tub and through the door, a wave of wild, white hair flowing behind her.

I followed her trail of discarded clothing, my cock growing harder, pulse beating faster with each step. Tuuli was already under the spray when I entered the bathroom, the large glass enclosure leaving nothing to the imagination. My bunny, on full display, her perky tits, that small waist, and those lean, creamy legs.

"Tito," she said, voice high, lit with wonder. "You have my favorite shampoo in here."

"I do." I ditched my shoes.

"Girlie soap, too."

"Yep." I yanked off my shirt, tossed it aside.

"And ladies' razors?"

"Yes."

"Why?"

"Just in case." I nixed my shorts and joined my girl.

She bent at the waist, one foot propped on the stool, and dragged a razor up her soapy leg. I turned on the second shower head and stepped under the warm flow, my guts, my ticker, my gray matter, a muddy fucking mess of emotion.

I didn't wash, intent on savoring every second of the show.

Humming a tune I didn't recognize, Tuuli finished her left leg and went to work on the right, her ass aimed my direction, no inhibitions, offering a view I was not worthy of, but damn well grateful for.

My steel-hard cock throbbed like a greedy son of a bitch. I gave it a stroke, hoping to appease the bastard. He only wanted more.

Tuuli set the razor back on the shelf and threw an inviting smile over her shoulder before stepping under the spray. I closed in, wrapping my arms around her middle, cupping those tempting breasts, and pressing my raging hard-on between us.

Her head rolled to the side, offering her sweet skin like a feast for the starving. I wasted no time tasting her shoulder, her neck, that sensitive spot behind her ear. The moan that rose from her throat set my blood on fire.

"Baby," I whispered against her neck. "I need you."

Tuuli

"I'm yours, take me," I begged, the contrast of his soft lips and scratchy beard driving me mad.

A deep, needy moan rumbled from his chest.

Seeking *more*, I arched my back, forcing my butt against his hard body, my chest harder into his grip. I loved the way he held me—resolute, tense, hungry, and vibrating with restraint.

A strong hand slid down my stomach, lower still, stopping when his palm cupped my sex and one finger slid along my folds, playing me in slow strokes, up and down, soft, then firm, forcing blood and need to the bundle of nerves that had the power to destroy me from the inside out.

One strong finger slid inside. I moaned, grinding against the friction.

Tito mumbled profanities into my neck, then turned me around and took my mouth, the silk of his tongue tangling with mine, his arms a vise around my waist, melding us together. The kiss ended too soon, his mouth moving down my neck to my chest, then lower, lower, nipping my waist, my stomach, my navel. Tito dropped to his knees, worshiping every inch of my skin with his lips, his hands, his heady profanities.

I curled my fingers through his wet hair. His eyes lifted to mine, lids half mast, dark with lust.

I swear he smiled before burying his face between my thighs, his tongue plunging between my folds. No playing around or working me up, he went straight to the main event, attacking my clit with tongue and teeth, sucking, then flicking, then grazing. My head fell back, my hips thrust forward, my legs weakened.

Strong fingers bruised my thighs. My lids slammed shut. I couldn't watch, the scene too much. His strong body, wide shoulders, wild hair, strong jaw working to please me.

He squeezed my inner thigh, urging me to open for him. I lifted my leg over his shoulder. He moaned in appreciation, diving deeper, his tongue moving lower, then inside me, a slow, heavenly penetration.

"Fuck. Fuck. Fuck," escaped my lips, driven by shameless abandon.

My loss of control snapped his last string of restraint, and he ducked his free shoulder, forcing my other leg up and over, and then he was standing, holding my hips, working his tongue inside me. My shoulders hit the cold tile, bracing me, and I was helpless to do anything but ride him, writhe against his face, absorb his sweet assault.

I ached. I burned. Nerve endings hypersensitive. Every muscle in my body coiled tight, to the breaking point, then released in one painful, soul-shattering, colorful explosion.

My cries ricocheted off the tiled walls. I dug into his scalp. My thighs tightened around his head. Tito absorbed my thrusts, licking and kissing through every electric pulse, riding the wave until it crashed to shore, a slow, shallow, ebb and flow.

"Fuck, that was beautiful," he rasped, sliding me down his body, stopping at his waist. "Curl those sexy legs around me."

I was a hot mess of skin and liquid bones. "I need a second to recover," I begged, although my legs obeyed his command, coiling around his small waist, bringing my core flush against his erection.

"Fuck, Bunny." He reached between us and positioned himself at my opening. I shifted my hips, eager for the stretch, hungry for his heat, greedy for the friction.

Hopelessly addicted to the connection.

Skin against skin. Breath to breath. Heartbeat for heartbeat.

He rolled his hips, entering me slow and steady, pulling my bottom lip between his teeth.

"Don't go slow," I begged.

"I want to cherish you."

"Fuck me now, cherish me later." I nipped his ear. "We have all night."

He pulled away, bracing me with one arm under my hips, cupping my jaw with the other. "We have the rest of our lives, you mean." A statement, rough and possessive, but I caught the flash of worry on his face.

Dear God, his vulnerability was a beautiful thing.

"Tell me that's true, Tito. Tell me we're forever."

"You want forever, baby?" He slammed inside me, then stilled. "I'll give you forever. I'll give you fuckin' eternity."

I curled my arms around his neck and rocked my hips, begging him to finish what he started.

The talking ended. Worry evaporated. His beast came out to play.

CHAPTER 19

Tuuli

"THANKS, TUULI." PASTOR DAVIES curled an arm around his wife and waved goodbye as they shuffled through the door, the cowbell giving a hearty rattle.

I waved. Delivered the fish and chips basket to table five, then checked the clock, my heart sinking with every shift of the red hand.

Tito and Tucker had been due home late last night. He'd sent a short text around midnight saying they were delayed, and I hadn't heard anything since.

Morgan, our new waitress, skirted around me, balancing a tray of empty plates, at the same time a group of loud, sun-kissed teens barreled through the door, roughing each other up and not paying attention to their surroundings. The largest of the group bumped into Morgan and sent her tray flying across the floor with a terrible clatter.

His face pinked with embarrassment, hers reddened in anger. They bumped heads, squatting at the same time to pick up the mess.

"Jesus. I'm so sorry." The boy hurried to stand and offered a hand.

Morgan swatted him away. "Step back. Just find a table. I'll get this."

I came to her aid at the same time Charlie barreled through the door, aiming his don't-fuck-with-me glare at the testosterone posse.

"Get these boys a seat, Toodaloo. I'll get the mess."

Had to give the tall kid credit. He didn't back down. Ignoring Charlie altogether, he dropped right back to his haunches and picked up every last dish he'd sent flying, despite the death stares Morgan aimed straight through his skull.

I settled his friends in the corner booth, checked on table six, then headed back to the rowdy boys.

"What can I get you to drink?"

They rattled off their orders, heads bowed in worship over their phones. As I headed to the counter, one of them mumbled, "Holy shit. I'd love to come all over that pretty face."

My spine stiffened.

A loud slam made me jump.

Someone yelled, "Jesus. Fuck. Shit."

I whirled around. Tito stood behind one of the boys, the mouthy one, I assumed, hand on his head, smashing his cheek into the table.

"Hey, Bunny." A playful smile greeted me.

I would never tire of the palpitations that hit every time I laid eyes on that face. "Grim."

"C'mere, baby." He jerked his sexy chin, gesturing me closer.

You could've heard a pin drop. I glanced around the diner and yep, all eyes were aimed our direction. My first instinct was to flee. Instead, I sidled up to Tito.

Not releasing the boy, he bent my direction and took my mouth in a greeting totally inappropriate for public viewing, but one hundred and ten percent worth the embarrassment.

"I missed you," he mumbled against my lips, eyes gleaming with mirth.

Releasing the kid's head, he bent low and commanded, "Apologize to Miss Holt."

The boy dragged a tongue over his bottom lip, eyeing his friends one at a time. He wanted to fight. He wanted to save face. Not one of his buddies gave any indication that they were going to back him up.

Tall guy warned, "This is Tango Rossi's place, Troy. Don't be stupid."

Troy's fists balled tight. Then he met my eyes. "I apologize for being disrespectful."

Tito patted him hard on the back. "Good man." He grabbed my hand. "Eat up, boys. Lunch is on me." Then he gave the table three raps with his knuckles, told the kids to have a good day, and dragged me through the swinging doors and down the hall.

Safely out of eyesight, he pinned me to the wall with a kiss that was playful and possessive.

I curled my fingers around the waistband of his jeans. "You're back."

"I'm back."

"You get the girl?"

He planted his hands on the wall above my head, wild eyes taking in every inch of my face, my chest, my hair like he couldn't get enough. "We got two."

"Are they okay?"

"They will be."

"You're amazing, you know that?"

His eyes flashed wide, meeting mine before his gaze dropped to the floor. I could swear he blushed, but then quickly recovered, distracting me with his killer smirk. "Clock out. Get your things. We have a date."

"My shift ends at eight. It's only noon."

"I'm tight with your boss. We worked out a little deal." He slapped my butt. "Hurry, now. I'll wait in the car."

With a cocky grin, he sauntered to the back door, then out, leaving me breathless and delirious with want.

I whirled around the corner, smacking nose to chest with a mountain of solid muscle.

"Sorry. Shit." Tango's arm clamped around my shoulders, grounding me until I steadied myself.

Rocky barreled toward us, dragging a Seahawks suitcase behind him. "Toodles! Guess what? Daddy said he's—"

Tango clapped a hand over his son's mouth and lifted him off the ground. "He's having a sleepover with his friend. Right, little man?" He jiggled his son playfully up and down. "You're having a sleepover. Mom and Dad are staying home for some much-needed alone time."

Rocky's eyes widened, two jungle-green saucers of joy. He nodded. His dad set him back on his feet.

"Grab your gear. Let's go." Tango held the door open for Rocky, then flashed me a devilish grin that would melt any woman's Fruit of the Looms. "See ya later, Tuuli." He stared at me longer than usual, an out of character softness to his features, then nodded and disappeared.

Weird.

Obviously, those two were up to something. Maybe they had a top-secret surprise planned for Slade.

I waved goodbye to Morgan, who still wore a scowl, then popped my head into the kitchen to shout, "See ya tomorrow," to Charlie.

"Have fun, Toodaloo! See ya." He shot me a wink.

When I made my way to the Mustang, Tito popped out of the driver's seat, jogged around to my side, and opened the door, muscles flexing, stretching the arms of his T-shirt in that sexy way you only see in the movies. Dark jeans hung low on his waist, hugging those virile thighs like a jealous girlfriend.

My entire body flushed with heat in one tempestuous heartbeat.

"Fuck, Bunny. Don't look at me like that. We'll never make it on time."

He dropped a chaste kiss on my forehead and waited for me to sit. "Buckle up."

I stretched the seatbelt across my chest and clicked it into place, looking up in time to catch Tito adjusting himself before sliding into the captain's chair.

"Where're we going?"

"Can't say." He stretched an arm across the console and squeezed my thigh. "There's a change of clothes for you in the back seat."

I looked over my shoulder. A light blue shopping bag sat right behind his seat. I pulled out the contents. A mint green, spaghetti-strap swing dress made of a cool, gauzy fabric, a silk cardigan, a pair of matching boy short panties, and a strapless bandeau bra were neatly wrapped in tissue paper. At the bottom of the bag sat a pair of strappy leather sandals. I didn't have to look at the tags to know the outfit came from a designer store that couldn't be found in Whisper Springs, Idaho.

"Tito."

He grabbed my hand and brought my knuckles to his lips. "It's over a hundred degrees where we're going. You'll be thankful for the light fabric. Put it on."

"Right now? In the car?"

"We'll be at the airport in thirty minutes."

"Airport?"

He only nodded, scratching his beard to hide his grin.

"You're making me nervous."

Tito

I'd never been so goddam nervous. Sweaty palms. Nausea. Hot flashes. Hundreds of times I'd danced with Lady Death, and never had I experienced such unease.

Fuck, I hoped the trip wouldn't blow up in my face.

Tuuli's left heel bounced over the top of her right foot, her hands pressed to the glass, that sexy-as-fuck halo of hair falling in wispy tendrils around her face. "I can't believe I'm in Vegas."

I couldn't believe my luck. My church girl in the City of Sin. Aphro-fucking-disiac on heavenly crack.

She turned, the loose fabric of her dress moving with her, the hem skimming the top of those creamy thighs. "What are we doing here?"

I met my beauty where she stood, shoving my hands inside my pockets to hide the tremble. "Before you become an official college student with your nose buried in a book twenty-four-seven, I want you to myself for a couple of days." Lie. Lie, lie, lie.

"This is the best surprise ever." She rose on her toes and pulled me in for a kiss, pressing those barely covered breasts against my chest, calming my storm with her breezy spirit.

I cupped her ass and squeezed, sneaking a grind before letting go. "This isn't the surprise. Come on. We have an appointment."

Those gorgeous blue eyes blinked up at me. She slid her fingers through mine and headed for the door, not a lick of fear or doubt on her face, shoulders relaxed, rockin' the shit out of that sweet dress.

When we exited the elevator, I wrapped an arm around her shoulder, eased her through the crowd, out the main entrance, and into the back of our waiting limo.

Two blocks from our destination, I broke out in a cold sweat. When we pulled into the lot, I flew out of the car and dry-heaved.

I could do this. I could fucking do this. Breathe in. *One, two, three, four.* Out. *One, two, three, four.*

When my head stopped spinning and my vision cleared, I looked up to find Tuuli staring, eyes worried, at the sign. FULL TANK TATTOO.

Before I could change my mind, I grabbed her hand and led her inside. The owner of the shop, Mick "Jackknife" Owens, came around the counter. "Moretti. Jesus H Christ. How long has it been?"

"Good to see ya, Mick." I grabbed his hand. We did the chest bump, shoulder pat before he pulled me into one of his signature bear hugs.

The guy stood six-three and carried his hard-earned bulk like a seasoned warrior. His handlebar mustache blended into a full, black beard that nearly reached his chest.

He let me go and pulled a shredded Metallica T-shirt over his bare chest. "This must be the lucky lady." Mick gave Tuuli a hearty handshake. "Mick Owens. Pleasure to meet you." His deep, throaty timbre fit the persona to a T. From bald head, to the leather pants and biker boots, the guy was bad-ass-biker, don't-fuck-with-me personified.

Tuuli stared at him. Unblinking.

I cleared my throat. "Mick, this is Tuuli."

Mick shot me a questioning glance, then nodded in understanding. "Well...let me see what we're working with here."

I dropped a kiss on her head and removed her cardigan.

Tuuli's pale face turned ashen. I shot her a wink and held her gaze, offering as much assurance as I could in my mild state of fear. Mick circled her and pulled the strap of her dress aside. With thick fingers, he traced her tattoo.

"Wait." She shook her head, the shock wearing off. "What are we doing? A tattoo?"

I stepped into her line of vision and tapped her chin. "Only if you want one. Mick here's the best artist in the business. You want that hate symbol covered, he'll turn it into something beautiful."

Her eyes welled, ripping my guts to shreds. "Really?"

I nodded. "Really, baby."

Her whole body trembled and she wrapped her arms around her middle in defense. "It hurts."

"I know. But if you want this, we're gonna do this together. You get inked, I get inked. Side by side. Nobody holding you down. You say stop, we stop. It hurts, you squeeze my hand. You cuss, scream, cry. You change your mind halfway through, we walk out of here. No hard feelings. You are one hundred percent in control."

"You're getting one, too?"

"Side by side."

"But...you...and needles."

I swallowed, forcing the fear from my voice. "I promised you forever. Ink is forever."

"Tito." Her face crumpled and tears breached her lashes.

I pulled her against me for my own benefit as much as hers.

Mick tapped on an art pad laid across his desk. "I've drawn a few pieces since we spoke last month, but the night is yours, so if Tuuli has some of her own ideas, we can sketch those up quick as well." He walked to the door, flipped the OPEN sign to CLOSED, and twisted the lock.

"Jazz!" he hollered. "Our guests are here."

A tall woman wearing biker boots, fishnets, ragged cutoff shorts, and a black leather bustier sauntered through the heavy red curtain. Her wavy black hair framed a set of jade eyes and bright red lips. She planted a kiss on Mick's cheek and offered her hand, first to Tuuli, then me. "Tuuli and Tito, right? Nice to meet you."

"Thank you for doing this," I said, eyeing the Grim Reaper tat covering most of her right arm.

"It's my pleasure."

"May I?" she asked Tuuli, placing a hand on her shoulder and moving to her back to inspect the ink. Tuuli pulled her hair out of the way, giving Jazz free rein to inspect. "Well. Good news is, I've seen worse." She pointed to a photo hanging on the brick wall. "See this one?"

Tuuli nodded, stepping closer to the framed picture. "That girl escaped a sex trafficking ring. They'd marked her neck with a barcode and the pimp's name in ugly, bold letters."

Tuuli leaned closer. The subject wore a ponytail. The black, gray, and red design started at the root of her hair and stretched down her neck and over her shoulders, a gorgeous, gothic depiction of roses, thriving amidst of a tangle of stems and thorns.

"That sweet thing cried through the whole first session. She was so scared, but she wanted to prove she was stronger than the pieces of shit who tried to beat her down. She's a regular client of ours now. Comes in twice a year. Runs a successful yoga studio on the other end of town."

"What do ya say, Bunny? We gonna do this?"

Liquid eyes met mine. "Bunny and the Beast?"

"Yeah, baby. Bunny and the Beast."

Tuuli

"You beast. Stop. Stop. I'm awake. I'm awake." I wiggled, a half-hearted attempt to break free.

Tito ended the tickle session, pushed to hands and knees, and dotted kisses up and down my spine. "Good. We've got important things to do today."

I yawned, then stretched, sucking in a sharp breath. My shoulder was sore, but I'd never suffered such a lovely burn. "What time is it?"

"It's almost noon." His thick, sleepy voice filled me with delicious, naughty plans, all of which required staying in bed.

We had spent all night at Full Tank. I had cried four times, not because of the pain, but because of the pure adoration aimed my direction every time I caught Tito staring at me. What he didn't know was that I had spent most of the evening in silent prayer, asking God to give him strength. He had paled the moment the guns were brought into view. He sweated profusely. He stayed silent, breathing deep, dying a thousand deaths with each punch of the needle. But he had stayed strong, and every time I reached for him, he'd held my hand and talked me through my own bouts of weakness. I walked out of that torture session a new woman with two new friends, and more in love with Tito than I ever thought possible.

"One more hour of sleep?" I begged into my fluffy pillow.

The mattress bounced, a sharp sting bit my ass, and a gruff voice ordered me to get out of bed. I rolled my head to the side and watched Tito stride to the bathroom, his bare muscles bunching and flexing, hypnotic and intoxicating.

Five minutes later, I untangled my legs from the opulent sheets, stumbled out of bed, and found my Grim standing in front of the bathroom sink, hands planted on the edge of the beige marble, head hung low.

A sight I would never tire of.

I hugged him from behind, curling my arms around his warm skin. He sighed, grabbed my hands, and squeezed them to his chest.

"Everything okay?" I pressed my lips to his skin.

"Perfect."

I lifted my face and traced the edges of his fresh ink. The outline covered his right shoulder blade, and when finished, would become a depiction of a mighty storm, where amidst the backdrop of black clouds, lightning strikes and blowing trees, a woman with seductive curves and flowing hair danced in a field, arms stretched to the sky, as if commanding the tempest. And if you looked closely, you'd see a beast with red eyes and jagged teeth hid in the shelter of trees, watching, waiting, enthralled by the tiny dancer.

"Thank you for this." I kissed the skin just below his artwork. His muscles coiled.

I shook my hands free of his grip and slid my fingers down his stomach, attending to each dip and curve of his tight abs. I moved lower still, through his patch of hair, to his arousal. He stiffened when I curled my fingers around the hot flesh, moaned when I stroked, once, twice.

"Fuck, baby." He grunted, hips flexing into my hand, the husk of his voice igniting elicit thrills.

"Thank you for loving me," I whispered into his back, working my palm up and down his length.

His breath hitched, head falling back on his shoulders, hand falling to his waist to cover mine, halting me mid-rub. "Tuuli. Shit, stop."

My body ached, heat swelling between my thighs. "I need you, Tito. I ache for you, everywhere."

"I know, Bunny. I feel it too," he rasped, guttural and desperate. "I bleed for you with every beat of my black heart."

His words coated my soul like warm maple syrup, sticky sweet and so satisfying. "Make love to me."

"You don't know how desperately I need that right now." He turned in my arms and cupped my face, fingers trembling, staring long and hard, searching for something. Words, or courage, or maybe both. "Marry me first."

My world stopped spinning. "What?"

"If I'm going to be the man sitting next to you every Sunday in that damn church, let me sit next to you as your husband. Let me be worthy of this body. Let me be yours forever."

Husband? Worthy? Didn't he know? I was unworthy. He was the prize in this relationship. "You are my forever." I gripped his wrists. His pulse thumped beneath my fingertips, a heavy, determined beat.

"Let's make it official."

"I'm too young," seemed the correct response, though the words sounded hollow.

"Too young. Too sweet. Too pure. We don't make sense. We shouldn't be here. But we are. Call it fate, divine intervention, whatever the fuck you want, but we're here. You're the only future I see. Let me make an honest woman of you."

I trembled, despite the heat between us. "Tito. It's too soon," I argued, again with the knee-jerk response.

He huffed, arms falling to his sides. "It's okay. We have the rest of our lives. I'll wait forever." With a sad smile, he scrubbed a hand over his head, then fisted his hair. "But know this. I won't enter that beautiful body again until you're my wife."

Oh. Sweet. Baby. Jesus.

"But we've already done everything," I huffed, frustrated. "What would be the point in refraining now?"

"Never too late to make things right."

"Why are you doing this?"

"Because you deserve nothing less." He left me standing speechless at the sink, and stepped behind the glass enclosure, his body disappearing behind a thick plume of steam.

He didn't want to be the demon who defiled the church girl. He wanted to be my forever in every way.

I twisted to see my reflection in the mirror. My tattoo, a beautiful stretch of wildflowers in my favorite muted spring colors, covered my shoulder blade and stretched across my back, delicate, feminine, and free.

I was young. I needed to find my own path. My own way. I needed to rise and fall, break and heal on my own. Become the best me I could be before sharing my life with someone. Right?

I had no doubt Tito would be patient. I had no doubt there were many storms in our future. What I knew, what he'd proven time and time again, was that Tito wouldn't carry me through those trials, he wouldn't come to my rescue. He would slap my ass, shout encouragements in my ear, and stand behind me until I conquered every lightning strike, tamed every gale force wind, and rose above every pounding pellet of rain. And no matter the devastation left in the wake of my storms, he would stand by my side and help me rebuild.

I stepped up to the glass, watching his form. He was graceful despite his bulk, angelic despite his demons.

A blessing despite my transgressions.

I dug a tube of all-day-wear lipstick out of my cosmetic bag, and in a gorgeous shade of dusty rose, wrote the three most important letters of my life.

Y.E.S.

Tito

YES. Scrawled on the shower glass, and again on the bathroom mirror.

Three simple letters that held the power to raise a man above the sky. I stalked through the bathroom, a herd of elephants stampeding through my chest cavity.

I grabbed my phone and shot off a group text.

She said yes! Get your asses over here.

Tuuli stood, back to me, bent over the bed, rifling through the suitcase I had packed. "You won't find what you're looking for in there."

She whipped around, a fucking blinding smile on her face. "How do you know what I'm looking for?" She pulled out a pair of denim shorts and dangled them on her finger.

"Don't put those on." Fuck. I could lock her in our room and keep her naked for the rest of our days.

"Why?"

"Because we're expecting company. And they're bringing your dress."

"My dress?"

I nodded. As if on cue, a boom, boom, boom rattled the door. Tuuli jumped, then snagged a T-shirt out of her suitcase, holding it against her chest. The damn thing did little to cover her intended parts, and I laughed at the innocent, panicked eyes flashing my way.

I hooked an arm around her waist and slammed her against my chest, dropping a kiss on her head.

She planted her hands on my chest, arching away from me. "What's going on?"

"Can I kiss you?"

A huff and an eye roll. So damn cute.

"Tell me something about yourself. Something big," she said, a small quiver to her voice.

"I'm getting married today."

Before she could react, I smacked her bare ass and scooted her toward the bathroom. "Go take a shower. The girls are here."

"Girls? What—"

"I love you, Bunny!" I shouted over her protest, closing her in the room.

I pulled a pair of sweats over my wet body and yanked open the door. Aida barreled through and captured me in a painful embrace. "Fuck, Tits. I can't believe you're actually going through with this."

Slade sauntered in behind, waited her turn, then hugged me long and hard. "Where's our girl?"

"Shower." I pointed a thumb over my shoulder.

"Good," Aida chimed in. "The guys are in my room, waiting. Now, go." She faked a kick at me. "We have lady shit to do."

Barefoot and bare-chested, I scrambled to the suite three doors down and let myself in. Tango and Tucker sat on opposite ends of the sofa, each holding an icy glass of amber liquid, each still sporting bed head and different versions of pajama pants. "The fuck you losers doing?"

Tango lifted his glass to the sky, his grin forced, his skin pasty. "Bachelor party."

Tucker laughed. "Hair of the dog."

Fuckers had spent the evening enjoying the City of Sin, while I sat on a torture bed of ink and needles. Wouldn't have traded places with them for anything.

Tango leaned back, stretching an arm across the back of the couch. "You sure about this, cousin? Don't have to do it in a church. She'll take you regardless."

"Never been more sure of anything. My girl deserves to get married in a church."

He held my gaze, assessing my mental competence, I assumed, then nodded. "All right then. I sure as hell never expected you to be the first, but damn, am I glad you're blazing the trail for the rest of us."

I clapped my hands and rubbed them together, dropping my ass on the couch between the two lugs. "Where's my drink?"

Tucker retrieved a third glass from the table at his side and handed the liquid courage over, raising his own to the sky. "To killer curves and silver daggers."

Tango lifted his glass. "To dancing queens and flip-flops."

I raised my own. "To thunderstorms and church girls."

Our crystal clinked. We swigged. We dressed.

Two hours later, I stood in front of the pastor, staring at my glowing bride, and I said, "I do." I'd never spoken truer words.

And when she kissed me. Fuuuuck. That kiss. Brought me to my knees. Tuuli followed, arms tight around my neck, laughing, crying, and trembling against me. I held her tight, and there, on the floor of the church, in the arms of my angel, I prayed, stumbling through a pathetic, yet heartfelt thank you to a God I'd long ago turned my back on.

Later that evening, after I'd given my wife multiple orgasms and she lay sprawled across my chest, she whispered, "You knew I'd say yes."

"No, Bunny. I expected you to say no."

She raised her head, her chin resting on my sternum, those killer baby blues blinking up at me. "But the church, the dress, you had to have planned months in advance."

"One month." I brushed a chunk of hair off her face. Damn, that pink glow dusting her cheeks was a boost to the ego. "I knew if you did say yes, I wouldn't be able to wait another day." I shifted, pulling her on top of me. She wasted no time straddling my hips, nestling her sweet spot against my growing erection. "I fucked up, though. I'd planned to propose at the Full Tank, not our hotel bathroom. Didn't predict what a mess I'd be."

She merely smiled, a storm raging behind that sleepy gaze. "It was perfect." Those delicious hips rolled, creating beautiful friction, lightning before the thunder. "We're married."

"Yeah, Bunny. We're married."

"Bunny and the Beast," she said, on a breathy sigh.

"That's right, Bunny and the Beast."

I'd never been more grateful to be alive.

THE END

Want to learn more about the
fight against human trafficking?
https://truckersagainsttrafficking.org

ACKNOWLEDGEMENTS

Madison. Thank you for sticking with me through this extremely slow-going, hair-pulling, soul-draining, gut-wrenching process. You are a blessing.

Julie. I love you. You are one of the most beautiful people I know, inside and out. Thank you for my gorgeous covers. Thank you for being my friend.

Felicia Moree. I've never met you, but I want you to know that your short-but-sweet posts on my FB page kept me going when I wanted to quit. And believe me, I wanted to give up at least three hundred times while writing this book. It may not seem like much, but for an author who struggles to be seen and heard, those tiny little bursts of encouragement are a lifeline.

My family. Just love. So much love, I could burst.

My readers. Thank you, thank you, thank you for spending time with my Triple T Boys and the women who rule their worlds.

Above all, thank you, Jesus!

OTHER BOOKS BY

TRUCK STOP SERIES
Truck Stop Tango
Truck Stop Tryst
Truck Stop Tempest
Truck Stop Titan

THE APOTHEOSIS SERIES
Aflame
Aglow

How To Kill Your Boss

If you enjoyed *Truck Stop Tango,* please share the book
with others and don't forget to leave a review.

CONNECT

www.krissydaniels.com

Facebook: @authorkrissydaniels
Instagram: krissydanielsbooks
Twitter: @kdanielsbooks
BookBub: @KrissyDaniels

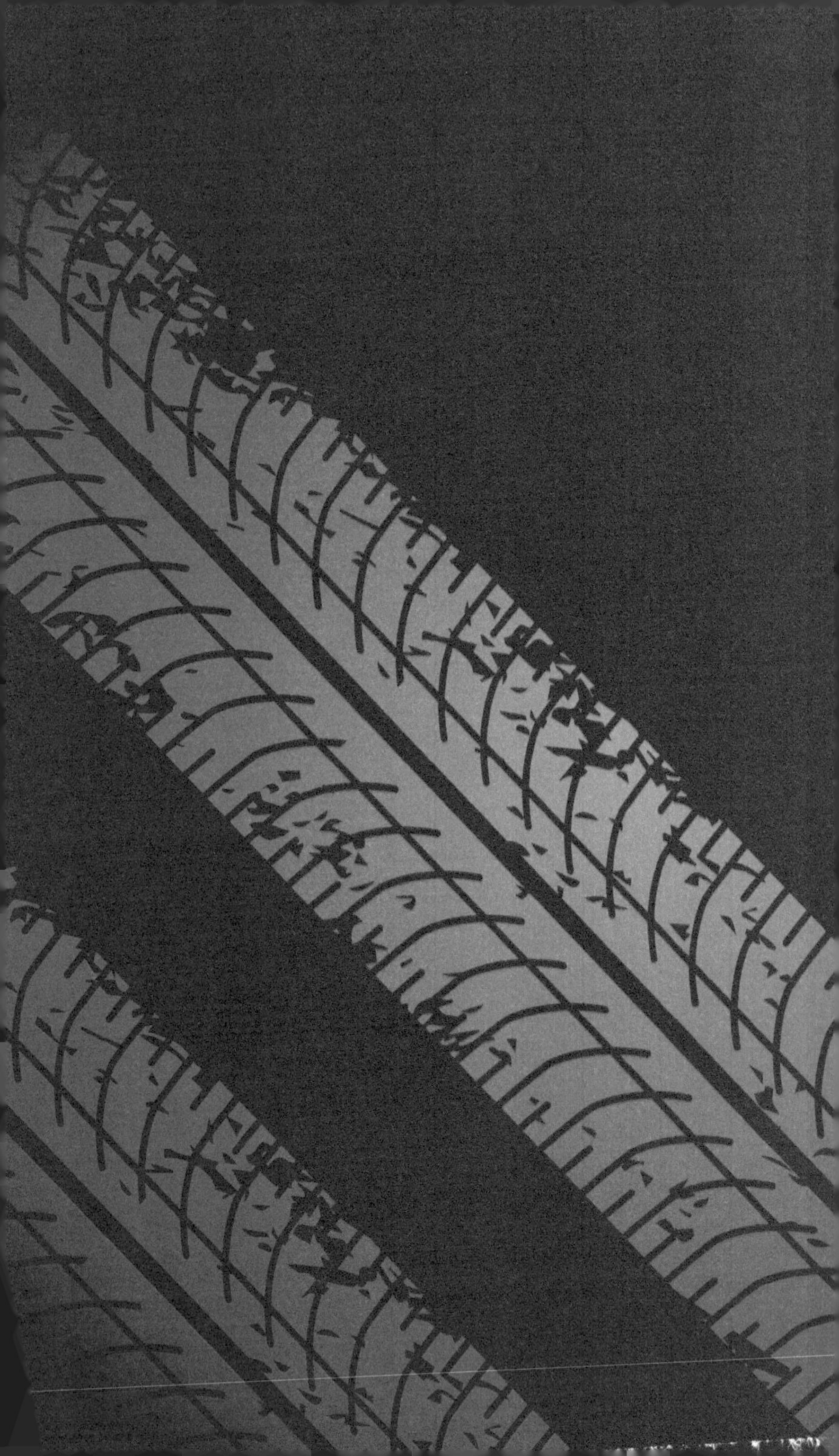